'If you've ever felt lon[...]
and just "wrong" thi[...]
LOVELY. Very funny, blisteringly honest, VERY sweet
on mother-daughter dynamics and ultimately hopeful'
**Marian Keyes**

'Much like the title, main character Sunny is a big
and bright character bursting with humour'
*Cosmopolitan*

'I was laughing from the very first page. *Sunny* is a big,
bright novel that radiates energy and warmth just like
the title. Sukh is such a fun and exciting new voice in
fiction. Give a copy of this book to all your pals!'
**Emma Gannon**

'Bracingly honest, funny and sharp . . . it took me back to
reading *Bridget Jones's Diary*. Fast, irreverent, but relatable'
**Adele Parks,** *Platinum*

'Hilarious and heart-breaking, enlightening and important.
I haven't felt so emotionally invested in a character
and her journey in a long time. Sukh's writing is funny,
sharp and so wonderfully descriptive that I really felt
like I was right by Sunny's side, rooting for her, for the
whole journey. EVERYONE needs to read this book!'
**Helly Acton**

'I absolutely loved Sunny! I wanted to high
five her on one page and hug her on the next.
A riveting rollercoaster of a read!'
**Heidi Swain**

'An honest, hilarious ride with a heart-warming message. Gorgeously written, and I so want Sunny to be my best friend'
**Jessica Ryn**

'Assured, clear, beautifully crafted. A triumph. Everyone should read *Sunny*. It's a funny, moving and important novel, and I loved every word'
**Stephanie Butland**

'What a gem of a book! So, so funny, warm and relatable'
**Lizzie Damilola Blackburn**

'Warm and laugh-out-loud funny with sharp observations on life. Sunny is the modern-day heroine we all want to know'
*Heat* **magazine**

'I loved Sunny, the hapless heroine of this heartfelt and hilarious book and I know you will too'
**Sarra Manning,** *Red*

'An ode to finding yourself amidst a life of other people's expectations: *Sunny* is funny and joyful and heart-breaking in equal measures. Sukh Ojla has created one of my favourite fictional heroines; brilliantly relatable and someone you cannot fail to root for. Highly recommended'
**Sarah Bonner**

# Sukh Ojla
# Sunny

HODDER*studio*

First published in Great Britain in 2022 by Hodder Studio
An Imprint of Hodder & Stoughton
An Hachette UK company

This paperback edition published in 2022

1

A CIP catalogue record for this title is
available from the British Library

Paperback ISBN 9781529356991
eBook ISBN 9781529356953

Typeset in Plantin Light by Hewer Text UK Ltd, Edinburgh
Printed and bound in Great Britain by Clays Ltd, Elcograf S.p.A.

Hodder & Stoughton policy is to use papers that are natural, renewable
and recyclable products and made from wood grown in sustainable
forests. The logging and manufacturing processes are expected to
conform to the environmental regulations of the country of origin.

Hodder & Stoughton Ltd
Carmelite House
50 Victoria Embankment
London EC4Y 0DZ

www.hodder.co.uk

For Mummyji and Daddyji, thank you for everything.

P.S. I hope this makes up for not being a doctor.

# Chapter 1

I wake up with a start, my hand automatically flying to my bag. It's still sitting right next to me, the long strap wrapped twice around my wrist – a habit I've picked up from my overly anxious mum, who insists on doing this whether she's awake or not. Safety conscious, as always. First, I check the contents, just in case. Second, I check my phone. No messages: thankfully nothing from the guy I've just snored my way through a date with . . . just a news notification from the *Guardian* app, which I happily swipe past. The news makes me anxious, especially when it launches itself onto my phone screen without any warning, but my extreme fear of missing out means I can't bring myself to *actually* switch off the notifications. And finally, I check my surroundings: my sole train-carriage companion is a crumpled man, fast asleep, snoring loudly, an Upper Crust baguette in each hand and a snail trail of drool running down his stubbly chin. Lovely.

The information board is nothing more than flickering orange neon nonsense, so I try to work out where the hell I am by looking out the dirt-flecked window; all I can see is a blur of trees and bushes. Instinctively, I know I haven't missed my stop, but there's not long to go. My mouth feels furry – a testament to the giant pitcher of sugary cocktails I downed earlier to make my date more interesting. My watch tells me that I have about ten minutes to transform into Sensible Sunny™. Not a moment to lose. There's work to be done.

Pulling off the black hair tie around my wrist, I scoop up my hair, which I painstakingly and expertly waved just a few hours earlier, and tie it into a knot. I'm aiming for the artfully messy vibe but one glance in the murky train window tells me I look more like Miss Norris, my Year 7 PE teacher. This isn't the first time I've asked myself this, but should I go to Turkey and get a hair transplant? Just for the front bits, to sort out the wonky hairline that I spend hours trying to fill in with eyeshadow and coloured hairspray whenever I go on a date. I must have done something pretty heinous in a past life to have been cursed with fine, limp hair on my head and thick, coarse hair on my chin.

I fish out a compact and then a pack of chewing gum from my bag, pop two in my mouth and chew ferociously to get the alcohol off my breath and the fur off my tongue, pausing momentarily to wipe off bright-red matte lipstick with a crumpled tissue and soothe my lips with an ancient tube of Eight Hour Cream – I've never really liked the medicinal smell of it, but beauty editors say it is a staple and who am I to argue? A quick wipe around the eyes with my little finger rubs in the concealer that has stubbornly settled into the fine lines underneath them.

Drunken Baguette Man is still asleep, dribbling and snoring away, as I reach into my bag once more for a pair of sturdy 100-denier tights. This is always the point when I desperately hope the CCTV isn't working and that anyone in the vicinity is either passed out or too drunk to care ... I start to slide off my trainers carefully and shift sideways, bunching up my tights at the foot. Anyone who has ever worn tights knows that this is not an easy task at the best of times, but it's torture with the stingy leg room, my lack of flexibility and a stomach that insists on getting in the way of the most menial tasks. I manage to put in one foot and then the other and start wiggling them up past my smooth calves and hairy thighs. (I don't see the point in shaving above the knee, you see – I jokingly referred to it as 'single-girl shaving' when I last saw my cousins, and one of them looked like she was about to be violently ill in response. Of course, all my cousins can afford to have laser done – they're probably as smooth as seals from the eyebrows down.) I shuffle lower in my chair, hanging over the gap like I'm doing some complex yoga pose, as I try to hoick the tights over my bum and my chub-rub shorts. I throw a quick glance towards Johnny Two Baguettes, to check he's still sleeping. I swear I just saw his eyelids flicker. *Shit, shit, shit.* Why couldn't I just have packed leggings? What a fucking nightmare . . .

'*We will shortly be arriving at Gravesend,*' booms the announcement, and at that precise moment, Johnny Two Baguettes's eyes shoot wide open. As quickly as I can, I shuffle my bum off the seat, the tights creaking where they're all twisted up. I slip my trainers back on, grab my bag and stand up, shoulders back, chin up, like I wasn't just scrabbling around on a gross train seat trying to get dressed.

'You look better without make-up,' I hear a gruff voice say.

'Sorry?' But of course . . . Who else could it be but Johnny Two Baguettes?

'I said you look better without make-up. You don't need it.'

Despite his bloodshot eyes and the glob of Brie on his cheek, I find myself, just for a split second, wondering if he might be The One. They do say that you meet him when you least expect to. And by 'they' I mean people who don't have a fucking clue.

There are a number of things I could say right now but I don't want to start an argument, so I settle instead for my second-best tactic: ignoring him and hurrying off the train as soon as the doors open.

On the platform, I can feel the relief of escaping Johnny and his baguettes. Here, it's only me and a few stragglers – all couples, of course; giggly drunken women hanging off bull-necked men in short-sleeved shirts.

'I want cheesy chips, babe. Rainbow Kebab will still be open, won't it?'

'How are we getting home?'

'Gave me the shits last time.'

'My phone died.'

'Should have ordered a pizza while we were on the train.'

'My feet hurt.'

Even as I roll my eyes at their slurred conversation – who says romance is dead? – I feel a familiar pang of loneliness.

Why can't *I* have someone to stand in line with while we wait for our respective kebabs?

With fifteen minutes to spare before the small supermarket closes, I leave the kebab couples behind and cross the road. Late-night, post-date supermarket trips are the best way to unwind. I have a set shopping list for these occasions:

- Ham-and-cheese sandwich with mayo
- Cheese-and-onion crisps
- A can of Diet Coke (everyone knows a can tastes better)

This is then followed by a quick look at the flowers to see if there is a yellow-stickered bunch that doesn't look too sad. Sometimes I buy two. Lilies for my mum and either roses or tulips for my room. Never carnations: the basic bitch of the flower world.

This evening, I linger for a moment by the glazed pastries in their plastic boxes, and I long for my local independent coffee shop back in London. I've not been back there since I left the city almost two years ago. Not that I could afford to go there on the regular at the time anyway. But occasionally, I treated myself to an almond croissant and a tea, sitting in the corner trying to perfect the alluring café-girl look while surreptitiously brushing crumbs off my cleavage.

Life at home is a bit different now.

Mum has a strict no-snacks, no-fizzy-drinks policy, which only serves to exacerbate my secret eating.

One of the many joys of losing your office job in London and having to move back in with your parents at thirty. I hope the automated system they replaced me with is living my dream life, with as many snacks as it wants . . .

Finally, I find my way to the snacks aisle for my routine slab of chocolate or Peanut M&M's and a giant bag of cheesy puffs. The bargain section is located at the end of the aisle, but there's nothing there today so . . . onto the booze aisle for my pre-mixed drinks. Two gins in a tin go straight into my basket, and I give the toiletries, books and stationery a cursory glance, then off I go to the self-service tills. I should be opposed to self-service tills, according to a recent article in the *Guardian*, but quite honestly the relief of not having to talk to anyone or let anyone see the contents of my carb-heavy basket is worth it. I wave goodbye to the laid-back, tired-looking security guard. And eventually, I'm out of there. Nine minutes. Pleased with my efficiency, I scurry to the front of the taxi rank, hoping the driver waiting there is someone who doesn't know my dad, for once.

No such luck.

I immediately recognise the electric-blue people carrier – it belongs to an uncle who lives just around the corner from my parents' house.

Deep breath, Sensible Sunny™. I slap on my smile as normal and slide open the door. I'm greeted by a shiny metal khanda hanging off the mirror, LBC mumbling in the background and a faint scent of spices and hair oil. Eau de Uncle.

'Hi, Uncle,' I say, trying to shove some joy into my voice.

'Hello, Sunny beta, all right? Why so late?'

'Trains were messed up.' I'm frighteningly good at lying – one of the very few perks of living a double life.

'I been checking the app and they said all fine, no problem on the trains tonight.'

Of *course* he's bloody checked the app.

'Oh, erm, I meant the other train, my connecting train.'

'You be careful, beta, it's Friday night, all the gorey go mad on weekends, drinking and fighting. Every week the same. I'm going straight home after I'm dropping you off. Your aunty worries about me, you know.'

'How is she?' I ask, more out of politeness than genuine concern, and desperate to distract him from looking up all connecting train times too. Aunty is his second wife, who he married within months of getting divorced. She is a quiet young woman he brought over from India. She's barely older than me. When I raised the subject with Mum she retorted, 'Well, at least he's married, unlike you.' OK, so she didn't say that last bit, but she didn't need to.

'Good, good. She want to work. I said why you want to work? I am working. I give you what you need, money, for shopping.'

I weigh up whether I should say something; according to an article I skimmed in one of those free London magazines, this is one of the seven warning signs of financial abuse. 'Well, you know,' I start, trying to be tactful but clear. 'She might want her own money for ... ladies' things ... like make-up.'

'She doesn't need make-up. Nowadays too many women's wearing make-up. I don't like it.'

Ah, here we go again. This is the second make-up-related comment in the space of half an hour ... Once again, I weigh up whether I should say something, but I'm really not sure Uncle would be able to grasp the fact that women don't *just* wear make-up for men.

Thankfully, we are already turning the corner into my street, so I keep silent and try my second-best tactic again: I've got my keys and purse ready for a fast getaway.

'How are Mum and Dad?'

'Good, thanks. Gurdwara keeps Dad busy and Mum's . . . soldiering on!'

'I must come and see them some time.'

'Anytime!' I say, my voice unnaturally high with relief that this mega-awkward journey is nearing its end. Until I spot that the meter isn't on . . . 'Sorry, Uncle, how much is it?'

'No, no—' He looks so horrified you'd think I'd just wiped my nose on the seat. Ah, yes. The infamous Punjabi tussle over who gets to pay. I have seen men almost come to blows over who picked up the bill in restaurants, and I've witnessed women refusing money from other women so vehemently that they were in danger of taking an eye out. It is always a matter of honour and pride and can last for up to half an hour . . . I seriously do not have the energy for it tonight. 'No, come on, Uncle.'

'No, no, I am not taking money from you, you are like my own daughter.'

I've never been very good at it so, wearily, I put the tenner away and bid him goodnight.

As expected, he stays in his car, headlights on, watching and waiting for me to walk the final two metres to my front door on the off-chance a wayward attacker ambushes me in my last few steps. As soon as I unlock the door, I turn to him and wave him off, my cheeks aching from a solid ten minutes of fake smiling.

★   ★   ★

My parents go to bed at 10 p.m. every night without fail, after my mum orders my dad to check all the doors and windows, and reminding him to take his statins, so it's no surprise that when I slip off my trainers, as quietly as possible, the house is pitch black. I listen out for any noises. Just the faint snores from their room telling me that like every other time, my parents are safely asleep.

I trudge up the stairs, managing to successfully avoid the squeaky step halfway up, holding my keys tightly so they won't jangle and give me away, while simultaneously feeling my way along the wall in the dark. It's like being a drunk teenager all over again, except I'm thirty and almost sober. Years of skulking around has meant that I've got it down to a fine art.

'Sunny?'

*Shit, shit, shit.*

'Hi, Mum.' I'm trying to keep my voice as surprise-free as possible.

'So late? Everything OK?'

'Yeah. Trains.' I know I said I'm really good at lying, but lying to my mum is harder – she can smell lies like no one else, so it's easier to lie in monosyllables. The trick to lying to my mum is never to give too many details and to get the tone completely bang on. Too happy and she will think I'm fooling around with a boy; too sad and she will think I'm on drugs. Despite years of lying to her about everything from the price of a new top to whether I've ever drunk alcohol, I still get a small twinge of guilt every time.

'Have you eaten? I was worried. You know I can't sleep if you're late.'

'I just heard you snoring.'

'I don't snore – must have been your dad.'

'I'm OK, Mama, go back to bed.'

Through the darkness, I can see her nod her head and wander back into her bedroom.

I close my bedroom door gently behind me, tiptoe around the floordrobe and collapse onto my bed fully dressed. I could fall asleep just like this, but as I start to drift off, my phone flashes, the glare penetrating my eyelids.

*Had a great time! Hope you get home safe! Would love to meet up again if you're up for it ...? Xx*

Ugh. Two kisses. Too much. Abort mission.

This is where the snacks come in. Sighing deeply, I pull my bag closer to me, tip out my haul and start assembling a crisp sandwich. With my ham-and-crisp sandwich in one hand, my phone in the other, I head straight to my Notes app to assemble a different sort of sandwich.

### The Shit Sandwich
*Hey [insert name],*
*Had a great time too! You're [insert generic compliment]! I don't really see us being more than friends, figure it's best to be upfront about these things!*

*Take care and good luck with the [insert reference to upcoming event or career milestone].*

For the third time this week, I fill in the necessary gaps, send the message and hurriedly put my phone on airplane mode. On a normal day, sending the text would leave me feeling relieved, but tonight I have no feelings left – I'm just wrung out and morose.

Looking down, I realise I've already eaten my sandwich. Double carbs tend to cheer me up, though not tonight, it seems. So, brushing off the crumbs, I reach over to my bedside table and silently extract my vibrator ... but on second thoughts, that would mean getting the spare duvet out of the wardrobe and I really don't have the stamina right now. Instead, I settle for good, clean ocean noises. Just as I'm falling asleep, my brain slaps me in the face, revealing to me the perfect comeback for Johnny and the Baguettes.

Every fucking time.

# Chapter 2

'I can see him.'

'Pardon?'

'I can see him, he's right there.' She looks in the direction of my right ear, her eyes glazed over slightly; her voice is fortune-teller dreamy. 'Oh yes. He's going to be someone *very* special. He's coming in *very* soon. *Very* soon. I'd say in the next three to six months.'

'Erm. Wow. Thanks.'

'Right.' She slaps her sturdy thighs, her voice now brisk and business-like. 'Time's up. You've done some great work. I don't think you need another session, do you?'

I nod a bit too quickly and reach for my purse, pluck out £35 (which has taken my balance to exactly -£456) and place it gingerly on the chipped IKEA table between us. After our first session a month ago, when I had gone to hand over the notes, she had told me off and asked me to place them on the table, muttering darkly that, 'Money holds energy. I don't want to pick up yours – this is powerful work, after all.' I should have known then that she was not a proper therapist. But at least now I also know to always place the money on the table so as not to *infect* her with my negative energy.

I bid the therapist goodbye and as soon as I'm out of her office – decorated with framed certificates and twee seaside prints in cheap frames, faded from years of sunlight blazing through her grubby, paint-peeling windows – I pull my phone out of my pocket and can't call Natalie quick enough.

'Hiya, babes!' Natalie's voice beams down the phone. I don't think anyone will ever be so happy to hear from me as Natalie is.

To look at, Natalie and I are an unlikely pair. She is tall, olive-skinned and long-limbed. I am short with the build of a marshmallow. The only physical trait we share is our fine, thin hair that refuses to hold any sort of style, and as a result we both have matching long bobs.

Natalie is a potty-mouthed cockney who is eternally curious about all things spiritual. I met her seven years ago. I'd just sold a load of stuff on eBay and had decided to spend my earnings on a silent retreat nestled in the North York Moors of all places. All the other women at the retreat looked like they could contort their toned limbs into *any* position at *any* given moment. The type of women who could boldly shimmy into a sheath dress without worrying about their arms looking like hams at Christmas time. They spoke in hushed, reverential tones; what I call 'a spiritual voice'. It's kind of breathy and husky and patronising all at the same time. While they daintily dipped organic carrots into violently lilac and lumpy beetroot dip, I was sitting at the end of the table with a glass of water, silently praying that no one could tell I'd scoffed two full-size Mars bars on the coach up.

At that moment, Natalie whirled into the room, late, in a pair of blindingly jazzy harem pants and the kind of strappy vest top I would *never* dare wear in public. She filled the room with the kind of cockney foghorn voice I thought only existed in *Carry On* films. If her voice was funny, her laugh was even better – infectious, deep and full.

'I've just come back from Ibiza, haven't I?' she declared when someone complimented her on her tan. I imagined her zipping around the island on a scooter, jumping off rocks into the sea, while all around her boys with eyes of liquid gold fell at her feet.

All the silent-retreaters were transfixed. She was loose-limbed and olive skinned while I was trying to ignore the fact that the waistband of my joggers was digging into my hips and the cheap, long-sleeved top I'd bought from Primark was making me itch.

I *hated* her on sight, of course. She was everything I wasn't: confident, unapologetic, comfortable in her own skin. But, on the penultimate day of the retreat, she saw me struggling with the almost-vertical hike and discreetly dropped behind the rest of the group to disclose that she could murder a glass of wine, thereby breaking the sacred vow of silence we had taken at the beginning of the week.

Now she's my go-to. My emergency contact. My ride or die. Despite the fact that she lives 200 miles away in Sheffield.

'My therapist just told me I am going to meet my soulmate in the next three to six months.'

'You fucking what?!' she screeches.

'She went all Sally Morgan on me.'

'But I thought she was gonna help you with your anxiety and that, not mess with your love life . . .'

'So did I.'

'Oh, well. Fuck her. It takes a while to find the right match, babes.'

'Yeah. I mean, she did at least diagnose me with depression and anxiety.' I pause for a second, remembering the moment she said it. The relief that washed over me. Everything clicked into place. That it had a *name* and wasn't just my 'personality'. And along with it, there was the shame. How had I not realised something so glaringly obvious for so long? 'So I guess she did do something. I dunno . . . Maybe I was hoping she'd help me get to the root of it all, or at the very least give me some coping strategies . . . All she did was tell me that the clothes-pegs thing meant I had OCD too.'

'The what?'

'When I put the washing out, the clothes pegs need to be the same colour as the clothing.'

'We *all* have stuff like that, babe.' Natalie's deep voice is comforting down the phone. 'I can't get up until the time either ends in a five or a zero. I don't think that's OCD, that's just one of them little things. Anyway, you never know, she might turn out to be right. Maybe you *will* meet someone at the wedding.'

I groan loudly. I've fantasised about meeting The One at weddings since I was fifteen. We'd bump into each other on the dance floor, my bangle would get caught on the sleeve of his kurta and in the process of untangling ourselves, he would fall in love with the way a faint blush bloomed across my perfect cheekbones. Cheekbones that neither fifteen-year-old Sunny, nor indeed thirty-year-old Sunny, possessed. Bollywood has a lot to answer for – especially heightening the romantic expectations of shy, chubby Indian teenagers from Gravesend.

'I doubt it. I met Ajay's mates at his birthday drinks. They're all *Wolf of Wall Street* types with tiny twenty-three-year-old girlfriends. And too-tight chinos.'

Next spring, Ajay is marrying Anjali, one of my best friends from uni, in a giant Indian extravaganza at a super-fancy venue near Richmond.

'Well, fuck 'em then. You know what I think about people in their twenties—'

'No one has anything interesting to say until the age of twenty-eight.' I finish her sentence with a quiet giggle.

'Exactly. Right now, there's a fella out there on a shitty first date or in a relationship with a right boring bastard wishing he could be with someone as sparkly and beautiful as you. You just gotta wait it out a bit longer.'

'Yeah . . .' I reply unconvincingly.

'And if not, me and you, we're gonna buy a bloody great big villa in Italy when we retire and get pissed on red wine every day and hire hot male nurses to wheel us about.'

I laugh at the image and feel the knot in my solar plexus loosen. I feel like I can breathe again.

'*Aloysius! Stop it!* Sorry, Sunny, my dog's eating something he's found in the park. What a knob. *Drop it!*'

Aloysius is a miniature schnauzer, one of those dogs that look like a grumpy old man and has the personality of one too. He hates children and loud noises. We have a lot in common.

'Sorry, babe, can I call you back?'

'Of course. Love you.'

In Poundland, I grab my usual selection of sweet and savoury snacks, two tubes of Nair (fuck waxing) for my arms for the upcoming family do tomorrow, a 'Happy Anniversary' card for my chachi and chacha, a box of dark-brown hair dye and a packet of vanilla-scented tealights.

My mind is still on the therapist and the crap she fed me in our four sessions. In our first session, she gave me a pad of A4 paper and a black biro and told me to draw a tree. I was terrified. I hadn't sketched anything since Year 8 art with Mr Williamson and I can't draw to save my life. I *hate* not being good at stuff. But I drew her a tree floating in the air with thick, uniform branches. She frowned at it for a few seconds and told me that the bare branches symbolised my loneliness. The floating tree? It proved I didn't feel safe or grounded.

At the time it sounded insightful. Now it just seems basic. Like a horoscope in the paper. And what was that stuff she said today about a soulmate coming into my life? But as much as I hate to admit it, there's a bubble of excitement rising in my chest at the thought of her 'premonition' coming true. I've already made a note in my Google calendar for six months' time. You never know . . .

The therapist wasn't *all* bad, *all* the time. She did teach me about 'transactional analysis'. The idea that, broadly speaking, all of us are either behaving like a parent, an adult or a child. That was useful. She also helped me understand why my ex was now my ex. According to her, I was *always* the parent in my relationships, unconsciously mimicking my own parents: worrying unnecessarily, being hypercritical and taking care of others, which meant that I was never taken care of. I'd gone straight home and got into bed fully dressed and cried about that for the rest of the afternoon. She was right. But how do I go about letting others take care of me when even the thought of asking someone for help makes me do a full-body cringe?

As usual, I walk home past a gaggle of Sikh taxi drivers, their moustaches waxed, polystyrene cups of steaming tea clutched in their hands, and I hear a deep rumble of laughter. Snatches of their conversation in Punjabi float towards me. 'This gurdwara committee is no good, I'm tellin' you. They are like politicians telling you what you want to hear so that you will vote for them. They won't get in this time.'

The last thing I want is to be recognised by an uncle, so I charge past, head down, eyes firmly fixed on the ground. By 'uncle' I don't mean a blood relative; I mean someone who knows my dad, who will grill me on what I'm up to, my job and educational achievements, in order to check if I'm a suitable match for his apparently perfect son. Usually, I'd get grilled about all these things by uncles and aunties at the gurdwara, but I only go for weddings or special occasions these days. Diwali, which was just last week, was full of all that. But I survived. I need to remind myself of that. I survived.

I love Diwali and everything it stands for: the triumph of good over evil and the reminder to fight for the rights of all communities, not just your own. I love the smell of fireworks and autumn thick in the air, the gurdwara lit with hundreds of strands of lights that cascade from the domed roof, and families lighting diyas outside the entrance, even though the anxious part of me always worries about dupattas catching fire. I enjoy seeing the familiar sight of the early-morning queues outside Virdee Stores for hot, sticky jalebis like molten-lava-shaped curlicues, sticking to the inside of the box, and my personal favourite: besan – blocks of smooth, sugary sunshine cut into cubes. Perfect with a hefty mug of strong but milky cha.

When I'm grilled by aunties, with their smiles that never quite reach their eyes, I always say I'm busy with work. A safe answer, seeing as work is king and busyness is the ultimate sign of success. They nod approvingly at this, while telling me it's important to make time for God, before moving on to their next unsuspecting victim. The real reason I don't go to the gurdwara is social anxiety. Or, more precisely, the fear of bumping into people I went to school with. The snooty Indian girls with the mirror-shine hair and the latest Kickers – the real ones, not the fake ones my mum bought me from Shoe Express. I left school almost half my lifetime ago but the sight of those girls – well, women – still fills me with dread, even though they're now mothers with at least two kids a piece and husbands who have sensible jobs and flashy cars. They still look better than me. Their eyebrows are perfectly groomed, their contouring on point and their salwar kameez elegant and perfectly fitted to their willowy bodies. Of course, it's easier to get a salwar kameez if you are under a size twelve. As a generous size eighteen, I have to get mine made. Or I get to choose from the two outdated, garish neon-purple ones gathering dust at the back of the shop.

This year, for Diwali, I stuck to my usual uniform of black leggings and a long, shapeless top that comes down to my knees. Accessories are a fat girl's friend. A small pair of hoops and understated make-up so I didn't look like I'd died the week before, but also like I hadn't tried too hard.

Sadly, though, I won't get away with this uniform for the party tomorrow – I'll probably have to wear one of the two Indian outfits I own that fit me at the moment. Something my perfect cousins don't have to worry about – a fact I'll be confronted with when I see them tomorrow at their parents' wedding-anniversary party. No doubt they'll be dressed as if it's their own wedding.

What a joy. I can't wait to be compared to Harrow's very own answer to the Kardashians.

# Chapter 3

Walking up the path to my house – a modest 1950s terrace with a brand-new porch built purely for shoe storage – I pull out my keys from my pocket, my Poundland goodies rustling at my side.

'Hi, Mama!' I call, stepping onto the mat and taking off my shoes.

'How was your meeting, puth?' Mum calls back from the kitchen.

I can't tell Mum I went to therapy. She already worries about my marriage prospects, which are dwindling as fast as my waistline is expanding. I told her I was going to meet a friend of a friend about a potential job at the council. It's always been a dream of hers that I work for the council, in any capacity. She just likes how it sounds. Unlike customer-service advisor for a furniture store, which is my actual job.

I follow her voice into the kitchen, where she's picking off dead leaves of coriander and chopping it up to freeze. Our next-door neighbour works on a farm and from time to time gives us a bunch or two of coriander or fenugreek. Sometimes, I wonder if it's the highlight of Mum's month.

'It was good, thanks. Very productive.' The lie slips smoothly off my tongue as I go to kiss her on the cheek, worrying that if I get too close she might be able to smell my deception.

She looks at me for a moment, watching me. 'You are distracted, puth?' she says, as though it's a question.

I simply nod towards her coriander.

'This will see us through winter,' she says immediately, easing the blue elastic band off another plump bundle of coriander, pleased with herself.

'Looks fresh. Do you want cha, Mama?'

'Chal, go on then, I've only had one cup today,' she replies solicitously.

'Kettle or desi?' I ask. Different occasions call for different types of tea. Standard tea – a teabag and boiling water – is for when you're in a rush or feeling lazy, and desi is for cold mornings and chilly autumn days like today when only a mug of strong, peppery tea will do.

I manage to extract the specially designated stainless-steel tea saucepan without dislodging the many other saucepans. I once tried to explain the KonMari method to my mum, taking each saucepan out and asking her if it sparked joy. She told me in no uncertain terms to never bring it up again. I reach for the loose-leaf tea brought back from India by a family friend and the mini pestle and mortar. Mum doesn't believe in using pre-made masala powders or those specially made stainless-steel tins to store spices. All her spices are kept in glass jars previously occupied by pesto, olives and strawberry jam.

I could do this with my eyes closed; in fact, I often did in my teens, waking up early to feed family members from India, bleary-eyed as I bashed the pale-green cardamom pods to reveal their black seeds, which always remind me of mouse droppings.

I plate up the biscuits as the tea boils. Custard creams for me and sugar-free digestives for Mum.

'Where's Dad?'

'Out asking for votes, where else?'

Dad has been out canvassing for the upcoming gurdwara presidential elections every day for the past two weeks from morning until night. This time around it's one of his oldest friends standing for president, a mild-mannered man who he used to work with at the factory before they retired. The election is in a week's time. It's always a tense time in our household, and indeed among the local Sikh community. Every time, I've voted for the person my dad tells me to vote for. It makes him happy, and I never know the difference between the two candidates anyway. There's always the threat of violence between supporters, often exacerbated by poison pen letters, alcohol and good old-fashioned machismo . . . *The West Wing* has nothing on gurdwara elections.

When I climb into my unmade bed, after Mum demands I 'rest after your big meeting', I open my bag and spread out my haul, scattering my duveted body with Peanut M&M's, toffee popcorn, two cans of Diet Coke (two for a pound) and a six-pack of cheese-and-onion crisps.

On autopilot, I take a quick scroll through Instagram to see square after square of throwbacks to luxury holidays abroad and immaculate minimalist homes in neutral tones and at least one photo of someone holding the keys to their new flat.

It's coming up to 5 p.m., the optimal time to post . . . the time when all my friends, with their perfect lives, boyfriends and kids on the way, will be checking up on the lives of other people. It's also the time when my exes, and all the guys I've dated, are staring at Instagram, waiting for the final hour of their dream desk job to end. Five p.m. is prime time for likes. I hate that I know these things, that it's *important* to me, but it's pretty much the only validation I get these days. I settle for a photo from when I went on holiday to Morocco a few years back. I look tanned, happy, carefree and, most importantly, slimmer, in a black summer dress with an embellished neckline. It's the picture I use on dating apps, as I've got a hint of cheekbones and I'm sitting down so you can't really tell how big I am. It says, 'I'm fun, but I'm not a party animal!'

The only reason I don't block exes or dates from Instagram is because they need to know I'm doing well, that I'm successful and have a life. Even though I don't.

After I've messed about with filters for a bit and googled quotes about travel, they'll never know the truth from my Instagram reality.

Surrounded by my Poundland buys, I type: 'We travel, some of us forever, to seek other states, other lives, other souls.'

I hold my breath as I press post and wait for the first like to roll in.

There it is.

*Ah.*

That familiar rush of dopamine.

I crack open the crisps as I read the comments.

*Omg you look great hun! Xx*

*Fitttt!*

*Love that dress! Where's it from?!*

I spot a like from a guy I once dated, who called himself 'ethically non-monogamous' – a fact he later admitted he hadn't bothered sharing with his long-term girlfriend. He was interesting, but it wasn't for me. Not at the time, anyway. These days, I wonder if it's more realistic to have a different boyfriend for each occasion, in the same way different drinks are suited to different moments ... One guy for the family events, the other for cinema dates and the other for essential life things like airport pick-ups and McDonald's runs.

I think about Michael. Does he still look at my feed? It's why I kept my profile public, so he could see that I'm absolutely fine without him.

He doesn't need to know that I'm in bed at 4.55 p.m., having just been dumped by my therapist.

I share the post to my stories and refresh a few times, checking if he's seen it.

This is how I know I still have feelings for him. This and the fact that I still check his horoscope (not in the paper; I don't trust those) when I read mine first thing every morning.

I unfollowed him because I thought it would help me forget him. It didn't. Six months later, I still check every few days to see if his profile is still private. It is.

But he never posted much when we were dating anyway. Sometimes he'd put the odd meme on his stories. Or a photo of him holding a mug of coffee or a protein shake, and I'd see a glimpse of his arm, pleasingly hairy and strong, and it would send such a strong pang of longing through me, like a shock wave. But I still won't contact him out of pure stubbornness, and he won't contact me because he's an emotionally unavailable prick.

I look down. I've already eaten three packets of crisps yet barely tasted them. I take a swig of lukewarm tea and push away the feelings of guilt that are bubbling to the surface as I survey the empty crisp packets littering the bed. I gather them up and push them into the bin, making sure they're hidden from view. The last thing I need is another of Mum's lectures about how difficult it is to lose weight as you get older.

I immediately download a thirty-day squat-challenge app and consider starting on Monday, but I force myself to get up. Damage-limitation time.

The app says to start at thirty squats, which seems doable. I try to ignore the perky Lycra-clad coach attempting to motivate me with her bland affirmations, her enthusiasm as fake as her tits.

I just about manage to complete the squats, fuelled purely by spite.

*God. If past me could see me now.*

I flop back onto the bed.

What would I have been doing in my previous life in London?

I'd probably have been getting ready to go out. Music blaring, wine poured, face mask on. Getting ready is always the best bit. The fizz of excitement about who you might meet. And then it's the Tube into town. Drinks, then dinner, more drinks. Then someone tentatively suggests shots and we all roar in agreement. Then there'd be the perilous Uber journey home, where you talk too loudly and brightly in a useless attempt to hide how drunk you are, just in case the Asian taxi driver knows your family.

Back then, even the hangover the next day was funny: the usual proclamations of 'never again', the double carbs and flat Coke and the day spent in bed watching something comforting and familiar that doesn't require any concentration.

Now my weekends consist of housework, doing the big shop with my dad and making endless cups of tea for the unexpected aunty who inevitably drops in without any notice. I'd forgotten the pure terror of sitting down to eat and then hearing the doorbell ring, followed by the military-like precision of removing all trace of our previous activity, while putting on a large pan of boiling water for cha, plating up two different types of snack (one sweet, one savoury) that everyone will stare at but no one will eat, while the uninvited guests and my mum make thinly veiled passive-aggressive jibes at each other.

'Sunny!' Mum calls sharply from downstairs. 'Have you finished resting? Time to get your suit ready for tomorrow!'

Chacha and Chachi's party will be celebrated in a function hall in Harrow. They're the branch of the family that have done well for themselves, the latest evidence of which is an eight-bedroom house somewhere outside Harrow. I preferred their old house in Hounslow, with its floral carpets and flock wallpaper.

They now live in a white-and-chrome nightmare, with a TV so big it distorts the picture, which serves only to enhance the nightmare vibe. My chachi Jaswinder, who used to only wear salwar kameez and pin her long hair in place with a selection of gaudy plastic clips, has now had her hair cut and coloured into a sharp, geometric rust-tinted bob. She now shops exclusively in River Island.

She looks great, don't get me wrong, she just doesn't look like my Chachi any more.

I stare, dejected, at my reflection in the mirrored wardrobe. One half of my wardrobe is full of Indian outfits that no longer fit me. My mum doesn't trust online shopping and thinks it's a scam, so all of my clothes have either been sent over by a kindly aunt from India ('Oof, I had to search *all* of Phagwara for a ready-made outfit that will fit her!') or came from tear-inducing trips to Southall where all the outfits were three seasons old and cost three times as much.

I pull out a bright orange-and-gold salwar kameez.

The tunic just about fits. It's a little tight around the tops of my arms, but if I drape the dupatta over one of them hopefully no one will notice. I pick out a matching fiery-orange bindi, chunky gold-coloured jhumka earrings, matching gold bangles and my trusty Punjabi jutti – the *perfect* dressy shoe in my opinion. They're flat, so ideal for my wide, almost-rectangular feet, and I can get away with saying that I'm going with a traditional look when really it's just because I can't walk in heels.

This will do. This will *have* to do.

# Chapter 4

'How long do I keep it on?' Mum says in a muffled voice.

'It's nearly dry, Mama. A few more minutes.'

I'd be lying if I said I didn't cherish the fact that the clay mask means Mum can't speak for a bit. It has already been a hectic morning – the party is just hours away, and my mum usually expends her nervous energy with a running commentary of what she is doing. On a normal day, either she is criticising me for not putting the washing out correctly, or she's telling me about a YouTube video she has watched about the many uses of fennel seeds. Today, however, she has been talking non-stop about what we need to prepare ahead of the party, what I should and shouldn't talk about and who I should and shouldn't talk to. This changes from family occasion to family occasion and is generally dependent on who has pissed her off since the last event. This time around I have been told not to be too friendly with the Glasgow contingent because they didn't invite us to a birthday party. We wouldn't have gone if they had, but that's beside the point apparently. The clay-mask idea came to me at the last minute, and it has been a stroke of pure genius.

Mum will never admit it, but she gets just as nervy as me about family dos, especially when it's Dad's side of the family. She's never gone into detail, but *I* know that she doesn't really like any of his brothers' wives. When you see them together, they are all laughter and hugs and smiles. She sends them all Christmas cards and remembers all their kids' birthdays. But

I recognise her discomfort in the tightness across her shoulders, in the way her usually generous, wide-mouthed smile becomes taut and practised.

Dad walks in half-dressed in a white vest and grey trousers, his neat little pot belly hanging over the waistband.

Mum opens one eye. 'Why aren't you ready?' she says, shedding fine flakes of clay onto her top.

'Where's my tie?'

'With your suit.'

'It's not. I've checked.'

'It is, I put it there myself. Look with your *eyes*.' She's glaring at him. Somehow she manages to be formidable despite the toothpaste-green face mask.

He trudges back up the stairs as she leans back and sighs exasperatedly.

'Found it!' he calls back down to us moments later.

Whenever we're about to leave the house, Dad will *always* start cleaning the car fully dressed up, vacuuming and polishing it with a selection of grubby-looking rags. It will *always* make us late and frantic, and will inevitably lead to a spat culminating in a stony silence on the drive to our destination, until my dad breaks the ice by offering Mum a boiled sweet from the glove box.

We don't apologise in this house. We offer food as a peace offering and you must accept it or be branded 'sensitive' – the *worst* thing you can be in a Punjabi family.

Knowing that my parents are going to find all sorts of reasons to delay us, I don't want to be one of them, so I leave my mum, with her face mask still on, and go and get ready. I'm already dreading wearing the outfit, but it's too late to change my mind now. I've got to hope my nice but subtle make-up idea will do the trick.

I think I'm making good time until . . .

'SUNNY!' Mum shouts at the top of her voice. My hand jogs, just as I'm lining my left eye, aka 'the tricky eye'. There's now a big black smudge where my almost-perfect flicky eyeliner was meant to be. I don't have the energy and we definitely don't have the time for me to start again. I reach for my dark eyeshadow instead. I guess I'll go for the smoky-eye look now . . .

Once I'm finally downstairs, my parents are already in full argument mode. What is it today?

I look outside to see if Dad is washing the car again but he's not there.

Oh *no*.

Dad has decided to polish his shoes *after* getting dressed.

'*What* are you doing now?' Mum click-clacks into the hall-way in her ancient kitten heels that I've been trying to get rid of for years.

'The card said two p.m. No one gets there on time,' he says, casually buffing his shoes with an oily chamois cloth.

'We are always late – everybody is always joking. And there is always traffic coming back on Sundays and you can't drive in the dark.' She turns to me. 'Suit looks nice, Sunny.'

'Very nice, puth,' adds my dad. 'Why don't you wear more often? Makes you look taller.'

'She is already tall enough,' Mum snaps back, checking the contents of her handbag.

'Mama, I'm only five foot four.'

'That is tall enough for girls. Do you have the card? Present?'

I hold up the gift bag, containing some sort of crystal orna-ment that my mum spent hours wrapping.

'*Who* celebrate their anniversary? Just because we are *living* in a white country doesn't mean we are *white*.'

This is one of Mum's most-used phrases. It's brought out when she sees Indian girls with dyed blonde hair, when my cousin called her firstborn Josh and when Asian people put their elders in a care home.

Mum is wearing a pale-green salwar kameez with fine gold embroidery on the hem and neckline. Her bun is held in place by a garish gold hairclip. The grey at her temples makes her look *distinguished*. Unlike me, she has pretty much been the same size ever since I can remember. She attributes this to her daily walks and the fact that she only eats one roti for dinner and hardly ever has dessert. I attribute it to her having more self-control than me. She grabs a hideous cardigan the colour of a cold cup of tea, with faux pearl buttons and floral appliqué patches on the front.

'Muuuum . . .'

'What?'

'Please don't . . .'

'It's cold. You are not feeling it yet, but *I* am, OK?' She buttons it right up to her chin.

'It's twelve degrees, Mama, I've checked. Why don't you put a shawl on instead?' Over the past few years, I've bought her an assortment of embroidered shawls – not those cheap pashminas that you get on Tottenham Court Road, two for £6, but properly nice cashmere ones from M&S or John Lewis. Of course, I have to lie about how much they cost. I can count on one hand how many times I've told my mum the real price of something. It's just not worth the hassle. And if she can't bear how much the shawls I've bought cost her, she'd have a *fit* if she discovered I'd spent over £200 talking to someone about my feelings.

Eventually we compromise, and she opts for a pale-gold shawl – last year's Christmas present – draped around her shoulders. It does a good job of hiding the monstrosity of a cardigan she's got on underneath.

'Mama, shall I do your make-up?'

'I've done already.'

Mum's idea of make-up is a cerise lipstick from Max Factor, a bit of powder and a dark-brown eye pencil. It took me years to persuade her to bin the harsh black kohl pencil she had been using since her twenties.

'Just a little bit, Mama, really light, a little bit of mascara maybe?'

'Nobody is looking at me, worry about yourself,' she says offhandedly as she neatly folds up a Kleenex and places it in her clutch. I don't push her further, knowing that this could very easily turn into a lecture about finding a husband.

Her beauty routine consists of Nivea cream twice a day, Dove soap (I had to wean her off Imperial Leather a few years ago and she will not hear of facial cleansers) and sometimes cutting off a bit of the aloe vera plant in the kitchen and squeezing out the goo to rub on her face.

'What are you doing now?' My dad appears in the doorway.

'Waiting for *you*.' She tuts at him.

'I'm waiting for *you* in the car.'

'Chalo, Sunny, get in the car. I'm going to check the back door and make sure the telly is on, make it look like we are home.

'Mum, we have a burglar alarm . . .'

'Shh, shh, get in the car.'

And, only forty minutes late, we are finally on our way.

As my dad pulls the car into the car park, I see an imposing red-brick building with a neatly manicured lawn already being destroyed by a gaggle of young boys running around in their party clothes, the knees of their trousers caked with mud.

'Nicer than their wedding day,' murmurs Mum, somehow managing to sound both impressed and disapproving.

I spot a few familiar cars in the car park, the personalised number plates a dead giveaway. They're all much fancier than ours, even though my dad has just caved and bought a Nissan Qashqai after years of holding onto his dilapidated Ford Escort. The Qashqai is my dad's pride and joy, but here it sticks out like a sore thumb among the sleek Audis and Mercedes that fill the car park.

We walk into the hall, which is festooned with white and gold balloons, our shoes sinking into the violently patterned carpet. The music is deafening, and it looks more like the Kardashians' Christmas Eve party than an anniversary party. Behind the DJ is a large screen displaying a montage of my chacha and chachi's life together. From shy and awkward teenagers to young adults at their wedding, back when my uncle wasn't even able to grow a proper beard and my aunt looked like a porcelain doll wrapped in a gold-and-pink sari and draped in heavy yellow-gold jewellery, a red bindi dominating her bird-like face. The photos morph seamlessly from grainy shots of newlyweds to my chachi holding a plump baby with a full head of fuzzy hair: their firstborn, my cousin, only a few years younger than me. Then there are Christmases, trips to India, more babies and a holiday to Disneyland – obligatory photo with Mickey Mouse. And finally, the latest addition to their perfect family: their German shepherd, Rocky.

As I bring my eyes away from the screen, back to the room, I spot Chachi making a beeline for us, dressed in a surprisingly revealing powder-pink sari that makes Mum stiffen with distaste. My dad is oblivious, as always, and is chatting away to a distant cousin about the price of gold.

'Happy anniversary, Chachi-ji. You look amazing!' I coo as I go to hug her.

'Oh, thank you, Sunny! You look nice in a suit – makes you look taller.' Out of the corner of my eye, my mum gives my dad a knowing look. Chachi grabs me by the shoulders a bit too tightly, before looking me up and down. I make sure my overly bright smile doesn't falter. The law of the jungle applies to my family. Never show weakness. They can smell it.

# Chapter 5

We're seated towards the front of the hall at one of the many large round tables covered in a snow-white tablecloth, which my mum stealthily rubs between her fingers, checking the quality. Flanked by my parents, I do some stealthy checking of my own, wondering if today might be the day my therapist's premonition comes true. But, sadly, it looks like I'm related to *every* man here.

Two of my cousins, Jasmine and Simran, float over in expensive-looking lehengas, their plump lips parted in polite smiles, showing off their perfect teeth, and their noses perfect thanks to Harley Street's finest. Not even a trace of the awkward, bushy-browed, buck-toothed cousins I used to play hide-and-seek with.

'Hi, Tai-ji, hi, Taya-ji,' they chorus in heavily accented Punjabi that makes me flinch.

'Hello, hello!' booms my dad, brushing crisp crumbs out of his beard.

'Hello, puth, all right? Look at you, so slim, both of you. Don't you eat?' my mum sighs wistfully.

'Oh my God, Tai-ji, I've put *on* weight,' says Jasmine, pinching a bit of smooth, unblemished skin at her waist.

I keep smiling. I hold my stomach in and sit up taller. *Show no fear, Sunny.*

'Where? I can't see,' proclaims my mum, grabbing Simran's slender arm and squeezing it. She looks to me for agreement. I just smile back blandly.

'Hi, Sunny!' They turn to me in unison.

'Hi, how are you? You look great!' I hug them both, catching a whiff of something expensive. They have that sheen only money can buy.

'So do you, I love the *simple* look, really suits you,' says Jasmine earnestly, giving me the same once-over her mum did.

'Oh, you know me, I'm low maintenance,' I say lightly.

They both laugh with their matching delicate, tinkling laughs as they toss their matching glossy, thick hair over their shoulders.

'So nice to see you guys – it's been *ages*. You should come over soon!' croons Simran.

'Definitely, I'd love that,' I lie smoothly, grabbing both of their hands and hoping they can't tell that I'd rather roll around on broken glass than spend any length of time with them.

As soon as they drift away, making promises of setting up dates, I eye up the crisps and nuts in the middle of the table. I didn't have breakfast because my outfit is tight enough and I didn't want to look bloated; this material isn't very forgiving. I look around to see my cousins now flaunting their midriffs in another direction. Everyone else is either taking selfies or having noisy reunions with people they only ever see at these parties, and the only people eating are kids who are being bribed/soothed with snacks, or old women who don't give a shit. My stomach growls in response. I'm neither a child nor an old woman, so I decide to fill up on orange juice instead. That seems acceptable, right?

I spot a steady stream of portly, moustachioed uncles making their way to one corner of the room.

Oh *hello*.

They're heading straight for a bar, tucked tidily away in the far corner. Sadly, ours is the kind of family where women are not supposed to drink, and even though we all do it privately, none of us would dream of drinking in front of our families. Apart from the Glasgow cousins; they seem to not give a shit. My mum blames it on their absent father. The rest of my cousins have set their Instagram to private so no snooping aunties can see photos of them dressed in their miniscule Boohoo dresses, getting drunk on cocktails at the Shard. It's another one of those unwritten rules, like keeping your boyfriend a secret until he proposes and pretending you're a virgin until your wedding night.

The barman has a *lovely* smile and broad shoulders that fill his waistcoat. His dark, almost black hair falls perfectly over one eye and frames his pretty features. I have an intense urge to push it back from his face. With my bum still firmly fixed to my chair, I allow my gaze to follow the barman as he pours perfect pints and laughs at one of the uncles' jokes.

Suddenly, in my mind's eye, we're in a bathroom cubicle. He's pushed me up against the wall. He's topless and kissing me all over. Moaning into my ear as he runs his hands over my breasts, kneading them gently, causing me to gasp so loudly I'm afraid the aunties queuing up outside, desperate for a wee, can hear me.

'Sunny! Sunny!' My mum thrusts her empty glass at me, before I even get to check out his name on his nametag, discarded on the imaginary bathroom cubicle floor, and then gestures to the jug of tropical fruit juice with it. I reluctantly turn my head away from my dreamy barman and fill her up.

Recently, whenever I've seen a guy like that, my mind has gone into a full fantasy-daydream sequence. I seem to plan my life out like I'm starring in a film in my head. It's like my special power, whenever I want to be transported somewhere else entirely, away from all the aunties and uncles and snooty cousins.

As soon as I turn back, I can see him flirting with one of the Glasgow cousins. Of *course* it's one of the Glasgow cousins.

'Ladies and gentlemen,' the DJ booms in a mock-American accent. 'We have a lovely surprise for you today. Please clear the dance floor and put your hands together for a very special performance for our lovely couple, Mr and Mrs Sanghera.'

The music switches to a remix of a famous 1970s Bollywood number, and every *single* one of my first cousins, except for *me*, walks onto the dance floor to take their positions. Even the ones who can't dance are up there shaking their hips to Lata Mangeshkar telling her lover to meet her by the shade of the peepal tree. I look at my mum, who is watching them, stony-faced. Everyone else in the room is cheering them on and whooping, filming them on their phones. Even the barman is staring at them, transfixed.

My stomach turns. I shouldn't have come. I could have made an excuse, but then I would never have heard the end of it from my mum. I wait for the dance to finish, trying to keep my gaze fixed above their heads so I don't have to see them shimmying their perfect bodies in time to the music, so I don't have to see everyone's enchanted faces staring at them like they're goddesses, and when it's over, I clap politely, my cheeks aching from the overly wide grin.

As soon as the starters arrive – the standard aloo tikki with far too much chilli, partly submerged in an assortment of watery chutneys – I tuck in. I'm absolutely starving by this point and don't care how I look. Mid-mouthful, Jasmine appears at my side, flicking her hair over her shoulder, a delicate sheen of sweat on her smooth brow.

'That was great,' I say, hastily swallowing a chunk of over-spiced potato, trying to sound excited and enthusiastic.

'Oh God, I was *sooo* embarrassed,' she says, in her typical faux-modest way, covering her mouth with a delicate, hairless hand.

'No, no, you were fantastic, we loved it!'

'What did you think, Tai-ji?' she says, addressing my mum.

My mum's smile doesn't quite reach her eyes and only I can tell that she's going to be adding my aunty, uncle and their whole family to the no-speak list alongside the Glasgow contingent.

'Very nice, puth. Very nice dancing.' She is barely looking at Jasmine, and I can feel her attention is really on me.

Jasmine turns back to me, seemingly satisfied with my mum's response. 'We would have asked you to be part of the dance, Sunny, but we *know* it's not your thing. Hope you don't mind!'

'No, of course not!' I shudder comically. 'Dancing in front of other people is literally my worst nightmare.'

It's not. I *love* dancing. They know that. When we were younger, I was always the first one on the dance floor, the one who made up dances to Michael Jackson songs and taught them all in our garden whenever they came over. We would all put on performances for our parents, who clapped along and cheered. Until my mum would grab me and put a black dot from her trusty black kohl pencil behind my ear to ward off nazar.

As soon as Jasmine leaves, gliding over to another table, collecting compliments like they're a tithe, I WhatsApp all my uni friends the same message:

*Gals, this is torture. I've just had to watch my cousins do a shitty dance and I'm not even allowed to drink. HELP xx*

I wait for a reply. Nothing. Which isn't like them. I wish I had someone to text, someone who was duty-bound to reply, like a boyfriend.

Before I can talk myself out of it, I take myself off to the bath-room, giving my mum some excuse about the food being too spicy, and as soon as I'm sitting on the toilet, the bhangra music just a muffled '*dff dff dff*' through the bathroom walls, I open up one dating app. It's almost a habit now – I know it's not good for me, or at least it's not something I *enjoy*, but it feels like a neces-sary evil – and, as though I haven't looked at it every few hours, I check my profile again to make sure the photos are bang on.

*No-nonsense thirty-year-old human woman looking for a kind, funny man with minimal hang-ups, the balls to text first and the ability to show emotion. As I am not a baggage handler, please make sure you have your s\*\*t together.*

With the therapist's 'predictions' popping up again in my mind, I get swiping.

We finally manage to extract ourselves from the party using the excuse of 'Sunday-evening traffic' – Mum's lie this time, not mine. As we say our goodbyes, I can feel her moving closer towards me, as though forming some kind of protective barrier between me and everyone else.

We bundle into the car, clutching giant boxes of Ferrero Rocher, waving and smiling until we turn the corner, then, right on cue, Mum announces, folding her arms: 'Now I have seen everything. Dancing like that, close, close, with her husband – she is the mother of three children! No sharam. White-people behaviour,' she tuts, shaking her head so violently her clip threatens to come undone.

Just as I predicted, Mum has a lot to say about Chachi's dancing at the end of the evening. Dad stares out at the road, not saying a word. He knows the best course of action is to keep quiet and let my mum come to a natural pause. She's like one of those spinning tops: she'll keep going and going for what feels like forever, until she wears herself out and gradually slows down, second by second, before falling over completely – all energy gone.

'Mum . . .'

'Not even *asking* you to do the dance!' she cuts in.

'Mama, it's OK, I can't dance anyway.'

'You *can*! They should ask you, anyway. Doesn't matter if you can't dance exactly like the skinny girls – they should ask!' My heart drops at that line. I'm glad she's in the front, and I'm just staring out of the window. 'Ever since they buying that big house, they looking down their nose at everyone else. I remember when they were living on just daal and roti.'

'I'm sure they didn't mean it.' Dad very much has a live-and-let-live attitude. I *definitely* don't take after him.

'I wouldn't have been able to rehearse with them anyway, Mama, they live too far away.'

'*This* is why you need to learn to drive.' She turns, looking at me in the way she might a bunch of wilted coriander.

Here we go again.

One of my Mum's *favourite* pastimes is pointing out my inadequacies. They are, in no particular order:

Not being able to drive
Being unmarried
Having uncontrollable facial hair
Being short-sighted
Eating too many snacks
Being fat
Buying too many clothes
Having short hair
Not being a doctor
Not owning a buy-to-let property
Not going to the gurdwara regularly

'I'll learn, I promise,' I lie. My anxiety is unmanageable at the best of times. I don't think me or any of the drivers of Gravesend will be safe with me disassociating behind the wheel of a death machine.

'All the other girls – even the ones younger than you – are driving now. They got their own cars; they're not scared or anything. Anytime they want to go anywhere, they just jump in their car and go! *Fut-a-fut!*' She clicks her fingers aggressively. 'I don't know why you are so scared—'

I tune out and lean back in my seat. Dad *hmms* and nods in all the right places.

My phone buzzes, waking me up from my daydream.

A WhatsApp from Elena from the girl's group chat, titled 'Chatty Cathies'. The group consists of Anjali, Charlie and Elena. We all met at uni. They're good fun, even if two of them have managed, rather selfishly, to land themselves long-term relationships. Anjali is the one engaged to Ajay, a clean-cut banker type; Charlie is in a relationship with the most boring man on the planet. And now Elena has met a guy who is absolutely loaded and spends her weekends going for fancy brunches in Instagrammable spots. Leaving me ... the only single one in the group.

Elena: *Hi @Sunny, love! How was the rest of the party? Sorry, I was having lunch with James's friends! All very nice! Told James loads about you all and he really wants to meet you!! Let me know when is good for you!! Xx*

I swallow my jealousy.

My phone buzzes again. It's a private WhatsApp from Natalie this time.

*Babes, just went on a date with such a great guy ... Got a few more dates lined up this week, but I think I could really like him! xxx*

A heaviness lands in my stomach, solid like stone; dread

mingles with shame as I automatically reel off identical messages to both of them:

*Omg so exciting!! Can't wait to hear all about it! Pretty free over the next few weekends :) xx*

What I really want to say is:

*Hi, babe, I don't want to hear your good news. I'm sorry, I'm just incredibly lonely and every time one of my friends tells me they've met someone nice, it feels like a failure on my part.*

*See, here's the thing.*

*I don't want to hear about your exciting, fizzy Bumble chats. I don't want to see screenshots of cute things your date has been saying to you. I don't want to hear how excited you are about him. I don't want to plan your hypothetical wedding with you.*

*Don't get me wrong, I will play the part of your best friend perfectly. I will give an Oscar-winning performance. I will slap a smile on and light up when you tell me about the plans you've made together. I won't even change the subject or talk about myself when you describe how wonderful his family is or how much his friends love you. But I can't be happy for you.*

*I will ask all the right questions and pretend to get excited when he takes you on a holiday where he will inevitably propose. When he messages me on Facebook to check your ring size and to ask me which cut of diamond you prefer, whether your style is modern or vintage, I will keep it a secret. I will be your unofficial wedding planner/bridesmaid/maid of honour. After your first dance, I'll be the first one to join you on the dance floor. Even though I'll be on my own, because despite the fact that you promised me I'd be able to bring a date, later you'll tell me you don't have the budget for 'everyone to bring a plus one' and that it's only 'partners allowed' because you don't want 'randoms' at your wedding.*

*And when you send me a photo of that first scan, I will know that this is the beginning of the end. You will move further away. Our lives will diverge. Our friendship will be reduced to a 'happy birthday' or 'merry Christmas' followed by lukewarm promises to meet up 'some point soon'. We will see each other at our friends' weddings but we won't get to talk, not properly, because by now you have a toddler and a baby: your hands are completely full. Our brief conversation will be full of gentle eye rolls at the pains of motherhood, but your smile will tell a different story. You will ask after me as an afterthought, though you're only asking to be polite, so I will laugh a bit too loudly and say, 'Oh, you know, the usual!' I'll make jokes about my failed dates, the awful guys I've met, the ones that are overly familiar, the ones who don't look anything like their photos, and I'll hope that you don't hear the hollow ring to my voice. But you don't – of course you don't. You've already moved on to talking about nurseries and going back to work and moving to a bigger house in the country.*

*Your news trumps mine. It always will.*

My friends would be horrified if they knew how I really felt. It would be the end of our relationship. So I say nothing. I always say nothing.

This will be my life, won't it? Left behind while my friends move on. I am *never* going to be able to afford to move out. I'll become one of those weird adult-kids suspended in a forever adolescent-like state. I'll probably end up wearing felt hats and novelty T-shirts. Everyone my age will have homes and partners and kids and maybe even holiday homes and grand-children. And I'll still be here. Still hiding my ASOS parcels from my mum. Still fantasising about travelling the world, while doing absolutely nothing about it. Never even allowing myself to *dream* about having someone to love. My parents will become more set in their ways. I'll start having dinner at 5 p.m. and get excited about the *Betterware* magazine. I'll become a martyr to my bunions, habitually wearing ugly shoes with plasticky looking soles. If the natural order of things comes to pass, my parents will die when I'm around 50. I will be left with a house that I can't bring myself to change. I'll become a recluse. Maybe even a hoarder. And I will end up as nothing more than a footnote in my friends' conversations, an anecdote . . .

'Do you remember . . .?' 'Oh my God, I'd totally forgotten about her!' 'Wonder how she's doing. Such a shame.' 'She had such potential.' 'Do you remember when she used to organise spa weekends? Dinners out? All our thirtieth birthday parties?' 'Yeah. Poor thing. She never did get married, did she?'

Natalie messages back immediately.

*OMG major fanny tingles!!! How are you, babe? How was that family do? Anything exciting to report?!*

'Sunny,' Mum says as we shuffle out of the car. 'All the time on the phone, *tik, tik, tik*.' She exaggeratedly mimics me tapping on my phone. 'Put it down and give your eyes a rest.'

'Yes, Mama,' I say absently – my eyes still on Natalie's message.

# Chapter 6

'What do you think, love?!'

It's one of those bright, cloudless autumnal Sunday afternoons: Elena and I are sitting outside a generic gastropub on the river huddled under a heater. They've somehow managed to decorate it for Halloween while keeping it classy. I've never understood the fuss about Halloween, though. The only way I can watch anything even remotely scary is if I watch it in the middle of a bright day, while on my phone, so I'm barely paying attention to it. My mum, however, loves Halloween, despite it being a peak 'white-people thing'. She circles it on the gurdwara calendar every year and starts stocking up sweets for trick-or-treaters in August. Which is remarkable, considering a few years ago she thought trick-or-treaters were starving children begging for food. She used to give them money and cheese sandwiches.

Right now, Elena looks like someone who is getting a lot of sex and very little sleep. She's glowing, yes, but her frequent yawns and the faint blueish tinge under her eyes betray her late-night love sessions. She is *always* the epitome of effortless glam; she dresses only in black, which suits her olive skin perfectly, and even without make-up, she looks luminescent with the kind of radiance that I need at least three different products to create. Even the blonde peach fuzz on her cheeks, visible only when the sun hits her face, adds to her air of effortless elegance.

'What do you think?!' she whispers again, breathlessly, checking over her shoulder in case James comes back to the table sooner than expected. Her eyes widen and fix on my face.

How do you tell your friend that her new boyfriend is giving you a severe case of the fanny flutters?

'He's great! You guys are great together!' I'm terrified that my higher-than-normal voice will give me away, but she buys it. Of course she does, she's in the New Love Cocoon™, where everything is great and the small irritations, like dropping the toast you just made or stepping in something wet while you're wearing socks, is just laughed off. Nothing can touch you in the New Love Cocoon™.

James is *hot*. Like someone-just-plugged-my-fanny-into-the-mains hot. When he looks at me, every hair (and there's a lot of them) stands on end. I hope it's not obvious. When I first saw Elena and James walk into the pub, time stopped. He's broad, but not too broad, and good-looking but doesn't know it. Add to that his liberal values, his concern for the environment and the fact that he's polite, doesn't interrupt and seems genuinely interested in me, he is *prime* fantasy material. *Plus* he smells like an angel. An angel I want to do all manner of unholy things with.

'He's so fit, I feel like he's *way* out of my league,' Elena says – hopefully she hasn't noticed the lust-filled drool threatening to roll down my chin.

'Oh please!' I laugh exaggeratedly. 'There is *no such thing* as leagues. And even if there were, you two would be in the same league. Top of the league tables. Premiership winners.' I'm running out of football metaphors to hide my awkwardness.

'Really?' Her face is alight with joy. I smile back, hiding my gritted teeth. 'Oh, I'm so glad you think so! It's *so* important to me that he gets on with my mates!'

'He's lovely!' I keep smiling and widen my eyes to really

show her how happy I am for her, for them. 'And it's so obvious he *adores* you! Shame he hasn't got any brothers!'

*Stop it, Sunny.*

Before Elena can start asking me who *I'm* 'dating' right now, James returns with a bottle of prosecco for us, two glasses and a beer for himself. All balanced expertly in his perfect hands.

*Don't look at his hands. Don't look at his hands. Don't look at his hands.*

Too late.

*Sunny. STOP thinking about his hands, like THAT.*

'Hope I'm not interrupting anything!' he says with a sheepish grin. I have to clench my jaw in order not to bite my lip flirtatiously. Why am I like this?

'I think you've got the Sunny seal of approval, babe,' Elena gushes as she threads her arm through his.

He beams at me as I hurriedly drink my prosecco.

'How's Gravesend?' asks Elena, daintily sipping from her glass. No wonder he loves her. She's so cute and lovely and perfect, she's like Bambi in human form.

'Well,' I say, thankful for the change of subject. 'We've just got another Poundland, so much the same. When are you going to introduce James to the delights of the Costa del Thames?'

Elena rolls her eyes and laughs. She and the girls visited once, soon after I moved back. I begged them to come and rescue me from the monotony of my life. They made fun of the modest town centre, and although I laughed along, I also felt a bit annoyed at how they sneered at the lack of shops and chain restaurants.

'What even is there to do round here?' they squawked loudly, eyes wide, looking around amused and baffled by the half-boarded-up high street. We ended up buying some bits in

Primark, then going to Caesar's for pizza and wine. I had asked for a table at the back to avoid being spotted by any of my mum's friends.

'Ah, yes, Gravesend's got the Pocahontas connection,' says James matter-of-factly.

'Oh my God, thank you!' I throw up my hands. 'Most people think she was made up by Disney!'

'I thought she was a fictional character!' chimes in Elena.

'When I was at school, they used to say she was buried under Kwik Save. Always made me so sad that she was under all those bags of broken biscuits.' Mum used to love trawling the aisles there, while I lagged behind her as a morose seven-year-old, distracted by the fizzy drinks and snacks I was never allowed to have.

James throws back his head and laughs – a generous, full-bodied laugh that makes my heart swell and my stomach flutter.

'Can you believe Sunny is single?! She's so funny.' Elena looks at James adoringly.

'No, *you're* so funny,' he replies, tapping her on the nose with his finger.

I grimace, hopefully imperceptibly. I don't want to draw attention to my singleness, not in front of the world's most loved-up couple.

'Sunny has *the* best dating stories. Tell him about the guy who had a meltdown in the park because he really wanted to go to M&M's World!' Elena leans forward, her hands laced together under her chin and ready for story time.

'Babe, that's basically the whole story.'

'No! It's just so funny the way you tell it!'

I take a deep breath and force myself into entertainer mode. It takes a full few seconds to make the switch. Within moments, Elena is clutching her stomach and laughing uncontrollably, and she keeps looking up at James as if to say, 'Isn't she so great? She's my funny friend!' And he's just looking back at her as though she's the most gorgeous thing he's ever seen in the world. Which, she is.

'Hi, Mama!' I call cheerily, carefully concealing my weariness – being an unpaid entertainer for Elena and her boyfriend has taken it out of me. I tuck my bag of contraband snacks, bought from the corner shop on my way home, under my rucksack and place them both gently on the stairs. I'm still trying not to picture Elena and James – their affection for each other made me feel like an intruder, like I'd just walked in on them in bed.

'It's raining. Why didn't you call your dad? He could have picked you up. You're going to get flu!' my mum admonishes me immediately. Mum's terrified of the rain and refuses to go out in it, drive in it or even open a window during it.

'It's fine, I didn't get wet,' I say, with a little flare of annoyance at her overprotectiveness and sudden irritation at her nagging.

She's in the kitchen engrossed in a YouTube video that my masi has sent her. 'Look, this doctor is saying put onion juice on your head and your hair will come back thicker,' she says excitedly without tearing her eyes from the screen.

'I'm not sure you should be taking health advice off a YouTuber.'

'He's a doctor!' she argues. Suddenly, she looks at me and examines my thinning hairline with such intensity that I have to turn away.

'What's wrong?' she says, her tone sharp, edged with suspicion.

'Nothing, Mama,' I lie, flicking through the leaflets for the local takeaways.

'Something happen?' she probes.

'No, no, I've got a bit of a headache, that's all,' I say, regretting it as soon as the words leave my mouth. The last time I made this excuse, she made me wear a turmeric poultice around my head, which stained my forehead yellow, making me look jaundiced. I hold my breath, waiting to see what outlandish remedy she comes up with this time.

She looks at me again, as though deciding whether to probe my emotions further or focus on the more important matter at hand – the headache. 'That's because your hair getting wet in the rain!' she says triumphantly, nodding to herself. 'Take two paracetamol and lie down.' Mum believes that painkillers are only effective if you lie down for a full twenty minutes after taking them – but I won't argue, because right now that's exactly what I want to do.

I trudge upstairs after taking a couple of unnecessary paracetamol and my heart sinks as I open the door.

My room is a Level 10 mess. It's long past the point of 'a bit cluttered' or 'could do with a tidy'. There are piles of clothes threatening to topple over, bags for life filled with old books and knick-knacks for the charity shop, and toiletries spilling out of drawers.

I quickly get undressed and pick up my fleecy pyjamas off the floor, give them a shake and pull them on. I should probably change the sheets, but this seems like an impossible task, so I give them an investigatory sniff. They will do for another day or two. I clamber into bed with my corner-shop goodies and open Instagram to spy on people infinitely more interesting than me.

I've got a new follower. GrantWells681.

Grant.

It's the same Grant I've been chatting to on Bumble for the past week or so. I'd been trying to find him on socials ever since we started chatting as part of my pre-date selection process. I've been burnt in the past when I've not bothered to do this. I once went on three dates with a guy who seemed charming in person, but after doing some online digging, I found out that he'd made a number of Facebook posts boldly declaring that he thought it should be illegal for women over a size ten to wear leggings.

Grant and I have already agreed to meet in a few days – I don't think I've got another 'talking stage' left in me. His Instagram profile is so dry so far, with just grainy pictures of landscapes and other people's dogs – but at least there're no overt fatphobia or racism. So far so good . . .

# Chapter 7

'Mama, I have to go, have you seen my keys?'

I'm feeling the familiar first-date nerves. Thankfully I'm having a good-body day. I'm wearing a pair of M&S control tights, which come right up underneath my bra and are doing a stellar job of keeping my lower half contained. I've gone for a new black wrap dress, which is low cut enough to distract anyone from the rest of me. I pull it up a bit before I run downstairs.

'Is that a new dress?' She clocks it straight away, of course.

'My keys, Mum!'

I'm in real danger of being unacceptably late if I miss the train.

'How much?'

'You've seen this before! It's old. I bought it in the sale last year,' I lie.

'I don't know, you spending too much money,' she says, before returning to reading the *Punjab Times*.

'Mum,' I sigh. 'Please can you help me find them?' I'm looking in all the usual places: worktops, on top of the microwave, in the cutlery drawer, by the front door, in her jacket pockets.

'Where you going again?' She raises her eyebrows, pulling what I think she thinks of as her 'innocent inquirer' face.

She's being deliberately obstructive now.

'MUM! I told you, Anjali's house.'

'Leh, I'm just asking, OK? Don't get angry, you'll get wrinkles.' She pulls an offended frown onto her face, but I can tell she's also secretly pleased with her line.

I'm about to come back with a reply, until I feel the cold metal of my keys in my jacket pocket – the *least* obvious place. 'Found them. OK, bye, Mum!' I plant a kiss on her cheek and give her a hurried half-hug before she can say anything else.

'If you kept them in the same place every time—'

'I know, Mama!'

I grab my bag and as I'm about to double lock the door, my mum shouts from inside: 'Remember to double lock the door!' She shakes her keys at me through the porch window. It's something she has insisted on, even when she's in the house, ever since there was a break-in five doors down ... in 1998.

By now, my heart is hammering and my underarms are damp. I'm going to get the nervous face sweats too, aren't I? I spend a few precious seconds checking and rechecking I have everything.

Purse, keys, travel card, travel make-up bag and emergency sanitary towel, even though I'm nowhere near due on.

Just as I'm putting everything back in my bag, the door swings open, almost knocking me over. Mum pops her head out and thrusts one of those blue bags you get from the Cash and Carry towards me.

'Here, take a banana so you don't get hungry on the way!'

'Thanks, Mum.' I can see in her eyes that this is both practical and her food-apology to me.

As I settle into my seat on the near-empty train, I take a few minutes to let my heartbeat settle before I touch up my make-up. I quickly look over my messages with Grant. He works with adults with learning disabilities. So this tells me he is

compassionate and mature. Grant is the eldest of three children. So he must be responsible. Ex-rugby player. As someone who likes to ogle muddy men with meaty thighs colliding
with each other, I approve. He's a Cancerian (so he's a loyal
homebody, although possibly somewhat intense). Doesn't list
the gym as one of his hobbies and there are no photos of him
doing CrossFit, so I'm hopeful that he has a personality and
doesn't spend all his time counting macros, unlike most men
I meet.

The messages are promising; he doesn't mix up 'their',
'they're' and 'there'. And *he* was the one who planned this
date, which makes a welcome change. He's keen, replies
promptly and he actually *said*, 'I'm looking forward to seeing
you.' I find myself feeling pleased about this until I remember
that this should be *normal* behaviour. Why is it that the bar for
men is set so low it's in hell?

My nerves ramp up as the train pulls into the station. I
walk up the concrete stairs from the platform slowly so I'm
not out of breath when I meet him. I take a few gulps of air
at the top of stairs to steady myself before I step onto the
busy street, full of well-to-do couples and their dogs queuing outside overpriced bakeries, arms laden with house-
plants. When I step out of the station, there he is. His hands
in his pockets, looking around. Suddenly, my nerves
disappear.

I've been catfished. His profile photos were either cleverly
angled or at least five years old. Or both.

I take a deep breath, embarrassed for all sorts of reasons
now.

*Keep smiling, Sunny.*

He half raises his hand as he walks towards me; he has a
strange, lumbering gait, and is that a . . . pleather jacket? I feel
bad for judging him already.

*Sunny, remember the good chats. Remember how he doesn't mention the gym on his profile. Remember that he has his own place.*

I try to bring back that feeling of hope ... but what is it about dates? Why am I always having to *talk* myself into liking men? Shouldn't chemistry kick in at this point if there's something there?

I weakly raise my hand, not sure what my face is doing. But he smiles and I see he has ... a massive mouth. He is 68 per cent mouth. And he's completely bald. Unlike in his photos, where he had a full head of hair and, *crucially*, no pleather jacket.

Internally, I'm rolling my eyes like mad. At myself, for being so judgemental. And at myself for being here at all. *Why* did I agree to going for lunch? Now I'm stuck here for at least two hours. And then we will probably have to go for a walk, or coffee and dessert.

'Hey,' he says. 'You're Sunny, right?'

I nod, not yet able to use my words. Why can't I use my words?!

'Great! Nice to meet you! Shall we get some lunch? Lunch still all right, yeah?'

I feel myself wanting to come up with an excuse – something like, 'Oh, actually, can't do lunch any more.' But I can't. Instead, I just nod, smile, nod again.

'Yeah, that's great,' I say finally.

After one of those embarrassingly long chains of 'Where do you want to go?' 'You decide', 'Oh, no, you decide' (including a brief interlude where he practically French kisses a stranger's dog, making me gag), we settle on one of those chain restaurants that Natalie calls Middle-class McDonald's.

As we walk in, I am assaulted by shrieking toddlers, exasperated parents and jaunty music.

Once we're seated, after Grant has awkwardly pulled my chair out for me, the back of it sticky with spilt drinks, I pretend to study the garishly bright menu, handed to us by an impossibly chirpy waiter, as if I haven't been here before.

'I think I'm going to go for the Big Brunch option,' I announce, after a few moments of fake-reading the choices.

'I'll join you, I think,' he says, with a cavernous smile. There's a sparkle in his eyes; he's friendly, but all I can focus on is his mouth. *What is wrong with you, Sunny?!*

'Very good,' the chirpy waiter says. 'White bread or brown for the toast?'

I feel myself relax, my shoulders loosen. Because I know this won't go anywhere and I'm not scared of any judgement, I go for the white-toast option. 'With extra butter, please,' I announce confidently.

Out of the corner of my eye, I see Grant grinning at me.

When the food arrives, we've barely said more than a few words to each other. We're just recapping everything we've said already on Bumble, as though proving to each other that we are who we say we are. He seems particularly keen to prove it.

As I tuck into my giant plate of food, slathering the butter on my toast, I let him drone on about his job as a support worker while thinking about what to cook for dinner tonight and whether it's best to do a big shop this evening or tomorrow morning. And am I too old for those glow-in-the-dark stick-on stars for my bedroom? Surely there must be a version for grown-ups on Etsy? Boring dates that aren't going to go anywhere are the perfect opportunity to catch up on life admin and daydreams.

'What about you? Do you enjoy your work?' he asks, dipping his toast into the yolk of his poached egg. I'm paying more attention to his food than to him and have no regrets about it.

'Erm, it's all right. It's not what I want to do long term, but it'll do for now.'

I don't want to talk about my job. I want to enjoy my hash browns in peace, Zippy.

'What's the dream job?'

Oh God. This. Bloody. Question. I don't have a clue, and every time I get asked it, I feel so utterly stupid for not knowing what I want. I contemplate telling him my fantasy of being a kept woman and spending the rest of my days baking and going to lunch. But I don't because that would make me come across as a gold digger. And I'd actually be bored after a week.

'I don't know. All I know is that it's not what I'm doing now. Nothing based in an office, that's for sure.'

'Yeah, that's what I love about my job.'

And he's off again, thank God. Extolling the virtues of no two days ever being the same and how passionate he is about making a difference. I'd admire him for this trait if he wasn't so bloody preachy about it, bragging about how many lives he's changed. By the time he's finished, my plate of food is demolished while his is still half full, and I've decided on enchiladas for dinner with sweet-potato fries.

'I like a girl who can eat,' he says, eyeing my plate.

'Sorry?' I say, purely to give myself some time to decide on how to respond.

'You know, I like a girl who enjoys her food. Has an appetite . . .' He winks.

Oh, dear God.

'Life is too short to diet,' I say, smoothly cutting him off.

As soon as he swallows the last mouthful of food, I look around to catch our waiter's eye. Unfortunately, there's been an influx of families, each with buggies the size of tractors, and the chaos of getting them all seated means there's no chance of getting the bill any time soon.

'That was pretty good,' he says, stifling a burp.

'Mmmm. It's certainly got busier since we arrived,' I reply flatly, still desperately trying to make eye contact with our waiter.

He smiles indulgently at a toddler who is waving at us from a nearby booth, white-blond hair sticking up in tufts, a smudge of avocado on his chin.

'Do you like kids?' Grant asks eagerly, following my gaze.

From the look in his eyes, I can tell he does and probably wants them, so . . . I lie.

'Oh *God*, no,' I exclaim exaggeratedly, as though I'm horrified by his question. 'Why would I want to push out a crotch goblin when there's wine to be drunk?! *And* what if it was ugly?! You can't even get a refund on it.' I shudder, hoping I've painted him a clear enough picture. 'You?' I ask innocently.

His eyes are wide with shock. He takes a deep breath before replying earnestly with: 'I love them. Can't wait to be a dad.'

I smile properly this time; I now have a good enough reason to turn him down without hurting his feelings, if he doesn't turn me down first.

'*Ah*, that's lovely,' I reply, trying to keep my voice light, while I'm turning back to see if I can make eye contact with a waiter. Any waiter at all.

'You've got a nice smile, really—' he says, completely oblivious to the fact that I don't really want to be here.

'Thanks! I'm just going to go up and pay,' I interrupt him, standing up.

As soon as he spots me heading in the direction of the counter, the waiter rushes over to us: 'So sorry, guys, can I get you anything else?' I feel sorry for him. He looks young. He looks tired.

I sit myself back down, beaming up at him. *My saviour. He's* the man who'll get me out of here. 'Just the bill, please!' I say, a little too brightly.

Without even a discussion, Grant hands over his card and pays the bill.

'Are you sure? I'm happy to split it,' I say half-heartedly, making sure not to press the issue *too* much.

He shakes his head, holding his hand up as if to say, 'No, no, I got this.'

As I stand up and get my coat off the back of the chair, he goes to grab it. 'Let me help with that!'

'Oh . . . erm . . . I'm good, thanks,' I garble, shrugging it on.

'Do you want to go and get dessert somewhere else?' he smiles at me, his eyes alight with something that looks a bit like hope, putting on his pleather.

*Abso-fucking-lutely not, pal,* I think to myself. 'Sure!' I say. 'There's a café across the road that's pretty nice.' The words tumble out of me and I immediately start kicking myself.

*WHAT. ARE. YOU. DOING. SUNNY?*

I can't take it back now. If I say I've just remembered I have to do something or be somewhere, it will be too obvious.

So, we sit for another ninety painful minutes over a dry chocolate-and-raspberry tart and watery tea, and as soon as he's drunk the last sip, I'm waving to a waiter for the bill once more before Grant can suggest another cup or even a drink at another bar. Because we've learnt that I cannot be trusted to say no even when I can't bear to spend another minute with this bore of a man.

This time, I pay. It is only fair and hopefully makes it clear to him that this *officially* signifies the end of the date.

'I had a really nice time,' he says when we're both standing outside the station. His arms are stretched out wide; he's going in for a hug. Suddenly, I panic – my eyes widening in shock-horror. Is he going in for a *kiss* too?

I move my head away from him strategically as his arms limply wrap around me, and I pat him a bit too aggressively on the arm.

'Me too!' My voice comes out abnormally high. 'Oh, that's my train pulling in now!' I say, without even turning round to check. 'Get home safe! Bye!' I practically shout at him as I back away and do an ungainly walk/jog to the platform.

Of course, it's not my train. There's no train here at all. My train isn't for another five minutes. I sink onto the cold metal bench, assessing my options.

I'm pretty sure I don't need to give Grant the Shit Sandwich. It was obvious that we had all the chemistry of a wet fart, so I text Natalie instead.

*Another dull-as-shit date. :| xx*

She replies as I'm getting onto yet another half-empty train:

*Oh babes! Thought he might be a good one! I'm sorry. :( free for a chat in an hour if you want to talk it out?! xx*

Immediately, I delete Grant's and my chat and his number, using the train journey as an opportunity to cleanse my phone of all the other numbers of men I've been on dates with over the years. Every single one of them has 'Tinder' or 'Bumble' where their surname should be. *Matt Bumble, Kevin Tinder* – one is even Joe Bum, because I was adding new numbers so regularly that I got lazy and didn't have the energy to add the crucial 'ble' onto the end.

I call Natalie the second I step off the train. It is my firm belief that everyone should have a designated post-date-debriefing pal. Natalie is mine. In fact, she's my pre- and post-everything pal.

'Hiya, beauts! Good timing, I'm just taking Aloysius out for a walk. Come on then, tell me everything. Why was he so bad?' she says eagerly.

'Ugh, just no, babes. Once again, old photos—'

'Why the *fuck* do they do that?!' she asks incredulously.

'God knows. Women are always given the blame for wearing make-up or using filters in their photos but what about men who post photos from at least five years ago? And I wouldn't mind, but he just ... Oh God, this is gonna sound *awful* cos I'm hardly a supermodel, but he was not ... conventionally attractive.'

Natalie cackles. 'Go on ... do your worst,' she says, egging me on.

'He had a *giant* mouth. It was just went on forever – at one point, I thought it might go all the way around his head. He looked like the love child of Zippy and Phil from *EastEnders*.'

Natalie is doing what she calls her 'asthma laugh', wheezing at my sorry situation. I can just imagine her, eyes closed, head thrown back, not caring about what any of the other dog walkers might think. I start laughing too, and eventually I'm so distracted by our chat that I completely forget that I'd planned to pick up some chocolate to comfort myself. Natalie has done the job so brilliantly all by herself.

'I'm thinking of taking a break from it all and just keeping a *lover*.' I whisper the last word, aware that there is an older Indian couple behind me. I know that, deep down, my relationship with dating, the way it makes me feel, is not healthy. But everyone else is doing it and everyone else seems to be doing it well, so I just keep thinking, 'This might be the last one.' Maybe casual relationships are the way forward.

Though maybe I won't be able to handle that either. I imagine myself explaining it to my mum, and all the masis when they ask why I'm not married yet. The horror on their faces. 'Masi, I'm now into casual lovers, actually. It's better for my health.'

'Do it!' Natalie shrieks excitedly – I'm still picturing my mum being consoled by all her yoga friends about my life choices. 'You deserve a bit of fun!'

It would never work; feelings would be hurt and these types of relationship only ever work in the movies, right? Still, how much worse can it get? Worth a try, maybe?

'Do you think— No . . . I'm being silly.'

'No, go on,' she urges.

'Do you think I'm unlucky in love because I once, *knowingly*, slept with a married man? Is this some sort of bad love karma?' I say in a small voice.

'Noooo! Sunny, this has absolutely nothing to do with that,' she coos soothingly. 'Besides you were, like, twenty or something, weren't you?! We all do stupid shit in our twenties. It's practically the law.'

'Yes. Yes. You're right. Oh crap, I'd better go, Nat,' I say, approaching my front door, bracing myself as always. 'Gotta pretend I've been wedding planning all afternoon.'

As I let myself in, Mum's bellowing on the phone in Punjabi. Maybe this means I can slink upstairs unnoticed and don't have to engage in chat about the little white lie I told her earlier to explain where I was going.

'Sunny! It's your masi. Come and talk to her,' she shouts from the living room.

No such luck.

'Sat sri akal, Masi-ji! How are you?' I chirp brightly, taking the phone and settling in on the sofa. All my masis are talkers, so I might as well get comfy, but I'm secretly hoping it's my mum's youngest sister – my favourite masi. Unlike my other masis, she doesn't take life too seriously and has no time for gossip – which is just what I need right now.

'Very good!' she replies. It *is* my favourite masi, and instantly I ease up a little. After the usual small talk, she asks me what's for dinner, and when I tell her I'm making enchiladas (thank you to Grant's dry chat for helping me with that decision), she reels off a recipe for salsa. She's an expert on Mexican cuisine now, apparently. She lives in California and is an *amazing* cook, and her Mexican daughter-in-law has taught her everything. I put on 10 lbs in as many days the last time she visited. I see my mum watching me as we chat, nodding encouragingly, a smile on her face.

Eventually, I replace the phone in its cradle, with a genuine smile for the first time today.

'How was Anjali?' Mum says, without missing a beat. Anjali is always my alibi. She's a safe bet: she's Indian and the only time they ever met, she was very polite. The fake Anjali I've painted a picture of for Mum is *so* perfect, educated and marriageable; she's the daughter Mum wishes she had – though she'd never say that to me.

'She's OK, just getting everything ready for the wedding,' I lie as I wash my hands. 'You OK with enchiladas, Mama?' I try not to make it too obvious that I don't want to linger on the topic of weddings for long: I can't deal with the inevitable conversation about my own lack of prospects today. Especially after Grant . . .

I stifle a yawn. God, even thinking of his name makes me sleepy.

'I'll cut the onions?' She pushes herself up from a chair. 'And you tell me about the wedding plans?'

'No, no, Mama, you relax. I'll do it.' I just want the kitchen to myself, so I don't have to put up with her nitpicking about the way I cut or peel vegetables.

She shrugs, and as she leaves the kitchen, reluctantly, my phone buzzes.

It's a number I don't recognise.

*Hey, hope you got home OK! Enjoyed spending time with you today but don't see it going any further I'm afraid. I'm looking to settle down with someone who wants kids and I know you don't want kids so don't want to waste your time. Hope you have a nice evening. Take care. G x*

Fuck.

Grant sent me a Shit Sandwich of his own?

The audacity.

# Chapter 8

'Thank you for choosing "How to Find The One". My name is Caitlyn Taylor and I'm here to tell you that your single days are almost over. Are you tired of being lonely, sad and single? Are you sick of being the only single one in your friendship group? Do wedding invites turn you green with jealousy? Do you resent having to hang around with couples? Are you sick of men not committing to you? Are you always the one before The One? Do you feel like you're the only single person on the planet and no one is ever going to love you and you will wander the earth lonely and dried up until you die alone and no one will put flowers on your grave?

'Well, you're in the right place.

'I'm here to help you find The One using your internal powers of manifestation. This is a method I have used myself in order to summon my soulmate, Gray, and we've been happily married for over four years now.

'Find a comfortable place to sit or lie down where you won't be disturbed for the next fifteen minutes or so.

'Ready?

'Breathe in and breathe out. In and out. Nice and gentle. You are a source of light. You are an empty vessel and within you, you hold the power to conjure your mate. Imagine your perfect partner. What does he look like? What qualities does he have? What job does he do? Imagine your life together. What does your house look like? How many children do you have? Is there a golden retriever? If you can dream it, you can create it.'

'Sunny!'

*For fuck's—*

'SUNNY?'

I turn the meditation track up louder.

'SUNNNNNNY!!!'

'HANJI . . .?'

I wait a moment. No response.

'Mum . . .? Mum . . .? MUM?!'

I sigh loudly, pushing myself up from the floor, which seems to get harder every year. I trudge downstairs loudly, only to find Mum glued to the TV.

'I call you so many times,' she says to me, looking straight at the television.

'What's happened?'

'I wanted to show you something on Sikh channel. It's gone now.' She waves her hand at me.

'Can I go then?'

'Chal, you're here now, let's have some cha. There's still some ladoo left over from Baksho's paath.' She's still looking straight at the TV.

By this, she means, 'Go and make me some cha, and bring me some ladoo too', so within minutes, I return with a tray with two mugs and a plate of ladoo on it. As I reach for a ladoo, my mum suddenly moves her head away from the TV to look me straight in the eyes with her razor-sharp stare.

'Why don't you have half?' she snaps.

'I didn't put sugar in my tea.'

'Everybody getting sugar these days. Even kids.'

My mum knows it's called diabetes, but it will always be 'sugar' to her. Just like hummus will always be 'chickpea chutney' and mozzarella 'the cheese in the water'.

I reluctantly split the ladoo in two, putting the second half back on the plate. Still it stares up at me, taunting me. My mum, however, relaxes and turns back to the television.

'They have a matrimonial show on one of the channels . . .' she says innocently, not looking at me.

'*Muuum.*' I don't like the teenage whine in my voice, but I can't help it; she brings it out in me.

'They're saying they have one hundred per cent success rate.'

'They would say that.'

'It's getting too late.' Her voice is suddenly wistful. Mum firmly believes that everyone should be married by the age of twenty-five, and they should have had at least two children by the time they're thirty. My failure to have done so can throw her into a melancholy at any moment, which often involves days of mournful sighs and not-so-subtle comments about how she wants to be alive to see her grandchildren. Inevitably, I always end up running out of patience and snapping at her, which then, inevitably, leads to a full-blown argument followed by a few days of the silent treatment. And so, the cycle continues.

'Look at the girls you went to school with. Kiran, she has two kids, both in school now. Reena is pregnant and even Gopi is engaged.'

'Gopi?! She used to sit at the back in the gurdwara and eat paper!'

Mum nods knowingly. 'Exactly. Her mum took her to see a pandit in Hayes. He told her to wear a silver bracelet and he put rice in her bra. Six months later, she's engaged to an accountant. We need to do something . . . Let me help you—'

Thankfully, before she suggests a visit to the pandit, the alarm on my phone jolts me awake.

'Right, Mama' I hastily down the dregs of my tea 'I need to leave for work.' I give the abandoned half ladoo a final wistful look – leaving my mum to her matrimonial show.

★    ★    ★

'If I lived closer, I'd love to take you out,' he purrs down the phone.

I look around the cold, cheaply carpeted office to see if anyone can hear us, but thankfully everyone seems too engrossed in their own calls to notice that I am on the verge of an eargasm.

I have a long-running phone flirtation with a customer called Andrew from the posh part of Edinburgh. He works as a freelance IT contractor. I don't know what that involves, or how much money he earns, but when he sent me photos of his damaged brand-new bespoke sofa, I could tell that he lives in a fancy Victorian townhouse.

He has an accent to die for, like the hot bloke in *Outlander*. Every time he calls, I have to stop myself from asking him to say 'Sassenach' in case I get done for gross misconduct.

Sadly, I must keep up my phone voice all the time in order to impress him, which is tiring. I'm not a snob but I've worked hard to flatten out my Estuary accent; it only comes out when I'm angry, or talking to Natalie. My voice is one of the reasons I am so good at cold-calling. 'I didn't expect you to sound like that,' my manager had said at my first job out of university when I was cold-calling businesses and trying to sell them toner.

I *haven't* told posh Andrew that I know he's married. And *of course* he's yet to mention it himself.

'This is like the film *Red*.'

'Don't they … end up together?' I say, knowing full well they do. 'Don't tell me you look like Bruce Willis.' Of course, I've googled him, so I know exactly what he looks like, where his last holiday was and how long he's been married. He has dark-brown hair and the kind of jaw that makes you want to lick it. And somehow, even though he lives in Scotland, he seems to have a slight tan in all his photos. On one particularly bleak night, after a few too many secret gins in tins in my bedroom, I may have put his photo and mine into one of those baby-photo generators just to see what our imaginary babies would look like. Don't judge me. I've got to find the joy in this job where I can.

'What's wrong with old Brucey?! What about the *Moonlighting* years?!' he says in mock outrage.

'What's *Moonlighting*?!'

'Oof. I'm showing my age. It's a TV show from the eighties. Google it. It's gold.'

I spot Sharon, my boss, out of the corner of my eye. 'I'm afraid I don't have any more updates for you on your replacement sofa at this moment, Mr Henderson, but I've got all your details, so as soon as I have any more information, I'll be in touch,' I say primly and efficiently.

'Your manager?'

'Yes, that's right.'

'What a cow. Tell her from me, you deserve a raise just for putting up with her.'

'I'll certainly get onto that straight away. Thank you and have a good day, sir.'

I hang up before he can reply and I smile sweetly at Sharon, a square-jawed woman with cropped bottle-blonde hair swept across her forehead à la Justin Bieber circa 2008.

'Oh! Didn't see you there!' I lie smoothly.

'Ready for our weekly catch-up?'

'Of course! Can't wait!' I lie again.

Sharon strides away in her nondescript court shoes. She's the captain of the local hockey team and takes the same no-nonsense approach to managing her team of seven customer-service advisors. She *insists* on a weekly catch-up, where we present our current cases and update her on their progress. My job is basically to lie to these poor customers who have issues with their high-end Italian furniture. And it's crucial we don't let on that it's really made in a factory just outside Harrogate . . .

You'd think that, given my double life and my expertise in lying, I'd be comfortable with deceiving strangers over the phone, but it makes me feel ill. The sofas are so expensive and so many of the customers save up for ages to buy one. I've had to stop myself from telling them to buy a sofa from one of those sofa superstores with the permanent sales instead. Sometimes, I've felt so guilty I've had to pretend I've been cut off before running to the loo to calm myself down. Once, Sharon took me aside to ask: 'Are you suffering from digestive issues?'

In this job, the only thing I have to look forward to (other than my flirty calls with Andrew, of course) is KFC Fridays, when Dean, the only man in the team, takes our orders and brings back fried-chicken loveliness. Thankfully, today is a KFC Friday.

Obviously, because Dean is the only man in the team, I have a bit of a crush on him. He's cute in a Peter Kay kind of way. Probably would if we were on a night out, despite the fact that he's what we used to call a three-pinter at uni (for anyone not well versed with this term, it means someone you'd only sleep with after three pints . . . You get the picture). Doubt he's very liberal, though. He's definitely the type to call the corner shop the 'Paki shop' . . . but at least he'd probably have the sense to say it only when I'm not around. So considerate. He wears paper-thin white shirts and black trousers to work every single day. He 'can't be arsed with fashion'. According to him, it's for women and 'poofs'. He calls everyone 'darlin'' and goes for a 'fag break' every ninety minutes. He's not my type *at all*, but he laughs at my jokes, and who doesn't want a man who brings them fried chicken once a week?

'What you having, sweetheart?' Dean asks, right on cue. 'The usual?'

'No, I'm on a diet,' I respond dejectedly. 'So, a grilled chicken wrap, no mayo and a salad.' I checked on the website in preparation this morning – this is the least calorific option.

'You sure, darlin'? No chips or nothing?'

My usual order is a Zinger Tower Burger, chips and a Pepsi Max. With a Twix and a cup of tea for afters. I looked at my calendar on the way to work and, because Anj's wedding is fast approaching, I've decided I should probably put an embargo on the double carbs. Half a ladoo was probably a wise move in the end too.

I was supposed to start my diet as soon as she sent out the save-the-date cards months ago.

'Nope, I'm being good, Dean.' I sigh.

'Well, don't think you're having any of mine,' he mutters as he types my order into his phone.

'I won't,' I say indignantly, but I'm already fearing food envy and regret.

As Dean heads out of the building, I gather up my clear plastic folder and make my way to Sharon's office. If she criticises me, at least I've got a dry chicken wrap to look forward to.

I knock lightly on the door.

'Come in!' Sharon beckons.

Inside, the walls are bare. The only hint at her personality is a sepia-toned photo of her on her wedding day in a ruched, shiny horror of a dress, arm in arm with Colin, an insipid-looking man with pencil-thin lips and an overly large Adam's apple, a look of pure terror on his face. I met him for the first time at last year's Christmas party and he just looks permanently terrified, so it's not simply wedding-day jitters.

'All right?' Sharon says in a way that suggests she doesn't give a shiny rat's arse how I am.

'Good, thanks, how are—'

'OK, so let's see what you've got on your desk.'

I place the folder down gingerly and clear my throat. 'So, there's the customer with the discoloured footstool, Mr Seedhouse.'

'Have you asked them what they've used on it?'

'Just the wipes that came in the leather-care kit.'

'Any photos?'

'No, they—'

'Can't make a decision without photos, Sunny. It's the rules.' She raises her eyebrows at me.

'Erm, yes, the thing is, he's an elderly gentleman and doesn't have a digital camera or a smartphone.'

'Can he get someone to take them for him?'

'Well—'

'I need to see photos before I can make a decision.'

'I don't think he's the type to lie . . .'

Mr Seedhouse is a sweet elderly gentleman who lives on his own in West Sussex. He calls once a week to check in, but mainly for a chat, and he's never kicked off about the poor quality of his footstool. He likes *Coronation Street*, dogs and his local football team. And he's surprisingly liberal for an old white man; he asked me what my pronouns were the very first time we spoke.

'We don't know that, do we?'

'Well, I've spoken to him quite a few times now and I'd like to think I *do* know him a bit,' I say defiantly.

'That's your problem, Sunny, you get too close to these people.' She's doing that thing where she leans back in her chair, observing me over the bridge of her nose – like she's a Bond villain or something. 'Too involved. I've heard you on the phone. You spend far too long with each customer, and I'm sure they love it – the old folk, the losers who don't have anything better to do – but you've got a job to do. And at the end of the day, you're costing the company money.' She takes a deep inhale for dramatic effect. I can see how much she loves this shitty job. 'You're going to have to start working harder. Now, let's set you some targets, shall we? We can review them at your next six-month review.' Without waiting for me to reply, she presses a button on her computer and the printer kicks into life. She fixes her watery grey eyes on me.

'How are things at home? Everything OK? Not hassling you to get married, are they?' she says with a chuckle.

I suppress the urge to scream. We're not all oppressed virgins living in terror of a forced marriage. She thinks that, just because she organised a morning of diversity training a few months ago, she is now the world-leading expert on Brown people. She probably thinks that racism starts and stops at the National Front putting a brick through your window. She'd never be able to grasp how nuanced racism is – and I can't imagine her ever getting to grips with what microaggressions are either, even though she is actually the world-leading expert in dishing them out.

'Oh God, no. I'm thirty. I'm over the hill, thank God,' I say with a lightness I do not feel. She looks at me like I've just admitted that I come from a family of camels.

I've worked here for almost a year and I'm still deeply uncomfortable being in a room with Sharon. I get the feeling that as soon you turn your back she will bad-mouth you to anyone who will listen. I know her type well. I went to an all-girls school. I can spot a snide bitch from half a kilometre away, like sharks can smell blood.

Eventually, she waves a sheet of paper at me. 'So, sign there to say you've read it. We don't want all your cases to be like that one with Andrew . . . from Scotland. That's been going on a long time, hasn't it? Have you still not resolved the problem?' She looks at me. Knowingly. Then she aggressively shoves the piece of paper under my nose and stares at me as I read it. The form has a list of objectives for me to hit within the next three months. It feels like a threat.

1. Reduce the average handling time for resolving customer issues to ten working days.
2. Increase customer service satisfaction by 10 per cent over the next quarter.
3. Returns and refunds training.

I hate this job. I have always hated this job. *My* only objective is to leave as quickly as possible, find something better, so I never have to see Sharon's jowly face again. I don't want to be *fired* from this job – no matter how much I hate it. I want to be able to walk out on my own terms . . .

But she's looking at me. So I sign the document, no questions asked. This is a stopgap. As soon as I find something better, I'm moving back to London, and this time I'll make it work. This time it'll be for good. There will be no rushing back to my parents' house if I ever get made redundant again.

If I stay here for much longer, I'm going to become as grey as the cheap wall-to-wall carpet. I'm not one of them. I'm not a muggle. Not at heart.

I back out of the office awkwardly and text Dean as I walk back to my desk.

Sunny: *Is it too late to change my order.??!! :(*

He texts back straight away.

Dean: *Usual?*

Sunny: *Yes pls x*

# Chapter 9

'I'll help you find a fella, it's easy!' Anjali shouts over the din of music and groups of people who have obviously been drinking all afternoon. I *hate* this bar in Old Street, but Anjali loves it. It's around the corner from her work and she always goes on about how she once saw a minor royal doing shots at the bar.

I've just been telling Anjali about my recent useless dates, for some light entertainment, as well as the 'Looking for Love Later in Life' article Mum dropped onto the kitchen table yesterday morning . . . which I'm pretty sure is intended for seventy-year-olds, not me . . .

'You're *so* funny, you should have no trouble finding a guy!' she declares confidently.

'Yes, of course, Anj, because all men want to date a clown.' I roll my eyes. She doesn't mean it, but any 'advice' from Indian Barbie sounds pretty condescending. Anj is barely five feet tall, with a button nose and dead-straight long black hair. She's so tiny that anytime we go on a night out, at least one man will try to pick her up. Quite literally.

She is never short of attention, not just because of her perfectly proportioned figure or her almost-black doe-like eyes, but because she exudes the kind of pretty naivety that draws men to her like a magnet. She even got hit on in Tesco Express once, the morning after a big night, hungover, eyes bloodshot, hair smelling like cigarettes. A guy followed her around the supermarket as she was searching for Berocca. She was weirdly flattered by it. I was on the verge of calling the police.

But in Anjali's world, you always get the feeling that nothing bad will happen. Even when I'm grumpy, like today, her enthusiasm and positivity are infectious.

Before I met up with her, I was already feeling a little frazzled. The Tube was packed with noisy families, tourists and, of course, couples. Couples everywhere.

But as soon as I saw Anjali, and she suggested the bar that I absolutely hate, I agreed – because sometimes she's like a tonic. Sometimes she makes me feel better. Or at least helps me forget my woes.

'What about him?' She gestures with her head to a tall, broad-shouldered guy in a grey T-shirt and jeans opposite us. I noticed him earlier; I can't switch off my radar. This is arguably one of the most exhausting things about being single: I'm constantly on the lookout, perched and scanning the horizon like a horny, desperate eagle. Even when it's the last thing I want. I've caught him looking over at us a couple of times tonight already. But I would bet my secret snack drawer that Anj is the one he's looking at.

She turns to me, her face lighting up with excitement. 'Come on, let's go say hi.'

'I'd rather shit in my hands and clap.'

'*Live* a little. Come on.'

She drags me to the bar – she's surprisingly strong for a woman less than half my size.

'Hi! This is Sunny, she's a fucking legend,' she roars over the noise.

'Hiya,' I say sheepishly. Feeling vulnerable. On display.

'Hi.' His reply is curt, looking down his nose at us. He then slides his gaze over my shoulder to scout the room. A tense few seconds pass; they feel like hours. It's obvious he's not going to say anything else. I can't bear to look at Anj's face. My own face is on fire.

The bartender hands him a pint of lager and as he taps his card, I break the interminable silence.

'Well, nice to meet you,' I say sarcastically.

'Yeah, yeah, have a nice night,' he replies over his shoulder, already sauntering off, his impressive shoulders tight under his T-shirt.

'Prick.' Anj is fuming.

'It's OK!' I say, immediately trying to calm her down. It *always* surprises me how behaviour like that comes as a shock to her. No one ever treats her like that. 'Most men are pricks, let's be fair.'

I look towards Anj briefly, but I don't want to see the pity in her eyes, so I try to get the attention of the bartender instead and order us gin cocktails.

'Anj.' I turn to her, authoritative. 'Go grab that table for us, yeah?' I nod towards an empty spot a few metres away. She shuffles off, her clutch under her arm. Is she relieved she doesn't have to comfort me?

As soon as the bartender sets my drink in front of me, I take a big gulp of the violet liquid.

'Here you go!' I set Anj's drink before her. My voice is bright. I whack a smile on my face. I just want us to change the subject, to move on to something else. But I can tell by the look in her eyes that she still wants to talk about *me*. She's eyeing me up and down.

'Babe, I've been thinking, do you reckon maybe you're single cos you're a bit ... *intimidating*? I don't mean it in a bad way,' she adds hurriedly. 'I would just *hate* for you to end up like Beena, all, like, aggressive and bitter.'

I can feel a lump in my throat. My heartbeat is racing.

'I'm not *fucking* intimidating!' I say a bit too loudly. I've heard Anj talk about Beena before – I've never met her, but every 'bad' quality Beena has that Anj has used as 'an example' to me always makes me think we'd get on really well.

She looks at me pointedly, like she's a schoolteacher doing her best to ignore my 'little outburst'.

'Maybe you're right.' I take a deep breath. I'm not intimidating. But Anj never likes to feel like she's wrong. 'I don't know any other way to be.'

'Men like to *lead* – let them take the initiative.' She places a conciliatory hand on my arm.

'I'd just like to have sex again before I die.'

'Well, that's easy! Go up to a guy, start flirting and see where you end up.'

I want to roll my eyes. I want to get up and walk away.

'Not that easy . . . and *I'm* not that easy either.' The more she talks to me about this, the clearer it is that she just doesn't get it. 'I still want them to be a decent person. Have respect and a sense of humour.'

'I think you're asking a lot of a fuck buddy.' She raises her eyebrows sceptically.

'Am I?! What? Basic decency and not a dickhead? Why is the bar so low for men?'

'Look. Are you on Tinder? Let's try that now! That's what people use to hook up, right?'

I sigh inwardly. She's one of those unicorns who has never had to do online dating. She meets people, and they fall in love with her. Just like her fiancé. 'Love at first sight,' he slurred at me the last time we all went out for dinner, after drinking a ridiculous amount of an eye-wateringly expensive red wine. He made it sound so simple. Maybe it *is* simple for other people.

I open the app and hand her my phone, rolling my eyes. 'Have at it, babe. Left for no, right for yes.'

I drain my glass, watching her as she frowns with concentration; she makes an L sign with both her hands in turn every so often, just to double check. She's always struggled with left and right. It's kind of adorable, really.

'Oooh, there's loads! God, they're fit.' She pulls the phone closer to her face.

'It's only because we're in London; you wouldn't say that if you were swiping in Gravesend. It's all racists or boys I went to Punjabi school with.'

'OMG!' She starts bouncing up and down in her seat, her eyes wide with joy. 'You got a *match*!'

'Ugh. Let me see.' I hold out my hand.

She shifts away, moving the phone out of my reach.

'Anj!'

'Wait, let me read what he's written!'

'If we're doing this, I'm going to need to get *properly* drunk. That cocktail was ninety per cent bloody ice. Prosecco?' I slap my hands on the sticky table.

'Ahhh,' she groans. 'I can't, lunch with the in-laws tomorrow.'

'You only saw them last week!'

'It's *every* week – some sort of tradition.'

I waggle my eyebrows at her.

'Oh, go on then!' She pushes her debit card towards me.

I down my drink and squeeze my way to the bar, which is now marginally less crammed with overdressed out-of-towners, all heels and buttoned-up polo shirts and too much aftershave

'All right?' A voice at my shoulder.

I turn to find myself face to face with grey T-shirt man again. He's a few drinks in; his body language is a bit looser, his square jaw is slightly slack. I feel myself bristle.

I keep my voice even. 'Hello again.'

'Having a good night?' he says casually, being all solicitous.

'She's engaged,' I reply flatly, staring him straight in the eye.

'Sorry?' He's just *pretending* not to hear to buy himself some time to recover.

'My friend. The fit one. She's taken. Sorry, mate.' I half turn away to catch the eye of the bartender.

'Erm. Right. Yeah.'

For a split second, I think he's going to correct me. That he's going to tell me I'm wrong. That he's *actually* interested in *me*.

'Shame. Two sambucas, please.'

I slide away from him, trying not to show my disappointment. Ashamed of how my heart leapt for a second.

*Get a grip, Sunny.*

As I head back over to Anj, I try to keep my head up, my shoulders down. I think of my mum correcting my posture, telling me not to slouch, to keep me distracted from thinking of stupid grey T-shirt guy, who I wasn't even interested in to begin with. Was I? I look back, despite myself, and see grey T-shirt guy's friend, who I hadn't noticed before, looking right at me. He smiles warmly. But he's wearing jeans that are skinnier than any pair I own and a polo shirt that is buttoned up right to his neck – not my type at all. Something about his vibe, though, reminds me of Michael. Without the thighs to die for.

I gingerly place the prosecco glasses on the table. 'I've been thinking, maybe I should just message Michael . . .' I splutter, barely thinking it through. Anj looks up from her phone sharply.

'You're not serious?!' I've never seen such disapproval in her eyes before.

Michael was the first guy I dated when I moved home, and the first guy, in a long time, that I thought I could be with. After a row of fun but weirdly sexless dates with him, I decided to broach the topic of where this was going. Which is when he told me he wasn't ready for a relationship after his recent divorce.

'Well, why not?!'

'Because he led you on and wasted your time?'

'He was just going through a tough time with the divorce, that's all. We actually got on well. He was fit.'

'There are *loads* of fit guys out there.'

'*Lies!* Look he's fit, he fancies me and he's funny. And he has thighs that I want to bite.'

'I thought you said you didn't sleep with him.'

'I didn't. But he used to send me progress photos of his "gains". And they didn't leave a lot to the imagination.'

'Hmmm . . .' She does the disapproving-big-sister look on me. 'I mean, I don't want to be the one to stop you, but it's for your own good.' She stares at me, really stern. 'I just know he's bad news for you. Remember how down you were about it all? Tell me you won't message him.'

I just wanted her blessing – now I wish I hadn't said anything at all. 'I won't, I won't.' I twist my prosecco glass around on the table.

'Promise?'

Between gritted teeth, I say: 'Yes, promise.' And without looking up, I turn the subject back to her. 'How's the wedding planning going?'

'Don't ask.' Anj rolls her eyes dramatically, brushing her hair off her shoulder with one hand. I can tell she's done this so many times before in response to this exact question. 'My mum is being her usual pushy self.'

Anj's mum is terrifying; she always looks pristine in a sharply tailored suit with a fresh blow-dry, and has a tendency to look over her glasses at you. I've only met her a few times – she lives in a giant house in a gated development in some Hertfordshire village. Last time I saw her, at Anj's thirtieth, she grilled me about my career ambitions and told me if only I did sit-ups, I'd look *so* much better, before gliding off to make one of Anj's primary-school friends cry after pointing out her adult acne.

'Go on . . .' I coax.

'She wants to invite about a hundred of her friends *and* she wants me to have seven bridesmaids.'

'I thought you weren't having *any* bridesmaids?'

'I'm not! If I wanted bridesmaids, I would have had you girls and my sister as the maid of honour.'

I've volunteered to look after the bridal emergency kit, which means I'll have to carry around a bigger bag than I wanted to, but I don't mind doing that for Anj. It'll give me an excuse to get out of photos. When I was twenty-three, I saw the idea in a battered old bridal magazine at the doctor's, and I added the essentials for desi brides: bindi glue, safety pins for errant dupattas. I thought I'd be needing it soon.

And I have needed it. Many times. Just not for me.

'I think you might have to put your foot down . . .' I trail off at the despairing look on Anj's face. 'Anyway, what's with these *weekly* visits to the in-laws?' I continue, shuddering for comic effect. 'I thought you said they weren't traditional.'

'They're not, but that seems to be the deal he's made with them. He's *allowed* to live on his own if he visits them once a week and calls his mum every day. I'm pretty sure he visits them during the week as well.'

'What about after the wedding? What happens then?'

'Well . . .' Anj starts. She's trying to be careful.

'Ahhh, I can see where this is going . . .' I'm keeping my tone as neutral as possible but can't stop the grimace spreading across my face.

'He's the only son, babe. And his mum expects his bride to live with them for a year.'

'A year!' I squawk, almost spilling my prosecco down my dress.

'I haggled him down to six months,' she says defensively. 'Six months will fly by.'

'Time only flies if you're enjoying yourself. Otherwise it fucking drags. As someone who lives with their parents, I can confirm this.'

She makes a sound like a wounded dog, burying her face in her hands.

It's my turn to be the big sister now. 'All I'm gonna say is, I went to secondary school with a girl whose husband asked her to do the same and they're still there seven years and two kids later.'

'But ... but maybe it won't be too bad ... She's pretty nice ... A bit stern and whatever. But it's not like it was for our mums' generation, not being able to leave the house without permission and all that crap.'

'How are you going to have sex, knowing your mother-in-law is sleeping next door?' I jibe jokingly. She buries her face in her hands again in complete embarrassment. Anj has always been prudish about sex talk; it gives me huge pleasure to make her squirm.

I pick up my empty glass of prosecco and hold the base up to my ear, pressing the flute up to an imaginary wall. 'Come on, Ajay, my son, we are wanting many grandsons,' I bellow in a strong Indian accent. Anj squeals, completely mortified.

As we step out of the bar to head our separate ways, Anj pulls me into a hug and slurs drunkenly, in her big-sister mode again: 'Now, what are you *not* going to do?'

'I'm not going to message Michael,' I reply automatically.

She pulls away from me as though to check she trusts me, and then she nods, satisfied.

# Chapter 10

'Your skin is very dry,' says the tiny Sri Lankan woman who is waxing my bikini line, her shrill voice interrupting my meditative breathing to distract me from the pain.

So . . . here I am, fanny to the wind, barely a week after Anj told me not to waste my time on Michael, getting my bikini line waxed after a whole two days of pre-hook-up preparation. We're meeting up – in a hotel – for one night. On the train back from drinks with Anj, I half-drunkenly scrolled through all the screenshots of our messages. (I'd obviously deleted his number – but left some trace of him behind, for Not-So-Sensible Sunny to discover at that precise moment.) We ended up messaging and then speaking on the phone for hours, with me hiding under my duvet so as not to wake Mum up. I ended the call looking up at the ceiling, my cheeks hurting from smiling and my throat hoarse from all the whispering. If it had been a Bollywood film, he'd have been outside my bedroom with a red rose between his teeth, confessing his love for me through the medium of song, dressed in a billowing white shirt and tight jeans.

Talking to him just reminded me of how *great* we were together – and he's not dating anyone, and he's still hilarious, and he's even learning Punjabi from some colleagues in his India office . . . He makes me feel *good*. We've spent a whole week texting each other, getting each other worked up. Even Mum has noticed and keeps commenting on my phone use. To the point where I had to invent an imaginary friend in

Australia to account for the late-night texting and calls too, just in case she heard them.

Mum, of course, doesn't know I'm here in London. She thinks it's a work trip – and she's not happy about it. Something she has been very vocal about over the past few days. 'But why can't they do the training in the office here? Why do you have to go to Swindon?' She insists I don't get paid enough for a work trip. And I don't.

Anj once recommended this place in Tooting. So far, this woman has efficiently pulled out all the hair from my legs, told me about the break-up of her marriage and advised me to steer clear of marriage entirely. 'Use men only to make baby!' she insists.

I let her go on, to distract myself from the pain of getting my overgrown bush ripped from my follicles. I'm pretty sure I can feel blood.

'Hmmm. *Very* dry.' She tuts disapprovingly as she smears slightly too hot wax in the fold between my leg and my groin. I gasp.

Do I need to add my vagina to my moisturising regime? This is the sort of shit they need to teach you at school, along with how taxes work and how to find a bra that doesn't stab you in the armpit.

'Is there . . . bleeding?' I'm trying to sound casual and not terrified. Not sure it's working.

'Little bit. It's nothing,' she says dismissively, applying wax to the other side of my upper leg.

I don't believe her for a second. Is Michael worth the pain? Is *any* guy?

He probably doesn't even care. He's been married before; surely he's seen a hairy bush?

Mind you, I looked up his ex on Facebook when we first met and she's a natural blonde, so probably doesn't have thick hair that grows in every direction.

I look over at the clock, starting to feel my heart rate increase with stress and panic. This was the only slot I could get and I'm cutting it fine. I can only hope the bleeding and the redness go away by tonight. 'OK, just the back now,' she barks, mopping her brow with the inside of her arm and sighing dramatically.

I flip over inelegantly onto my front; the rickety table I'm lying on creaks as I try to get comfortable. The flimsy paper roll sticks to the bits of wax on my legs.

I dutifully hold my arse cheeks apart so she can wax my *actual* rectum. As she drones on about her ex-mother-in-law, I think of what my mum would say if she knew I was paying forty quid for a stranger to get down to eye level with my fanny.

Mind you, what would she say if she knew I was spending the night with a man in a hotel? A man I can't even talk about to any of my friends, apart from Natalie, because they won't approve. Natalie is the least judgmental person I know, and although she was surprised when I told her, she agreed that a bit of 'how's yer father' would do me some good.

I've also taken a day and a half off work for 'minor surgery'. I kept it deliberately vague and looked solemn as I told Sharon so even she knew not to pry. At first I felt bad about lying and pictured her watery eyes on me when she gave me my targets. I'm on thin ice, and we both know it ... but, right now, this *does* feel like minor surgery. And she can't fire me for a medical procedure, right? I'm pretty sure she can't, but I make a mental note to look up the Employment Act anyway.

I get up from the table gingerly, relieved and a little light-headed and buzzy because I've not eaten since this morning, and even then I could only manage a few mouthfuls of cereal. Mainly nerves, but also strategic because I don't want to be bloated for later. My plan not to eat carbs after 5 p.m. failed after only two days when I gave in to Mum's cajoling to try her new naan recipe.

I wait for the woman to leave so I can get dressed, but she's not showing any signs of going anywhere.

She just stands and watches me, which feels even more intimate than when she was nose-to-fanny tweezing out an ingrown hair. I hobble out of the salon, crotch burning. Is this what Kings of Leon meant when they sang 'your sex is on fire'? There also seems to be rather a lot of leftover wax sticking to my knickers, which is making each step I take agony.

I almost walk past the hotel completely. It's like a dingy-looking version of a Best Western, with a meagre car park out the front and some old Christmas decorations hanging limply across the doorway. I walk into the lobby, where I'm greeted by a tired Christmas tree, and try fruitlessly to get the attention of the receptionist, who I can spy in the back enthusiastically tucking into a Pot Noodle. I clear my throat a few times and it's only the fact that I'm on a tight schedule that forces me to say something.

'Excuse me.' I look in the opposite direction so I can pretend I haven't seen her shovelling a Pot Noodle into her face.

She saunters to the desk, straightening her blazer and wiping her mouth with a napkin.

'Hello. Checking in?' she asks wearily, not making any eye contact with me as she lazily moves the mouse around.

'Yep. The surname is Sanghera.' I try to inject as much urgency into my voice as possible in the hope that it wakes her up from her stupor.

'How do you—'

'S-A-N-G-H-E-R-A.'

She types it in slowly. It takes all my willpower not to vault over the desk to do it myself.

'Hmmm . . . I don't think— Ah, yes. I found you. Check out

is at eleven. Wi-Fi code is on here. Room four. Down the corridor and turn left.'

I practically snatch the key card out of her hand and march to room number four.

The room isn't the worst hotel room I've been in. It's a little tight to walk around, dark furniture, TV on the wall, a desk built into the wall with a small chair, a full-length mirror, small shower room. I press down on the bed lightly before sitting on it. Yep, that's an old mattress; the springs squeak slightly. At least it's clean.

Time to get to it. I set the timer on my phone for an hour. I open all the windows to get rid of the slightly musty smell and unpack everything, laying it on the bed, claiming the side that is furthest away from the door. I massage oil into my bikini line in the shower and with a bit of persistence get the flecks of wax off. I then moisturise with an expensive lotion Anj got me as part of a set for Christmas (I've been saving it for a special occasion) and do my hair and make-up in record time.

I've gone for a slightly sixties vibe. Like a sexy Asha Parekh meets Dusty Springfield. Nude lip, thick eyeliner, multiple coats of mascara and a ton of backcombing for the hair.

Should I light candles? Maybe not. It might look like I've made too much of an effort. Plus, I've just emptied half a can of Elnett to keep my hair in place. So instead, I turn on the bedside lights and place the sleek and expensive-looking vibrator that Natalie got me for my thirtieth in the drawer on my side of the bed. This is a surprise . . . but from our messages I get the feeling he would be into it. My phone buzzes.

Michael: *Nearly there. What's the hotel like?*

I look around the room again and notice the peeling wall-paper in the corner and the smudge of fingerprints at the bottom of the mirror.

Sunny: *Erm . . . basic!*

Michael: *Hope you've not nicked all the toiletries already.*

I've already scouted this out, obviously. But I'm afraid in this case I have to say to him: *It's the kind of place where everything is nailed down.*

Michael: *The toiletries aren't the only thing that are getting nailed ...*

Michael: *Wait, that's bad. Sorry.*

Sunny: *Haha that's awful, even for you!*

Michael: *Need anything?*

Sunny: *Don't forget condoms! How far away are you?*

Michael: *15 mins.*

Shit. I set another timer on my phone for ten minutes and down a cheap miniature bottle of wine I got earlier. I brush my teeth carefully so as not to mess up my make-up but thoroughly enough so he doesn't smell the booze on my breath.

When I'm done, and when I've got about three minutes to spare, I give myself a last-minute cursory check. My hair has an effortless wave that takes a *lot* of effort to get right; the same goes for my make-up. I give my face a double spritz with fixing spray so it stays put. It won't. Of course it won't. I pull the tags off the negligee I've bought and pull it over my head. Not bad for £9. A quick zhuzh of the hair, a bit more perfume.

I look at myself in the mirror and pull out my phone, opening up the camera. I take a few mirror selfies of me in my negligee and send one of the many to Natalie. It could just be the lighting and the mirror but I'm sure I look a bit slimmer.

Natalie's reply comes instantly – I've told her what time everything is planned for, so she knows when she needs to be on standby. In this moment, I'm glad I told her – even if I've told no one else – because I need a boost in text form.

*Baaaaabes, you look SMOKING! Have fun, be safe and I can't wait to hear all about it!!! Loves ya xxx*

I put my phone on the table and turn to look around the room. I feel a bit exposed, a bit lonely, for a moment. I've never met a guy at a hotel before, so I don't quite know what I'm meant to do. I'm trying to be daring for once. After all the calls and texts Michael and I have exchanged, I've got my hopes up about what's going to happen tonight – this could be amazing or a complete let-down. Whoever named it 'casual sex' did not take this into account.

*Don't think about it, Sunny,* I tell myself, before switching on the telly, so if he walks in now it looks as though I'm nonchalant, like I haven't spent half the day preparing for this.

Michael: *I'm in reception.*

'Oh, balls,' I say out loud to the empty room. I didn't think this through. Of *course* he's not going to just walk in. I have to go and get him.

It rather ruins the effect that I had hoped to create: me casually lounging on the bed in skimpy lingerie as he enters the room. Once again, life gets in the way of me becoming the sex kitten of my dreams.

I text him back hurriedly – *Be down in a minute* – as I pull on my jeans and jumper over the negligee and stuff my feet into my trainers.

Right now, I'm feeling 100 per cent less sexy, with my negligee all scrunched up under my jeans and the lace rubbing against my skin unpleasantly. They don't show you this bit on TV.

My heart is pumping away like it wants to break free of my chest.

As I walk towards reception, my nerves suddenly kick up a notch. My legs have gone weird. They're heavy, leaden; each step feels like I'm wading through treacle. I can't quite catch my breath.

Because when I turn this corner I will see him.

For the first time in nearly a year.

\* \* \*

He's standing in reception and it's like one of those moments in a film when the background fades away and all you can see is each other. Except the lobby is packed with a large group of Italian students all chattering away loudly, playing music on their phones, dressed in shiny puffer jackets, so it doesn't last long before the moment is interrupted by raucous, childlike laughter at some TikTok video.

But he seems to ignore them and looks straight into my eyes, and I really hope my face is doing what it's supposed to – looking all casual and relaxed, like this is the most ordinary thing in the world, rather than stunned because I'd forgotten how *incredibly* good-looking he is. And tall. And broad.

Even in his nondescript navy waterproof jacket, I can see how broad his shoulders are. I gulp.

'Hello,' he says, laughing slightly.

Is he nervous?

'Hi.' I am full-on beaming now. My heart feels like it's in my throat; I'm excited rather than terrified.

I approach him but have no idea whether I should hug him or kiss him or both. I settle for a friendly hug; his short hair is slightly damp and sitting up in spikes from the rain. He hugs me more tightly than I expected, and I wonder if he can feel how fast my heart is beating. When we break apart, I grab his arm and lead him to the room – turning away from him to catch my breath once more.

'I don't know what you're talking about,' he says as we wander through the dull halls – the wallpaper looks like it hasn't been changed in about fifteen years. It's the kind of wallpaper my aunties would think very trendy, timeless. 'This place is all right. The way you were going on, I thought it would be like the Bates Motel.'

'It's pretty dingy, though, don't you think?'

'I think you're fussy.' He winks at me. He slips his hand into mine and gives it a reassuring squeeze.

'Here we are.' I present the door to our room to him, and he raises his eyebrows in boy-like excitement. He's so cute when he does this – I forgot this expression, after all this time.

I watch as he scopes out the room. I wander past him immediately and sit on the bed, pretending to watch *Coronation Street* when really I'm just super conscious of every movement he's making. He's opening all the drawers. Doing exactly what I did. But he's completely unembarrassed about doing it in front of me. Then he opens the drawer next to where I'm sitting – the cabinet I've dubbed my bedside table.

'Did that come with the room?' He looks at me quizzically.

*Oh God.*

The vibrator.

I bite my lip to stop myself from smiling so much, my eyes crinkling, threatening to flood with tears of laughter, and all of a sudden I'm having difficulty breathing. It's nerves, and laughter, and everything all combined.

*Fuck.*

It suddenly hits me that I don't really know him that well, do I? And yet here I am in a hotel room with him. The rush of excitement laced with sudden, newly realised fear is making me a bit lightheaded.

'Hello,' he whispers huskily. It's like he's just switched on the 'sexy' mode. He leans down to kiss me.

'Hi,' I whisper back, my heart now pounding so hard against my chest I think I might pass out as I turn my face up to him.

He pulls me up and we look each other in the eyes and kiss properly. It's nothing like the snatched kisses at train stations I remember from when we were dating. I lean against him to hold myself up. My cheek presses into his hard chest, and I'm hoping he can't feel me trembling. He hesitates for a moment, as though he wasn't expecting something as emotionally intimate as a hug, and then his arms wrap around me, keeping me in place, and eventually I relax into him. I can feel my body loosen, and I'm starting to feel completely comfortable with him here.

He goes to take off my jumper, and pulls it up over my head, then he undoes my jeans and runs his hands gently over my shoulders and collarbone, making me shiver. Abruptly he turns me around, grabs my breasts, nuzzling my neck.

Well . . . someone must have a good memory because this is exactly what I described during one of our frantic late-night sext sessions.

He starts to whisper into my neck; all my nerves tingle.

It's all moving too fast, too quick.

I want to go slower, but I don't say anything. I let him lead.

I step out of my jeans as he unbuttons his shirt. He pushes me gently onto the bed and lowers himself on top of me, his weight heavy and reassuring.

He puts his hand under my chin and pulls my face up towards him, his lips meeting mine. For a minute, I imagine myself floating above, watching us, as though we're in some sort of film, seamless, sexy.

I can't get *enough* of his kisses – and I can feel a steady build of adrenaline, of heat, rising in my stomach. He smells of rain and minty shower gel.

When he pulls away, I can't bring myself to look at him. He's too handsome; it's like looking directly into the sun. Instinctively, I drop my shoulders so he can pull down the straps of the negligee and bra.

'What's this?' he says, staring intently at my breasts.

*Oh fuck.*

*He's found a nipple hair. He must have found a nipple hair. Shit. I thought I'd got them all. Pointy, witchy bastards.*

I bring myself to follow the line of his eyes, cringing, before I realise, with such deep relief, that he's looking at the tattoo of the lotus flower between my tits. A gift to myself for my thirtieth.

'What do you think?' I say, half nervous that he's going to say he doesn't like it or, worse, that he'll *actually* find a nipple hair.

He doesn't say anything at all, but he traces the lines of the tattoo between my breasts with the tip of his tongue before taking my nipple in his mouth. I had, cleverly, already anticipated this, so my arms are firmly by my side to prevent my tits from migrating into my armpits. And when he pushes the negligee up, I automatically suck in my stomach.

'Relax,' he whispers, looking up at me.

*That's easy for you to say,* I think, *when you look like the love child of GI Joe and Captain America and all I can think about is how many of my chins you can see. I hope it's nothing like when I accidentally open the front-facing camera on my phone.*

*Think sexy, Sunny. Think sexy.* He starts to kiss my belly and I squirm and will him to go lower. I can't keep my stomach sucked in that long. When I imagined him kissing me all over, when I imagined this night, I didn't really mean *all* over . . . He sits back on his heels and roughly pulls my knickers off and I have to fight every instinct not to cover myself with my arms. I'm telling myself to hold still.

He settles himself between my legs and I can't bear it. It's too good. It's too much pleasure. Is that a thing? I almost want to text Natalie right now to ask her. Maybe I'm overly sensitive because I haven't had sex in so long. I try to hurry him along because I won't be able to climax – I'm feeling too self-conscious. I feel exposed, cold, so I guide him by his shoulders to kneel between my legs before lying on top of me.

Suddenly, my mind is running so fast. Again, it's all moving too quickly, isn't it? Maybe I wanted us to chat a bit first, to catch up, to find out a bit about him and his life outside this dingy hotel room. Would it all then be a bit more organic . . . even though we both know why we're here?

'Condoms?' I whisper urgently.

'Yeah, in a bit.' He's not focusing on me for the moment. He's concentrating on positioning himself perfectly between my legs.

And then I stiffen as he enters me, but I let him. For a bit.

Until he picks up speed and I place my hands on his chest. His eyes are on my body. His eyes aren't on me.

'Michael, stop.' I look at him. 'Get a condom!' I repeat urgently.

'I'm not going to come in you.' He looks me in the eyes now, trying to soften my worries with his gaze, and he pulls himself down to start kissing my neck and I feel what little resolve I had crumble instantly.

'I know,' I say, softly this time. 'But I don't want to risk it.'

'But you feel so good,' he murmurs into my neck, as though that's a valid reason.

But it's been so long since someone has said that to me and it's been forever since someone has wanted me, my body, so utterly and wholly, that I let him, and I ignore the small voice in my head telling me this is risky, a mistake, that I'm worried, and instead I just make sure that he isn't doing all the work and push my hips up to meet him.

He's strong and doesn't tire easily, and for a while I lose all track of time. I lose myself in him.

But then, almost as quickly, it feels like it has gone on for too long, and my mind begins to wander. I'm counting the seconds, and my hips are hurting and I'm starting to feel sore and I'm running out of breath.

I don't come. And, more crucially, he doesn't either. He stops moving on top of me and slowly gets off – I can see his forehead is slicked with sweat, but it's almost the only indication that he's been doing anything physical for a long time. I pull the covers over me; he grabs a water bottle from his bag.

'Do you want some?' he asks, before taking a sip himself, and I drink thirstily. I can tell he's watching me for a moment, maybe still thinking about us, and what we've just done. When I hand it back, he finishes it and climbs under the covers beside me.

# Chapter 11

His alarm blares and he shuffles out of bed immediately. In the end, we didn't get to sleep until 4 a.m. It's his weekend with the kids, so his mind is already on other things. I stay incredibly still. I don't want to interact with anyone on three hours of sleep, let alone someone as hot as him. And I think he probably thinks I'm still asleep, which is good because I've slept with my contacts in, and my face feels so puffy it might have doubled in size overnight. As soon as the door to the en suite closes, I grab my phone. Natalie messaged me last night, just before midnight.

Natalie: *How's it going, babes??!! Hope you're having fun and being safe. I want to hear EVERYTHING* 😊 *xxx*

My mind jumps back to Michael. We had sex for a second time. And yet again there was no condom. But it's too late to say anything now.

I take a deep breath, knowing that when I tell Natalie she'll be able to make sense of why I feel a strange kind of dread in the pit of my stomach.

Sunny: *Best. Sex. Of. My. Life. So much fun but I think the last time we had sex it wasn't safe. I'm gonna have to get the pill ffs.* 😞

My message reads so calmly, but even as I type the words I know I'm not being honest with her. Or myself.

Natalie: *OH FUCK. Yeah! Get to a Boots ASAP. You'll be fine, don't worry!! You might feel a bit rough for a day or so but that's about it. Let me know how you get on. His decision or yours? Xxx*

Sunny: *His . . . sort of. But I didn't say anything.*

Natalie: *He should pay for it then, OK, babes? You shouldn't have to put up with all the consequences. Xxxx*

I reply with a heart emoji and hear the shower being turned off. I'm just running my fingers over my chin to check if any hairs have sprouted overnight when Michael emerges out of the shower, a tiny towel wrapped around his waist; a fug of steam, backlit by the bathroom light, makes him look like a character in a soft-porn video, and I have the most intense urge to jump up and lick the water droplets off his chest.

'Shower's not bad. How'd you sleep?' he says, collecting his clothes off the floor. I wonder if I can tempt him back into bed.

'That's not a bad view,' I say, playing it cool.

He chuckles, then returns to the bathroom but keeps the door open and I can see his reflection in the bedroom mirror. I stare at my phone – searching for where the nearest Boots is – while secretly watching him as he fusses with his hair. He catches me looking and I jerk away, feeling blood rush to my face. He puts his shoes on without a word. I'm still staring at my phone.

'See you soon then?' I chime, as he hefts his bag over his shoulder. I don't like my tone of voice, desperate and pleading. I want him to want me like he did last night.

'Yeah, see you soon,' he says, and he winks at me as he lets himself out.

'I'd like to get the morning-after pill, please,' I say assertively but quietly.

I'm in a small, crowded Boots on Oxford Street. I purposefully chose this one in the hope that it would be empty, so the chances of me bumping into someone from Gravesend were almost zero. I stood outside for a full five minutes pretending I was on the phone just to work up the courage to come in, saying over and over again in my head: *I'm an adult. There's nothing to be ashamed of. I'm an adult. There is nothing to be ashamed of.*

I marched up to the counter with my head held high and my shoulders back and waited for the pharmacist to come out from behind the partition.

And of course the pharmacist is Asian. I can't believe I'm about to get told off by an uncle. His tag says Imran. He's slightly chubby, with a patchy beard and glasses, and he clears his throat awkwardly when I ask for the morning-after pill.

'OK, follow me,' he says, and leads me to the side, a little way from the counter. Out of the corner of my eye, I see two women buying meal deals and Quavers, pretending not to look at me. For a second, I picture one of them as my mum, watching me from a distance. My stomach drops at the thought of her – at the thought of having to go home. But it's not her. Of course it isn't.

He asks a few cursory questions, and I can tell he is deeply uncomfortable with dealing with me. His stiff manner and stilted words are a dead giveaway.

I hold my nerve and answer the questions succinctly, and he hands me a laminated sheet of A4 card with some questions about my medical history on it and I skim it quickly, keen to get out of there as soon as possible.

Believe it or not, I've never needed to get emergency contraception before. I'm normally so responsible, insisting on partners getting tested before we even sleep together. I remember girls in Year 10 taking the morning-after pill and bragging about it the next day at school. It had seemed so grown up, so glamorous. Right now, it still feels strangely like a rite of passage even though I'm fifteen years late to the party.

'So, erm, there's this version, which is £29.99, and this version, which is the Boots' own version and is £16.99.' He holds out two different packets in front me, his eyes firmly fixed on his hands. He's not looking at me at all.

'What's the difference?'

'Nothing. They are both as effective as each other,' he says, clearing his throat.

'I'll take that one then.' I point to the Boots version.

The whole transaction is carried out without us even making eye contact.

I settle into my seat on the bus to the station and send Natalie a photo of the packet.

*Oh babes, get it down ya! Totally forgot, I'm meant to be seeing my brother and his girlfriend tonight but speak to you soon? This weekend? xxxx*

I want to speak to Natalie about it *now*. To make it seem real. To analyse everything I'm feeling because I can't quite figure it out. She's my closest friend – and the one who always just gets it without me having to explain over and over. I think about calling someone like Anj, but I made a promise I wouldn't message Michael and I can't bear her disapproving tone again.

I have that after-sex glow, that sexy tiredness, the ache between my legs, but there's an edge to it all as I take the pill, washing it down with lukewarm water.

Instead of taking my make-up off on the way home as I usually do after a date, I have to put some on to look less tired, otherwise my mum will have a million questions, and I don't know if I can think quickly enough to come up with the necessary lies. I pat in a bit of concealer to disguise my under-eye circles.

After a detour via Aldi to pick up halloumi for dinner, I unlock the front door at just gone one. Halloumi is my mum's favourite – she loves a mezze platter with hummus, roasted veg with garlic, quinoa salad, halloumi pitta, spicy potatoes and tzatziki. It feels like my way of saying sorry for lying, even though she'll never know.

I can hear her before I step onto the doormat.

'Don't you think the table will look better here?' she says from the living room.

I can only guess that they are rearranging the living room, or at least my dad is, and Mum is purely there in a supervisory role. I seem to have caught them mid-argument, which, for once, I'm relieved about because it means I won't get grilled about my evening.

'Let's leave it where it is,' Dad sighs as I enter the room. He looks at me imploringly.

'Why don't we try it? We can always move it back?' I step in, as though I've been here all along, and Mum nods vigorously, pointing to me with her hand and glancing back at my dad, like, 'See, be more like Sunny.'

'I'm going to put the shopping away and then I can help,' I say diplomatically, backing out to the kitchen.

'What did you get?' Mum shouts.

'Halloumi!' I shout back from the kitchen, gulping down a sick feeling in my gut.

'Oh, my favourite! Very good!' She smiles at me, and for a second everything feels all right. If I ignore the jagged edge of guilt piercing my gut.

# Chapter 12

Early one drizzly morning on my way to the train station, I spot a familiar figure leaning against an ancient Volvo. I stop abruptly and squint as the man stands and smiles when he spots me.

'Michael!'

Clutching a bouquet of plump white roses the same colour as his shirt, he walks hurriedly towards me. His hair is soaking wet and his face a picture of delight as he approaches me. I'm frozen to the spot, my mind working overtime to figure out what he's doing here.

'Sunny.' He gently strokes my cheek and I go to open my mouth to ask him what he's doing here, but he stops me by kissing me tenderly on the lips, before breaking away and getting on his knees.

'I am an idiot, please forgive me, Sunny,' he says in broken Punjabi; he frowns as he trips over the words. 'I was scared of telling you how I felt, but I'm not scared any more. I love you, Sunny!'

I whip round, scared someone might hear him, and to my surprise there is a crowd of smiling people applauding us and cheering his declaration of love. I look back at him, all six feet of him in his see-through shirt, and kiss him passionately as the crowd roar their approval.

'Who is sending you messages now?' asks Mum suspiciously, snapping me out of my daydream. Of course it was a daydream. I'm actually sitting in the kitchen, washing up after helping Mum to make a whole load of paneer spring rolls – it's nearly Christmas and Mum likes to stock up the freezer in case of unexpected visitors. When I was living in London, the only things I kept in the freezer were potato waffles and vodka.

'They're saying on YouTube that looking at your phone all the time makes your face look old ...' she says disapprovingly.

'It's no one,' I say hurriedly and turn my phone on silent. The only reason I had it on vibrate was so I didn't have to keep looking at my phone to see if Michael had messaged.

It's only just gone 12 p.m. on a grey Sunday, but it's already getting dark, so the Sunday scaries are setting in – work has become the thing I dread the most, despite my phone calls with Andrew and the old man with the discoloured footstool. I know it's only a matter of time until I have to leave, until Sharon actually fires me, and I can't quite face the thought of being at home with Mum every day until I find something else ...

'What you are worried about?' Mum says directly.

'Nothing, Mama,' I reply, unsure as to what she means. For a second, she looks at my face, analysing me. But when I say nothing else, she lets it drop, a frown still lingering on her brows.

Mum and I have both got our heads covered as Mum has Sukhmani Sahib on. That's her Sunday ritual: light some incense in the morning while she's praying and then put the Sikh channel on at twelve to listen to Sukhmani Sahib while we do chores. She says it's supposed to bring you peace and dispel any fears. Normally it works; even if I don't understand the words, the low, melodic rumble of the granthi reciting the verses is often soothing in itself. But not today. The combination of the festive blues, not hearing from Michael and the perpetual bloating from the morning-after pill is making me feel worse than usual.

This time of year always feels daunting. No matter how much I prepare for it. I don't know if it's because it always seems like an anti-climax or because I use it as another occasion to take stock of my life, which inevitably leads to yet another bout of the blues that doesn't shift no matter how much panettone I shove down my throat.

Thankfully, there is no Secret Santa taking place at work; instead, we're going out for lunch at the local pub next week. We had to decide what we wanted to eat back in October. I went for the turkey, seeing as we won't be having it on Christmas Day.

We put the tree up on 1 December, the placement of it causing another almost-row between my parents. We splashed out on a new tree – artificial, of course – from Argos. The year they moved into their first home together, Mum insisted they have a proper tree . . . but she was so distraught by the dropping needles that she brings it up every single year. I picked up some new decorations from Wilko and discreetly disposed of the ratty tinsel that had graced our old tree since I was a child. Now we have perfectly coordinated pale-gold decorations, with a delicate star balanced on top.

Then, of course, Dad and I have our Christmas ritual of watching *Ben-Hur*. It's why one of my very first crushes as a little girl was Stephen Boyd, who plays Charlton Heston's childhood friend. All thanks to his ruggedly masculine good looks and his dimple. Never has a man looked so good in sandals.

On Christmas Day, we usually all pitch in. I cook; Mum and Dad peel the veg.

'What do you want for Christmas dinner, Mama?' It's only two weeks away and normally by now I would have already got Mum's sign-off on the menu, even though we have the same thing every year.

'Oh, whatever you want,' she says offhandedly. 'Something simple – don't go to too much trouble. Let's not eat too late,' Mum continues. 'It gives me gas, then I can't sleep. And only main meal and pudding. I already have crackers. And the chocolate money.'

She buys those chocolate coins as soon as they're in the shop, sometimes as early as September. There are three large bags hidden away behind a huge sack of lentils. She thinks I haven't found them, but she's been hiding them there for years. I don't even like them, but Mum enjoys the novelty of them. We don't do big presents, just little tokens. Due to Mum's giant scarf collection, this year I've decided to forgo getting her another one and have bought her a fancy hand-care set with cotton gloves, cream and exfoliator. I bought Dad some smellies and a shoe-care kit. She'll still grill me about the price and tell me off for spending money on them.

'How about,' I say, already knowing the answer, 'a roasted veg tart, sautéed sprouts, honey-roasted carrots and parsnips, stuffing and gravy?'

'Perfect. Very nice.'

'And then for pudding, apple pie and custard?' Once again, I already know that she'll agree to this.

'Good. My favourite.'

Once Mum has settled herself back into watching the TV, I let myself open up my messages with Michael. We've been texting on and off. More off than on. He's been quiet. I'm running out of excuses to make for him. We *said* it was just sex, but it felt like so much more.

Now I don't know what to do. My feelings for him came completely out of the blue. But he's not even suggested we meet up again. There was a flurry of messages after our night together, and the glow afterwards lasted for almost a week – for me anyway, despite the feeling that lingered in my gut.

I keep trying to remind myself that he remembers things about me – the way I like to be kissed. But when I don't hear from him, when I'm just staring at my phone, like right now, willing him to message me, I can't stop my mind from screaming that he doesn't like me.

I feel so grey, so lethargic. And I don't think it's because it's December and it's cold and rainy. There's something else going on, something else beneath it, something that I can't quite see because it's half hidden in the shadows. I feel like I'm wearing a very thin mantle made up of all my past rejections.

Once again, I'm good enough for a night of fun but not good enough to be the girlfriend. It happens every time. Natalie always blames it on men, on the men I date, but I'm common denominator here, and it's hard not to think I'm the problem, that I'm the reason that these men treat me this way.

I picture my mum and wonder what she would think of me if she knew what I was doing. Pining over a guy. A white guy who has kids, who is learning Punjabi one word at a time, who had sex with me without a condom. If she knew that my worth, right now, was so tied to his attention, I wonder what she'd say.

It's easy for people on the outside.

I can just hear Anj's disapproving big-sister voice in my head again, telling me he's a waste of my time. I close WhatsApp and open it again seconds later.

I shouldn't, but I can't help myself, like when you *know* you shouldn't scratch a mosquito bite, knowing it will make it worse in the long run, but you do it anyway for the short, sweet seconds of relief.

*Hey, how's your Sunday going?*

# Chapter 13

Dean is standing in the smoking area on his tenth cigarette of the day. The bags under his eyes tell me he was out last night . . . on a Sunday.

He's in his standard uniform of semi-transparent white shirt, black trousers and a liberal splash of Davidoff Cool Water. I'm tempted to ask him if I can have a cigarette, but I don't have my smokers' aftercare kit on me (perfume, chewing gum, travel-sized mouthwash and hairspray), so instead I settle for breathing in his second-hand smoke in the hope that it will have a similarly calming effect.

It's one of those oppressive grey afternoons when the whole sky looks like one giant smudge of charcoal and the day is dragging, which is why I followed Dean out in the first place – I could feel myself falling asleep at my desk. One of Sharon's kids has a dentist appointment, so there's very much a 'teacher's off sick and the substitute teacher hasn't turned up' vibe, and with only a few days left until this Christmas party, no one's getting much work done anyway.

'Expecting a call? You've been staring at your phone all day,' he says, pointing to my phone with his cigarette.

'Just checking if someone's messaged me.'

'Oh yeah, special someone, is it?' He nudges me and winks.

'Apparently not. Just another timewaster by the looks of things . . .' I start, warily, having never spoken to Dean about 'guy things'.

'Thing about blokes is, if they're interested, they'll let you know, and if they're not, well . . .' He trails off, giving me a conciliatory smile.

I tip my head sideways at him, trying to communicate wordlessly that I'm not really up for this conversation right now.

He laughs. 'Listen, what are you doing tonight?'

'Erm. Nothing. The usual. You?' *Please don't ask me out. Please don't ask me out.*

'Fancy a quick drink?' He sees the frown on my face. 'Oh! Nothing like that. Just think you could do with cheering up. Plus, I could do with a bit of hair of the dog.' He smiles, baring his stained teeth and silver crown.

Yeah. *Definitely* don't fancy him any more. Even if he does enforce KFC Fridays.

'Don't you have a Pot Noodle and a wank to go home to?'

'Oh, there she is! Cheeky cow.' His hearty laugh descends into a hacking cough.

When I get back to my desk, I go to call my mum from the loo to tell her I forgot that it's someone's leaving do and reassure her I won't be back late and that I'll be safe and yes, I do remember I promised her I'd help her make samosas tomorrow.

The White Horse is a squat red-brick building; it's part of a chain that tries a little too hard to be something it's not, with its exposed brick walls and giant lightbulbs. Apart from a few solo businessmen in shiny suits nursing pints of lager, scraggy tinsel and too many fairy lights, it's empty.

'Grab a table. I'll get these. What are you having?'

Dean is already halfway to the bar before I can shout, 'White wine spritzer with lemonade, please!' It's not the coolest drink in the world but I can't go home drunk. Especially if we're making samosas tomorrow – they require my full attention.

He comes back with a whole bottle of wine, a pint of lemonade and a Peroni.

'*Dean*, I'm gonna be off my face!'

'It's a spritzer, it's like juice!' He laughs as he mixes the wine and the lemonade together and slides the glass over to me.

'Happy fucking Christmas.' He clinks his drink with mine and I down half the glass thirstily.

A few hours later and Dean is sipping on a Coke and I am feeling pleasantly loose-limbed, having drunk the best part of a bottle of wine. Dean has been tucking into a messy burger with a side of chunky chips and onion rings. I've gone for loaded fries. I'm yet to find a combination of food I love more than potatoes, cheese and meat.

'Can I interest madam in an onion ring?' He places the ramekin of golden onion rings between us.

'No, thanks, I only like the crappy onion rings from Iceland, and those look homemade.' I frown, inspecting them.

'Surely homemade ones are better?'

'Not in this case. You see, what happens is, you bite into the onion ring and the onion slithers out, burning your mouth, and all you're left with is the empty, greasy batter . . . sheath.'

'You really know how to put someone off their food.' He puts an onion ring down and goes for another bite of his burger.

My phone buzzes in my pocket and I whip it out immediately. It's just the girls – sending pictures of their Secret Santa gifts from work. My heart drops.

'Can I give you some advice?'

I look at him, not sure I want to take any KFC Friday Dean advice at all. But I shrug.

'If I was you, I'd forget this guy. You've got loads going on: you're attractive, you know how to have a laugh, you're smart – you give Sharon a run for her money. If he can't see that, if he isn't biting your hand off to take you on another date, then he really ain't worth the shit on your shoe.'

For a second, I want to laugh – at the fact that Dean is actually being all serious for once in his life – and then I want to hug him. Because, for a second, I feel like he's right. Like I actually believe the words he is saying about me.

I feel my phone buzz again in my pocket, and I go to switch it off. I catch sight of the time on my home screen, the background a picture of me and Mama from last Christmas – our plates empty, our stomachs full.

It's already 8.51. '*Fuck*. It's late.'

Dean checks his watch. 'It's not even nine, what you on about, woman?'

'No, no, I said I'd be home early.' I wipe my greasy hands on a napkin and reach for my coat. 'Trains aren't very regular this time of night. Thanks so much for dinner – and the advice.'

'Well,' he says, standing up. 'You're not getting the train at this time of night. Come on, I'll drive you.' He doesn't wait for a reply, but walks in front of me, holding the door of the pub open too. At first, I feel a little wobbly on my feet after the gigantic spritzer, but the cold air and the walk to the car sobers me up instantly.

On the drive, I don't know if it's because we're having such a laugh listening to old-school garage or because I'm more drunk than I realise, but I completely forget to tell him that he needs to drop me off on the main road, so he's already pulling up outside the house.

My heart starts to beat a little faster, but I'm still distracted – by the music, and by the fact that I've had a *nice* evening for the first time in ages. Out of the corner of my eye, I think I see the net curtain twitch in the living room, but I can't be sure.

'Oh fuck.'

'What?'

'My mum.'

He peers out of the window. 'Just tell her the truth – I'm a mate from work.'

'Yeah, she doesn't believe men and women can be friends.' I don't want to explain it all to him, but I'm glad that he already sort of gets it. 'Fuck it. It's too late. I'll have to face the music.'

'Well, listen, you need to keep your passport on you. I saw this documentary on—'

'Whoa, whoa!' OK, I spoke too soon about him getting it. 'Dean, she's not going to ship me off to India to marry me off to a stranger.' I laugh, despite the fact that I feel like I'm about to throw up and shit myself simultaneously.

'Well, good luck anyway.' He reaches across to hug me.

'What the fuck are you— Keep your hands on the wheel, mister, I'm in enough trouble as it is.'

As I walk up to the door, I realise I probably smell of cigarette smoke and white wine, but it's too late to check if I've got any chewing gum. Besides, Mum's not stupid. She knows people only use chewing gum to cover things up.

I open the front door slowly and quietly, hoping she's on the phone to one of her sisters or engrossed in a Punjabi news bulletin. No such luck.

'Sunny?' She pops her head into the hallway, swaddled in a thick dressing gown and slippers.

'Hi, Mama,' I reply warily, not looking at her, concentrating on taking my boots off. Hoping the longer I avoid eye contact, the more sober I'll seem when I finally look at her.

'Who was that man who dropped you off?' She's deathly calm. She's going to blow at any moment.

My throat constricts, and a wave of irritation floods me. I don't want to have this conversation with her tonight. I wish I could just tell her the truth and she'd believe me. If I really wanted to, I could just go upstairs and ignore all of her questions for the night; I weigh up what her reaction will be. I feel like a kid who's been caught cheating on a test.

'Someone I work with.' I'm careful not to call him a friend in case she thinks he's a *boy*friend.

'I'm not stupid—' she begins, and I feel an unexpected surge of anger spread across my solar plexus. My carefree night out with Dean is already a distant memory.

'I never said you were. Goodnight, Mama.' I walk upstairs, my back tensed because I'm half expecting her to lob a flip-flop in my direction like she used to when I was a kid and I talked back. She was always careful that it didn't actually hit me, but it was enough to shut me up. I can't believe I just talked back to her – a tidal wave of fear threatens to overwhelm me. Why do I still feel like this when I'm thirty years old?

I stop myself from going full teenager and slamming my bedroom door. Instead, I lie down on my bed, fully dressed, and find hot tears streaming down my face, soaking my pillow. I breathe out; I don't know when I last took a deep breath.

'Sunny! Don't think I don't know what you're up to!' she shouts up the stairs.

She's saying this to get me to talk, but I don't rise to it. I don't have the energy, and even if I did I wouldn't know what to say. My mum has never seen me with a boy before. I know there's a lecture coming, so I grit my teeth and quickly get my noise-cancelling headphones off the bedside table. The muffled silence drowns out her voice and I focus on calming my ragged breaths, praying for the knot in my gut to loosen.

# Chapter 14

The next morning I trudge downstairs, a familiar leaden feeling in my stomach, ready for a telling-off from Mum. It's better to get this bit over with. In the past I would have hidden in my room until lunchtime, but it only prolongs the inevitable. I feel a stab of annoyance that I can't even enjoy my precious day off.

The smell of frying onions hits my nostrils as I open the door to the kitchen. The soothing sounds of Sukhmani Sahib and the smell of incense mingle with the aroma of toasted jeera. It's not even Sunday . . . which means she must be doing all she can to calm herself down.

'Hi, Mama,' I say softly.

'Hello.' No nickname, no puth, no beta. That's not a good sign. She's frosty. I hold my breath as I wait for the axe to fall.

'Eat something,' she continues, not looking at me. 'Then we are making samosey.'

It's best to stay quiet when she's like this, so I pour myself a bowl of Rice Krispies, making sure I make as little noise as possible to avoid giving her any more ammunition. I sprinkle a teaspoon of sugar on top, drown them in cold milk and retreat to the living room to eat them with a teaspoon; I'm firmly 'team small spoon', not only because it means that food lasts longer that way, but also because it reminds me of being a kid – weirdly comforting.

I turn on the TV and it automatically pops up with the Food Network channel, presented by a mumsy-looking redhead, ex-city girl, now apparently overjoyed to be living on a ranch and making muffins for all and sundry. I don't buy it for a second.

'How long are you going to be?' Mum pops her head into the living room; her tone is sharp enough to make me stand up immediately, almost knocking my Rice Krispies out of their bowl. 'We do not have all the time in the world.'

I take a deep breath and follow her into the kitchen-diner. On the large, rectangular table covered with a garish plastic table-cloth, she has placed two ancient stainless-steel tea trays, a small bowl full of something that looks like wallpaper paste, a plate of covered pastry rounds and a glass bowl of samosa filling. The smell makes my mouth water.

I know my place here.

I wash my bowl, teaspoon and hands thoroughly and dry them before sitting at the table, where my mum is already curling each pastry round into a perfect cone, the two ends of the pastry poking up like rabbit ears; her hands are both deft and gentle. She places them delicately on a tray. I pick them up and fill them with the potato-and-pea filling flecked with jeera and onion, making sure to fill right into the sharp point of the cone.

'Make sure you fill the point of the cone. We don't want just pastry.' Her voice is devoid of its usual warmth, her eyes firmly fixed on the pastry.

I push a single pea right down into the cone and fill it up gently, preferring to use my hands rather than a spoon. I place the filled open samosa on the second tray; she picks it up, inspects it to see if there is enough filling inside and gently dabs on the paste – a mixture of flour and water – and seals the parcel of potatoey goodness.

We are four samosas in when she finally breaks.

'I know what you were doing,' she says to the samosa. 'A mother always knows.'

Instantly, I am seven years old again, caught stealing straw-berry Hubba Bubba from ASDA with my cousins.

She sounds more disappointed than angry, which is always worse.

'You are *lying* to me. We brought you up better than that.' She pauses to remove some filling from a samosa I have overfilled in a panic. 'What if something had happened? What would we do? Did you think of that? Did you think of *me*?' Her voice has been rising steadily and even though I thought of so many things to say to her last night, I never expected her to be so reasonable, so calm. I'm thrown off balance.

'I told a friend where I was,' I reply lamely.

'Friend? Which friend?' she demands, looking at me finally.

'Anjali,' I lie. It's best to choose an Indian friend.

'You are telling *friends*, but not *me*?' She's looking at me now, for the first time.

I open and close my mouth uselessly; normally our argu-ments are more like a contest to see who can shout the loudest and they usually end with me storming out and slamming as many doors as possible.

'I was so worried I didn't sleep at all last night,' she sniffs, talking to the samosa once again. Ah, the guilt trip – this is more familiar territory. I decide against mentioning the fact that I was home well before her bedtime and that I could hear her snoring when I got up for a midnight wee.

I sigh. Not knowing how to play this, I decide to be honest – well, slightly honest anyway. 'Mama, you're always going on at me to get married. How am I supposed to make that happen by staying *in* all the time?' I'm too scared to look at her in case she hits the roof. My heart is beating audibly in my chest. I concentrate on filling another samosa, grateful for something fiddly to focus on.

'It is time for you to get married, and I want you to have choice. I don't want to get anybody else involved. I know everybody is finding husband online.'

'*Everybody?*'

'But I am your mum and I want to see who you are meeting.' She looks at me again. 'I want to know they are right enough for you. You're my daughter.'

'What? You want to . . . meet them?'

I envisage my mum sitting in a corner of Pizza Express spying on me and my date, watching us through two holes cut out of the *Punjab Times*.

'No, no. You talk to them first. I don't know what you kids talk about these days. But show me them first. I can help you choose. What about Tindle?'

My heart drops immediately. What on earth is happening right now?

'What?'

'Jassi's grandson met his fiancée there; they talk about it all the time in the yoga group. Very good place to meet eligible boys,' she says, looking proud of herself, as though she's come up with the best idea.

My heart is sinking so far it's now falling through the floor. I wish I could follow it and disappear right now. Is this an alternate reality? Is this one of my nightmare-fantasy sequences?

I'm sitting here making samosas with my mum and my mum is talking about Tinder. Did I die last night or something? Did Mum kill me with her flip-flop without me realising?

'Puth, do you have it on your phone? The Tindle?'

I hand over my phone as if in a trance, watching myself do it from a great height. But I come to my senses as she grabs it and instinctively grip it more tightly. She wrenches it out of my hand easily.

I open the app for her and feel my face redden as she eyes up the men's profiles – thankfully, no one is holding a fish or worse. 'Are there any more?' she asks, clearly disapproving of Kevin, thirty-four, from Swanscombe. With face tattoos.

'Yes, Mama,' I reply, and swipe for her. She frowns, shaking her head.

I swipe again, until I catch a glimpse of a guy revealing a little bit too much in his sweatpants and I swipe past as quickly as I can. 'What was that?' Mum asks.

'Oh, just a glitch, it does that sometimes. You know, Mama, why don't we try something else?' I pull my phone away from her view for a moment, and log into an Asian dating website, hoping it won't make me want to cry inside quite as much. I created my profile ages ago, but now I need to make it Mum-friendly as quickly as I can. I replace any photos of me wearing a low-cut top/bright lipstick or with a drink in my hand with a photo of me at a wedding, with my cousins and on a family holiday to New York.

'Here you go, Mama.' I show her my newly censored, Mum-appropriate profile. She's frowning.

'Take this one down,' she finally says, pointing at the one with my cousins.

'Why? It's a nice photo. It's from Ravita's wedding.' It's also from a few years ago when I was half a stone lighter.

'They might think you are someone else . . .'

She means a potential husband might prefer one of my pretty, slim cousins to me. She has a point. Nonetheless, it still stings, and I delete the photo.

'What happens now?' she says impatiently.

'Well, now you wait for someone to message you, or you can message someone first.' Hoping that this is the end of this excruciating conversation.

'No, no, wait. Let the boy message first . . . then?'

'Then you . . . talk, and if you get on, you meet up.'

'Where? Pub?!'

'No, no!' I say as quickly as possible. 'A café, maybe a restaurant,' I lie.

'Hmmm, OK. Show me some boys then.'

I pass her my phone hesitantly and point to my list of matches. She puts her glasses on and scrolls in silence, her fingers fumbling on the touch screen. With every passing minute I'm getting more anxious and the cereal I just ate is threatening to make a reappearance.

'These are all apne?' she says, peering at the screen over her glasses. I still don't know whether she is long- or short-sighted, or, indeed, what she needs these glasses for at all. By 'apne' she means Sikh, Punjabi and of the same caste; quite literally *ours* or one of us.

'I don't know about caste, Mama. But they're all Sikh.'

I hold my breath, awaiting a lecture about caste and the diffi-culties I will face if I marry into another caste. When I was sixteen, I remember her warning me that if I chose to marry out of caste, neither she nor my dad would come to the wedding.

But surprisingly it doesn't come. Good. Because I don't think my view on caste and casteism being an utter crock of shit, not to mention anti-Sikh, would go down well now. She's probably saving it for later, though. She gets to the end of the list.

'Bas? That's it?'

'That's it, Mama. There's not a huge pool to choose from.' Within your criteria, I want to add. I shrug, feeling slightly vindicated, and lean back, waiting for her next move.

'Now what?' She frowns as if her future son-in-law is going to pop out of the screen like the Genie in *Aladdin*.

'Now we wait.' I exhale, realising I have no idea when I last let myself breathe.

'OK. No more secrets, teek aa?'

'No more secrets, Mama,' I lie, relieved but still a bit shaky from the weirdness of it all.

'And tell me where you going and with who, OK?'

'Of course! I'm going to put these in the freezer,' I say, gesturing to the samosas. As I get up and walk away, I feel like one of those characters in a movie on death row who gets a call from the governor pardoning them at the eleventh hour.

# Chapter 15

'Babe, she was swiping on Tinder! She called it "Tindle".'

Natalie's wheezy chuckle down the phone is contagious and soon I'm laughing too, drawing some looks in the cereal aisle. I decided to go to the big ASDA straight after work to pick up some bits for Christmas, but mainly because I couldn't face going straight home. Mum and I had got through potentially the most awkward day of our lives, but I wasn't running to get back to it all yet. Supermarkets are my love language. Even if I don't buy anything, there's something about the orderliness and soporific muzak that calms me down. This is a twenty-four-hour ASDA with a sizeable clothing and homewares section, so it's in the upper echelons of supermarket-dom.

'I always thought your mum's love language was feeding people, but maybe it's actually acts of service. If you think about it, babe, it's very open-minded of her . . .' Natalie brings me back to the moment, and the topic, at hand – my mum and my dating apps.

'Well, yes and no,' I reply. 'She's got some ground rules: he's got to be Sikh and Punjabi, of course, and have a good job, come from a *good* family and—'

'Did you explain how Tinder works?'

'Do you think it would even be possible to explain how Tinder works without my mum wanting me to get rid of my phone completely? We moved onto the Asian dating website pretty quickly.'

'I guess that's more up her street. Maybe it's good to approach it in a different way.' Natalie is in her problem-solver mode. 'Try being a bit more open and less judgy about it. See what she comes up with. Try not to make your mind up so quickly about someone. We all do it.'

'It's just bloody weird,' I say, wandering through the world-foods aisle, balking at the prices. 'My whole life she's been telling me to stay away from boys and not even look at them and now she's *swiping* for me. I've got emotional whiplash.'

'Isn't this what you always wanted, though, babe? To be able to talk to your mum about stuff like this?'

Is this what I've wanted? Mum never got involved in my love life at all because, as far as she was concerned, it didn't exist. She lectured me on marriage and prospects, yeah, but it felt like we had a clear boundary. Now nothing is quite matching up to what I'd expected.

'Not really,' I say, after a while. 'I mean, I want her to like whoever I end up with, but now she's poking her nose into every part of my life . . . I've never had that before. You don't get it – I don't want to chat about boys with Mum. It's *embarrassing*.' I don't want to get into the fact that being best friends with your mum is peak White-people-behaviour.

'You never know, babe, you might actually meet someone you like. They do say that mums always know you better than anyone else . . .'

I sigh. 'I don't know if that's the case when you live two completely separate lives.'

'Well, if nothing else, it might be good to take your mind off Michael.'

The mention of his name immediately transports me back to the hotel room, but instead of reliving that post-sex glow, I just feel a bit shit.

'Has he been in touch?'

'Do memes every few days count as being in touch?' I chuck a packet of chocolate Hobnobs in my basket. I don't want to admit to Natalie that I'm the one who initiates contact, then I feel stupid and delete his number, and that every few days he'll WhatsApp me a meme, but when I try to strike up a conversation, he vanishes and doesn't ever ask after me. Ever.

'Bin him, babe. Enough already! Yeah, he's hot, but he's also an emotionally unavailable douche.' I can just imagine her rolling her eyes at him.

'I know, I know . . .' And I do know it, but I can't quite bring myself to cut him off.

'Imagine if *I* was dealing with someone like him – you'd tell me to block him.' She's not wrong, but I'm too embarrassed to admit my feelings for him to myself, let alone to someone else. 'Come and see us soon, please? Sheffield misses you.'

Relieved to no longer be talking about Michael, or my mum, I promise her I'll come up soon, after Christmas – but with the cost of Anj's hen do and the wedding coming up, it won't be for a while.

'I miss you. Give Aloysius belly rubs from me, all right? Love you.' I hang up, and as Natalie's picture vanishes off my screen I feel flat, completely deflated.

'Sunny . . .?'

My head whips up to see a glamourous Indian woman towering over me in a sleek pair of knee-high boots. It takes me a few seconds to place her.

'Mandeep! Hi!' Even in my shock at seeing her, I manage to put on my phone voice.

'Oh my *God*.' She waves her hand in the air like she's just told the most hilarious joke and is batting her laughter away. 'You look *exactly* the same as you did at school!'

This would be a compliment if I didn't have a monobrow and frizzy hair all throughout secondary school. Mandeep Bains was in the same year as me – she was Miss Popular, captain of the netball team, head girl and was once in the local newspaper for raising funds for a local hospice. She managed to do all of this while looking perfect. If we were in the States, she would have been prom queen.

'How *are* you?' She cocks her head to the side and furrows her brow – or at least tries to but can't because of what I can only assume is Botox.

'Good! Good! Moved back recently . . .' I keep my voice even, trying not to give anything away. People like Mandeep hold onto your every word and save it away for the future. Even after all these years, I don't trust her.

'Oh yes, I heard you were back from London and that big, big city life. Your mum and dad must be *so* happy to have you home.'

'Yeah, yeah, of course. How are you? You look great!' I'm being genuine here; she looks immaculate. Everything about her screams money, from her expertly blow-dried hair to her boots to the elegant rings on her wedding finger. I seem to be surrounded by women like this, whether it's my cousins or this blast from the past in the cereal aisle.

'Oh my *God*, stop, I'm *so* tired!' She flicks a curtain of thick chocolate hair over a slender shoulder.

I notice she doesn't say 'you look great' back, but it's not surprising. I'm wearing a bobbly, shapeless New Look jumper, once black but now a dull, greyish blue.

'How's married life?' I nod towards the ring with its diamond the size of a gobstopper. She's been waving her hand around like she's been swatting a fly for this whole conversation; it seems only fair to give her what she wants.

'Oh *great*.' She elongates her 'r' in an attempt to sound

elegant, but it just reminds me of the Frosties tiger. 'Ravi is *so* busy these days – he's away with work at the moment but my boys keep me occupied. What about you?'

'I'm single.' I smile but hit a roadblock. I'm racking my brains for something to say that might make my life sound somewhat glamorous – but between the furniture place, living with Mum and Dad, and constant dating, I've got nothing.

'You're dating?' She tilts her head and flashes me a smile that says, 'There's no hope for you so I'm just going to smile and hope it's not contagious.'

I nod. My teeth are gritted together, but if I keep my eyes wide and bright, hopefully she won't notice.

'I'm sure you'll meet someone soon. Bet your parents are piling on the pressure! But it is *good* to focus on your career before marriage and all that.' She smiles again as if to say 'Girl Power' before asking, 'What do you do?'

I take a deep breath, my smile as firmly fixed as possible. 'Erm, I work in customer services . . .' I wish I could lie to other people as well as I lie to my mum.

'Oh . . .' Her eyes widen slightly. 'Cool!'

I'm expected to have *made something* of myself by now – I can see it in her face. Her eyes shoot to my basket and suddenly her expression softens, as though my shopping basket of chocolate Hobnobs, jumbo tampons and Christmas-branded cheese puffs communicates more to her about my life than the words I am actually saying. She has not changed.

'Listen.' She begins to move away from me and pulls out her phone. I half imagine her texting someone for an emergency get-out. 'We should go for coffee sometime! Are you on Facebook?'

'Yes.' Of course. Someone like Mandeep never leaves without setting up a coffee date. She probably doesn't know how to just say 'bye'. 'Just type in my name and I should come up!'

My relief that this charade is coming to an end is making me lightheaded. She click-clacks away from me and, not for the first time, I wonder what it must be like to be pretty. Right now, I'm wondering more specifically what it must be like to be Mandeep.

I still have to buy a few things, because I've only got my impulse buys in my basket at the moment – but I head straight for the self-service till and pay because I can't bear the thought of continually bumping into her around the shop.

As I walk home, I feel like I'm that girl again – the unpopular one from school, with the monobrow and the frizzy hair, Mandeep and her crew walking behind me, queens in their own little world, looking like they've just stepped out of *Asiana* magazine. Back then, I always thought that when I grew up, things would be different. Mum used to tell me not to worry about those other girls and to focus on my studies so that when I grew up, I'd have everything I ever wanted. I should have known then that it was just the sort of thing you said to children to cheer them up, to give them hope.

# Chapter 16

'Baaaabes! We miss you!' shouts Charlie, always a bit aggressive and loud when she's had a few glasses of wine.

Their merry faces fill the screen – we're on FaceTime and I'm in the one tidy corner of my room. I've managed to put on a bit of make-up for the first time in weeks, even if I haven't showered today.

Christmas was the usual quiet affair, with the obligatory row about Dad hogging the gravy and Mum telling me off about spending too much money on their presents – but with all the stress of the 'festivities', Mum has only been asking me about the dating messages every few days, rather than every minute like I expected. She did, however, spend a few evenings between Christmas and New Year looking through photos of me, suggesting new 'Mum-approved' ones for me to put on my profile.

New Year's Eve was spent with the Harrow branch of the Sanghera clan, complete with obligatory present-gloating (they all got matching Apple Watches for Christmas) and a mammoth cheese board heaving with cheesy goodness. Thankfully, I'd managed to talk Mum out of bringing the huge pot of saag she'd cooked the day before. I couldn't blame her; our get-togethers used to involve everyone bringing a hearty dish, not nibbling daintily on cheese and crackers. Dad spent most of the night glancing towards the kitchen, hoping that there would be some 'proper' food on the way.

I spent most of the Christmas holidays wondering what Michael was up to. New Year came and went without so much as a 'Happy New Year' message from him, let alone an 'I want to see you again'.

Charlie, Elena and Anj are at Charlie's house, getting ready to go out. I've told them I'm 'coming down with something'. It's easier than telling them the truth: that I've been finding it harder and harder to get out of bed lately. That I feel like that cartoon character who's followed around by a dark cloud wherever he goes.

'Why don't we do a spa weekend?' I suggest, almost impulsively, feeling guilty that I'm not there. Seeing as I've been spending more time in bed than a Victorian lady with malaise, getting away for a bit would be a good thing.

'Yes!' they chorus loudly.

'How about sometime in February? It's such a shit month.'

'SPA BREAK! SPA BREAK! SPA BREAK!' chants Charlie, knocking back a glass of rosé as big as her head.

'Oooh! A Galentine's thing!' Anj squeals, clapping her hands.

'You guys have actual boyfriends – Valentine's is your holiday. Let us *single* girls have Galentine's to ourselves, please!' I joke.

'Valentine's is shit, doll.' Elena sounds weary.

'Has something happened?' I ask, concerned with also a smidge of . . . what is that? Hope? Schadenfreude? Jeez.

'No, no! Things are *great* with James! It's just the pressure, isn't it? We've decided we're going to go away later in the month. Maybe Florence or somewhere,' she says offhandedly. Like it's nothing.

'Oh, yes, just Florence or somewhere, darling! No biggie.' Charlie imitates Elena while flicking her hair. Crushed together in the phone screen, I can see they're having the best time. Their eyes fuzzy with alcohol.

'Do you want to organise it, babe?' asks Anj, staring down the screen at me. She knows I'm the natural-born organiser.

'I'll give you three guesses and the first two don't count. Week after next? Maybe stay over on the Saturday and come back on the Sunday?' I say quickly, because I won't be able to afford two nights away. But I need something to look forward to and my temporary dip is fast becoming a rut. Hopefully having something to plan will take my mind off Michael and his fuckery.

They quickly check their calendars on their respective phones. Charlie's face is right up close to the camera as she scrolls to her calendar app and taps energetically at the screen.

'Yesss!' They chorus again, holding their glasses aloft.

'Babe, we've got to go, otherwise we'll be late for dinner.'

We end the call in a flurry of goodbyes and love-yous and have-funs.

If there's one thing I know, it's how to get a bargain. I am terrible at bartering in person. I must be the only person who went to Morocco and bought everything at the asking price. But I'm good at sniffing out a deal and putting my white voice on when talking to strangers on the phone.

Within an hour, I've managed to bag us a weekend at a spa on the outskirts of Berkshire, an easy train ride away from Paddington – three-course dinner, breakfast and a treatment each for only £99 per person, down from £129.

And within two hours, I've drawn up a document complete with timings, links to potential activities, spa treatments, local pubs and clubs, the number of the local cab company and train times.

Next, I need to practise the lie I'm going to tell my mum, while asking for permission to go away for the weekend without giving her the opportunity to say no. This is a fine art.

Every child of immigrants knows that you *have* to choose a time when your parent is in a good mood and start going above and beyond. But it's crucial that you don't butter them up too much, or they'll get suspicious.

Also, you *have* to mention it far enough in advance that they have time to get used to it, but not so early that you have to deal with weeks of them complaining about your absence or hundreds of questions about who is going to be there. When I finally feel ready, the lie embedded in my mind, I get up and wipe my make-up off before heading downstairs. Thankfully I remember just before my foot hits the last step that I told Mum I'm sick in order to score myself an afternoon in bed.

'Why are you out of bed?' demands Mum as she decants saag from a yoghurt container.

'I just need some water.' I pull a glass out of the cupboard.

'Don't drink cold water. That is why you getting sick in the first place.' She tuts.

I sigh, put the glass back and reach instead for a sachet of Lemsip. 'Mama, Anjali and her mum and some of her cousins have invited me to go on a spa weekend with them . . .'

'To do what?' she asks, puzzled.

'A spa, you know, steam room, massages, that sort of thing,' I reply casually. 'It's a few weeks away, but just thought I'd let you know.'

'Who is going?' she frowns.

'Me and Anjali and her sister and her cousins and her mum.' She's nodding so far, but I hurriedly add: 'Ladies only.'

Once again, Anj is always a safe bet for Mum. She has an inherent mistrust of white girls, believing that they will corrupt me. Little does she know, I'm the so-called wild one in this group, and I'm always the first to suggest shots.

'Hmmm. Check if your swimming costume still fits,' she says warily, and I head back upstairs, Lemsip in hand, feeling half victorious, half worried about where the hell I'm going to find a decent swimming costume in the dead of winter. 'And if you get messages on those apps, you must tell me, OK? I am helping you.'

'Yes, Mama,' I say, through gritted teeth.

When the spa trip eventually arrives, the train journey passes in a blur of gins in a tin and giddiness, and I've momentarily forgotten about Mum on Tinder and Michael and Sharon and my shitty job. These girls, who seem to have so few cares in the world, who don't seem to take anything too seriously, are exactly what I need today. At least there's no chance of anyone launching into a deep and meaningful conversation. We're the annoying group of drunk women that I would normally tut and shake my head at silently as I turn the volume up on my headphones. I told the girls we were getting an earlier train so they wouldn't be late, a trick I learnt from dealing with my perennially late parents. The girls carry me along with their excitement.

In addition to the tinned cocktails, I bought a selection of crisps from M&S before we got on the train because I don't want us to turn up completely battered. And I nicked a few plastic glasses and a handful of napkins and ancient lemon-scented wipes from Mum's picnicware cupboard. I'm always prepared.

'Our mate's getting married!' says Charlie excitedly to the group of elderly friends across the aisle from us. She points to Anj, who ducks her head shyly and groans.

'Let's do a toast! Here's to the bride-to-be!'

'And to our organiser, Sunny!' adds Anj, smiling at me.

'To Sunny!'

'Thank you for getting us a good deal, babe!'

I raise my plastic glass to Anj, and to myself, beaming.

'What treatments are you having, hun?' continues Anj, delicately nibbling on a spicy tortilla chip.

'A full-body massage,' I tell her. 'Which means I'm buffed and buttered to within an inch of my life. I've spent upwards of two hours de-furring my body from the eyebrows down to my hairy toes. And even then, I didn't finish it all!' I wail, dramatically throwing my head back, getting into the spirit of the day.

Anj and Charlie chuckle with deep belly laughs, but Elena is frowning at her phone.

'I'm sorry, I just need to check in with work quickly,' she mutters, making to get up.

'El,' Charlie looks at her. 'Put your bloody phone away, we're on a spa break. We're supposed to be relaxing!' She grabs Elena's phone, holding it out of reach. Charlie closes her eyes and touches her index finger to her thumb and hums, 'Ommmm.'

I clench my jaw slightly at this and look over at Anj, wondering if she's feeling uncomfortable too. But she's laughing along with the others, and she's actually Hindu, so maybe I'm being a bit oversensitive.

When we arrive at the sleepy, rural train station, like something out of one of those 1940s wartime dramas, Charlie announces: 'Shall we get an Uber?'

I jump into organiser mode immediately, claiming my role within this group. 'There's no Uber here. I've booked us a taxi,' I declare. And the taxi pulls up next to us almost instantly, as though I've summoned it with my mind, and we all pile in, giggling like teenagers, gin still swirling round our system. It looks like the crisps I got haven't gone very far.

We eventually pull up to the hotel fifteen minutes later – a fancy-looking Edwardian building surrounded by acres of well-manicured gardens that I already know we're going to be too hungover to explore.

We stumble into the lobby, which is all dark wood panelling, dark carpets and flock wallpaper, squishy sofas I want to dive into, high-backed leather armchairs, books – so many books – and giant lamps looming over the chairs. A couple of older patrons are having tea, reading books and newspapers. For a split second, I wish I were here on my own so I could spend the whole weekend tucked into a little corner in an armchair with a pot of tea and assorted biscuits. The girls suddenly feel too loud, too high energy for me right now.

We're by far the youngest people here, which hopefully means no screaming kids in the swimming pool.

We approach the reception. The desk is decorated with giant, fat-bellied pewter vases overflowing with white lilies.

'Hello, we'd like to check in, please. The booking is under the name Sunny Sanghera,' I say quietly but firmly, purposefully deepening my voice.

'Hmmm . . .' The woman behind the desk taps in the details, tap-tap-tapping away. After a minute, she says, 'I can't seem to find it. How are you spelling that?'

I spell it out slowly and clearly.

'Did you book directly with us?' she asks. I sense a bit of cool detachment from her, no doubt because she suspects we booked at a cheaper rate from one of those discount websites. Snooty bitch.

'No, we booked via spasearchers.com, one of those discount websites. Would you like to see the email confirmation?' I'm getting a little nervous now and I daren't look at the others. After what seems like an interminable silence, she looks up at me.

'Oh, that must be why. We'll need to keep a credit card on file – a charge that will be released. It can take up to forty-eight hours.'

'Of course.' I hand over my card, hoping no one can tell how panicked I was. I'm the organiser – I'm always the organiser and I've never messed up before.

'Thank you – here are your rooms: twenty-two and twenty-four. They're on the second floor, down the corridor and past the therapy rooms.'

The room allocation has already been decided. By me. I don't think I could share a room with Charlie – she's far too full-on at the best of times, but the deal breaker was the fact that she's a morning person. So, it's me and Elena in one room, and Anj and Charlie in the other. We're all on the same floor and in adjoining rooms, so we troop down the thickly carpeted hallways, the wheels of my cheap suitcase getting stuck in the carpet.

'Meet in the hallway in fifteen?' Elena asks us all as we let ourselves into our respective rooms. 'We could go to the sauna.'

'Oh.' I shake my head. 'I've still got to finish de-furring myself. You guys go down, though – I'll be as quick as I can.'

'Oh God, Sunny. I bet you can't even see it,' groans Charlie.

'Easy for you to say, your leg hair's blonde. Mine is as dark as my soul.' I laugh.

Charlie shrugs and heads into her room, while Elena and I do the same.

As we step in, we 'oooooh' and 'aaaah' in unison, and I smile with relief.

'Do you mind if I take the bed closest to the door, darling?' she asks, inspecting the headboard for dust.

'Of course not!' I dump my bag on the bed by the window and sit beside it, bouncing on the mattress slightly.

The room is generous, although it's not exactly to my taste, with its fleur-de-lys-print carpet and stripy wallpaper. But it is comforting and cosy. I earmark the overstuffed tub chair for reading and tea drinking, imagining myself on my ideal solo holiday, while Elena unpacks her perfectly packed suitcase. She pulls out tiny wisps of clothes and matching toiletry bags full of high-end skincare. Everything is coordinated and sleek, just like her. I'm too embarrassed to take out my ancient Primark wash bag, so instead I busy myself having a nose around.

'Ooh, there's a bath! Oooh, Elemis!' I exclaim before realising that I don't *really* want Elena to see my overexcitement at all this stuff either. It's probably nothing to her – Elena frequently stays at the Mandarin Oriental in New York.

I bound out of the bathroom to see that Elena has stripped completely naked and is slipping into a tiny black swimsuit with cut-outs. I do a little double take at how comfortable she is with her nakedness. She's not trying to keep a towel wrapped around her while also trying to wiggle into a costume, like I always do. She's just posing, openly, in front of the mirror with a slight frown on her face as she studies herself intently.

'You look great, babe,' I say reassuringly as she looks over her shoulder to examine her tiny pert bum in the full-length mirror.

'I'm just *so* bottom heavy,' she groans. 'I've always struggled with my thighs.' She grabs them both, giving them a shake. It takes all my strength not to point out that at least her thighs don't rub against each other when she walks. I just will her to stop talking.

'Honestly, you look amazing in that swimsuit. You'd look amazing in a sandwich bag. Seriously.'

She shrugs at me. Takes a selfie of herself. 'I'm sending this to James,' she says matter-of-factly.

'How is he by the way?' I ask casually.

'Oh, amazing. He's just got a new promotion at work and we're going to Babington House to celebrate next week.'

'Ahhh!' I inject some excitement into my voice, as it seems the right emotion for the moment. 'Tell him congratulations from me!'

'I will.' She twists her thick hair into a messy bun at the top of her head. 'You know, he's a big fan of yours . . .'

'Yeah?'

'Yeah, he was like, we should have her round for dinner.'

'Well, tell him to introduce me to one of his fit mates and I'm in,' I say, half joking.

'Oh, Sunny, I wish.' She shrugs her shoulders, keeping her eyes on her hair in the mirror. 'They're all taken – he was literally the last one.'

And there it is again. That stone at the pit of my stomach. She doesn't notice my disappointment because her phone has buzzed – and she's already giggling away. I'm starting to wonder if Mum actually will do a better job of finding me a partner than I've done so far. I roll my eyes at myself. If Elena knew I'd let my mum get involved in my dating life, she wouldn't believe it

'Take it that photo was a hit?' I say lightly.

'Look!' She thrusts the phone into my face, not caring about whether I want to see it or not.

*Looking beautiful, babe! I want to take you away somewhere hot, just so I can see you in it.*

I raise my eyebrows, pretending to be impressed, when I'm actually just imagining James and me on a beach somewhere, sipping margaritas.

She lets out a little squeal of delight and I bite the inside of my cheek.

'Well done on the hotel, darling, it's so cute!' she gushes, pulling her phone out of my hand and putting her clothes on over her swimsuit. 'You should be an event organiser or something, you're so good at it.'

I'm itching to be on my own so I can unpack. Being an only child means I have never had to share a room with anyone else and doing so makes me uncomfortable, like it's an invasion of my privacy. Even when I was younger, and my cousins would come over and we'd all sleep in the same room, I was never able to settle. And now, since I've moved home, my bedroom is my sanctuary, albeit a messy one that needs redecorating, but a sanctuary nonetheless.

'Might be worth looking at. You can't work in customer services your whole life.' She looks at me pointedly.

'I wasn't planning to.' I chuckle, but her comment stings. 'Anyway, better make a start on the deforestation. See you later, yeah?'

'Why don't you just get waxed? After a while, it comes back so much finer.'

I want to tell her the truth: because I can't bloody afford to, Elena, and unless I'm getting laid regularly, there's no point in spending the money. But getting laid has now turned into an annual event.

'Oh, I just haven't found a decent waxer in Gravesend,' I lie.

She finally leaves with a cheery 'don't be too long, darling' over her shoulder and I sit still on the bed until I hear her knock on the room next door. They're all chattering away, their voices carrying along the corridor as they head down to the spa.

I sink back on the bed. Finally, I can breathe. The bed, even though it's a single, is not stingy and is the perfect firmness. I stretch out and feel the knot in my stomach that I didn't know was there loosen slightly. I luxuriate in the silence. It's perfect. God, I love hotels. The anonymity, the comfortable bed and someone else making it, the lack of clutter. I like the blandness – I find it soothing. I could easily nap right now but I don't want to keep the girls waiting.

I run my hands over the thick cotton sheets and think about the Michael hotel. It would be so nice if we could come somewhere like this. For a whole weekend. Rather than that dingy inner-city hotel that made me want to stand in a hot shower for ages afterwards.

I imagine him. Michael. In a hot shower. With me . . .

I snap out of it; I've got a job to do, and I'm meant to be here to forget about Michael and his fuckery. I jump up, put my bag on the bed and unpack quickly, hanging up the plain black dress I plan to wear later in the wardrobe, laying out the make-up and jewellery to go with it on the table, and setting my trusty black ankle boots and thick tights on the floor next to it.

I take out my razor, a bottle of conditioner (I've not used shaving cream for years; instead, I use a cheap coconut conditioner to shave with), two brand-new tubes of Veet and some tweezers and put them by the bath. I'm exhausted just thinking about how long this is going to take. If only Victorian swimming costumes were still in fashion, I wouldn't have to worry about all this.

I set a timer on my phone for thirty minutes, put a nineties garage mix on Spotify and get to work. I use the razor for my lower legs, shaving my toes carefully. I spread the Veet on my thighs with the plastic spatula and waddle into the bedroom, trying not to let my thighs touch, and lay a towel on the bed. I then lower myself down onto it gingerly, keeping my knees in the air, legs apart, like I'm at the gynaecologist. I set a timer for fifteen minutes; I always leave it longer than suggested. The strange, sulphuric scent fills the room and I play *Candy Crush* until the timer goes off. When I'm all done, my legs feel slippery smooth. And I'm seven minutes ahead of schedule. I've got this down to a fine art.

I get into the black tummy-control swimsuit I bought from M&S just for the occasion, after taking Mum's advice. It was in the sale, probably because it is so frumpy – and because it's so frumpy, Mum thought it was fine. I pose in front of the mirror, just like Elena did earlier, adjusting it so it covers my arse and boobs without making either of them look saggy.

After a good ten minutes of posing and sucking my stomach in, scrutinising myself from every single angle, I realise no amount of ruching is going to make this swimsuit situation any better.

What if the towels aren't big enough?

What if there isn't a robe that fits me?

What if I have to wander about the spa with the robe open like that character from *Little Britain*?

I start to panic, my breath growing shallow and raggedy. I shove my face into my hands, not wanting to look in this mirror for another moment.

*Come on, Sunny. Come on, Sunny.*

I check my phone, and there are already three messages from the girls in our group chat.

Anjali: *Where are you, babe?!*

Elena: *Hurry up! There is literally no one here!*

Charlie: *Are you having some alone time, you dirty cow?!*

I consider not going down at all. I could say I'm sick or that I suddenly came on my period, then I could just sit and read the new Marian Keyes that I've been saving for this weekend. I could eat my stash of secret snacks, have a gin in a tin and watch telly and then take my time getting ready and just meet them for dinner in a few hours. Maybe, by tomorrow, I'd have a bit more confidence. I could go down early before anyone else and then have my massage. As soon as the thought pops into my head I dismiss it.

*No. I have paid good money for this weekend. I can't hide away.*

I head to Google and type: 'AFFIRMATIONS TO HELP BOOST YOUR CONFIDENCE'.

I keep scrolling until I find the right ones – ones I can actually hear myself saying, and possibly believing – then I stand in front of the mirror, where I repeat this one line.

'I love my body and I love myself. My body is a gift. I treat it with love and respect. I love my body and I love myself. My body is a gift. I treat it with love and respect. I love my body and I love myself. My body is a gift. I treat it with love and respect.'

I chuck on jeans and a top, and after a long inhale, like I'm about to dive underwater or something, I open the door and head down to meet the others.

# Chapter 17

'How's the dating going, babe?' Charlie asks me from the other side of the steam room. I'm feeling a bit better for the moment – because of course there *was* a robe that fitted after all, and the spa area *was* empty. It's now just us four in the aromatherapy steam room.

There are three different aromatherapy experiences to choose from: Relax, Revive and Reinvigorate. We're in Relax, which consists of a combination of lavender and patchouli from what I can tell. I can just about make out Anj's outline amid the fog. I can *Relax* in here – maybe thanks to the aromas, or to the fact that if I can't see Anj, no one can see me, meaning I also don't have to worry about Anj scrutinising my face for signs of Michael-related lies, and I can let my stomach hang out.

'Yes, tell us!' Elena chimes in, like she's getting comfortable for story time. 'We could do with some goss in our lives.'

'Oh, nothing much to report.' I close my eyes and tilt my head back. I decide I won't mention Michael at all – then it won't be lying.

'Did you get in touch with Michael?' Anj probes, and I swear to myself. Can she sense it? That I broke my promise?

'Which one is Michael again?' asks Charlie. 'There's so many I can't keep up.'

'There's not been *that* many!' I protest.

'Darling, you've been on a different date every week since you split up with erm . . . what's his name . . .?' She trails off.

I hold my breath.

'You showed us a picture of him – tall, quite muscly . . .'

'Yep. *That's* Michael.' I picture him, tall, broad, standing in reception at the dingy hotel, gut tightening as I sound his name.

'Did you end up messaging him?' asks Anj again gently. I can tell she's trying to help me open up, as though it's just me and her, as though she *knows* I messaged him and she's trying to catch me out.

Sitting unseen in this Relax room feels way more stressful than watching my mum swiping through Tinder.

'Hold on. I thought that was over and he didn't want a relationship,' Charlie jumps in immediately.

'He doesn't, *didn't*. I decided not to go there. Not worth it.' I'm even more grateful for the clouds of steam being pumped into the tiny room right now. My face would be a dead giveaway.

'Good, he was *nowhere* near good enough for you. Even as a fuck buddy.' Charlie's voice is firm. I know she means well, but I can't help being irritated by her.

'Ah, I'm proud of you,' Anj says, but I can't tell if she's proud or if she just doesn't believe me. 'It must've been *really* hard because you really liked him, didn't you?' Something about her pitying tone grates on me.

'Well, yes . . . he's my type, after all. Tall, beardy, emotionally unavailable.'

'All men are emotionally unavailable, though. We can't expect them to be everything, can we?' says Elena.

'I don't think I'm asking a lot for a man to be able to express how he feels!'

'Why don't you just get a fuck buddy, darling?'

I'm almost tempted to tell them about Mum and the apps. It is pretty funny in an absurd kind of way. Besides, it feels weird to keep something so major from them. But then I play out their various responses, and I don't know what would be worse: them laughing at me or pitying me for letting my mum take charge of my love life.

'It's not that easy. I am literally *unable* to have casual sex with a guy without catching feelings.' I'm thinking of Michael again. That fug of steam behind him as he got out of the shower. *That* was meant to be a hook-up, but I can't get him off my mind. They, of course, don't know that. 'I'm truly disappointed in myself.'

'That's not feelings, darling, that's hormones. Mother Nature's way of tricking us into having babies.'

'Well, Mother Nature is an absolute dick.'

'Who've you been having casual sex with anyway? Why haven't you told me any of this?' Anj asks, sounding half offended, half intrigued.

'No, no,' I lie quickly. 'I'm just . . . I just mean generally.'

'I don't get why it's so *difficult* for you to find someone. Maybe it's because you're looking online,' Charlie chirrups. I twist my hands around each other.

'Wow,' I say, after a short pause, with a lightness I don't feel. 'You sound like my mum.' I feel tears threatening to spill over. I try to take a deep breath, but the steam is too dense, and I end up coughing.

'God, I don't miss dating,' continues Anj, oblivious to my cough-crying.

'Being in a couple isn't that great, Sunny . . .' Charlie trails off, changing tack suddenly.

'Oh no, *babe*, what's going on?' asks Anj, concerned.

'Oh, nothing serious. I'm just *bored*,' Charlie sighs. 'Wish I was the one going on dates. He's just always . . . there. Stroking my hair, touching me. Sometimes it's a bit full-on.'

'What a monster,' I mutter under my breath.

★   ★   ★

When the steam room becomes unbearable, we leave and go our separate ways: Elena has a hot-stone massage booked in and Charlie and Anj go for a swim, which means I finally get to be alone until dinner. I practically run to the changing room and throw on my clothes, barely bothering to dry myself off properly. I don't want to waste any precious moments of my alone time. I'm guessing I have about an hour to myself.

As soon as I get in the room, I check my phone.

No messages. Not even from Mum, who has been forwarding me WhatsApp videos about how to prep your skin for your big day and telling me to update my dating profile to mention I have a Punjabi GCSE, as though that might encourage 'the right kind of boys' to get in touch.

There's that sinking feeling in my stomach again. Michael hasn't been in touch for ages now. I flop down on the bed. The excitement of being alone is gone and I'm just deflated. Maybe it's simply because I'm not relaxed yet; it always takes me a few days to relax on holiday, so I can hardly expect myself to get there in a matter of hours. Or maybe it's because of what Charlie said in the steam room; voicing my biggest insecurity. Why *is* it so difficult for me to find someone? I play it over and over again, feeling the shame and anger and something else, something more than sadness, rise up in my throat.

By the time we head down to dinner, we're already pleasantly tipsy after pre-drinks in Elena's and my room. The gins in a tin were a little warm so I filled the bath with cold water and put them in there: two tins each (on offer at four for the price of three). Even though she wouldn't approve if she knew I was drinking so much alcohol, Mum would certainly be proud of my resourcefulness . . . so at least there's that.

As we strut down to dinner in dresses and heels, I feel great, part of the gang – the unpleasantness of earlier all forgotten.

My hair is behaving itself and because, for once, I wasn't doing my make-up on a train, I've done a good job. I look good. I *feel* ... tingly. Alive. My smile isn't forced, and for once I'm in the moment and I'm enjoying it. I've already WhatsApped some selfies to Natalie, who firmly agreed I looked hot, and I wanted to send a picture to Michael too – but I can't bear the thought of it going left unread and unresponded to.

Dinner is from a set menu – the usual gastro pub-style fare – and despite the stuffy look of the dining room and the starched linens, the portions are hearty, the wine and the conversation are flowing, the steak is perfect, the chips are triple-cooked and the service is impeccable. We even get complimentary coffees and petit fours at the end. 'Complimentary' is like music to my ears, because halfway through our second bottle of wine, the price starts to dawn on me. I'd forgotten this isn't all-inclusive, and the thought of the bill is sobering me up.

But, thankfully, when the waiter wanders over to ask if we want anything else, Elena offers to pick up the tab for the wine, and I breathe a silent sigh of relief. After much protesting, we let her, because out of all of us, she is the one with the highest-paying job.

We leave the dining room, me arm in arm with Elena, Charlie and Anj with their arms around each other's waists, all of us swaying a little. I'm more than ready for my bed – the combination of rich food and booze is making my eyelids heavy, and I am picturing my night ahead, wrapped up in that bed in my fleecy pjs. It's the sort of night my mum dreams of, with an Ovaltine at the ready.

'Girls?' Charlie stops in the middle of the foyer. We turn to look at her. 'Fancy a club?'

*God, no.* We all look at each other.

'We can't go to bed just yet – it's only ten!' Charlie pushes.

I *knew* it'd be Charlie to suggest this.

After carefully considering all of our facial expressions, Anj says diplomatically: 'Maybe we can go for a bit?'

Has Anj ever been to a club with Charlie? There's no going to a club for a *bit*.

'Yes, fuck it, darling, girls' night out!' Elena jumps up and down like a child.

'Come on, Sunny!' Charlie turns to look at me, her eyes glazed. 'You can sleep when you're dead!'

She's drunker than I thought.

'Well, luckily for you lot, I have prepared for this.' I pull my phone out, trying to summon up the energy to deal with the next few hours.

'*Course* you have!' Charlie hugs me tightly, tripping over my feet.

'OK, so there is one club in the town centre. It's a ten-minute drive away; I'll book us a cab. You guys go grab your coats. Elena, can you get mine, please? And if you need a wee, go now or forever hold your piss.'

# Chapter 18

Fifteen minutes later, we clamber into a people carrier. You know you're in a white area when even the cab drivers aren't Asian. As I plug my seatbelt in and convince the girls to do the same, I feel the buzz of *being spontaneous* ripple up through my chest, and suddenly I don't care that Charlie is making me stay up late. Suddenly, I'm young and light and free.

We drive through countryside for ages and, almost out of nowhere, turn into a town that looks like it could be a mini-Gravesend, except there's not an Indian person in sight. And there, in the centre of the main high street, is Club Altitude. Dark-fronted, the sign in italic font. Proper classy. Sandwiched between a Subway and a vape shop. The burly, bald-headed bouncer chewing gum lets us in with a terse nod and an 'Evening, ladies.' And we walk in, pay a fiver each to the bored young woman at the cloakroom. We can hear the nineties R&B blasting through the speakers.

The club is more like a bar with a dance floor. A few suspicious-looking locals turn their heads as we walk in. It's not too busy, has sticky floors, red-and-black walls and enough mirrors to make you feel disorientated. I locate all the exits and do a headcount, before we make a beeline for a semi-circular booth decorated in black faux leather and chrome.

'Right, SHOTS!' I declare.

'Yes! She's back! This is the Sunny we know and love!' Charlie punches the air. For a split second I want to punch her.

'I'm too *old* for shots!' protests Elena, scrunching up her face as her eyes fix upon the teenage girls shuffling awkwardly from one foot to the other, trying to look cool.

'You're bloody not! This is Anj's pre-hen-do night out!'

I raise my eyebrow at this. No one told me.

'Not tequila, please!' says Anj fretfully as she unwraps her scarf from around her neck.

'Sambuca?'

'Oh God, no, even the word makes me want to gip.'

'Baileys?' I'm running out of options.

'Fuck it, you'll get what you're given!' Charlie roars as she drags me to the bar.

'Noooo!' Anj protests in the distance.

'Four sambucas, please, mate!'

'And some tap water, please!' I add hurriedly.

'You look lovely tonight, babe,' says Charlie. 'So nice to see you all dressed up for a change and having a laugh.'

'Ahh, thanks,' I reply, unsure how to respond to her backhanded compliment. 'You look lovely too! *Everyone* does, don't they!'

'I reckon you're gonna pull tonight. I can feel it,' she says knowingly, giving me a hard nudge with her elbow, trying to wink but blinking instead.

We carry a tray full of shots, a plastic jug of cloudy water and glasses back to the table. A couple of guys are hovering close by in matching tight chinos and pastel shirts. I can see from here that Anj is doing her best polite-but-not-interested face, holding her hand up with her engagement finger on display in the most awkward, obvious way possible.

'Hello, lads, I'm Charlie.' She sounds as though she's about to do a business deal. 'And *this* is Sunny, she's the single one.' She nudges me again.

The two guys smile awkwardly at me and then nod. One of them seems shy, uncomfortable; he's looking at his feet – and I know exactly how he feels. The other one starts practically leering at Charlie.

'Come on, girls.' I begin handing out shots, doing my best to ignore the men completely.

'Can you take a photo of us? Can you take a few?' Charlie waves her phone at the man leering at her, and suddenly she's pushing us girls together, forcing us to pose on either side of the table. Instinctively, I angle my body away from the camera and half hide behind Anj.

We knock back the shots and I head to the toilet – I just need to get away, be alone for a moment – but by the time I come back, the club seems to have got busier, with groups of spotty young people knocking back vivid-coloured drinks that glow in the dark. Anj and Elena are ignoring the club completely, looking intently at something on a phone.

'Anj is just showing me the decor for the wedding!' Elena shouts.

'Ooh, let me see!' I move my attention to Anj's phone too.

'Oh, don't worry, phone's about to die, babe,' Anj replies.

'Who's coming to the hen party? Not long now!'

'The usual suspects: my cousins, obviously you guys, some of my friends from school and ... ugh, my mum made me invite Beena. Literally don't even know where to seat her, somewhere *far* away from me.'

Before I can ask Anj more about Beena, I catch sight of Charlie at the bar talking to the man from earlier, before tottering back over to us, all sparkly-eyed with a bottle of prosecco and four glasses.

'He bought us some fizz,' she announces proudly, pouring it out into glasses, spilling practically half the bottle on the already-sticky table.

'A toast! To the bride-to-be!' shouts Elena.

'To the bride!' we chorus.

Once the whole bottle of prosecco has been demolished, much more quickly than expected – I'm not sure if that's because of how much Charlie spilled, or how desperate we are to get drunk – the energy starts to lull, and Anj has run out of wedding stuff to tell us about. So, Charlie, Elena and Anj are all sitting round the table texting their boyfriends. Their eyes don't look up from their phones once. I feel like a complete lemon. For a moment, I contemplate texting Michael. The bubbles have gone straight to my head, and I take myself to the bathroom for a moment and start scrolling through all his messages. My eyes can barely focus on the screen, and suddenly I'm hitting record on a voice note, looking at myself in the mirror. I should have taken a toilet selfie while I still looked good and my make-up was intact.

But then, out of nowhere, the opening bars of 'Bootylicious' blast through the speakers, and I rush out of the toilet and see the girls all look up from their phones, like they're being called back to the mothership, and as we make eye contact with each other, we yell excitedly and make a little impromptu dance floor by our booth. We're singing along loudly.

By the end of the song, we're out of breath, sweaty. As I squeeze myself back into the booth, I spot Charlie snogging a tall guy with a shaved head metres away from our table. Her arms are hanging loosely around his neck, she's pushing up against him, his hand on her arse.

Elena is watching too. As soon as the next song finishes (the DJ is firmly fixed on early-2000s hits now), Charlie staggers back over to us, arm in arm with the man.

'Where did you go?' shouts Elena.

'This is Jack!' Charlie yells. 'He used to be in the army. Feel his muscles. Go on. Feel his muscles, Sunny!' Before waiting for any kind of response from me, she grabs my hand.

'I'm OK, thanks.' I pull away.

'Why are you being so *rude*?' she demands, eyes fixed on me. Jack looks sufficiently awkward, but his arms are still wrapped around Charlie.

'I'm not.'

She rolls her eyes as she turns away.

'I'm going to get some fresh air,' I mutter to no one in particular. 'Mind if I . . .?' I catch Elena's eye and nod to the pack of Silk Cut on the table. She shrugs, so I take one out of the pack and head to the smoking area out the front, now full of people who look much younger than me.

I realise how tired I am, how much my feet hurt, how much my head hurts. I wish there were somewhere to sit out here.

'Excuse me?' I ask a youngster, who looks like he's over-joyed to be up past his bedtime. 'Can I borrow your lighter?' He nods, like a rabbit in headlights, and hands it to me. I light my cigarette. 'Thanks!'

I lean against the wall and take in a deep breath. The first inhale instantly makes me dizzy. To think, I used to smoke twenty a day at uni.

'You know it doesn't count if he's not in the same postcode.'

I turn around and Charlie's there, grinning, a cigarette hanging loosely from her fingers. I hand her my cigarette so she can light hers.

'Let loose. What's wrong with you?' Charlie says. It seems she's happy to be having a conversation with herself. 'I know you disapprove,' she continues irritably.

I shrug and think about not saying anything at all – maybe she'll lose interest. She doesn't want my approval anyway.

'I dunno, babe,' I say eventually, as Charlie leans against the wall too, to stop herself from swaying. 'It's just . . . not fair on John, is it? I'm not judging, but . . .'

'You slept with a married man, for fuck's sake!' Charlie shouts it as loudly as she can.

'Bloody hell.' My heart is in my mouth and I can feel eyes on me from around the smoking area. 'That was years ago. I was twenty-three! It's not the same thing. I wouldn't do that now.'

'Oh, it's just a bit of *fun*!' Charlie's frowning. 'I'm not having an *affair* or anything. I'm just having a laugh.' She throws up her arms, almost toppling over. I grab her elbow to steady her. 'You're so miserable all the time, Sunny. It's like moving home has actually turned you into your mum. Why can't you just cheer up!'

'Is it any wonder with you and your little *digs*?' The words are out of my mouth before I realise, and I hear the edge in my voice. Out of the corner of my eye I see Elena and Anj tottering towards us, cigarettes in hand.

Charlie looks like she's been slapped and, suddenly, you couldn't stop me if you tried.

'Do you need me to jog your memory? In the steam room earlier? "Oh, Sunny, why is it so hard for you? Why are you so unlovable, Sunny? What's wrong with you, Sunny?"'

'That's not what she meant.' Anj's voice is faint, competing with the roaring in my ears.

'I'm not some . . . some . . . fucking . . . performing monkey that you can call on to entertain you any time you're bored in your perfect fucking relationships.' I wheel around and face Charlie, almost going over on my ankle. 'Oh, it's so hard for me, my boyfriend just loves me so much. Boo-fucking-hoo. Leave him then. See how easy it is out there. When every decent man is taken, and everyone treats you like you've got the plague just because no one wants to be with you.'

'Maybe if you spent less time flirting with other people's boyfriends you wouldn't be single,' Charlie spits.

'What?'

A look passes between Elena and Anj.

'What?!'

It feels as though everyone in the smoking area has gone silent. Like everyone is watching.

'It's . . . we've just noticed that sometimes when we're out, you can be a little . . . overly friendly with our partners,' says Anj carefully.

I look from Elena to Anj and back again, trying to process what I've just heard. 'Are you for fucking real?!' My voice is harsh, high-pitched with shock.

'I don't think you *realise* you're doing it, but yeah, we've all noticed it,' says Elena quietly.

'And you've obviously all talked about it. Is this what you did the other week when you got together? Talked about me behind my back?'

'It's not that deep, babe, come on . . .'

'No, it obviously is.' I'm shaking now. 'So, I make an effort with all your boyfriends even though they're as boring as fuck – yeah, they are – and it makes me some sort of homewrecker? Yet Charlie is out here actually *getting off* with another bloke, practically *humping* him all night, and that's totally fine? Oh, well done, Charlie! It's all a bit of fun!' I clap loudly in mock applause. I don't care who can hear me.

'I have not been—'

'Look, girls, girls, we've all had a lot to drink—'

'Yeah, let's call it a night.'

'Fine by me,' I snap. 'I was ready to go home ages ago.' I stride back into the club for my coat. For a split second I think about grabbing their coats too but decide against it.

When I return empty-handed, with my coat already wrapped around me, their faces are a picture of mild shock. I stare back belligerently, daring them to say something.

Elena rolls her eyes and mutters something like 'childish' under her breath, but clearly with the intention of being heard, as she passes me to get her coat.

I turn to hail a minicab across the street so Charlie and Anj can't see that I'm crying. As soon as the cab pulls up, I open the door and sit in the front, then open the window and stick my head out. They clamber into the back seats, all snug. I can hear them talking quietly and Charlie crying and whimpering.

'Would you mind turning the music up?' I bark to the cab driver, and he does as he's told.

I walk as quickly as I can to the hotel room. They're all following a few feet behind, talking in low voices. It's like being back at school. Feeling misunderstood, never quite knowing the right thing to do or say, helpless and excluded and betrayed by the girls in Year 9 who you thought were your friends.

I unlock our door as quickly as I can, expecting Elena to follow me in, but she doesn't so I just let the door close behind me. I don't turn round to check. I fold myself into bed, curling up into a ball, wanting to be as small, as invisible, as possible, and I shut my eyes so tightly that the room stops spinning. I wait, listening for Elena, but she never comes in.

I realise I can't feel anything any more. There's just a blank space inside me where rage should be.

# Chapter 19

I wake with a start. My heart is pounding. My eyes feel like they have rolled around in cat litter. My brain scrambles to figure out where I am. The duvet feels too light and fluffy to be my own, and I can't hear Mum rattling around in the kitchen.

Then the memories of last night come flooding back in flashes. Charlie's blotchy, tear-stained face; Anjali's mouth twisted with disappointment; the silent cab ride home; swallowing my tears until they formed a lump in my throat. I look over to Elena's bed, and her little snuffly snores tell me she is out for the count. I turn very slowly onto my side to reach for my phone until my stomach lurches violently.

Oh, *great*, this hangover is worse than I thought.

Seven fifteen.

I squint, turning the brightness down on my phone, as it's threatening to perforate my retina.

Of course. It doesn't matter what day it is; I always wake up at around now. No one sleeps past this time in the Sanghera household. And for a moment, I actually wish I was back there, sitting at the kitchen table drinking cha with Mum and Dad. I check my call log, my heart suddenly racing with fear. But thankfully no drunken phone calls were made. It's a relief; I've got enough to deal with right now. I don't want to face the girls this morning, so I check the National Rail app for a way out. The first train to London isn't until 9.30. I could pack quickly and creep out. Maybe even squeeze in a quick breakfast. The thought of food makes me feel queasy.

It would mean missing out on the full-body massage I've already paid for and was very much looking forward to. But the thought of having breakfast with them and then the long journey back, making polite but strained conversation, fills me with dread.

I open WhatsApp to message Natalie; she will know what to do. She always knows what to do.

Then I see there's a message from Mum.

*Hope spa is good. Tell me about any messages.*

Before I can even let myself get a bit annoyed at this, I see there's a WhatsApp from Michael.

My heart skips and skitters in my chest.

*LOL.*

I scroll up and see that he left me a voice note in the early hours of the morning.

I feel a sense of victory that I managed to resist the temptation of messaging him last night. Admittedly, it was probably just because I was too drunk, or too focused on my friends being dicks to me.

I burrow down in the duvet to muffle the sound and press play.

My drunken slur fills the room.

It's not from him.

It's *me*. I remember a flash from the evening – recording a voice note before the call of 'Bootylicious' distracted me . . .

*Fuck.*

I scramble to turn the volume down but end up dropping the phone. A fire creeps up my chest, across my face. My heart is going to explode. My arms have gone numb. Am I having a stroke?

I look over at Elena to see if I've woken her. No. She's still sleeping. I roll carefully onto my side and lower myself to the ground; my urgency to hear the voice note overrides my hangover's desire for me to remain very still.

I half tiptoe and half stumble to the bathroom, using the wall to steady myself.

Oh God, is this alcohol poisoning?

I've only had it once before, at Charlie's twenty-first. We went to Strawberry Moons and were bought shots of vodka by a couple of Russians. Bad. *So* bad.

I fumble for the light switch and manage to find the bathroom-mirror lights the first time. Thank God for fancy hotel lighting. Right now, fluorescent lighting would have sent me over the edge. I lower myself onto the loo and lean my head against the cool edge of the sink, closing my eyes briefly. Then I press play again.

*'Hiiiiiii, Michael . . . it's meee . . . Sunny . . . in case you don't have my number saved any more . . . I am having a GREAT weekend by the way . . . thank you for ASKING. Anyway, you're probably already in bed cos it's like ten p.m. and you've got to wake up early and be boring with all your CrossFit buddies and do a million burpees and meal prep and drink fifteen protein shakes.'*

At this point I laugh far too hard at my own joke – a wheezy, Muttley-esque chuckle.

*'Is that why you weren't interested? Because I'm not fit. And we can't talk about fucking macros together? You know we first met on a dating app, right? The thing is . . . I just don't understand why someone would go on a fucking dating app and then not want to date. Why would you date if you weren't ready to date? Just . . . have a wank or call a mate or watch a movie or . . . get a fucking hobby . . . We had such a nice time, but you always give off mixed signals.*

*'Remember that picnic? In the park? Ages ago. Like our second date. Course you remember, you remember EVERYTHING.*

*Like everything I have ever told you. Like who does that unless they really care about someone? Like the neck kisses – I told you I liked those once – literally ONCE – and ... and ... actually I'm fucked off with you – the whole not wearing a condom thing was bang out of order, like, I could be pregnant or have an STI and you don't even have the DECENCY to check if I'm OK. I'm not crying cos of you, I'm not upset, OK? I'm just drunk and I'm not used to it cos I don't really drink any more like I used to. Anyway bye, Michael. You won't hear from me again. Have a nice life.'*

The impact of my parting shot is somewhat lost as I hear myself whooping at the opening bars of 'Bootylicious'. That song will now be forever ruined. The worst thing is his response.

*LOL.*

I stare at it, taunting me.

I can't even share it with the girls and have a laugh about it because they don't know anything about him any more – they don't know I'm still thinking about him. Instead, I send both voice notes to Natalie with the message:

*Guess who got really drunk, properly fell out with her mates and sent Michael TWO DRUNKEN VOICE NOTES. Kill me now pls. xxx*

I lean my head against the sink again and close my eyes. Michael's *LOL* etched on my brain. I want to climb out of my skin with shame. If I was alone, I'd get back into bed and sleep for hours, but I'm too scared to go back into the room in case Elena is up. Heaving myself up from the loo, I look in the mirror, assessing the damage. My usual morning puffiness is worse than normal, my hair is sticking up like Edward Scissorhands', and my eyes are bloodshot because I didn't take my contacts out. I wash and dry my hands and carefully take out my lenses, eyes watering. And my mouth feels like it's lined with fur.

I turn on the shower and gingerly step into the bath, terrified my legs are going to give way any second. I'm hit by a sudden image of me slipping, cracking my head open and being found, naked, by Elena. At least I'd get some sympathy that way. As soon as the warm water hits my skin a pungent mix of hairspray, cigarette smoke and sweat fills the air. I turn up the temperature. The water is close to scalding but it's doing its job, blocking out my thoughts of last night.

I wash my hair twice, scratching roughly at my scalp, and slather on conditioner while I scrub myself raw. By the time I get out of the shower, Elena is still asleep, but I've formulated a plan.

I quickly and quietly get dressed in a dark corner of the room. I shove my wet hair under a hat, grab my book, a large pair of sunglasses and a can of Diet Coke and breathe a sigh of relief as I slowly close the door and walk along the deserted corridor to the lobby and to the exit. It's a crisp, clear winter's day, the sky the colour of sapphires. The blast of cold air instantly wakes me up. An elderly couple amble slowly arm in arm along the well-kept path, but there's hardly anyone else around. I smile at them benignly from under my sunglasses.

I wander around the back of the hotel and sit on an ornate wooden bench by a disused fountain. It's so quiet I can hear the birds singing, accompanied by the occasional rumble of a car in the distance. I close my eyes and lean back, trying to focus on the quiet, but my brain is fuzzy with anxiety.

Soon I'll have to face the girls.

I try to concentrate on my book but give up after reading the first paragraph three times; the words leap across the page. I scroll through Instagram – anything to distract myself from having to face the others. I hurriedly flick through my feed, past photos of girls I went to school with looking dead on their feet with a grinning, bright-eyed toddler attached to their hip. As always accompanied with a saccharine caption.

*Nothing like mornings with my sweet boy, Alfie. Growing up so quick. Love you, bubba xoxo*

I'm almost tempted to comment, 'He can't read your comment, you fucking idiot,' but instead, I take a photo of the book I can't read with the fountain in the background and upload it to Instagram.

There's still no reply from Natalie on WhatsApp. But there's Michael's last message to me, the solitary *LOL*, still taunting me. I could just block him; it wouldn't be the first time. But it wouldn't block him from my memory. I briefly consider knocking my head against the bench in the hope that might do the job.

*Sorry about that – alcohol had been consumed. Have a good day!* I hit send.

I feel stupidly proud of myself for not adding a kiss on the end, then delete our chat, his number and all the screenshots I've taken over the past few months.

In the dining room, a tired-looking young waitress with dark hair scraped back in a tight bun greets me cheerily.

'Some of your party are already seated.' She rummages around for a menu and I see that Charlie and Anj are talking animatedly over a cooked breakfast. Before I can ask for a separate table, the girls turn to look at me, then at each other. The waitress is already leading me to the table. I follow her, my heart thudding, my jaw tense.

'Morning.'

'Morning.' They wear matching tight smiles.

'Where's Elena?' I busy myself with taking off my coat, so I don't have to look at either of them.

'Having a facial,' Anj says coolly, taking a sip of orange juice.

'Cool. I'm going to get some . . .' I trail off. They don't care what I'm doing. Normally I love a breakfast buffet: I have a system of how to approach it. Savouries first, then granola, yoghurt and fruit, and finish off with pastries. Always save the best till last. But today I'm panicked, so I grab whatever's closest to me, bypassing the weird toaster that looks like a mini-BBQ.

I sit down facing the two of them with my bowl of fruit and a raspberry yoghurt. I eye up their glistening fat sausages and crispy fried eggs with envy. The air is dense with unspoken words; all of a sudden my throat feels like it's closed up and I'm incapable of making a sound.

'Do you want some juice?' Anj gestures to the jug. When she fills my glass for me, I watch Charlie out of the corner of my eye nibbling on a piece of toast, her eyes carefully averted from the table.

'Someone should be coming over to take your order, if you want a cooked breakfast. I can—'

'I'm OK, thanks, don't have much of an appetite,' I lie, spearing a chunk of apple with my fork. An unbearable silence descends on the table. I'm itching to look at my phone just for something to do, but that would be rude. I can imagine them exchanging looks while I scroll. Anj puts down her fork carefully and reaches out for my hand.

'Guys, I think we need to clear the air after last night . . .' She takes Charlie's hand too, and for the first time since I sat down, Charlie looks at me, directly, her large grey eyes already glassy with unshed tears.

My stomach clenches tighter.

'I know some . . . stuff . . . was said last night . . . in the heat of the moment . . .' Anj looks at me for a bit too long and I feel my cheeks redden. 'But we'd all had a bit too much to drink, and we all say things we don't mean when we're pissed . . .' She looks from me to Charlie and back to me again.

I manage a nod and a quiet, 'Mmmhmm.' I press my lips together tightly, in the hope that it will stop me from unleashing the anger building up inside me.

'If I said anything to upset you, I'm sorry but . . .' I look at Charlie, her tone apologetic, as a single fat tear rolls down her cheek.

'I'm sorry but—' isn't a fucking apology. I look at Anj, and I can see in her eyes that she knows it's barely an apology too, but she says nothing.

Charlie is looking at me, waiting for me to reply. I nod, conjure up a small smile.

'I'm sorry too. You're right, we were drunk and, you know . . .' I say with a small shrug. Anj exhales and her shoulders visibly drop.

'Oh, I'm so glad we could sort this out, girls.' She beams melodramatically, squeezing my hand. 'It would be such a shame if we let a silly thing like that come between us. We've been friends for so long.'

I nod again, wondering if that's a good enough reason to stay friends with the women Charlie, Elena and Anj are becoming.

# Chapter 20

'So, you said on the phone last week that you were feeling a bit lost?' The therapist's voice is calm but direct. She's new – and I'm hoping she's a better fit. I need a good fit right now.

I had to tell Natalie everything that happened with the girls. The journey home was a nightmare; it was so awkward I could barely breathe, and the voice note to Michael just made me feel completely shit – it's been weeks since then, but I'm still thinking about it all the time. As soon as Natalie heard the whole story, she immediately insisted that I give therapy another go. She's been in therapy since she was eighteen and goes through therapists like I go through giant bars of Fruit & Nut. This is someone who was recommended to her by a woman she met on a yoga retreat in Sri Lanka. She's more expensive than the first therapist, so I'm hoping we can wrap this up in six sessions. I am balls-deep in my overdraft and still have to buy a new dress for Anj's hen do next month, which is the only thing she's talking to me about at the moment. All my going-out clothes are far too old and tight for public consumption.

'I never did have the best sense of direction,' I reply drily.

She doesn't say anything. Instead, she purses her thin lips slightly and looks down at her A4 notepad. It's still got the price sticker on it. For some reason, this really pisses me off.

'Do you often use humour to mask your feelings?' She cocks her head, her mouth turned up in the faintest of smiles.

I wait for her to carry on talking. She doesn't. To my horror, I realise she's waiting for an answer.

I want to say yes, yes, I do actually, Wendy. Because life is a bloody struggle, and we could all do with a laugh. Also, aren't all fat people supposed to be funny? That's the age-old trope. Fat, jolly person who has a great sense of humour to make up for their physical shortcomings. Get on board. I don't make the rules.

'I guess . . .' I say weakly, hoping she'll drop it.

'It's a very common defence mechanism,' she says, not unkindly, though I still feel myself blush like I've been caught out. But I'm not backing down.

'Well, you have to develop a sense of humour if you're fat. Especially if you're not pretty. That's why so many attractive people are so dull. They've never had to try, have they? Mind you, I'd rather be interesting and ugly than fit and boring as . . . hell.' I smile, proud of myself for not dropping an F-bomb. She continues to stare at me and nods her head slightly, like she's trying to figure me out. Which I guess she is. I just wish she'd hurry up about it, as we've only got ten minutes until the end of the session.

'Is that how you see yourself? As ugly?' She speaks softly – which is annoying, because it means I really have to focus on her. She's making a few notes on her pad. Her elegant fingers move swiftly across the page. Will I ever get to see the notes she's writing about me? I make a mental note to google this when I leave.

'Well, I know I'm not a supermodel. I look all right in the right light, with a bit of make-up on, but you wouldn't want to see me first thing. I look like a manky toe. And a hairy one at that.' I finish with a little laugh.

Wow. Not. Even. A. Smirk.

'I want to explore this idea that you see yourself as unattractive. Where do you think that idea comes from? Because you're clearly very pretty.' She says it like she's stating a fact. Are therapists *allowed* to say stuff like this? She crosses her legs, her pen poised, one hand under her chin. I can feel sweat bloom under my armpits. My breathing quickens.

'Erm ... I ... I've always thought it, I guess.' My voice breaks slightly, trying to ignore the last bit she said.

'Even as a child?'

'Oh, well, no, I was a cute kid. All rosy cheeks, big brown eyes. Up until the age of about seven. Seven till nineteen were my ugly-duckling years. Then I discovered make-up and GHDs and threading, and I transformed into a ... slightly less ugly ... swan, I suppose ...' I trail off. I'm not really here to talk about this. I want to know why I feel so sad all the time, why I'm always dating guys when I know it won't go anywhere, why I never enjoy time with my friends. I'm sick of feeling like I'm the broken one.

I just want to feel light and joyful, if such a feeling exists outside movies. I'm not even that fussed about being *happy*; I'd settle for not feeling like absolute rubbish.

'When you tell yourself that you're unattractive, whose voice is it?'

She's really not letting this go.

'It's mine.'

'No one has ever told you you're unattractive?'

'They've told me I'm fat – that's the same thing to them, right?' I cross my arms and stare out of the window at the dark, cobbled street.

She looks at me, blinking slowly. 'I have some homework for you.'

My heart leaps at this – I love a bit of homework.

'With this large piece of paper and this pen, I want you to draw a spider diagram and write down all the words you use to describe yourself. Bring it with you next time.'

I look at the piece of paper in front of me. At first, I see Mum's face – stressed about me not being able to drive and not owning a buy-to-let property, and trying to hide her sadness when another one of her friend's daughters is getting married. Then I see Anj and Charlie and Elena, laughing without me – maybe even at my expense. A few months ago, we were best of friends, weren't we?

Then, the words jump out at me.

*Lazy.*

*Failure.*

*Boring.*

*Sad.*

*Lonely.*

*Unwanted.*

*Unworthy.*

*Numb.*

*Nothing.*

I take the paper and pen, and stuff them in my bag.

# Chapter 21

'Anybody message?'

Not even a 'good morning' these days.

At first, I think she means Michael – and my heart starts racing, because he's all that's been on my mind since the spa weekend. But then she clarifies: 'On the Tindles?'

Mum means the dating apps. Of course she does. It has become her new favourite thing. While I've spent days moving from bed, to sofa, to work – enjoying only KFC Fridays with Dean, who, besides Nat, seems to be the only person who just lets me be myself at the moment – Mum has been thinking about my dating life an unreasonable amount.

Last week, I made the mistake of telling her about a guy I was chatting to before we'd even arranged to meet. Partly to get her off my back and partly because I got overexcited. I thought, for a stupid second, that all the worries I'd been wanting the therapist to fix might actually have been fixed . . . by a message. From a guy. On a dating app. With a profile my mum might even approve of.

Hari (short for Harinder) was a self-confessed 'spiritual type'. Originally from Newcastle (cute accent, tick), he now lives in Richmond, working as an acupuncturist and massage therapist. Not only did he know his star sign, his rising sign *and* Vedic star sign, but, crucially, he didn't live with his parents and was looking to settle down, according to his profile.

This got my hopes up, but, most importantly, it got Mum's hopes up too. He ticked all of her boxes, and all of mine, so he and I swapped numbers and messaged pretty much non-stop for a day and a half. Almost enough time for me to forget about Michael,

But just as I was about to ask about his life path number, he hit me with a semi-flaccid dick pic, so I had to shut him down immediately and delete all trace of him from my phone in case Mum got her hands on it. When she asked me when I was going to see him, I had to tell her he was about to move to Scotland. My mum has made it clear I can't move any further away than the Midlands, even for marriage.

Since then, she's been asking every single day if there's someone else on the cards.

She's waiting at the bottom of the stairs as I come out of the loo, dressed for her weekly yoga class in dark joggers, a floral top and one of her beloved cardigans.

'Mama, I'm going to be late for work!' I race down the stairs holding my pre-menstrual boobs in my hands.

'Yes or no?'

'Yes, but—'

There *is* another guy now, but I don't want to show my mum too much in case it doesn't go anywhere. She was so disappointed that Semi-Flaccid and I didn't get married, even though we'd only just started messaging, so I daren't tell her that me and this other guy, Jag, have been talking for days already, in case she calls to book the hall.

'Who is he?' she demands, looking over the banister at me as I run around getting my stuff together.

'Look, we've only just started talking. Please don't—'

'Show me, quick, *quick* then.' Her hand is reaching in front of her in a grabbing motion, gesturing impatiently for my phone.

I look up at the ceiling, praying for it to give me strength to deal with this before I have to deal with Sharon at work too, and I open the app to click on his profile. I put it on airplane mode first, in case she accidentally sends him a wink or something. I watch her nervously as I finish tying my laces, then throw on my coat and scarf.

She's nodding, her eyebrows set in a slight frown, her lips held tightly together. She's giving nothing away.

'Hmmm ... Jag ... tall, handsome ... *divorced?*' she says eventually.

'Nope. Never been married.'

'Job?' she asks the phone directly, and I reply with: 'IT, works in London.' He does *something* with computers, but I don't know what, and I didn't want to ask in case he thought I was thick.

'Live in London?'

'Yeah,' I lie instantly. He actually lives up the road in Bexley, but I'm worried if I tell her that, she'll start making enquiries of her own at the gurdwara.

'Bye, Mama, I really have to go or I'll miss my train.' I prise my phone from her fingers – and her eyes, for the first time, look up at me.

'OK, go, go! Here, put this in your bag.' She picks up a small tin of pineapple chunks in juice from the table by the door and passes it to me. My favourite. A peace offering.

'Thanks, Mama!' I kiss her on the cheek and practically run out of the door before she says anything else.

Jag and I have been chatting for just under a week. From what I've seen so far, he is cheeky, funny, the same age as me, speaks fluent Punjabi and when my mum said, 'Hmm ... tall, handsome,' what she meant is he is HOTTER THAN THE SURFACE OF THE SUN.

We swapped numbers and had a quick chat on the phone, and I've already managed to find out which part of Punjab his family are from; he's not from either of my paternal or maternal ancestral villages, so no chance of accidental incest.

Now that my mum knows about him, she'll expect me to push things along a bit, but I'm not a big fan of endless messaging anyway. I always feel like messaging for ages before meeting up can create a false sense of intimacy and heightened expectations followed by a very disappointing date, where you realise you only got on via messaging, and in real life, the man in front of you is not actually as funny in real time. I once went all the way to Broadstairs to meet a man who was hilarious over WhatsApp but had absolutely no chat in person. I think he'd got all his jokes off Google, or had his friends reply for him. It was a very long and boring date, plus he had the sort of soporific voice that made it pretty much impossible to stay awake and I had to leave after ninety minutes, telling him that my non-existent cat was in labour. It took me longer to get there.

As I jump on the train, a message buzzes in from Jag. It says, simply, *Good morning*, but I feel a flutter in my belly. Rather impulsively and impatiently, squidged between two businessmen in suits heading to work, I decide to make my move. With Jag, that is. I open up the Notes app and draft a few different versions before settling on:

*Fancy meeting up for a drink sometime soon? X*

Nice. Cool. Doesn't appear too keen. (I'm aware that drafting a message in Notes isn't necessarily impulsive, but it's the most impulsive I do, OK?)

*Yeah cool.*

I am inordinately proud of myself for waiting a full fifteen minutes before replying.

*I'm pretty free this week ... Thursday?*

I'm 'pretty free' every bloody night now that I have three fewer friends than I started off the year with. Of course, Anj, Elena and Charlie are still very much in my life and on my WhatsApp group, but they've not bothered to message me directly once. It's *all* about the hen party.

Suddenly, my mind is racing to Anj's wedding – what if Jag and I are a thing by then? Maybe I could bring him along. Mum would love that, wouldn't she?

I fantasise about the faces they'll pull when they see me walking in with him.

*I can do Thurs.*

*Cool. Where do you want to meet?*

*Up to u*

OK, so this is not a great sign. He's not bothering to plan this. But I can hear Natalie in my head telling me to give the guy a chance. Maybe he's busy or distracted; I know he's already at work. And anyway, it's probably better that I choose. At least that way I know that I will like it. Plus, it takes the pressure off – I'll know where the loos are, which is one less thing to worry about. The usual it is then.

*How about the Royal Oak in Greenwich?*

This has become my usual spot for taking dates; it's far enough from Gravesend to ensure we don't get spotted by any nosey aunties, but close enough that if I end up having a great night a cab home won't be too eye-wateringly expensive.

I often wonder what the staff must think of my never-ending revolving door of disappointing dates. I'm just hoping we don't have to add Jag to the list of them.

*Cool*

I feel my heart sit heavily in the pit of my stomach; he's not as chatty or as forthcoming as he was last night. If it wasn't for the fact that I think Mum might actually like him, and the fact that she keeps asking about dates, maybe I would have ghosted him or just not bothered replying. I can't face having to come up with some story about why I just 'didn't get the vibe' with him. Mum doesn't understand 'vibe'.

*6pm OK? I have an early start the next day.*

I can't tell him Mum expects me home by a certain time. *Yeah.*

*Hi Mama,* I type out my message, feeling like I'm offering someone a promotion or something. *Meeting Jag on Thursday. Have fun at yoga. Xxx*

'But where are you going to meet him?' she says later that day, like she's some kind of TV detective.

'At a café near work,' I lie. She doesn't know that there aren't cafés near the office. And I can't tell her that we're going to a pub.

'Don't eat too much, OK? And don't talk too much. You remember what happened to Raji? The boy's family said no because she talked too much.' I roll my eyes, but she's concentrating on checking a tray of toor daal for stones.

My mum has never dated. She met Dad on their wedding day and had only seen him from afar at another event before that. But somehow, she's giving me advice on dating etiquette?

'Make sure you ask him his surname and about his family, how many brothers and sisters, OK? Too many brothers means too many sisters-in-law.' She looks at me knowingly. Dad is one of five brothers. Mum doesn't get on with any of the wives.

'OK, Mama.' I try not to sigh in exasperation, knowing how awful she had it when she came to the UK, living with all of Dad's brothers and their bitchy, spoilt wives who didn't lift a finger. Mum had been brought up not to question anyone or anything, and so she kept her head down, kept the peace, until she and Dad had saved up enough money to move out. I think that's why she's so happy to boss me and Dad around now – she's making up for lost time.

'And if he say to you let's go somewhere *else*, don't go with him, OK?' She peers at me over her glasses, her gaze piercing.

'Erm . . . OK,' I mumble. And then it hits me. She's giving me The Talk™. Or at least the closest we're ever going to get to it. I'm thirty. I thought I'd got away with this.

I bury my face in my giant mug of tea.

'These modern boys they are . . . it's not like it used to be. Things are very different now. They are only after one thing . . . and then they leave the girl when they get what they want. So not even kissy-kissy—'

'*MUM!*'

I can't walk out because I'm eating and leaving food on the plate is a cardinal sin in this house – the repercussions would be even worse than The Talk™, trust me – so I flick through the Aldi leaflet in a bid to distract myself, but I'm barely able to concentrate on the special buys.

*One day you will be able to laugh about this, Sunny,* I tell myself. One day. Maybe not in the near future. But one day. I hope.

# Chapter 22

'So, how was that spa thing of yours the other week?' Dean asks as we're standing outside in the smoking area after another long day of wrangling with customer-service policies and Sharon's passive-aggressive comments about 'resolution times'.

'Oh, fine,' I say flatly, taking another swig of Diet Coke.

'Pull the other one,' chuckles Dean. 'You've had a face as long as the M6 for the past few weeks. Don't think I don't notice these things. Come on then, tell ya Uncle Dean, what is it? Boy trouble again?'

I scoff.

'. . . Girl trouble?' he says, his eyes widening.

'No, you perv.'

'Mum trouble?' he says, looking at me knowingly. 'Or is that the same as boy trouble now, seeing as your mum is playing matchmaker?'

'Piss off. And who's fault is that? It's just friend trouble,' I reply.

'Ahhh.' He sighs, putting out his cigarette on the low wall we're leaning against, immediately lighting another. 'Sorry, mate.' He wafts the smoke away with a meaty hand.

'Can you smoke in my direction, please, for fuck's sake?' I say, inhaling deeply. 'I'm second-hand smoking here, thanks.'

My phone buzzes and when I see it's Anj, an involuntary groan escapes from the depths of my weary soul.

Anjali: *Hi girls, thought I'd check in before the hen! Hope you're well! Can't wait to see you!!! Xxx*

Elena: *Counting down the days, darling! So exciting* 😊

Charlie: *Arghhhh!!! SO EXCITED, BABE! Just bought the most PERFECT dress for it too!*

'Bad news?' Dean asks, watching me intently.

'Ugh. No. It's just a . . . friends WhatsApp group I'm in . . .' I put my phone in my pocket.

'I don't suppose these are the *friends* who've made you so miserable lately?'

I lean my head back and stare at the sky, half wishing we were still talking about my mum being my new dating coach, because the sorry state of affairs with Anj and the girls makes me feel a bit sick. I give him a quick rundown of the argument at the club and the breakfast the next morning – every awkward moment of it is etched onto my memory.

'Fucking hell, that's a bit rough.' He rubs a hand roughly across his forehead.

'Yeah. The thing that's freaking me out the most is that I would actually be OK with not seeing them again. I'd be a bit sad, but I don't think I'd miss them. Does that make me a heartless bitch?'

'Look, I dunno a lot about girls, but if you're saying you're all right with not being mates with them any more . . . sounds like the decision is made. Here's what I think: either sit 'em down, talk it out and see what happens, or, if you're not that fussed about them, cut your losses and move on. If you can't be yourself around them, then it sounds like they're not worth it.' He leans back, and starts coughing violently.

I look at Dean, simultaneously disgusted by his hacking cough and also wondering how on earth he suddenly seems like the wisest person in the world. Nat has told me again and again that 'life's too short to go around pretending to be someone you're not' – I thought she meant with dates; I didn't realise she might mean friends I've known for ten years too.

'Well . . . thanks for the sound advice, Dean, but now I've got to go on a date with a guy my mum wants me to marry.'

'Serious? I thought she was just helping you find dates.'

Solemnly, I respond with: 'I've got my wedding dress in my bag.'

His face is suddenly terrified, and I can see the guilt in his eyes.

'Don't worry, you'll get an invite, seeing as it's all your bloody fault.'

Six o'clock comes and goes. I've been watching the pub's front door every time it opens, and most of the time it's a whole crowd of friends, searching for a place to sit down and unwind after a day's work. They keep looking over at my table, wondering, probably, why I've got a booth all to myself.

I pull out my phone so I don't have to keep making eye contact as each new person comes in with their huddle of friends, or with their girlfriends or boyfriends.

Six ten. And there's still no sign of him.

I check my WhatsApp, turning my Wi-Fi and my 3G on and off, even though I know I've had connection this whole time. He hasn't messaged me at all. I read our chat for the fifteenth time in the past few minutes in case I missed a vital message or something.

There's no message and he's not online.

How long do I wait?

At 6.15, a message flashes up and my heart leaps. I scramble to unlock my phone:

*You like him?*

It's Mum. My heartbeat settles back down. I feel a tiny surge of love at the fact that my mum checked in at all, but then a creeping sense of fear – what if he stands me up? What will I tell Mum then?

*He's not here, Mama. He is late.*

*OK.*

I want to rant, to tell someone how annoyed I am, but I can't say all that to my mum. What if he ends up being The One, and Mum will just remember him as the guy who made me wait forever and really annoyed me. She'd never forget it. Or she'd find some way to explain his behaviour based on something I did.

I check my make-up in my compact for the umpteenth time and wish I'd ordered something stronger than a white wine spritzer. The pub is now crammed full of people, shoulder to shoulder at the bar. The noise is louder, and I'm searching for his face in the crowd in case he hasn't spotted me – the only person hanging out in a booth on their own.

'All right?' says a voice right next to me.

'Fucking hell!' I grip my chest as my heart threatens to punch out of my ribcage.

I look up to see Jag, in a dark jacket and black jeans, a bit more beardy than his photos but no less handsome. Definitely handsome enough to turn my mind blank for a few seconds.

'Sorry, didn't mean to make you jump,' he says with a chuckle. I note his even, white teeth and shy smile. Oh *God*, I fancy him. I half feel like calling Mum right away to tell her but stop myself – because I haven't jumped into an alternate universe just yet, even if sometimes it feels like one.

'What are you drinking?'

'White wine spr— Just white wine. Pinot Grigio. Please. Large.' I remember that I'm supposed to be annoyed at him for his lateness, so I stop grinning and look him right in the eye, daring him to challenge me. But he just lopes right over to the bar and runs his hand through his hair, checking himself out in the mirror while he's waiting to be served.

He's taller than I expected. And he has a cute bum. A little on the skinny side, though, and there's something about the way he carries himself that makes me think he might not be as confident as he first seems.

Then Sensible Sunny kicks in. No apology? Instantly, I feel myself putting up a guard. Not quite a shark-infested moat, more like one of those low walls that you get around gardens in suburbia.

'Here you go,' he says, planting my glass in front of me. The wine slops over onto the table as he slides into the booth with his pint of lager.

'Cheers,' he says gruffly, without looking at me. He raises his pint to me, and for a moment I feel like he's treating me like one of his mates, rather than someone he's on a date with – but, picturing myself going home to my mum and telling her what a disaster it was, I smile and nod and continue to give him the benefit of the doubt.

'You look nice,' he says blandly. He's still not quite making eye contact with me. I keep trying to lock eyes with him, get a sense of him, but his gaze slides off to the side instead.

'Thanks,' I say blandly in return. I'm getting that sinking feeling; my mind is already whirring for stories to tell Mum. We've never done this before – she's never known when I've been on a date, so I've never had to make up a lie about the date *itself* . . .

'Better than your photos,' he says, his gaze still skirting around me.

I'm so momentarily stunned by his rudeness, I can think of nothing to say. Mum and I handpicked the photos on my dating profile together . . . so it's the Mum-friendly version of me that my Tinder dates never normally get to see.

'Bit early to start negging, isn't it?' I put my glass down harder than I mean to and it spills over my hand. He finally looks at me with a frown.

'Sorry?' He even looks cute when he frowns, for God's sake.

'Are you? For which bit? Being almost half an hour late or the backhanded compliment?'

'I . . . what? I . . . you're just really pretty, you know. I mean, your photos are nice, but in person you're . . .'

*Oh God. I've totally read him wrong.* For a split second, I'm wondering if Mum has the magic touch.

'What's negging?'

'Never mind,' I say hurriedly, a blush creeping up my neck.

'Oh, and yeah.' He nods to his beer, his fingers tapping on the table awkwardly. 'Couldn't find anywhere to park. Took me ages to find a spot. I ran out of battery and was worried you'd have left.' He looks up at me from under his thick lashes and looks so apologetic that I have to force myself not to smile.

'Right.' It's a perfectly legitimate excuse – I don't drive, so I'd have no idea – but he still hasn't said *sorry*. I say sorry to everyone, about anything – even things that aren't my fault. It feels outrageous to me that he won't even apologise for keeping me waiting here like a lemon.

I catch him glancing at my cleavage.

'I'm glad you didn't. Been looking forward to this. I mean it though, you're fit,' he says neutrally, as though he's deciding whether he wants tea or coffee.

'Thanks.' I want to continue to be outraged, but whenever he pays me a compliment, however small or superficial it might be, I can feel myself relaxing, softening a bit. I decide to be kind back, rather than grill him further on his parking credentials: 'You're not bad-looking yourself.'

With that, there's a hint of a smile from him, and he holds my gaze for a few seconds longer than he has before. This feels like progress. He's finally warming up; it's just nerves. The chat at the beginning of a date is always a bit stilted, right? I'm sure even the world's greatest couples had awkward chat at the beginning of their first date.

And then: 'You think? Now I've got a semi under the table.' He smiles cheekily and shifts in his seat.

'Pardon?!' I shriek, my eyes widening like saucers, and then I laugh despite myself. Partly out of complete and utter shock and partly because I like his forthrightness.

'It's not often I meet an Indian girl like you . . .'

'Yeah? What are Indian girls normally like then?' I cross my arms, fully aware that it's accentuating my cleavage; I catch him looking again. He's subtle, but not as subtle as he thinks he is.

'Bit stuck-up, always asking a million questions, wanting to know how much you earn . . .'

As much I want to defend my fellow Indian women, it sounds like he's previously dated all my cousins . . . it's exactly what they'd say.

I take an imaginary clipboard out of my bag and push my imaginary glasses up my nose. 'Ah, yes, I've been meaning to ask you, how much *do* you take home each month? And if it's less than £70K then I'm afraid this interview is over.'

He laughs loudly and shakes his head. A faint spark goes off somewhere in my nether regions. 'Talking of checklists, we'd better check we're not related.' His face turns serious all of a sudden.

'Good point, you don't want to be getting a stiffy over your cousin. Surname?' I smile at him, trying to lighten the mood.

'Johal,' he states matter-of-factly – actually looking me in the eyes now.

'Do you have family in the Midlands?' I narrow my eyes, feeling like a sassy detective in an ITV drama. I vaguely remember a distant cousin of my dad's with the same surname.

'Doesn't everyone?' He shrugs, his eyes still fixed on me.

'True. Whereabouts?'

'Nottingham, I think.'

'Hmmm,' I reply thoughtfully. 'We're related to Johals but they're in Wolves. So I think we might be safe. See, this is the stuff you don't have to worry about when you date gorey.'

'Do you date many gorey?' He seems surprised.

'Actually, I *only* date gorey.' I cross my arms, daring him to challenge me once again.

'Indian guys not good enough for you?' He's back to looking at the table now – I can't tell if he's shy or awkward, but his voice is light, playful.

'Well, if you can find me one who is taller than me, doesn't love his mum too much and doesn't expect me to live with his parents after marriage, then we can talk.' I raise my eyebrows at him in mock defiance.

'I can see you're gonna keep me on my toes. My last girl-friend was white,' he says, as though it's a secret he's been holding close to his chest. 'I had to end it, though – she just didn't get it. I even introduced her to my mum – my parents are pretty cool like that – but she called her by her first name and didn't even take her shoes off.'

I grimace. 'That's not her fault, though! You should have prepped her! Take your shoes off, don't call anyone older than you by their first name and never refuse food even if you've just eaten.' We laugh at that, nervously – but for a moment it feels at least like he kind of understands.

Another couple of wines later and Jag is looking cuter and cuter. He's relaxed a bit now and, unlike most men I know, he lets me makes jokes without feeling the need to top them. We've discussed the usual topics: work, previous relation-ships, dating disasters. He doesn't seem to mind his job – he's happy with the stability it provides – and he's only had one serious relationship, which ended three years ago, and since then he's been on just a handful of dates. I bank all this information to tell Mum. I'll leave out the serious girlfriend bit; I doubt she'll approve of that.

And he's looking at me. He's looking at me like he wants me – the kind of look Charlie, Anj and Elena are so used to getting from every guy. The kind of look no one has given me for years. Right now, I feel attractive. The voice that normally tells me to stop doing this or that to look better is no longer there.

I wonder if other people are looking at us. Can they tell?

Now we're onto the most important subject of it all: our Nando's orders.

'Medium fino pitta, no caramelised onion chutney with chips and coleslaw,' I say with an air of finality, daring him to challenge me.

'Peri-peri or normal?'

'Normal.'

He grunts in reply and nods his head as if he's thinking about whether that's acceptable. In between sips of wine, I laugh. I think about my chat with Dean earlier and our dinner weeks ago – it wasn't a date at all, but I felt relaxed there. I'd been so worried that I'd never find that with someone I could actually be romantically involved with, but Jag, even after the shaky start, seems to be coming out of his shell. And I can be myself – I can talk about food without seeing any judgement in his eyes. I can make jokes without him being a dick. And he's cute, flirtatious, a bit cheeky – which we all know is my thing.

I'm even picturing myself going home and telling my mum that he's nice, that we had a good time.

'What's yours?' I ask, giggling, unable to help myself.

'Half a chicken, chips and peas.' He says it seriously, like this is an important conversation that deserves his full attention. I like that.

'Classic.' I nod in mock seriousness. 'Heat level?'

'Gotta be extra hot . . . a bit like—'

'Don't say it! That's cheesy, even for you!'

We settle into an easy silence. The pub doesn't seem as busy any more, and I lean back in the booth, pleasantly drunk, any shred of self-consciousness now dissipated. I am dying to ask him when his birthday is so I can figure out his star sign. It's where my mind runs to whenever I'm starting to wonder about a guy – there's so much their star sign can tell me. If only I could vet everyone on their star sign before we even get on the date. I dated *three* Capricorns before I realised they were all humourless pricks.

But I can't ask him outright what his star sign is, so I ask, simply: 'So . . . when do you turn thirty-two?'

'October,' he replies, as though he's asking a question. His voice goes up at the end.

So, he's either a Scorpio or a Libra. This means he's either *very* sexual and mysterious or he's indecisive and fun . . . Right now, with the wine sloshing around, my heart jumping every time he smiles, I'll take either.

'Sorry, I'm just going to pop to the toilet. Back in a sec,' he says and gets up. He pulls his shirt down with both hands in a way that reminds me of shy boys at school, and I decide that not only is he cute, but that maybe he doesn't know it. It doesn't quite go with the super-forthcoming cheekiness he gave me earlier, but he's nervous . . . We'll see where it goes.

I look down at my phone immediately. One is from Mum:

*Sunny, is he ready for marriage yet?*

And one is from Natalie:

*Do you fancy him? Xxx*

I hastily reply: *It's too early to tell,* and, *Yes, and he's cute enough to forgive for the lateness.*

'You hungry?' He's back, standing by the booth, backlit by the pub. He looks broad, tall.

'I could eat.' I shrug nonchalantly.

'Come on then. I know a place.' He helps me gather my bag and my coat, and as I slide awkwardly out of the booth, I half tumble into him. 'Easy there,' he says, grabbing me gently by the shoulders, and I mutter, 'Sorry,' shyly into his chest. Up close, he smells like Tom Ford and soap and all of a sudden I feel my heartbeat in my vagina. I've not felt like this for a while . . . since . . . well, I'm not going to think about Michael now. I concentrate on walking in a straight line as I follow him out of the pub, and as we're met by the cold wind, he puts his arm around me and pulls me a touch closer.

# Chapter 23

As we're heading out of Nando's, arm in arm, my belly full with medium fino pitta, no caramelised onion chutney, chips and coleslaw, his with half a chicken, chips and peas, I ask myself if it could really be this easy. It would make a great story for the kids. Mummy and Daddy went to Nando's and the rest is history. We knew straight away that we were right for each other. It wasn't all plain sailing, though – Daddy was almost half an hour late. And he'll say, 'I was worth the wait, though, wasn't I?' and I'll roll my eyes jokingly, and our kids will grow up wanting what we have and none of them will sacrifice their happiness in order to make someone love them.

'Well, I'm going this way.' I stop and point vaguely behind me towards the train station. Now would be the time to kiss me . . .

'You don't want to get the train home, I'll drop you off,' and he nods his head in the other direction – presumably towards his car.

'You sure?' I ask, secretly relieved that I don't have to get two trains and a cab, and also glad that I might get to spend a little bit more time with him. And I'll get to see his car – Mum might be interested in that.

'Yeah,' he says brightly. 'Gravesend's not that far from me.'

We walk the short distance to where he's parked, and I wonder if we look like a couple. I catch our reflection in the building opposite as we're waiting to cross the road. I reckon we look good together. I allow myself a small smile. But when he catches me looking at us, he looks away too quickly for me to read his expression in the distorted glass.

He presses his car keys when we reach the car park, and the lights of a silver Audi flash. As he goes to open the passenger-seat door, he suddenly pushes me against the car, firmly but gently, and leans down to kiss me so quickly I don't even register what's happening. We bump noses a bit and I'm breathless from walking so quickly, so I break it off, pulling my face from under him before he can get going.

'What?' he asks, his voice firm but I can sense a smidge of hurt there too.

'Nothing . . . I . . . you took me by surprise, that's all.'

'Why are you surprised?' he says, tucking my hair behind my ear. I panic momentarily that he's going to see the length of my sideburns and do a runner. 'You've been teasing me all night, flirting, flashing your cleavage.'

I act indignant. 'I don't know what you're on about!' I flutter my lashes as I look up at him, secretly glad that at least he's noticed my efforts.

He grabs my wrist and pulls me into him and kisses me again, but I'm ready for it this time. Better. Much better. His mouth travels down to my neck. I let out a small, involuntary moan.

'God,' he breathes into my hair, 'you're so horny.' Ugh. Who says 'horny' any more?! I make a mental note to run this by Natalie when I update her later. His breath is hot against my ear, he presses himself into me. I suck in my stomach automatically and stick out my tits, so he's distracted. As his mouth finds mine again, he runs his hands down my waist and I thank all the gods and deities that I had the foresight to wear control tights. He grabs my bum, giving it a squeeze. *Definitely* a Scorpio.

It's all so teenage, making out in a car park, that I want to laugh. I hate myself a little bit as I giggle involuntarily.

'Oi, oi! Nice one, fella, get in there, son!' a small group of lads chorus as they go past, beers in hand. They break into a football chant a bit further down the road.

As he gets ready to drive off, he does that thing where he puts his arm across the passenger headrest as he looks out of the rear windscreen to reverse. There are fireworks going off in my crotch. We head out of Greenwich towards Gravesend, and the city roads turn into longer, quieter roads – and Jag is focusing; he's wearing his driving glasses. He's a good driver. He doesn't talk much – the odd comment here or there – but he's checking his mirrors, indicating when he needs to. He's not driving too fast at all – my mum would be pleased. I spend the journey watching him, in a non-creepy way. He just snogged me up against his car; I think I'm allowed to watch him as he drives me home. He has a nice profile. And nice hands. Long fingers and neat nails and not very hairy. Is it too soon to hold his hand at the traffic lights?

*Yes, yes, it is, Sunny, you idiot. Keep your hands to yourself.* There's no traffic at this time of night, so, disappointingly, we get to Gravesend sooner than expected. As we get close by, about ten minutes away, he turns off before the roundabout.

A bubble of panic rises up and threatens to choke me. 'Erm, Jag, this is the wrong way.'

Oh God, he's going to kill me.

He's going to kill me and dump my body and everyone we know is going to blame my mum for allowing me to leave the house, for letting me meet this guy.

'I know. Sorry, I just . . . I want to kiss you some more and I can't do that outside your house, can I?' He grins, pulling into a deserted layby surrounded by overgrown bushes and litter thrown from passing cars.

As he turns off the engine, I feel fizzy with excitement.

He undoes his seatbelt before leaning over to unbuckle mine, lightly brushing my breast as he does. I don't know if he meant to do that, but it makes me gasp anyway. He cups my cheek, moving his hand up to my hair. Oh God, are we going to have sex in his car in a layby?

'I don't want to . . .' I can feel my excitement change colour.

'Calm down,' he says softly. He's trying to reassure me, but I don't feel reassured. 'It's just kissing.'

He moves his hand from my cheek down to my breasts. I flinch slightly.

'Erm. Nope,' I say boldly.

'Oh, what? Come on.' He sounds like a teenager who's had his Xbox confiscated.

'No! Not on a first date,' I protest, batting his hand away firmly.

'But they look so good.' He bites his lip as he openly ogles them. I cover myself with my hands instinctively, feeling like I'm swatting away a toddler going for cake.

'Come on, Sunny,' he says, and I realise he's used my name for the first time this evening. 'Just let me touch them once . . .'

'No!' I bat his hand away as playfully as I can manage.

'Can I put my head between them?' He leans his head on my shoulder.

'Absolutely not, you pervert!'

I laugh despite myself, for what feels like the millionth time this evening, at the absurdity of his request as I push his head away.

'Fuck, you're such a tease,' he says, pulling away with a grunt of frustration.

'I don't do that kind of thing on a first date,' I say primly.

'How about a goodnight kiss then?' He swoops in before I have a chance to answer and kisses me so gently I almost push his head between my boobs myself.

As we approach my road, he asks, before I have to say anything, 'Where do you want me to drop you off?' I direct him to the opposite end of my road, so we don't go past the house at all, just in case Mum is still up.

'I've got cousins that live on this road,' he says matter-of-factly. This does not surprise me at all.

'Thanks for the lift home and dinner. I had a nice time.'

He looks at me again, like a scolded puppy, and mutters, 'I wish I could kiss you again,' before saying, more loudly, 'It was fun. Let's do this again.'

While I'm walking away from the car, I'm very aware he might be watching me, so I concentrate on walking in a straight line. I rearrange my face into a more neutral expression as I approach my front door, trying to hide the girlish grin that has been threatening to blossom across my face all evening.

'Sunny? I didn't hear the taxi – you didn't walk from the station, did you? It's dark!' Mum is in the doorway to the kitchen in a fleecy dressing gown.

I can't tell her he dropped me off. She would not approve of me getting in a car with a strange man, even one she's vetted.

'No, of course I got a taxi, he just stopped the car a bit further down.'

'Next time, tell them to stop outside the door, OK? It's not safe.'

'OK, Mama. Why are you still up?'

'I couldn't sleep. I'm making hot chocolate. How was he?' she says lightly, turning back to the kitchen.

I tense up, thinking about the kiss by his car, the kissing in the layby. I can't tell her *everything* that happened. She probably thinks we spent our whole time talking about our hopes and dreams, our families, our future life together. I don't want to disappoint her with our chat of messed-up past relationships and Nando's. I follow her into the kitchen, quickly looking in the mirror in the hallway to check my make-up is still intact after all the intense kissing. It's held up surprisingly well.

She's already heating up the milk for the hot chocolate on the stove.

'Go on, beta,' she says, 'tell me everything.'

After a deep breath, I launch seamlessly into the story of the dream date. If you think about it, this is like those interpreters with the headsets at the UN. Except I'm not translating into German, I'm translating into 'Mum'. I tell the story seamlessly, replacing the white wines with orange juice, the chicken pitta with a veggie burger and the passionate kisses and dirty talk with a chaste handshake. I can tell she approves by the fact that she doesn't interrupt me – she's watching me intently, smiling at odd moments too. When I'm finished, she sets a mug of hot chocolate in front of me like it's some kind of reward.

'Did you find out his surname?' she says, her face serious once more.

'Yeah, it's Johal.'

'Your dad has a cousin who is a Johal – we will have to check that they are not related. You can't marry someone you are related to!' She smiles at me like she's making the funniest joke in the world, and I can tell her mind is already running towards planning the wedding, who to invite, who not to invite . . .

'We don't have to rush into anything, Mama.' My voice

quivers with nerves and panic, imagining myself sitting next to Jag at our wedding – and even though I don't want to get married right away, I can picture it, I *can* actually see it. So much for me taking a lover. I mean, I knew there would be no such thing as soon as Mum got involved, but now I'm wondering how much I want this and how much of this is what I think I *should* want.

'No rush, but why wait?' She shrugs, slurping her hot chocolate. 'You like each other. Good family. Never been married. Good job,' she muses.

'Mama, I've only met him for a few hours – it's not enough to know if we like each other, really,' I say, the words tumbling out like a waterfall. She shrugs again, as if to say, 'I don't believe you,' and before we can get into it, I say, 'I'm sleepy, Mama,' and yawn ostentatiously before using my distraction technique: 'How was yoga class?'

Her yoga class is a hotbed of gossip and intrigue and I let her ramble on about so-and-so's daughter-in-law who has run off with another man; I nod and gasp in all the right places.

As I wander upstairs to bed, my mind is racing with all the excuses I can give my mum for why Jag and I can't get engaged next week. Maybe I need to make up some kind of fake minor surgery for him . . . an ingrown toenail? A hernia? A dodgy appendix? Just to buy us more time.

*Hope you got home safe. Thanks for a nice evening :) x* I text him as I pull the duvet over my head.

Immediately, he sends back the devil emoji.

I wait. Nothing else.

Maybe he is just shit at messaging. Maybe he just pressed the wrong emoji or something. Everyone says men are shit with their phones, right?

# Chapter 24

Everything seems easier when you meet someone nice, doesn't it? The commuters and their jabby elbows don't piss me off so much, and it doesn't bother me that I don't have a seat. The walk to the office along an A road doesn't seem nearly as polluting or depressing either, and the thought of seeing Sharon at some point today feels more like a minor hiccup than a massive pain in my backside.

Work passes by much more quickly than normal. Sharon is busy 'on calls' all day, so barely makes an appearance and isn't breathing down our necks like usual, which probably adds to the carefree vibe. I keep checking my phone, not because of Michael this time – I'm barely even thinking of Michael – but because of Jag. He hasn't messaged me today, and I am determined not to message first. I was the last person to text, and I have more pride than to become a double-texter. In an attempt to stop me looking at my phone obsessively, I shove it in my desk drawer. But then I open up the drawer to check it again. But only twice . . . an hour.

'Right, Sunny,' I say to myself, under my breath. 'If you catch up on all your work and sort your inbox out by lunchtime, you can check your phone.' As a result, I manage to catch up on all my outstanding work and have an empty inbox by lunchtime. Feeling pleased, I pull out my phone.

Still no message.

I organise my drawers and email sexy Scottish Andrew to tell him there is no further update on his sofa. He doesn't reply, which is unlike him. I update Natalie on the lack of messages and try my best to ignore the uneasy feeling blooming in the pit of my stomach.

He's busy.

He's lost his phone.

He's dead. He's got to be dead, there's no other reasonable explanation.

By the time 5 p.m. rolls around, I have taken screenshots of our messages to decode later to see if I can figure out where it all went wrong, and I've already deleted our chat and his number.

I walk to the train station, no longer buoyed by the idea of a bright future with Jag by my side, and flop into my seat, feeling drained all of a sudden. Then a message pops up.

*Hey.*

I'm so embarrassingly relieved that he's messaged me that I swallow my annoyance and convince myself it's OK to reply straight away. He can see I'm online anyway.

*Hey yourself.*

I will not call him out on the fact that he hasn't messaged all day. I refuse to be naggy and high maintenance. I am a cool girl. Woman. I am a cool woman. I'm going to play him at his own game and not ask any questions and see how long it takes him to make more of an effort.

*hows u?*

Great. 'Hows u' – the text equivalent of nails down a blackboard.

*Good, thanks. You? Busy day?*

When I get home via the corner shop to stock up on illegal snacks, the first question my Mum asks is whether I've heard from him. As much as it annoys me, it feels good to share this with Mum; I'm just glad he *has* messaged, so I don't have to lie about yet another thing.

'Yeah, he's really busy with work but he messaged me just now.' OK, so half a lie. 'What's for dinner, Mama?'

'I made paneer earlier. Your dad is staying overnight at the gurdwara.'

Dad's friend won the election and as a result he is now on the gurdwara committee and in charge of security. He and some of the other members take it in turns to patrol the grounds overnight after a spate of break-ins a few years ago.

'Blocks or loose?' I'll eat paneer in all its forms – paneer tikka, shahi paneer, muttar paneer – but I have a soft spot for paneer that hasn't been pressed into blocks and is crumbly, a bit like scrambled egg, lightly spiced, with peas adding a little sweetness. My favourite way to eat it is rolled up in a hot buttered roti.

'Chal. Go upstairs and get changed. We will eat in front of *Gardeners' World*.'

It's just after 7 p.m. and I'm halfway through a Twirl when the landline rings. At this time in the evening, it can only be an aunty calling for my mum. I pretend not to hear it so I don't have to speak to whichever aunty it is and endure a lecture on the virtues of getting married young or the successes off her offspring.

My mum answers, and from her tone I can tell it's my chachi, the one she doesn't like, the snooty one with the fancy anniversary party. My mum has three different phone voices. One she uses for the doctor's office – it is polite and deferential – one for people she doesn't like and one for overseas calls, which comes close to breaking the sound barrier. She's never got over the habit of shouting down the phone when calling India, even now that the quality of phone calls has improved and is exactly the same as if she was calling an aunty down the road.

She's congratulating my chachi over and over again. I creep out of my room and lean over the banister to hear her more clearly. From the sounds of it, someone has just got engaged. Yes, definitely an engagement – she's rolling out the old 'daughters are another's wealth, and they must leave us one day' line. I roll my eyes and try to figure out who she's talking about; Chachi's daughters are far too young to have got engaged – by modern British-Asian standards anyway.

'Yes, well, things are looking up for Sunny too . . .' my mum says loftily.

I nearly drop the Twirl on the carpet.

'Hmmm . . . We are talking to them at the moment.'

*We?!* Who is this 'we'?! And who is 'them'?! She'd better be speaking French because there is no *we*. I slowly creep around and lower myself onto the top stair, careful to miss the creaky floorboards.

'It is all in God's hands, of course, but he is from a good family, has a good job . . . Hmmm . . . You know how it is with kids these days . . . I don't like to get involved. She has found him herself. On the internet . . . Hmmm . . . Hmmm . . . It was different in our day, as you know. But you have to let the children do what they want – they grew up here. I said, "We will support you, puth, just make sure he is a good person, that's all I ask."'

I roll my eyes hard. The lies are coming thick and fast now. They move on to gossiping about another relative and I go and lie down on my bed, desperately trying not to give in to the temptation of a stress nap. The rest of my snacks remain in their blue plastic bag, forgotten.

My phone buzzes.

*Nah, not really.*

Nothing else. Does this man not understand how conversations work? This is like pulling teeth, but I remind myself of all my friends who say their partners are crap at communication and good at other stuff and you need to train them as if they're unruly puppies. I need to learn to compromise and not ask too much from one person. I remember a married friend saying that every relationship has one leader and one follower. With me and Jag, I am definitely the leader. I have no problem taking control. And take control I shall. I fire off another reply, not bothering to wait the requisite amount of time.

*Just looking at my calendar for the next few weeks and I'm quite busy. Just thought I'd check if you still want to meet up.*

*Yeah, course. When?*

Finally! I pretend I'm looking up cinema times, even though I've already planned this and three other options in case he doesn't go for the cinema. I've looked up film times at a cinema that is close to both of us but not so close that we will bump into anyone we know.

*Next Friday? Maybe we can go to the cinema? I quite like the look of* Avengers, Mission: Impossible *or* A Star Is Born.

Mission: Impossible? *Not heard of the others.*

*Great. There's a showing at 6.50?*

I feel satisfied for now. This is progress. I head to his Facebook page to see if I can figure out when his birthday is before we meet up; maybe it can explain why he's so crap at messaging. I scroll down and see that people posted birthday wishes on his page in 2016 – 24 October. Shit. He *is* a Scorpio. I look up our compatibility.

The phrase 'too many differences for it to work' jumps out at me. Intense, hard-working and secretive. Our overall compatibility score is 48 per cent. Well, that's almost a 50-percent chance of it working out. I'll take those chances. I once knew an Aries and a Capricorn who had been married for over twenty years. Anyway, sun signs are a very reductive way of looking at compatibility according to Natalie. What I really need to know is his rising sign, but I'll need the time of his birth for that. And even I can't weave that into a conversation without looking like a creep.

I'm googling unlikely astrology matches when my mum calls me to come downstairs. I shake the crumbs off my top and wash my face and rinse my mouth out to rid it of any evidence of snacking.

'That was your chachi,' she announces as I walk into the kitchen.

'Yeah?' I act surprised.

'Jasmine is engaged, getting married next year. He is an accountant.'

'What? She's only . . . twenty-two!'

'Twenty-three. It is the right age to get married. I told her about you, that there is some talking going on.'

'Mama! Why are you telling people?'

'Your chachi is not people . . . So, what is he saying about marriage? Cut some salad.'

'Mum, I've only met him once!' I say as I get the chopping board out.

'And? You still don't know?!'

I'm trying hard to keep the panic out of my voice, and I change the subject quickly. 'How did Jasmine meet her fiancé?'

'Friend of a friend did an introduction. Very good way to do it.'

Ah-ha! That's code for they've been together for ages and met on an app or in a bar.

'Ask him next time, OK? About marriage. I don't like keeping secret from your dad. And we have to redecorate before you get married, so we need good notice.' She says this with an air of finality.

★ ★ ★

We eat dinner in front of the TV, with *Gardeners' World* on of course, and although Mum would never admit it, I swear she has a crush on Monty Don. I'm zoning out and in a carb coma from the roti when my phone buzzes. I pick it up excitedly and even Mum glances over with a tiny, gleeful smile on her face, but it's a text from Anj.

*Hi babe, hope you're well! Sorry haven't been in touch! Been sooo busy with wedding prep! Can't believe it's the hen do already?! See you tomorrow xx*

In all the drama of the non-messages and now my cousin getting engaged, I haven't even had a chance to think about seeing the girls tomorrow for the first time since the spa weekend. I think about the dress that has been hanging on the back of my bedroom door for weeks to remind me to stick to my diet, ready to be squeezed into tomorrow – I bought it hurriedly from ASOS and didn't have time to get anything else. Natalie kept sending me pictures of other dresses:

*Babes, with boobs like yours, THIS dress is the one. I'd never hide them away if I had your tits. Xxx*

But all the dresses she picked out were the wrong colours, with short sleeves or off-the-shoulder numbers, and they didn't go with the 'pastels' theme. Pastels make me look like day-old sick.

*Fuck the theme – you should wear what you feel comfortable in,* she insisted. And yet there it is, the cheap pale-pink wrap dress I ended up settling for, which feels like its sole purpose is to cling to my rolls, hanging on the back of my bedroom door like a polyester tent.

As I try to focus on Monty Don and his crocuses, all I can feel is rising dread, threatening to cut into my windpipe.

# Chapter 25

I walk into the famous pastel-coloured dining room from the wood-panelled lift, remembering to look up because apparently it makes you look more confident and like you belong. I keep having flashbacks of last night's dream, where I walked into the restaurant naked, with every single person laughing at me, while my teeth fell out, cascading like an avalanche down my naked body. It's safe to say, even compared to walking into a restaurant naked, I have never felt more out of place than I do here, with its chandeliers and its £300 salt-and-pepper sets made of rare wood. The only time I've been in here before was to use the loo. I stride deliberately towards the dining area, stomach in knots, smiling benignly at the retail staff, hoping they won't notice that I cannot walk in heels.

Anjali's sister, Chandni, who does something important in the City, is the one who insisted that we all wear pastels. Probably to match the décor. Anj's whole family are big in something to do with imports/exports. My whole family are into eating fried chicken and arguing about land back home. At uni, Anj lived in a flat her dad bought for her in Marylebone, while I shared a damp three-bed in Newham with an assortment of mice and two couples who couldn't keep their hands off each other, even at mealtimes. Anj was the first middle-class Indian person I ever met. Before her, I thought all Indian immigrant families were like mine and worked in factories and on building sites in order to scrape a living together.

At uni she was like the rest of us, drinking until the early hours, delighting in impromptu booze-fuelled trips to Brighton. But suddenly a few years ago, she began to change, dressing in designer clothes, hanging out with her rich pals, wearing *actual* diamonds. She went from loving nothing more than karaoke in dodgy bars and drinking watered-down cocktails until closing to becoming a more polished version of herself. Now she only goes to the poshest of clubs and restaurants.

When Charlie and I called her out on it a few years ago, after getting very drunk and very loud, she confessed she was husband-hunting and had to 'act like a lady'. I've only met her fiancé, Ajay, a few times, but he also does something that I don't really understand, in insurance. All I know is that whatever he does pays him enough to buy him a luxury flat in Zone One and expensive holidays every other month. And, crucially, a massive rock for his fiancée. It cost as much as I make in a year.

I spot the group of mainly Indian women at a long, rectangular table. Even from here, I can see they're nothing like me. How do rich people get that sheen? Are they dipped in something? A kind of coating? I am mesmerised by their freshly blow-dried hair that surrounds them like a vapour when they shake their pretty heads.

Normally Charlie and Elena would have waited outside for me so we could walk in together. They know I hate walking into places by myself. I was tempted to message them to ask if they could wait outside for me, but, seeing as we haven't spoken since the spa weekend, I didn't know how my message would be received. So here I am, walking naked into a restaurant, on my own.

Anjali spots me and waves; she's at the head of the table in a pale-pink knee-length dress, discreet diamonds winking at me from her ears and wrists. My stomach knots itself even more tightly; I didn't know that was possible.

I scan the room for Charlie and Elena as Anj totters over to me daintily and throws her arms around me. I reciprocate somewhat stiffly. I spot the others halfway down the table, deep in animated conversation with some women I don't know.

'Sorry I'm late, the trains were fucked,' I mumble apologetically into her impossibly shiny mane of hair.

'It's OK! I'm so glad you're here,' she mutters into my frizzy hair, which is approximately 80 per cent dry shampoo – I didn't have time to wash it because I spent so long trying to find the right shapewear for this bloody dress.

I smile politely. She seems to have either forgotten the events of the spa weekend or has decided to put it behind her. I've certainly got no desire to rehash the events of last month – that was enough confrontation to last me a lifetime.

Anj points to an empty seat about halfway down the table, opposite Elena and Charlie.

Here goes.

I mentally gird my loins and plaster on a smile.

'Hiya!' My voice is unnaturally bright and high.

Elena greets me enthusiastically, but I know Charlie well enough to see that there's a forced politeness to her smile.

'You look lovely,' says Elena – she sounds genuine. 'I don't think I've ever seen you in pink before.' I stop myself from saying, *Yes, that's because I didn't have a bloody choice.* Both Charlie and Elena are in caramel-coloured dresses. I'm pretty sure they've also had their hair professionally done for the occasion. Looking down the table at everyone else, it seems I'm the only one who missed the memo on that.

'Thanks, you both look really nice too. Love that necklace, Charlie, is it new?'

'Um. Yeah. John got it for me for our anniversary.'

'Oh, *happy anniversary*! It really suits you,' I lie. It looks like something Hyacinth Bucket would wear down the WI. I'm struggling to find anything else to say, but thankfully at this point a handsome, dark-haired waiter asks me if I'd like some champagne and I answer so enthusiastically he looks completely taken aback.

I'm sandwiched between two glamorous women. I overhear one of them announce to her neighbour – a painfully thin woman with cheekbones that are threatening to pierce through her skin – 'Manoj doesn't want me to work, you see, there's really no need.'

'Hi, I'm Sunny, nice to meet you.' I turn to my other neighbour.

'Sarina. I'm a cousin of Anjali's.'

A little spark of recognition goes off in my brain. Anj seems to have dozens of cousins and every weekend one of them gets engaged or married or has a baby shower.

'Ah, yes! Anj said you've just had a baby! Congratulations! You look wonderful for someone with a newborn. I don't know how you manage it with all the sleepless nights,' I say sincerely, in a friendly tone of voice.

'We have a night nanny,' she replies in clipped Oxbridge tones, managing to sound both condescending yet polite.

'Of *course* you do,' I mutter under my breath. When I open my mouth to ask about her job, she's already on her phone, tapping away furiously.

The table is dotted with stands full of dainty crusty sand-wiches and cakes; I could eat at least two of them myself. The glistening pastries are dusted with icing sugar and the fat scones are begging to be split open and slathered in clotted cream and jam. My stomach growls aggressively; I was too nervous to eat breakfast. And I was too scared to get a snack from the train-station café in case I dropped food down my dress. Pastels are not a messy eater's friend.

But as a fat person, you *must* eat the least out of everyone at the table. That's the rule. So, I reach for the elegant champagne flute. *OK, Sunny, you're gonna have to perform your way through this.* I wish Natalie were here – she'd be knocking back the champagne, piling her plate high with sandwiches without even a modicum of embarrassment. Her joyful Barbara Windsor cackle would echo through the elegant room, turning heads.

'Hello, I don't believe we've been introduced, I'm Sunny.' I hold out my hand confidently to the glamorous stay-at-home woman to my left.

She smiles warmly and takes my hand. 'Nikita. Pleased to meet you. We've just been discussing our outfits for the wedding. Who are you wearing?'

'Oh, erm, I'm getting something made. Our tailor is on it,' I finish quickly, hoping I sound posh enough to seem like I would have a private tailor.

'*Oh,*' she says, wrinkling her nose, confused.

'Yourself?' I ask hurriedly.

'Sabyasachi, of course.'

'Of course!' I echo with an earnest smile. I only know who Sabyasachi is because Anj has been banging on about wearing one of his creations at her wedding for years.

I am normally so good at this. I talk to people for a living, for God's sake. But these women are reflecting myself back at me and all I'm seeing is a sad, fat, unattractive woman with all the charisma of dog shit. I think of that spider diagram my therapist told me to draw and feel that if I stepped into each of these women's minds, I could probably fill every inch of white space with unflattering adjectives.

I look surreptitiously around the room and see that everyone is either engrossed in conversation or taking endless photos of the tiny sandwiches and cakes, all fitting the pretty pastel theme as instructed by Chandni. Everyone apart from one. There's one woman who is actually eating, wearing a shiny emerald blouse cut so low you can see a sliver of the delicate black lace of her bra. All of the others look identical with their straight, waist-length hair and discreet jewellery, like they're related to the Kardashians. Apart from her. That's not to say she isn't attractive; she's pretty, with a square chin and thick brows and a broad, straight nose. She has short hair, cropped close to her skull, and a septum piercing, a collection of tiny studs running down her ear. She's talking animatedly and laughing loudly at something – a joyful, dirty laugh, not dissimilar to Natalie's. I am captivated by her lack of self-consciousness. She turns and looks at me directly and smiles warmly.

I smile back.

Anjali's sister, Chandni, stands up. She's wearing an off-the-shoulder powder-blue dress; even heavily pregnant she manages to look neat and put together. In her delicate hands she has a small sheaf of ivory-coloured note cards.

'Hi, ladies!' she drawls in her affected Home Counties accent. 'Thank you so much for coming together to celebrate my baby sister's wedding. Anj, I'm so proud of you.'

I find it odd when people say they're proud of the person getting married. Are they proud of them for getting married? For unlocking the ultimate achievement? Or just in general?

My mind, for a second, jumps to Jag – I wonder if I'll hear from him today.

'You're the best little sister I could ask for. Even though you always took my things without asking and used to go crying to Mum when it was your fault in the first place.' The other women titter and I join in, but her speech is drier than a stale rice cake.

'It seems like only last week that we were playing weddings in Mum's old saris and now you're getting married for *real*.' The women do a collective *coo*. I place a hand over my heart, hoping that'll do the trick, despite the fact that Chandni's simpering tone makes me want to cave her head in with an ice bucket.

'I couldn't have asked for a more perfect brother-in-law than Ajay. He's kind and generous and *sooo* caring, and he's going to take such good care of you.' I clench my jaw at that. 'He's going to be an *amazing* uncle to this little guy.' She caresses her belly gently, eliciting another round of 'ahhhs' from the group.

'I wish you and Ajay a lifetime of happiness, and I know I speak for everyone here when I say that no one deserves this more than you. So, without further ado, please raise your glasses to the future Mrs Ajay Vaswani!'

I catch Charlie's eye and she's gently dabbing away tears. Give me strength.

I feel a gentle, warm hand on my arm and turn to see the woman in the emerald blouse beaming at me. 'Hi, I'm Beena, do you mind if I join you?'

*This* is Beena. Anj has always seemed mildly obsessed by Beena; she brings her up all the time, as though she's the epitome of a cautionary tale. I half expected her to have horns and a tail, but, standing in front of me, she's like sunshine, and I warm to her instantly. I don't know if it's because of her smile or her flat vowels and Northern accent.

'No, of course not! I'm Sunny, nice to meet you.' Up close, I can see an intricate line tattoo disappearing into the collar of her shirt. 'I love that colour on you!'

'Thanks! I thought *fuck* the theme. I haven't let someone tell me what to wear since I was at school. You having a good time?' she says, sipping her champagne, scanning my face, a wry smile playing on her lips.

'Erm, yeah!' I say uncertainly.

She laughs. 'Bullshit.' Then she lowers her voice and leans in conspiratorially. 'I saw your eyes glazing over during that speech.' I press my lips together hard to stop myself smiling.

'Was it that obvious?'

'Only to someone who was also practically bringing up their scones. Talking of scones, why aren't you eating?'

I pause, not knowing whether to be honest.

'Give us yer plate. They'll only go to waste – you know none of this lot will eat them.'

She piles my plate high with sandwiches and pastries before grabbing another plate and helping herself to a fruit scone.

'How do you know Anj then?'

'Our families have known each other for years. You?'

I start to say, 'We're best friends,' but the words stick in my throat. 'Uni.'

'Not your scene either, is it?' she says through a mouthful of scone.

'Am I *imagining* the judgement?' I gesture to the rest of the room.

'You know what's real and what's not,' she says, studying my face.

'I'm guilty of being too sensitive, so I can never tell. My first instinct is to always doubt myself.'

'Beena?' Another voice chimes in. I turn around to see another woman, tall and elegant. 'I didn't recognise you with the new hair ...' The woman trails off, looking at Beena's almost-shaved head with barely concealed disgust.

'All right, Tasha. This is Sunny. Sunny, this is Tasha; we were at school together.'

'Hi, Tasha, nice to meet you,' I say, trying to be friendly, but really I want to have a go at her for the look she gave Beena. I can already feel myself getting defensive over this woman I barely know.

She ignores me and zones in on Beena.

'Are you looking forward to the wedding? We're going to make a weekend of it. It's been sooo long since Kishan and I had some time away, so we thought we'd stay in town. Maybe Soho House.'

'Nice. Macaron?' Beena tilts her head towards the cake stand.

'Oh, no, I can't eat any more.' She clutches her stomach and puffs out her cheeks.

'Back in a minute. Too much champagne,' Beena says, wiping her mouth with a napkin and getting up to leave.

Another woman – they're all beginning to look the same to me – greets Tasha enthusiastically; they air-kiss either side of me and start having a full-blown conversation over my head. I lean back slightly to make it easier for them.

'I'll have to go on a diet before the wedding or there's absolutely no way I'm getting into my lehenga.' Tasha pinches a roll of 'fat' at her waist, which is actually just skin.

'After Ethan was born, I did paleo – no grains, only meat, fish or eggs – and I dropped a dress size in two weeks,' she announces proudly.

Silently, I place the rest of the smoked-salmon sandwich that I've been nibbling back on the plate. I never really know how to react when women half my size call themselves fat and wail about their lack of self-control despite their visible clavicles and concave stomachs. Thankfully they eventually drift off towards the other end of the table.

'What did I miss?' Beena plonks herself next to me and drains her glass in one.

'More diet talk,' I say through gritted teeth.

'Bloody hell. Here, drink up. Then let's get out of here.'

'We can't . . .'

'Why not?'

'It would be rude!'

'Would it? Having the time of your life, are ya?' She raises her eyebrows and cocks her head at me.

'Well, no . . . but it's still in full swing . . .' I splutter. She continues to stare at me until I'm forced to look away. I look down the table at the women, all deep in conversation with each other. Anj is surrounded by a few of them and she is in her element. Charlie and Elena are at the opposite end of the table, taking selfies with a few of Anj's cousins. I turn back to look at Beena, who is knocking back another glass of champagne. 'Fuck it,' I mutter and drain my glass, my brain already thinking of an excuse as to why I'm leaving so early.

'That's the spirit. If I know one thing, it's that these women are more interested in themselves than anything else. French exit?'

'Sorry?'

'Follow my lead. Grab your bag.'

She stands up and walks casually towards the doors. I follow her, willing myself not to turn around to see if anyone has noticed us. She walks past the lift and down the stairs quickly. I'm breathless from trying to keep up.

'I've never done that before!'

She looks back at me impishly. 'Fun, innit?' She laughs. I laugh with her.

Out on the street, she grabs me unexpectedly and hugs me.

'Congratulations, you've just successfully completed your first French exit!'

I giggle, giddy from the champagne and our audacity.

'Wait, I need to get out of these shoes,' I tell her, the balls of my feet burning. I lean against a wall and reach into my bag to get out a pair of fold-up ballet pumps. The pumps have such a thin sole it feels like I'm walking on the pavement barefoot, but I'm so relieved to be out of my cheap heels that I don't care.

'Now, this is a very important question – choose carefully. Maccies or Five Guys?' Beena says solemnly.

My stomach rumbles in response.

'Maccies. Every time. Let's go to the one on the Strand,' I say with certainty.

'Hun, I'm sooo proud of you,' says Beena in an uncanny impression of Chandni.

'Don't! I'm gonna wet myself,' I shriek as we weave our way down towards Trafalgar Square.

We order our meals at the giant screen and select table service. It's predictably busy but I spot that my favourite seat is empty, in the corner on the ground floor where I can hide away but still look outside and people-watch. I spot a small group of women drunkenly stumbling along the pavement, all kitted out as if for a wedding in smart dresses, hats and heels. I like to think they've escaped an equally heinous event and smile as one of them dances to non-existent music.

After we order, Beena and I hurriedly make our way to the table in case it gets snapped up by one of the many families of tourists milling around aimlessly.

I feel my shoulders drop for the first time since I woke up.

'What do you do for work?' I ask, intrigued. Anj has barely told me anything about Beena, beyond her hairstyles or 'unconventional' life, which could mean anything at all, really.

'All sorts. I run a magazine, I have my own fashion line, I DJ and I'm thinking of training to be a tattoo artist.'

'Wow. I mean, I didn't think you'd work in HR, but you're, like, even cooler than you look.' Thankfully the server brings over our food at just the right moment to interrupt my major fangirling.

'I used to work in law, if you can believe it,' she replies with a grimace.

'No way!'

'Yep.' She stabs the paper straw through her drink. 'Did everything my parents wanted – uni, all of that. Woke up on my thirtieth birthday and thought fuck this, I hate my life. Jacked in the job, sold my flat, put all my stuff in storage and went travelling for a year.'

'I don't think I've ever been so jealous of anyone in my life.'

'I'm making it sound really simple; it were terrifying. I had absolutely no idea what I wanted to do. Everyone around me were saying that I were making a massive mistake and I'd regret it. *Including* Chandni.' She practically spits out her name.

I roll my eyes. 'Why am I not surprised?'

'Is Anj a *close* friend of yours then?'

I sigh heavily.

'Uh-oh. I smell a story.'

'It's a long story, but I'll try to make it short.'

She leans forward and rests her chin on her hand. 'I bloody love story time. Take as long as you like.'

I find myself telling her everything. It unravels out of me like a dropped ball of wool. About the spa weekend, Michael, my mum vetting my dates and Jag. She listens intently without interrupting. I can feel my heart beating, and it feels for a moment as though I'm reliving everything over and over again.

'Sorry, we've only just met and I'm pouring out my heart to you,' I say awkwardly when I've finished and there's no more food or drink left on our table.

'Can I give you a hug?' She stands up, her arms already outstretched. I give a small nod and stand up. She steps over to me and hugs me tightly, placing her chin on my shoulder. I feel my body relax and so does she because she laughs quietly. When she pulls away, my eyes are wet with tears and so are hers.

'You've gotta make sure your choices are your own. Even if you *think* they're your choices, there's no harm in questioning them. You know what's right for you, it's just whether you're ready to acknowledge it.'

I nod, unable to say anything for a moment.

'I've been where you are,' she says frankly. 'If you ever need a little getaway, I've got a spare room – my flatmate moved out a few months ago, so if you need space to work out what you need, it's there.' She looks at me to make sure it's registered. 'How do you feel?' she asks, gently taking my hand.

'Lighter. And like you need to invoice me for your time.' I laugh weakly.

# Chapter 26

Today, I've woken up feeling better than I have in weeks thanks to some deliciously buttery parathas I had last night when I got home, and Beena, despite the slight guilt at the way we left the hen do. In bed, I scroll through Instagram and see on Anj's Insta Stories that she went to a bar with Charlie, Elena and a few of her cousins. She looks happy and drunk so I'm hoping she didn't notice us sneaking out early. I'd be lying if I didn't feel a touch of FOMO at not being there, even though I would've hated every minute of it. Before I go downstairs, I message Anj partly to thank her for a lovely time, out of politeness, and partly to figure out if she saw us leaving:

*Hi love! Hope your head isn't too sore this morning! Had such a lovely time* 😊 *Sorry had to leave early.*

I need to come up with an excuse so that if she did notice she can't get too angry with me. Food poisoning is out because we were all eating the same thing, period pain seems too obvious, so I decide to go with migraine. You can't be annoyed with someone if they have a migraine.

*Had a migraine brewing all morning – thought it might go away on its own but it was getting worse and didn't want to worry you. But it was so nice to meet so many of your cousins before the wedding. Can't wait xxx*

I send it, and immediately start googling 'how does karma work?' because I really do not want to *actually* start getting migraines.

Then my phone rings.

It's Anj.

I stare at it for a few seconds before answering it, remembering at the last minute to put on a slight sick/tired/migrainey voice.

'Hi, babe.'

'Hi, love, just thought I'd check in on you – you feeling better?' She's somewhere loud and is shouting to make herself heard.

'Yeah, a bit better, thanks. How are you?'

'Not gonna lie, my head is sore this morning, but I had so much fun. I didn't even notice you'd left until we went to a bar!'

I feel a stab of sadness at that, until the relief washes it away.

'I saw you were getting on with Beena . . .' she continues.

'Oh my *God*, she's amazing, why have I not met her before?'

'Listen, babe, that's kind of the reason I called. Please don't take this the wrong way, but just . . . I wouldn't get too close to her. You know what I've said about her before? Well, we've known her family for years, our parents have been best friends forever. She's a bit odd. I wouldn't have invited her, but our mums are really good friends and I kind of had to. I don't trust her.'

'What do you mean, a bit odd? She was nothing but friendly to me . . .'

'Hmmm . . . she has a nice side to her. She used to be OK, then she had a breakdown or something and left her job and went backpacking. We used to hang out a fair bit, but after she came back from travelling, you couldn't even have a glass of wine without her banging on about migrants or some tribe in the Amazon. Then she kind of cut us all out, shaved her head, and now she's turned into, like, this weird cat lady and lives on her own in South Norwood.'

As someone who lives in a house where I have to get dressed to go to the loo, this sounds like bliss to me. But it's no surprise that Beena isn't someone Anj would get on with.

'Just ... be careful. I'm not sure she's a good influence. I just wouldn't want you ending up like her, you know? She's really messed up her life. She had it all for a while ...'

'Right ...'

'Anyway, I'm just about to meet some friends for brunch and thought I'd check in.'

Her pause tells me it's Charlie and Elena. My gut twists.

When I hang up, I see there's a message from Beena.

*Hiya love! Hope you're OK this morning and having a lovely Sunday* 😊 *was so so lovely to hang out with you yesterday! Let's do it again please?! Sending love xxx*

The tightness in my gut softens, and I feel Beena's shine swim through me.

My bed is a mound of brightly coloured georgette and other scratchy materials designed to make me never want to take my leggings off ever again. I stupidly made the mistake of telling my mum that I was trying on outfits for Anj's wedding, and now she's downstairs with a cup of tea and is expecting a fashion show. I'm only half an hour in and I'm on the verge of tears.

I pull a dusky peach-and-gold salwar kameez over my head and make my way downstairs to the living room where my mum is waiting like Tyra Banks. If Tyra Banks watched the Sikh channel. I give her a half-hearted twirl, unable to look her in the eye.

'What do you think, Mama?' I say, hopeful. She peers at me over her reading glasses.

'Little tight, henna, under the arms. It's pulling.' She gets up and tries to pull the fabric down, but it's not budging. 'Let me see from the back. Hmmm, no, doesn't look good.'

'Thanks, Mum.'

'Take it off and let me see if there is any material.' I go to leave the room to get undressed. 'Take it off *here*, we are all the same!' She settles herself back down on the sofa.

'I need to go and get my top, it's cold,' I lie. She doesn't know that I got a lotus flower tattooed on my sternum a few months ago and would flip her lid if she ever found out. Not least because it cost £250.

'What are the other girls wearing?' she asks when I come back down and hand her the kameez.

'Doesn't matter what they're wearing. They're skinny, they don't have any problems. They can just pick something off the rack and be done.'

'Hmmm, no material. They never leave any extra,' she complains, turning the kameez this way and that. 'You take after your dad's side. They are all *heavy*. Even the women.'

My heart thuds in my chest. I should be used to this – I know she'll always comment on stuff like this – but whenever she does, it takes me partly by surprise and I don't know why. She is very careful not to say fat or moti to me after I pulled her up on it a few years ago, but she'll still never fail to comment on someone's body. I guess she's only saying what we all think. When I walk into a room or meet or even see anyone, that's the first thing I look at or notice. That probably says a lot about me too.

'What else have you got? What about that green one your masi sent?'

'It's too old, Mama.'

'You've only worn it once.'

'Yes, but two years ago and fashions have changed since then.'

'Let me see anyway.'

I think about arguing back, but it's pointless, so I trudge back upstairs and push the clothes to one side. I collapse onto my bed, deflated, and google 'plus size Indian clothing UK'. I am presented with a selection of tunics that even my mum wouldn't be seen dead in. I haven't been shopping for Indian clothes in the UK since I was a teen, when a bulldog of a woman in a shop on Green Street looked me up and down and announced loudly to the whole shop that they didn't stock my size. To get her back, I didn't pick up a roll of fabric I accidentally knocked over. That showed her.

'Sunny! What you doing?' Mum shouts up the stairs.

I slide off my bed and pick up a long, flowing green kameez and pray that the tight churidar trousers will fit over my calves.

It fits. I look pregnant. But it fits. I have a back-up.

'That's better!' my mum exclaims as I show her.

'I think I'm going to go shopping next weekend, Mama. I might find something nice.'

'You should have said earlier; your masi could have sent something, but now there is no time. You could get the same thing in India for less than half the price. You always leaving things to the last minute.'

'When are you seeing Jag again, puth?' she says casually as I make myself comfortable on the sofa to watch a repeat of *Bake Off*.

Shit. I forgot we talk about boys now. I don't think I'll ever get used to it.

'On Friday,' I say shortly.

'Going for coffee?'

I quickly weigh up whether I can say cinema or if she will be against us being in a dark room together. I decide to risk it.

'Cinema and dinner . . .'

'Oh. Me and your dad used to go to the cinema when we moved out of the family home. Every weekend. Until VCR came out.' A little smile plays on her lips. I let her reminisce. 'Have fun, puth.'

I wait for the inevitable words of caution, but they never come.

# Chapter 27

My cousin Jasmine has just announced her engagement on Instagram with a photo of her and her fiancé. He looks identical to every other young Punjabi lad I've seen: manicured beard, slicked-back hair and designer everything. She's wearing a black off-the-shoulder dress, looking immaculate as always. Her eyes are slightly red and her nose a girlish pink from crying tears of joy. I try to read the lengthy caption all about how she knew Arjun was the one and how she has dreamt of this forever. I give up halfway through.

I comment in all caps: *I CAN'T WAIT TO CELEBRATE WITH YOU!!!*

It's hard not to compare yourself to your cousins. Maybe I wouldn't feel as bad if I had something to be excited about, a job I loved or holiday plans. I really hope she doesn't ask me to be a bridesmaid. Her sister and her cousins from her mum's side look like models and I'll probably look like a half-melted snowman next to them.

If I'm still single by the time she gets married, her mum will be insufferable, so naturally Jasmine's news has put an awful lot of pressure on today's date with Jag. Great.

I keep trying to think of Beena's words – and wonder if Jasmine's life is the life I want. Or more the life my mum wants me to want.

I start typing out a message to Beena but stop myself. I can't bother her with everything little thing that gets to me.

Even though we've got into the habit of messaging each other every day, I don't want to be the clingy friend.

I shower and carefully roll a low-cut dress up and place it gently in my bag so it doesn't crease. I don't want to look like I'm making too much of an effort for Jag – and it's only the cinema. I treated myself to a selection of new perfumes from a cool little independent shop online. The one I choose is a bit more floral than I would like and smells a bit like rose incense, but I love it. I read somewhere that rose increases love, so I dab a little on the inside of my elbows and I've put a tiny rose quartz in my bra to double my chances. I don't intend on letting him touch my tits, so I think it's safe there, but I'm wearing my best bra and I've plucked my singular witchy nipple hair, just in case . . .

I'm in Lake Como. With a guy. With Jag, actually . . . and the sun is setting, and he's looking at me like I'm more beautiful than the view . . . I know! And before I can even catch my breath after looking out at the mountains and the calm of the water, he pulls me towards him, before taking me by the hand and leading me down the terrace. The sun has set and the only light is from the moon and the candles on the dinner tables – we're the only customers left . . .

Then I hear the soft notes of a piano playing 'At Last' by Etta James. And he guides his hand behind my waist, and leads the way as we dance . . .

OK. So, fantasy is not quite reality here . . . because I'm at the stuffy cinema and he's late again.

But I *can* deal with this.

I grew up with two chronically late people – it's probably why I like to be early for everything.

It's clearly not spring in Lake Como here. The temperature has dropped and I shiver, but I don't want to go in by myself.

Instead, I watch the other couples walk quickly into the warmth. At least it's not windy or raining, so my hair still looks good. I check my make-up and teeth for the umpteenth time and force myself to take a few deep breaths. Then I spot him, walking casually, and *slowly*, towards me.

God, he's still so cute in that scruffy way. I try not to stare at him and focus on standing up straight, sucking in my stomach.

Etta James is still playing in my head.

'All right?' He nods at me, a small smile playing on his lips.

'All right?'

Is he going to kiss me?

He leans down and brushes my cheek with his lips.

I blush.

'Yeah, fucking traffic.'

'You should think about getting public transport. This car seems to be a nuisance. Let's go in,' I say lightly, trying to ignore the disappointment that settles in the pit of my stomach at his lack of apology. Or a proper kiss.

The dark foyer is full of young couples.

'Do you want popcorn or anything?' he asks, not looking at me as he taps away on his phone.

'I'll have a medium salty popcorn and a Diet Coke, please,' I say confidently, after convincing myself not to say no out of politeness – he hasn't offered to pay for the tickets, so I might as well get my money's worth. We walk over to the brightly lit counter where we're served by a sullen boy who looks like he can't be much older than fifteen.

'Aren't you going to order anything?' I nudge him.

'No, I'm cutting back on snacks, I need to lose a bit of weight,' he says, patting his non-existent belly.

I feel myself flush.

'That's seven ninety-nine,' the teenage sales assistant says.

'Fucking hell,' he mutters under his breath as he taps his card on the reader.

I feel a stab of guilt. He's acting like being here is a chore.

As we take our seats, I thank him. He acknowledges this with a cool 'no worries'.

My mind is racing. Have I done something wrong? I feel panicked. Have I read this *whole* thing wrong? He's been quiet on WhatsApp, but he was never that chatty anyway. I think about my mum, who's probably already writing the invite list, finalising the design on the velvet invitations. She thinks he makes me happy. She wants me to be happy.

'Is everything OK? You seem a little quiet,' I say carefully, trying not to show the hurt in my voice.

'Yeah, fine. Just tired, innit,' he says to his phone. He doesn't sound tired at all. He sounds bored. He sounds disinterested.

I'm glad we're in a dark room so he can't see my heart breaking on my face. The fact that I'd let myself hope, given him a chance. This was not the second date I had envisaged. Did I *imagine* our first date? The flirting, the kissing, the teasing?

He plunges his hand roughly into the popcorn without asking and starts chomping it noisily as the trailers start. I can't concentrate on the film. How am I going to get through dinner, if I'm the one forced to make all the conversation?

For a second, I imagine my mum sitting a few seats back, watching us, imagining us enjoying our cinema trip in perfect harmony, when really my eyes are trying not to blink out tears, and he's flicking from the film to the phone to the box of popcorn.

By the time the credits roll, I've convinced myself that I just want to go straight home.

We emerge blinking into the bright fluorescently lit foyer.

'I'm going to the loo,' I say. I duck into a cubicle just as I feel tears prick my eyes. Part of me wants to message my mum, the person who, inconceivably, is the most up to date with the whole Jag situation, but I need time to work out what I'll tell her. Instead, I message Natalie.

*Nat, second date with Jag. He's being so weird. I feel like he's mugging me off. What do I do?! Xx*

I powder my nose to help tone down the tell-tale redness and decide I'll tell him I'm going to give dinner a miss. Because of a headache. Then at least I can leave with my dignity intact, despite the fact that he's made me feel shit. I try not to think about breaking the news to Mum.

In the corridor, he's nowhere to be seen.

I wait a few minutes; he's probably gone to the loo himself. But a few more minutes pass and there's still no sign of him.

I walk into the foyer. Still no sign.

He's done a fucking runner. He's left. He's walked out.

*Wow.*

I stride towards the exit, head up, looking straight ahead, ignoring the couples walking into the next viewing hand in hand. I feel my breath quicken as I push open the double doors, bumping into a man and not apologising to him because, honestly, fuck men. Fuck the lot of them. The useless, lying bastards.

No more dating for me. No more Michaels, no more Jags. I pick up the pace in the direction of the train station.

'Oi! Sunny! *Sunny!*'

I whip round. He's right there, half hidden in the shadows.

'Where were you going?'

'Home.' I keep my voice even. I don't want to give him the satisfaction.

'I couldn't get any reception, so I came outside.' He waves his phone at me as though it's the most obvious explanation in the world. I can see a smile curling the corners of his lips.

'Right.'

235

'Did you think I'd left you?' He's smiling properly now, in a cheeky way, not a smirky way.

I shrug, not knowing what to say.

'You're mental.' He puts his arm around my shoulders. 'Come on, let's get some food, I'm starving.' I can't tell him now that I'm not hungry, that I just want to go home, because he'll think I'm sulking. My heart is hammering; I feel stupid, embarrassed. My rage is washed over by a deep sense of shame.

Dinner is painful. The conversation is stilted and we spend a lot of time looking around the restaurant to avoid looking at each other. I try to force down the sadness with a gulp of my wine. The spaces between our conversation are the width of the Darién Gap.

Out of the corner of my eye I see another Indian couple, dressed in all black and all over each other. She's got that long, glass-like hair, like the woman in my fantasies, the woman I want to be. He's got an impressive beard and a tidy pagh. She laughs sweetly as they pose for a selfie. They look so comfortable together. It's like seeing an alternate reality. He touches her waist lightly and she leans into him. I force myself to look away and I stare at my plate instead.

When the waiter comes to clear our plates and asks if we want to look at the dessert menu, Jag jumps in before I can and says: 'Shall we go then? I'll drop you off.'

He drives in silence for a bit until: 'What's that perfume? Don't wear it again.' He's staring straight ahead, his nose wrinkled in disgust. 'Are you trying to tell me something?'

'Sorry?' I'm genuinely confused at what he means.

'With those boots.'

He gestures with his head towards my DMs, still not looking at me.

'Lesbian boots, aren't they?'

I laugh nervously, unsure if this is his idea of a joke, not knowing what to say.

'Don't get all sensitive,' he says. 'It's only a joke.' He's suddenly become vibrant, animated, now we're in the car, now this date is coming to an end. But he's a dick. He's being a dick.

I want the car seat to swallow me whole. I want to be on my own. I contemplate pulling him up on it all, but I don't trust myself not to cry in anger and frustration, so I sit in silence for the rest of the journey.

There is plenty I want to say, but I am a woman in a car with a man I do not know. Not really. A man who has already proved he can seamlessly switch from being charming and funny and flirty to . . . this.

His attitude today, his comments, remind me of other men I've dated before.

And I realise, right now, how alone I am. In a car. With a man. On a dark road.

As soon as I'm in the front door, I take a few deep breaths and slip off my boots. I want to scrub myself raw in the shower. I want to forget about tonight. I'm on the verge of tears.

'Sunny? You OK? How was it?' Mum is in the kitchen again, waiting for me. Of course she is waiting for me. She's wiping down the worktops – part of her night-time ritual.

'Not good, Mama,' I reply with a deep sigh, feeling, for once, like I'm actually being open with her – like I'm actually telling her what I feel. I can't lie. I feel too broken to lie right now.

'Why? What happen?' She looks alarmed.

I think about telling her everything: about him ignoring me; about the car journey home. But just as the words are starting to stream out of my mouth, I swallow them back down.

I haven't been there before. I haven't told my mum everything like that before. What if she tells me to try again? What if she says I must have done something wrong? If she makes it my fault.

I take a deep breath. There's only one lie that will get me out of this. I'm not proud of myself for it, but the words tumble out of my mouth before I can pull them back: 'He's got a kid, Mum.'

Her eyebrows shoot up. She slams the bottle of Dettol spray on the worktop with a resounding, 'What!?' The shock and hurt in her eyes almost make me confess the truth. Almost.

'He just told me.' I nod sadly. 'Never married.' I have to lay it on thick; if the imaginary child was the result of a failed marriage, there's a small chance she might overlook it, but a secret illegitimate child – absolutely no chance.

'He didn't say anything before?' She sits down at the dining table. I feel a twinge of guilt at her shocked expression. But I think about myself, sitting in that car, with that man. And I am glad that this lie, no matter how bad, will mean I won't have to be there again.

'No, I had no idea. He didn't mention it before.'

'Kanjar kisse thah da!' It takes a lot for my mum to swear and for a split second I am almost tempted to laugh at her outburst.

'Don't worry, there are plenty of nice boys.' She beckons me and hugs me tightly and I almost burst into tears, but I don't want to worry her.

'I thought he was a nice boy, good family.'

'You can never tell, though, Mama,' I say wistfully.

'This is true.' She nods her head sadly. 'Chalo. Never mind, heh? Have you eaten?'

'I think I'm just going to go to bed, Mama.'

'Your dad bought some besan ... your favourite ...' She looks at me with a knowing smile and I smile; she knows it's my weakness. 'Why don't you just sit here and eat it with me?'

I get a plate, break off a few cubes and settle myself down in a seat opposite her. I think about making an excuse, finding a reason to be alone upstairs, but her face looks concerned – her eyes are telling me she's worried about me, and I decide to stay put. She doesn't talk, for what I think is the first time in my whole life ... ever.

We just sit, and we eat, and we listen to the Sikh channel in the other room. And I gradually find myself growing calmer. My heart beats more slowly. That feeling in my stomach, it doesn't dissipate, but it mellows.

# Chapter 28

The next day, I'm making my way on the Tube to Mile End. Anjali's sister has booked an actual Bollywood choreographer to help us with the dance for the wedding reception. I don't quite know when this became a thing at weddings. All I know is that one day we were watching bhangra dancers and the next day we had to *become* the bhangra dancers.

The song has been chosen and Chandni has instructed us to learn the words because we will be lip-syncing. This started a whole 'Sorry, we don't speak Indian' thread from the white contingent in the 'Friends Dance' WhatsApp group, which boiled my piss so much I muted them for a whole twenty-four hours.

I just screenshotted the whole thing to Beena. I didn't want to dump on her, but I felt like she'd get it, seeing how well she understands Chandni and her friends.

*Fucking hell* – Beena had texted back. *You go show them how it's done. What idiots xx*

Despite their behaviour, and the fact that Beena won't be there – she flat out refused to be part of the dance – I'm excited about the rehearsal. I love the song, and even though this is the remixed version, it's still a classic. I remember dancing to it in my cousin's bedroom, wrapped in her mum's bright pink-and-gold chunni with the little mirrors.

The venue is a trendy dance studio in East London. I'm the first one there, as always, and I sign in with a bored-looking receptionist who barely glances at me. I flatten myself against the wall as a large group of impossibly tiny dancers swarms past me. They're all limbs and sleek buns and concave stomachs and neat belly buttons.

I'm wearing my black high-waisted gym leggings, which I bought for Zumba a few years ago in the hope that they would contain at least some of the jiggle, and a baggy off-the-shoulder top because I once read in a magazine that they draw attention away from your 'problem areas'. (If only it was simply problem *areas* and not a whole problem *body*.) As well as, of course, an industrial-strength over-the-shoulder boulder holder to keep the twins in their rightful place.

Natalie's constant refrain of 'Sunny, embrace your curves! You're beautiful' rings in my ears.

Moments later, they all bundle into the reception area: Charlie, Elena, Anj's friends from school, Jo and Abi, and Chandni, of course, looking immaculate as always. They're all babbling excitedly among themselves, their faces pink from the cold.

'Hi, Sunny!' chorus Charlie and Elena. They're trying hard to make an effort, but they don't come over to hug me. It's not just the physical distance that tells me things are still strained between us. It's the smiles that don't quite reach their eyes and the polite nods, as if I'm nothing more than a neighbour they only see at the charity cake sale once a year.

'Can someone open a window, please?' Chandni says accusingly as we file into the dance studio and are hit with the smell of old shoes and body odour. We all shed our layers; they're all in tiny spaghetti-strap tops and cropped leggings.

Oh great. Mirrors. I didn't think about the mirrors. A whole wall of them. I position myself at the back.

The door swings open and a tall, thin Indian man in a shiny teal tracksuit saunters in. He surveys the room, hand on hip. His neat handlebar moustache and thick, gelled-back, shoulder-length hair gives him the look of a Bollywood villain. Chandni rushes over to him.

After a whispered chat with Chandni, he walks into the middle of the room and claps his hands loudly twice.

'OK, ladies, my name is Vish. I'm a dancer, choreographer and all-round badass,' he drawls in a voice that is a curious mix of Mumbai and LA. 'We are going to give the bride and groom a dance to remember, and after this, I *guarantee* the single girls will have men falling at their feet and you married ones . . .' He looks around the room and pauses for effect. 'Your husbands won't be able to keep their hands off you.'

He twirls and pops his hip and bites his finger in a parody of a seductive woman. The girls giggle. A generous laugh escapes my lips. I like him.

'So, let's see what we're working with here. Does anyone have any dance experience?'

Everyone mumbles 'no' and I look at the floor. I can feel my heart quicken and I push down the panic that's threatening to bubble up to my throat, as I'm reminded of the Zumba classes a few years ago, and all my PE lessons years before that.

'Don't worry, I am used to working with beginners. I worked on *Monsoon Love*, the new Divya Sharma movie, and let me to tell you . . .' Again, he pauses for dramatic effect, lowering his voice. 'Can't. Dance. For. Shit.'

'Nooooo. Oh my God,' Chandni says, scandalised.

The white girls and I look on nonplussed. My knowledge of Bollywood films is limited to the ones that my dad and I used to watch – the black-and-white ones with dimple-chinned movie stars and their doe-eyed, satisfyingly plump co-stars, seemingly comfortable with their soft upper arms and round bellies. I caught a bit of a recent Bollywood film at my cousin's house and couldn't believe how raunchy they are: no more near-miss kisses; there was full-on grinding and humping! And the clothes . . . I wear more in the bath.

'Anyway, have you all listened to the song?'

'Yes,' we all chorus dutifully.

'Then let's get started. We've got a lot to get through and only two hours.' He shrugs off his tracksuit jacket, revealing a tight white T-shirt.

As he presses play on the sound system and the thud of drums fills the room, my heart lifts and my feet start tapping automatically. The bass kicks in, melding with the soaring vocals of a woman singing about going to dance for her lover.

'Oh my God, Sunny, you were *so* good!'

'I didn't know you could dance like that!'

'Have you ever taken lessons?'

'You could *totally* have been a professional!'

I'm practically skipping down the street. Despite that being the most exercise I've done in years, I feel light, my muscles are tingling, my ligaments are stretched and energy is flowing through my veins.

'All right, girls, calm down, it was a pretty straightforward routine,' chimes in Chandni with her signature eye roll. I don't say anything at all but file the anecdote away to tell Beena later.

We slowly make our way to the tiny pub where we are having a well-deserved drink and dinner. We're all giddy from the adrenaline of dancing and laughing for the past two hours, still humming the song. Even the tension between me, Charlie and Elena seems to have lessened as they walk either side of me – we're not quite arm in arm, but it's certainly not as awkward as it was before.

The pub's open fire casts a warm glow in the bar. A few punters turn to look at us, a gaggle of giggling women. We make our way to the back; bottles of prosecco are ordered, and some overpriced mineral water for Chandni. Menus are perused.

I relax into the padded bench, relieved that I've managed to bag myself a seat at the end of the table. Another example of subconscious fat-girl behaviour, so that if you need to go to the loo, you don't have to do the embarrassing scooch across the seat while everybody watches. I let the bright chatter wash over me and bask in the post-exercise glow.

'What are you getting, babe?' asks Elena, interrupting the beginnings of a daydream where I become the world's first plus-sized Indian dance star.

'Maybe the chicken pie with mash and greens?' I reply, as if I didn't spend ages perusing the menu the night before. 'What about you?'

'Hmmm, that looks good.' Elena frowns at the menu. 'I think I might go for something *lighter*, maybe the salmon bowl. I don't want to eat back all the calories I've just burnt off!'

I am immensely proud of myself for not putting her straight about how calories work; in the interests of harmony, I just smile and nod.

'I'd like to do a toast!' declares Charlie. 'Here's to our best friend's wedding and doing the best Indian dance ever!' She does a little head wobble on the word 'Indian' and knocks back the prosecco. I look over to Chandni, as the only other Indian person in the group, but she's smiling indulgently, sipping her mineral water.

After we've ordered from the cute Irish barman, who charms us into getting a bottle of red *and* white wine and some even *more* expensive mineral water for Chandni, Elena carefully chimes in with: 'I was thinking of wearing something Indian, but I don't want to offend anyone.' Her eyes are on me and Chandni, waiting for our reactions. But before we can say anything . . .

'Why would it offend anyone if the whole *theme* is Indian? Isn't it?' says Charlie, knocking back another glass of prosecco.

I laugh, sure this is a joke. Everyone turns to look at me apart from Chandni, who is busy tapping away on her phone, completely oblivious.

'It's an Indian wedding, not an Indian-*themed* wedding,' I say pointedly, looking at their nonplussed faces. 'Just like a church wedding is a church wedding, not a church-*themed* wedding.'

'We went to an Indian wedding a few years ago and our next-door neighbour lent me and Mum some saris,' says Jo excitedly, not acknowledging a word of what I've just said. I wait for it but don't say anything just yet, knowing white people use saris as a catch-all term for Indian clothes . . . 'They were gorgeous!' she continues, as the other girls look at her excitedly. 'Like those embellished baggy tops and MC Hammer trousers!'

'So, they weren't *actual* saris?' I finally say, disbelieving, my heart in my throat. All eyes turn to me.

'Well . . .' Jo looks at me. 'You know what I mean. They look like pyjamas, don't they? Quite hard to pull off, I think, but they looked great on me.' She starts laughing inanely.

'Salwar kameez.'

'Hmm? Sorry?' She's now got the hiccups from laughing so hard – she raises her eyebrows at me as if I'm interrupting her fun.

'It's actually called a salwar kameez,' I repeat, making sure I'm smiling as I say it. I feel a slight, imperceptible shift in the atmosphere and I press my nails into the palm of my hand to remind me to stay calm.

'Right, well, *I* don't know, do I?' She looks to her friend Abi to back her up, laughing awkwardly.

'Well, now you do. The top is called a kameez and the "MC Hammer trousers", as you so creatively put it, is the salwar.' I try to keep my tone light, but it's hard not to let anger creep into my voice.

'I wasn't told that!' she says defensively.

'Yeah, I don't think it's that big a deal,' chimes in Charlie, leaning over Elena for the bottle of prosecco.

'But you should learn that ... it's only polite ... That ... that would be like me calling Morris dancing the waltz or the ... the ... I'm ... I just think ... it's rude to wear another culture's clothing as, like, a costume and not even bother to learn what it's called.'

'Do you know what you're going to wear, babe?' Elena asks me in a soft voice.

'Well, seeing as it's an "Indian-themed" wedding, I thought I'd get my MC Hammer trousers out,' I reply, my voice dripping with sarcasm.

'Babe, babe, Sunny! What's got into you? Why are you getting so angry?'

'I'm not, I'm just saying!'

'It's not Jo's fault,' says Abi quietly.

I look over and see Jo's eyes fill up, before the tears spill prettily onto her rosy face.

Great. That's all we need.

I can tell she's already won. I never know if I'm in the right or not. But I'm not apologising. I can't. Elena scrambles to find a tissue in her bag.

'I'm fine, I'm fine,' Jo sniffs.

'OK, who's having the salmon bowl?' The cute Irish barman seems to appear out of nowhere brandishing plates of food. Oblivious to the charged atmosphere, he chats away to Abi who seems to have caught his eye. Everyone solemnly settles to eat, and slowly but surely a low hum of conversation starts up again. I can't bring myself to meet anyone's eye so I look down at the delicious-looking pie with its golden pastry lid and half-heartedly pick up my fork, even though there seems to be something hard and spiky stuck in my throat. I take a swig of prosecco to dislodge it.

'I'm sorry if I've offended you in some way. I really didn't mean to,' Jo says in a half-whisper. The polite thing to do here is accept her apology, but the words stick in my throat. I can't look at her, at any of them. I just nod at my plate. My face is burning, my heart is going to burst out of my chest.

'Ah, let's just forget about it and be mates! We all say things we don't mean in the heat of the moment!' slurs Charlie, turning away and rolling her eyes.

Sometimes my anger terrifies me, the way it shoots up my spine like a hot snake trying to escape through the top of my skull. In that split second I imagine grabbing her by her pretty ponytail and slamming her drunken face into the table until her nose shatters. The phrase 'red mist' doesn't even cover it. I take a few shaky breaths while I decide whether to say something.

'You know, Charlie, just because you've collected a few Brown friends along the way, it doesn't mean you get to decide what is and isn't OK.' I stare at her as she stares back at me in disbelief, her mouth slack with shock. I look down the table and catch Chandni's eye.

'You're making a scene, Sunny,' she says, with a look of such naked disgust that it tips me over the edge.

'Oh, you can fuck off an' all,' I explode, my Gravesend accent coming through. It's like I've thrown a grenade into the middle of the table. She squawks in response.

Unable to look at any of them, I reach down to gather my bag and coat and scarf and walk to the exit on shaky legs, bumping into chairs as I go.

The cold, biting wind is a balm to my cheeks, which are so hot that I feel like they're actually drying out my skin, like I've been sitting indoors with the heating on too high. I walk around the side of the pub and lean against the wall, my legs threatening to give way. I don't know how long I stand there.

My mind is racing, thinking of the things I wish I had said. I wish I had told them about being made to wear a salwar kameez on World Book Day in primary school and being laughed at and called a 'freshie' by the Indian kids and a 'Paki' by the white kids. Yet when all my white friends use Indian clothes to play dress-up, they're seen as beautiful, perfect, can do no wrong.

My chest feels tight as I practically run to the Tube and down the escalator – anything to make me forget what just happened. All sound is cut out. I can't hear a thing. I feel like I'm underwater and the rest of the world is above the surface, unable to reach me.

As I sit down in a half-empty carriage, I realise I didn't even pay. I would normally message Nat, but I'm not sure she'd understand.

I open up the group chat, wondering if I should type something, but then I see a new message from Beena:

*Hey, dancing queen! How did it go today?! Can't wait to see you shake that ass at that wedding! xx*

She signs off with a GIF of Aishwarya Rai in *Devdas* looking coy as she dances. As soon as I get off the Tube, I send her a voice note giving her the lowdown. It ends up being a six-minute rant and I sign off by apologising multiple times for leaving her a podcast. But having told Beena, even though I barely know her, I feel calmer. My helpless anger has transformed into righteous anger because I know she'll get it.

When I get in, Mum's soaking fenugreek seeds in a large glass bowl. The minute brown pebbles remind me of the stuff at the bottom of fish tanks.

'What's that for, Mama?' I keep my voice light.

'Making hair grow. I'm going to put the water in a bottle and use before shampoo.' She covers the bowl with a dinner plate. 'How was dance rehearsal?' She pronounces it more like 'wrestle'.

I grunt non-committally in reply as I preheat the oven, making sure to empty it of the tava and multiple oven trays.

'What happen?' She's always had a nose for a story. She'd have made a great private investigator.

'Erm, nothing ... it was fine,' I say, grabbing a pack of battered onion rings out of the freezer – I've been dreaming of a beige dinner ever since the train home. 'What did you have for dinner? Roti?'

'Something happen, isn't it?'

I busy myself buttering two slices of white bread. I don't know how to explain to her what just happened – insensitivity? Cultural appropriation? I don't want to call it racism. When my mum first came to the UK, she was spat at in the street, had rocks thrown at her, all because of the colour of her skin.

'Is it Jag? Did he send message?' The concern in her voice makes me turn around to face her.

'No, no. Nothing like that ... It's my friends. Charlie and Elena and Anj.'

'You had argument?'

'Yeah. Yeah, we have. They're not very ... It's nothing, Mama. I don't think I want to be friends with them any more,' I say quietly, hoping she doesn't probe further. I sound like a child who has just come home from school after a fall-out, and tomorrow it'll all be OK again. Except this time, I don't know if it will be. I think of what Dean and Beena have said – about getting to choose my friends, about things being my choice and not someone else's.

I can feel tears brewing. My mouth is dry, my throat tight.

'People change when they get older, puth. Sometimes you think, when you're young, we are going to be friends for life. Then your friend getting married, moving house, you get busy. It's OK, it's normal, acha?'

She hasn't got it. But I haven't told her the whole story – I never have. I've always painted my friends to be perfect, because if they were anything less than that, Mum wouldn't think them worthy of me at all.

I exhale loudly and turn to her, but she's already got her head buried in the latest copy of *Punjab Times*. I hug her tightly.

A message from Elena flashes up:

*Hi. Your share of the meal came to £27. PayPal or Monzo is fine.*

# Chapter 29

To my immense relief, Mum hasn't mentioned marriage since the disastrous date with Jag. Even after her frenemy, Shindo, announced that her youngest daughter, who is a good few years younger than me, is engaged to be married to an engineer from Canada. She also doesn't mention anything about our chat last night, preferring instead to gossip about a woman at her yoga group who has decided to start wearing bright pink lipstick only a few months after her husband died suddenly on a trip to India.

As much as I never want to see the girls ever again, even Anj, I'm still duty-bound to go to the wedding. But Beena will be there, which means at least there'll be one friendly face. She sent me a string of messages and an equally long and ranty voice note backing me up last night, ending with her shouting, 'DON'T LET THOSE BITCHES GASLIGHT YOU!'

I decide to practise the dance for Anj's wedding in my bedroom while it's still fresh in my mind. The least I can do is be the best dancer there. I pull on my wedding outfit to get the full effect.

I'm only halfway through the song when my mum shouts my name.

'What are you doing up there?'

'I'm practising the dance for Anj's wedding!'

'Sounds like you are going to fall through the roof! Come downstairs before you damage the floorboards.'

'Can you go into the kitchen then, Mum?' I say sullenly.

'Why? Plenty room here.'

'But . . .'

'I want to see too – don't be silly, show me!' she demands, turning down the volume on the TV.

Downstairs, I reluctantly find the song on my phone, get into position, one hand on my hip, and press play. I practise the moves half-heartedly, self-conscious of my jiggle, purposefully making my movements less dynamic so I'm not accused of being too sexy. Mum divides her attention between me and a YouTube video on Ayurvedic remedies for knee pain.

'You need to lift your feet more. And wear your chunni across your . . .' She signals to my chest as I stop the track.

'Mum,' I whine, a little breathless. 'They are what they are. I can't do anything about them.'

My mum has what I call tidy boobs. Whereas my cups over-floweth and threaten to burst out of my clothing at any given point; I had uncles (who aren't actually my uncles) staring at them as soon as I hit puberty, forcing me to wear long, baggy jumpers, which inevitably made their wives comment on my weight.

'Hmmm,' Mum says, now looking me straight in the eye. Her expression is soft, and I can tell she thinks she's being kind. 'After you were born, I put on a little bit of weight, but I had a wedding to go to, so I bought knickers from BHS, and they are tight but look very *smooth* under clothes . . .'

'I have shapewear, Mama—'

'OK, that's good, wear it to the wedding,' she says, turning back to YouTube, as though her job here is done.

'Puth, get me my notebook and pen. Your dad is saying his knee is hurting.' The sentence has barely left her lips when she notices Dad pulling into the driveway. 'He is going to live a long, long life.' I can't quite read her tone when she says this – it's half solemn and half wistful.

My parents have always slept in separate beds and don't show any sort of outward affection towards each other, but that's pretty normal for their generation. The first time I went round a white friend's house, we snuck into her mum's room to play with her make-up and I looked at the double bed with the pale-pink padded headboard and asked where her dad slept. She looked at me funny and said they slept in the same bed.

I didn't know why it felt wrong, but it seemed shameful somehow.

Although no one says it, I know my mum's family think she married beneath her. I hear it in the way my bibi sighs when she looks at my mum or strokes her long hair. She is fond of her son-in-law and says he's a good man, but she regrets not standing up to her late husband, my bhapa-ji, and insisting she marry someone else. Maybe she doesn't see the way my dad gives my mum's shoulder a little squeeze when she makes him tea or the way my mum never buys anything for herself without buying something for my dad too.

'Hello! I've got prashad – it's still warm!' Dad appears in the doorway of the living room, his hands cupped around a small parcel of kitchen towel, which he unwraps as I hastily cover my head and cup my hands to receive the sweet golden mixture of sugar, butter and flour.

'Just a little bit, Dad!'

'Oh, come on!' He frowns at me. 'You used to have two servings when you were little.' He drops a generous dollop into my hands.

I close my palms, touch them to my forehead and mutter, 'Waheguru,' before eating it far too quickly.

'Anyone call?' he asks, sitting heavily in his designated armchair.

'Nobody. Did you have langar?' Mum watches him as he gently rubs his knee.

'Yes, but very early . . .'

I smile. This is code for 'I could eat again'. I leave to wash my hands before I get butter from the prashad on my outfit. My mum rubs the butter into her hands like my bibi does.

Before I change into my standard at-home outfit of Primark leggings and whatever top is long enough to cover my arse, I decide to post a selfie of me in my outfit on Instagram Stories. I grab a couple of bangles and a matching green bindi, shake out my hair and find a filter that makes it look like I have make-up on.

Heading back downstairs, my dad asks me: 'What is the dance you are doing?'

I can tell he and Mum have been talking about it from the way Mum doesn't turn round when he asks, as though she doesn't want to give anything away.

I play the song on my phone and Dad starts nodding his head to the music, a big smile on his face.

'Chalo,' Mum says. 'Sunny, let's eat, it's getting late.'

'Puth,' Mum says, soft and snappy all at once. 'No, that goes in the other cupboard. Leh, how long have you lived here and still putting things in the wrong places?' Whenever it comes to cleaning up in the kitchen, Mum becomes fierce, barking instructions, because things have to be put back in a certain way. I know the places for everything – the plates with the green flowers around the edge always go under the plain plates; the small spoons always go in a separate place from the big spoons – and yet, every time, Mum changes something and acts as though it has always been that way. I look at the pan in my hand, knowing full well it has never lived in the cupboard she's indicating, but I do as I'm told. There's no point arguing.

'Puth,' she says again after a few minutes of silence, once she's satisfied I've put the pans in the right places, 'I think we should look for another boy.'

She's not looking at me; her hands are in the sink, scrubbing another pan with a Brillo pad. Her eyes are fixed on it so intently, I'm not sure she's even sensed that I've frozen to the spot.

I had thought that Jag and the fact that he had ultimately been a disaster might be the last time Mum bothered trying to get me to date people. I thought it would be the end of my dating altogether. I'd told myself I was done.

'OK,' I say slowly, desperate not to make a wrong move.

'Yes, so after you have finished, give me your phone. If we need to, we try Tindles again. Maybe better boys there.'

I nearly drop the pan in my hand.

'Mama, we don't need to do Tinder – the Asian dating website is much better,' I say, meaning 'much less likely to send you dick pics'.

'Hmm, I do not know what we can trust after Jag, all that lying.' She shakes her head in disbelief, still not looking at me. I gulp down a glob of guilt. I still feel bad about that lie, and I don't know why. Not because Jag didn't deserve it – I couldn't face seeing him again – but because I never told Mama exactly why he wasn't right. Now, if this next guy isn't right either, what do I tell her this time?

'OK.' I nod, barely able to say anything else. Mum nods firmly, her eyes now on me.

When we sit down at the kitchen table, Mum puts her hand out and makes a grabby motion for me to pass her my phone.

'Mama,' I say, moving my chair over to sit right beside her. 'Let me show you.'

Before I get to her, I turn my Tinder radius to within one mile, to make sure we *really* minimise the possibility of finding someone my mum would deem 'appropriate'.

When we see a white guy who works in a coffee shop, I know instantly he is not what my mum is looking for in a son-in-law. Even if my mum's using dating apps, she is still intent on finding me a good Sikh Punjabi boy. He looks kind of cute, but also like the sort of guy who might start a conversation about my bra size or something, so it's a relief when Mum says, 'No,' quickly and firmly.

'No,' she says again when we see an Indian guy who looks about twelve, wearing a *Mario Kart* T-shirt. 'Too young!' Mum exclaims, once I've already swiped past.

But then we land on another guy, who makes it very clear in his profile that he is 'thirty-three, looking for love, Sikh, fluent in Punjabi and a self-confessed mummy's boy lol'. The mummy's boy thing immediately puts me off – it's a red flag for me. As is the 'lol'. But, Mum seems to like it. Mum *loves* mummy's boys.

'Puth,' she says, almost whispering with excitement. 'He is *perfect*. Tall . . . Handsome! Punjabi! And he looks like a very good boy.'

I peruse his photos. His name is Rav. Nothing incriminating. Nothing that will put Mum off him on the spot.

As I swipe, a few seconds later I get a message saying we've matched.

Mum claps her hands in glee. It's like she's firmly got to grips with Tinder, and I don't know whether the idea amuses or horrifies me.

'*Talk* to him.' She hands the phone back to me, and I'm glad for this at least. I had been having visions that she'd start messaging him herself.

*Hi, how are you?* I type. *Let me know if you fancy going for a drink sometime.*

I keep the message completely PG, just in case Mum wants to assess my work, but there's nothing salacious I'd want to say to him anyway. He looks nice, but I'm just not . . .

I can feel my stomach turning, and I don't know why – a queasiness that has just come out of nowhere.

*Hey. Yeah, that'd be nice. I'm in Gravesend, where are you?*

Oh *God*, I stall. I'd almost forgotten I'd set the search area so close in the hope that it'd minimise suitors … now I'm potentially going to be dating someone who lives just round the corner. I'm surprised I don't already know him.

*Me too. Shall we meet further afield though?*

*Yeah. Good idea. London?*

Once we've firmed up a plan, I relay it all to Mum. She nods. 'Good, that is good,' and ends with, 'Don't let that one silly boy put you off. You deserve someone good, a good boy.' For a moment, my heart does a little flip. She doesn't notice. Then she gets up from her seat and heads to the living room, where Dad has woken up from his nap and is talking particularly loudly on the phone about potholes for some reason. She turns back to me and gives me a thumbs-up. I've never ever seen my mum do a thumbs-up before, but a little part of me feels a bit better about this date now.

I know I'm only really doing this for Mum. I'm just doing it to get her trust back, or to keep her happy, or to keep her from telling me to get married right away. But still, talking about boys, even half honestly, with her, feels like a whole different world. It feels for a little bit like she might in some ways understand me.

I know what my mum is looking for in a boy – she's made that clear for years – but I can't yet figure out where my needs end and my mother's needs begin.

# Chapter 30

'So why are you single then?' Rav is staring at me intently over a beer that he has barely touched since we got here.

It takes all my willpower not to roll my eyes at this question. I hate it with a passion. I think I hate it even more than, 'Where are you from then?' There is no good answer to it. You might as well as ask me, 'So what makes you so deeply unattractive to men that you, at the grand old age of thirty, have never had a long-term relationship?'

I just shrug in response, wanting to tell him what an idiot he is for asking this question at all. But he simply replies with: 'Ahh, you're one of them picky ones.' He's leaning back in his chair like he is God's gift or something. I knew when I met Rav at the train station that we would not . . . gel. It's nothing to do with how he looks; he's smart, well dressed and didn't lie about his height. He just has this air about him, as though he's the most special person in the room – I think this is probably the mummy's boy thing. The fact that he has probably been told, his whole life, that he *is* the most special person in the room. I've never been told that. And look how balanced I am.

'What's wrong with being picky?' I say, unable to help myself. 'Isn't that just a euphemism for having standards? Also, as far as I'm aware, only women get called picky. Not men. What does that say about society? That women should know their place. Settle for what they can get. Not get ideas above their station.' I press my lips together, well aware that I've said too much for a first date. For the first time in forever, my mind properly jumps back to Michael. While there was so much not right about my relationship with Michael, at least he always had something interesting to say. I don't think he ever asked me the 'Why are you single?' question once.

'Whoa. I was just making conversation.' He throws up his hands in a gesture of surrender. His eyes are wide in shock-horror, as though I've just said the most outrageous thing.

I'm beginning to think I *hate* dates. This bit at least. When you're trying to figure each other out, like two positive magnets repelling each other. Two dogs sniffing each other's arseholes.

I have to remind myself that Mum likes the look of him. Good job. Tall. Punjabi. But I wish she was here to see all this first-hand. She'd probably ask him about his relationship with his mother and be completely charmed when he says the phrase, 'She'll always be my favourite woman,' forgetting that the whole point of this date is to get *me* to become his favourite woman.

I take a deep breath – I can feel bubbles rising in my stomach and my chest, my anxiety and annoyance combined. I'm drinking orange juice today – I didn't feel like having to hide the smell of wine on my breath, because I know Mum will be waiting for the debrief once again.

'Anyway, what about you?' I smack a smile on my face, telling myself to get through the evening, give the guy a chance. 'How long have you been single?'

'Not long,' he says, looking down at his beer like a scolded puppy. 'Do you have a type?' he asks, stifling a burp.

'Erm. Tall, dark and handsome,' I say lamely, instead of the truth, which is: built like a brick shithouse, liberal, open-minded and doesn't balk at a bit of hair pulling in the bedroom.

'Well, I'm two out of three.' He winks suggestively.

'Ha.' I half scoff, half laugh, hoping he didn't see the pretty obvious rolling of my eyes. 'What about you?'

My eyes wander away, surveying the rest of the pub. We're in a nondescript gastropub in Central London, full of City bankers dressed in suits, downing pints at the bar. I'm already scouting out the other guys here, wondering if I could start chatting to anyone at the bar to escape. But when was the last time I actually ended up chatting to a stranger in a bar without them mugging me off? I remember the guy from that bar in Old Street. The one with eyes for Anj. Not me. Never me.

I can tell I'm being a bit of a cow and probably coming across as standoffish. But I know as soon as I meet someone whether we will click. I think we should normalise having a thirty-minute grace period where you can walk away after half an hour with no hard feelings.

'I like curvy women; you know, not skin and bone. Hate skinny girls. I like *real* women.'

And there it is. I realise I was expecting him to say something like this.

'As opposed to three ferrets in a coat?'

'What?' He looks genuinely confused.

'You said real women. All women are *real* women . . . you know . . . regardless of their body shape.' I can feel myself getting my loudspeaker out once more.

'You know what I mean,' he says, waving his hand dismissively.

'So, do you live on your own?' My back is beginning to ache from carrying this conversation.

'Nah. With family.'

Of *course* he does. What mummy's boy doesn't?

'Me too. Who can afford to buy these days?!' I grimace, wondering if we can maybe bond over this at least.

'Oh.' He rolls his eyes casually at this. 'I've got a couple of properties. I want to get a proper property portfolio. Make my first million by the time I'm forty. I'm on track.' He analyses the surprise on my face. 'I thought you'd have a house too; thought maybe you were renting it out and living with your parents.' I honestly could not think of anything worse than owning my own home yet *choosing* to live with my parents.

I really should have vetted him with a phone call before the date. Now I'm stuck here for at least a few hours.

'You know, it's really stupid not to invest in property,' he says to me. 'You could be making so much money right now.'

I refrain from saying anything, but a whole speech pops up in my mind. If I go there, my voice is just going to get louder and louder until everyone in the bar is looking at us. A few beers later, he tells me all about how much he *loves* Dubai and I barely manage to stop myself from saying I'd rather never go on holiday again than go to the hellish, overheated shopping centre that is Dubai.

When I don't say a word back, just smile and nod, he takes it as an invitation to pull out his phone to show me photos. Oh great. I nod politely while he shows me identical tall, shiny glass buildings and photo after photo of him in loafers with no socks. I know it's the fashion and maybe I'm old, but all I can think is that his shoes must stink.

By the time I've finished my glass of orange juice and he's finished his pint, I say, 'Well, I better go, I've got an early start tomorrow.' It's 8.30.

'Oh, yeah, that's OK. Let's go to the station.' Something in his expression tells me he might be mildly disappointed at this, and it feels like the biggest shocker of the night. I thought it was crystal clear that we. Did. Not. Click. I don't think I've ever been so bored and frustrated all at once in my life. And I live a life where I have to remember where to put the pots and pans, and spent years sneaking up the stairs in the dark, hiding gins in a tin in my underwear drawer.

We say goodbye – me a bit too brightly – at the station. I almost go to shake his hand. He gives me one of those awkward side hugs you give your aunty so that there is no genital contact. We're both getting the same train, because we live ... as feared ... just round the corner from each other. At the platform he heads up to the front of the train, half expecting me to follow, but I stay firmly in the middle.

By the time the train is pulling out of the station, I've already messaged Natalie the unhappy news.

Natalie: *Oh Sunny! I was hoping he might be The One! I thought he might be like the Sikh fella from* The English Patient*! Any chance of a second date?! Xx*

Natalie is obsessed with the character of Kip from *The English Patient* and thinks all Sikh men are as dashing and handsome and romantic. I feel bad bursting her bubble, but she needs to know that the majority of Sikh men I've dated have an unhealthy attachment to booze and their mothers.

Sunny: *No, babe. He definitely wasn't like that. I think 0 chance of a second date. Xxx*

Natalie: *Noo! That's sad. You don't reckon it was your bad love karma from pirate boy, do you?!* 😔

A few years ago, I left a man in a bar. Told him I was going to get us a drink but just left. In my defence, he was obsessed with pirates, and that wasn't going to go anywhere good, was it? Now, I can't help thinking that *this* is the reason I am still single.

'Hello, puth, all right?' Mum's cutting up a collection of wedding invites tonight. Most, if not all, wedding invites have a line or two of scripture in them and my mum cuts out the words carefully to burn them along with other religious materials like leaflets from the gurdwara. She believes this is the most respectful way to dispose of them rather than chucking the whole card in the bin with the used tea bags and onion peelings.

'How was it?' she asks excitedly. Her eyes light up when she looks at me, and for the briefest of moments I feel terrible that I'm coming home with bad news. But then I quickly remember Rav and the date and his 'Why are you single?' question, and I shudder all the terrible feelings away.

'Oh, Mama, *not* good,' I say, pausing for dramatic effect.

'What happen? What did he do?' She looks around almost as though he's here, as though she's ready to take him head on, and I want to give her a hug. But I've got to dish out my lie first.

'Well.' I take a deep breath. I've decided my lie. I can't tell my mum there was 'no chemistry', and quite frankly she'd love that he has tonnes of property and wants to be a millionaire. So there's only one way out. 'He was drunk when he turned up,' I say disapprovingly, shaking my head for effect.

'Hawww!' Mum's eyes widen in horror.

'Yep.' I nod slowly. 'And he carried on drinking. Two whole pints. That's why I left so early.' I sigh heavily to signal my disappointment.

'Good!' Mum stands up and puts her hand on my shoulder reassuringly. 'You did the right thing. You can't marry a sharabi. They never change. Your masi married a man like that and look at her. He never worked, always asking her for money and shouting.'

I feel bad for besmirching Rav's name, but the alternative would be seeing him again and I can't put myself through that.

'I agree, Mama. Good that he showed his true colours from the beginning.'

266

'Chalo. Doesn't matter. We'll find another boy,' she says, sending a shock wave of dread through me. I know I've been kind of enjoying Mum being involved . . . but after Rav, I'm not sure I can take another date. 'What did you eat? I made beans toast. Left some for you.'

'Nah, I'm OK, Mama, I'm going to bed. I'm really tired.'

But she's already heading for the kitchen.

'OK, OK, I'll eat,' I say, placating her. There's not much Mum's masala beans on toast can't cure.

I'm already drafting the Shit Sandwich text as I wait for the toast to pop up.

'You know, puth, I been thinking,' Mum says, as she puts the plate of beans on toast on the table in front of me. 'It is *good* you are not marrying the first boy you are meeting. Marriage is for life – it is good you are looking for someone just right for you. You deserve happiness.'

I look up at her – and I know she's saying this in the context of Jag being a secret dad, and Rav a drinker, but I can still feel my heartbeat relax for a moment.

# Chapter 31

Mum has been tiptoeing around me for a week since the date with Rav, as though she doesn't want to upset me, as though I'm a fuse ready to blow.

She's never been like that with me – which tells me she can sense something is wrong.

There was an immediate sense of relief after Mum's reaction to the date. But the next day, I could barely move because reality came crashing back.

I'm still living at home, in exactly the same position I was in a year ago. Except now I have friends I can't trust, friends I can't even bear to be around, who are all living the lives they always wanted, and I'm here, forgotten again. And Natalie, the only friend who seems to actually get me, lives miles away. Half the time it feels as though she lives only in my head. I think about Beena, and all the changes she made in her life – but I'm not *brave* like that, and I definitely don't have the right-shaped skull for a crop. I can't imagine packing everything in – sacking off that horrid job with Sharon (even if Dean is a mild drop of comic relief in my life right now) and ditching the dating and the marriage stuff for good. I've been sitting in my room for days – going to work, coming back, forcing myself to be alone. I've been staring at that piece of paper the therapist gave me – it was goading me with its bright, white blankness. But this week, I've managed to cover it in words. Those words that popped up in my head. Words about myself.

I've been ignoring the therapist's emails to make another appointment, and have instead put my faith in YouTube astrologers, trying to make sense of how I've been feeling, and searching for a clue in the stars as to when everything's going to change.

After work today, where Sharon actually left me alone (because I think Dean told her I was 'going through things', though I have no idea how he would know), I just want everything to stop for a bit. Sometimes, I'm ploughing through everything fine and then it hits me.

The train station is deserted tonight; there's not even a guard around. It's almost dark. I make my way to the benches bolted into the ground. I don't remember when I started feeling so tired all the time. Was it before Rav? Before Jag? Or is all this because of them? Because of Charlie, and Elena, and Anj?

I drop heavily onto the bench.

I look around, alone, and it's like I'm suspended, like I'm floating really high up on this platform. And out of nowhere I feel that emptiness bubble up. I'm confronted with a carousel of disappointing dates, all the men I've dated over the years, from the M&M's guy, to Michael, Jag and finally Rav. I think about Charlie's face across the table after the dance rehearsal. The way she looked at me as though she didn't even know who I was. I see my mum, her face full of hope when I come home now. How excited she is when she thinks I'm *actually* talking to her. Letting her in. But, while I'm not lying completely, I still can't tell her the truth. Will I ever be able to tell her the truth?

Half the time I don't know if I'm even being honest with myself, let alone anyone else.

The hollow starts deep in my belly and simmers up slowly yet determinedly to my eyes. I start to cry. Not a solitary tear.

I am no stranger to crying in public; I have shed a quick, silent tear while listening to a sad song, reading about an abandoned dog or once on the top deck of the number 73 bus on my way home when I finished *The Kite Runner*. But today, I can't stop them.

'Sunny, get a grip,' I mutter under my breath, wiping my tears away. I can feel a tightening in my chest. I pull out my period app. I must be due on. That's the only explanation.

My app screams back at me an answer I already know. Nope. I'm a good couple of weeks away from shark week.

I roll through a series of other reasons – could it be a full moon? I swear I always feel out of sorts on a full moon. I open up my astrology app, hidden within folders and folders on my phone, so no one comes across it and ridicules me for believing in astrology. Nope. There are no extraordinary planetary alignments today.

Is it because I'm hungry? I look in the emergency snack pocket of my bag (one of the reasons I love a big bag) and fish out a small packet of slightly melted chocolate-covered raisins, but I can't bring myself to open them. I can feel the tears streaming down my face, eyes screwed up small, so the platform looks bleary.

If it's not my hormones, horoscopes or hunger . . . then that means it must just be me.

I try to regulate my breathing – I imagine my mum's favourite exercise: breathing through one nostril and out the other, and I try it, hoping that focusing on something might help bring me back to myself.

I hear Mum's voice, calming and soft: 'In one, out the other,' over and over again. But it's not helping.

I scroll through my phone aimlessly, all the messages blurring into one. I can see Anj's wedding group, and a sickness fills my stomach. The wedding is just three weeks away now.

When she first got engaged, it seemed forever away. I had so many plans, so many ideas. I'd go there with a guy, even if Anj hadn't given me a plus one. I'd look stunning in an outfit I *wanted* to wear, not one that I had to settle on because of my body.

I wanted to feel glamorous for once, be the fun, flirty Sunny that I am in my daydreams, in my carefree fantasy world. I wanted to be the fun, flirty Sunny Anj and Elena and Charlie always expect me to be. Confident and in control and not jealous at all of her best friend getting married to the love of her life (even if he is a boring banker).

I hover over my chat with Natalie on WhatsApp. I hit the call button next to her name. I steel myself to hear the call tone ring out, to be left with nothing but silence and my own thoughts.

But she picks on the third ring.

'Hiya, babes!' Her voice is bright and cheerful, and instantly I feel a tiny bit lighter.

'Hi, you free for a quick chat?' I try to keep my voice soft and carefree. I don't want to worry her.

'Of course, my darling, I'm just on me way to the tip! Had a massive clear-out of the garage at the weekend and I can't wait to get rid of this shit. Aloysius, get *down*. Sorry, babes, he's just trying to crawl into my lap as per.'

I can imagine chubby little Aloysius trying to clamber over the gear stick into Natalie's lap. He's the only dog I've ever loved. When he was sick last year, I actually got on my knees and prayed that he'd get better.

'I can call back later . . .' I say out of politeness, not really meaning it. I want to talk to her now. I don't want to be left with the silence of the platform.

'No, no, what's going on? You sound down.' Her voice is calm, measured. She's always been the person I turn to. She *gets* it. She has always understood. Where I've needed to say a million things to others, I only need to say a few words to Natalie.

'I can't stop crying,' I say quietly. 'I'm at a train station and I'm just sitting on a bench and I can't stop crying. I don't know what's wrong with me. Something is wrong with me.' I look around. I'm still alone at the station. I'm grateful for the privacy, but I can't help feeling that the rest of the world is going on with its life, while I'm sat here, crying my eyes out on a cold bench.

'Has something happened?'

'No, nothing.'

'Are you due on?'

'Nowhere close.'

'Is it the full moon?' she asks, and I want to hug her for it. I want to hug her for caring about the things I care about.

'No, nowhere close.'

'Oh, babe.' There's a quiver in her voice. 'Is it . . . do you think it could be depression?' she says gently.

I take a deep breath before I reply, thinking about the first therapist and my diagnosis of depression and anxiety – thinking about the words she said, matching up to the feelings I'd felt for so long. My hand reaches into my coat pocket where I feel the piece of paper, folded up, adorned with all the things I hate about myself. The words circle in my mind. 'It doesn't feel like it. I don't know what it feels like.'

'Do you think it might be time to see another therapist? A proper one? Not a bloody medium masquerading as a therapist?! I know you saw someone else too, but . . . maybe it's time to find someone new, if that's not helping?'

'Yeah. Maybe. I dunno.' I sigh. I can't think of anything else to say.

'Look, Sunny, you might not want to think of solutions right now, but there's a great therapist my mate goes to see in

South London. I can get the details off her. Make an appointment as soon as you can.'

'Yeah,' I reply flatly. 'I'm sorry.'

'For what? For being human?' She waits for a reply, but I don't say anything. I can feel tears continuing to fall down my face. A lump rises to my throat, making it hard to speak, hard to breathe. 'Don't be ridiculous! You've got nothing to be sorry for.'

I don't reply. I can't say a word.

'Sunny?'

'Yeah?'

'Let's make a plan to meet up soon, yeah? I miss you. And I think a change of scene might be good for you.'

'I miss you too,' I reply, barely able to form the words through the silence that fills my mind. 'Look, I've got to go, my train's here. But thanks, OK?'

'Are you sure?' I can hear worry pierce Natalie's words. 'I can chat for a bit longer – I've just parked up.'

'No, no, it's OK. You're at the tip.'

'I've always got time for you,' she says softly.

'I know. I'll call you later, OK?'

'OK. Love you,' she says, and I press the red button to end the call, because I can't say anything back.

I put my phone in my pocket. For a moment, I think about messaging Beena again, wondering if she might understand. She felt like a kindred spirit, someone who has been where I've been. But I don't. I don't want her to have to feel like she needs to be there for me, when really she doesn't know me at all. And yet that conversation in McDonald's was more uplifting than any time I've spent with Anj, Charlie and Elena in the last few years. But I can't call her *now* . . . Imagine, calling her now, with tears streaming down my face. She'd run a mile. Wouldn't she?

I stare out at the platform as a train approaches and passengers pile out of the doors, with only one or two people jumping on. They wander past me, as though I'm not even here, as though I'm completely invisible.

I want to be at home. I want to be on my own. But I don't want my mum to worry about me. I don't want her to ask questions. So I just sit, and I stare. Waiting for a change. Waiting for something to change.

# Chapter 32

'Sunny?' Mum knocks on the bathroom door. 'Sunny?'

I ignore her. I'm in the shower. The world feels distorted, unreal, hard to understand. I'm standing here with tears rolling down my cheeks. It's been like this every day. It's been like this for weeks.

I keep telling myself I'm fine. I always get like this, don't I? And then it always gets better. I cheer up. I laugh about my shit dates with my friends. I laugh with my friends about living with my parents.

I'll just laugh about it all.

'Sunny, shall I make you a cup of cha before work?' Mum calls, louder this time, but I still don't respond. 'I am going to have some. Come and sit with me, heh?'

I've never known my mum to be this persistent – usually she'd just tut and walk away if I don't respond – but as she reminds me about work, I realise with a sickening clarity that I can't face it today. It's taking all my energy to stand under the shower rather than to slump into a ball in the corner, letting the water beat down on top of me.

'Puth?' Mum is waiting outside the bathroom when I come out in my towel, and I nearly scream. For a second, I'm worried she's going to spot my tattoo, before realising it's completely covered. I make eye contact with her. She's not scrutinising my body, but still, she hasn't seen me in a towel since I was a child, so I rush straight to my room, feeling energy fill my legs for the first time in forever.

'Mum! I'm fine,' I reply, not feeling fine at all, wondering if she can hear the lie cracking my voice. 'Just a bit of a headache, OK?'

'I'm making cha, puth,' she says. 'Come have some before you go. Or tell work you are sick. You working hard. They will be OK for one day.' I think I'm one sick day away from being called into the office for another 'serious chat' with Herr Sharon.

As she wanders down the stairs she says, 'Sometimes I have a headache too. You need to rest when you have a headache.' Her voice is soft, as though she means something else entirely. As though she knows that when I say 'headache' I don't mean a headache at all.

I sit on the bed in my towel and get under the covers. I can't face work, but I can't face staying at home either, with Mum hovering over me, asking what's wrong, offering me food, trying to get me to open up.

I text Dean:

*I've got a migraine – can you tell Sharon?? Can't face calling her up.*

When I'm fully dressed, I head downstairs, trying to hold myself up as straight as possible so as not to attract any more attention. I look fine. I look like Sunny, don't I?

'I'm going to work, Mama,' I say. She's sitting at the kitchen table with a cup of cha for her, and a cup of cha for me. She looks at me, gestures towards the mug, nodding at me to sit down.

'If you are not well, don't go in. This will make you feel better,' she says, meaning the cup of cha, meaning the chat with her. But right now I can't think of anything worse. I can't face talking to Mum, telling her I'm OK, that everything is fine.

'No, Mama, I'm OK. I feel better after my shower. I've got to go to work – so much to do.' I grab myself a cereal bar, wave it at her, hoping she'll be satisfied that this means I'm eating.

'OK,' she nods. 'I make sure your dad is OK then.' She tries to hide the disappointment in her face that we won't be spending the whole day together, drinking cha, watching the Sikh channel, and a nub of guilt grates at my temple.

As I'm putting on my shoes, my mum shuffles past me and heads into the garage. When I'm outside, I see she's taking her usual spot as dad's supervisor, while he does his annual clearout of the garage. Mum is already muttering darkly about his beloved jars full of rusty nails. They both wave goodbye as I head past them, now mid-argument about whether we need to keep the lawnmower even though there is no lawn any more. Something tells me Mum will win this round too. But this time, I can feel Mum's eyes linger on me longer than usual.

I walk at normal speed until I get around the corner, when I slow down. I'm not going to work, not today. I'm not going back home. But now, I have nowhere to go. All my friends are at work. I could go into London but that would cost me money I don't have.

If I turn back now, Mum will realise I've lied to her, and I can't face that. Or I'll have to tell her the truth about how I'm feeling. And I can't face that either.

I walk towards the town centre, wandering aimlessly until I find myself outside the gurdwara. I haven't been since Diwali and, as it's mid-morning, it seems like a safe time to go unnoticed. I cover my head with my scarf as I enter the gate and push the heavy wooden door open. I crouch down, putting my hand on the cold marble floor, before touching my hand to my forehead.

As I take my shoes off and wash my hands, I look around nervously. It's empty. I fish out a pound coin from my purse, the reassuring hush soothing my nerves.

As I make my way up the cold marble steps, I still don't see anyone else. I pause at the entrance of the diwan hall, placing my bag on the ladies' side of the hall, scanning the room to see if any of Mum's friends are around. Only a handful people sit cross-legged at the sides of the high-ceilinged room, some with their heads bowed, as the giani recites from the Guru Granth Sahib, his voice a low, resonant hum that fills the otherwise silent room.

I walk quickly down the aisle, my feet sinking into the plush royal-blue carpet. I feel self-conscious; I feel like I'm being watched. I stand for a few seconds in front of the Guru Granth Sahib, never knowing what to pray for, feeling guilty that I only come here when I *want* something.

My mind goes blank for a second and then I remember that piece of paper with all the words I think about myself scrawled all over it.

As the words obscure my mind, I recite slowly, silently, '*Please, please, please, God, I'm so unhappy,*' as I bow down, my knees creaking loudly. I deposit a pound coin into the golak and bow my head, touching my forehead to the carpeted floor briefly. I lever myself up before scurrying to the back of the hall, sitting down with a thump and leaning back against the cool wall.

When my heart rate slows after a few minutes and I realise that no one is paying any attention to me, no one is watching, I feel my body soften, my muscles relax, and I take a few slow breaths. I allow the giani's words to flow over my thoughts. With a start, I recognise a couplet that my bibi used to recite every morning. I mouth the words alongside the giani and find myself crying once more, letting the tears fall, doing all I can to keep my breathing even. Not a single ladylike tear but hot streams, and an intense, all-consuming ache that feels like my ribcage being torn in two.

I bow my head.

A couple of older women pass me, dressed in identical cream salwar kameez and chunnis, muttering to each other about having langar. My stomach growls in response but I decide to go without in case I bump into anyone I know.

As everyone files out to langar, I sneak out of the doors. I wander down to the river to walk through the gardens, where I hung out during my summers as a teenager and tried my first bong during my emo phase. There's now an outdoor gym and a new play area. It's empty apart from a few clusters of elderly Sikh men. All in their uniform of checked shirts, gilets and turbans. Some of them are slowly ambling along the path around the small lake and others have commandeered the benches. Their loud debates about politics both here and in India make me smile despite myself; so calming, so familiar.

I find a message from Beena on my phone:

*I'm still fuming about those girls from your dance rehearsal!! How have you been? Shall we catch up before the wedding? We could go there together??*

I want to reply, but the thought of going to the wedding at all, even with Beena, makes me feel sick.

And then a new one from Dean:

*Have told Sharon ur off sick today – apparently she's thinking of banning KFC Fridays – is that even legal??? Shall we speak to our union rep?? I reckon she just wants u and me to suffer. I knew she hated us ... Maybe we could sack off this job and work somewhere else? I'm so done with Sharon. How u doing, matey?*

An offhand comment full of kindness like 'How u doing, matey?' from someone I used to think had the emotional understanding of a cucumber is enough to tip me over the edge. I stuff my phone into my pocket and buy myself a strong tea in a polystyrene cup from the rundown café at the edge of the lake instead. I add three sugars to warm me up and settle down on a bench to look out onto the murky Thames. I take a photo and think for a second about posting it online, on

Instagram, but the thought of Sharon seeing it, or Anj or the other girls, makes me pause. I send it to Natalie.

*Couldn't face going into work. So sick of feeling shit. How are you? xx*

She replies instantly:

*Come up to Sheffield. You sound so fed up and me and Aloysius would love to see you!! Do you good to have some time away xxx love you heaps, pal xx PS. You can finally ride around in my ridiculous convertible!!*

I know she's right. I want to be anywhere but here, so, on the spot, I make the first proper decision I've made in a while. And, with Beena's words of wisdom in my head, it's a decision I'm making for me: I look up the trains on my phone for that week right away.

But the tickets are extortionate. It's cheaper to go to Marbella than get the train to Sheffield. The National Express it is. I book the tickets on the spot.

When I get home, Mum's ears prick up as soon as she sees me, like she's waiting for something.

'Mum, I'm going on a work trip this weekend,' I say immediately, because it's easier than telling her I need to get away for my own sanity. That sometimes being here at home feels claustrophobic. That if I stay in the house a minute longer, I'm going to lose my mind.

I watch as her eyebrows furrow, and she observes my face closely, as though asking my face what the truth really is. But she doesn't say anything. She simply nods. And for that moment, I want to thank her. I want to hug her for not asking anything else. But I don't. I just head upstairs and start shoving some things into a bag.

Later, as I go downstairs to make dinner, I overhear her talking to Dad. Even though I can't make out everything they're saying, I'm familiar with the tone of their voices. It's the same hushed tones they used when they were worried about me going to uni and living away from home for the first time. The same hushed tones they used when I was at school, worried to walk home on my own. I crouch down on the top stair to hear them better.

'. . . Sleeping too much . . . headaches all the time.'

My dad just 'hmmms' in agreement.

'She doesn't talk to me . . . stressed . . . always quiet. It's like someone has done black magic. I never see her smile . . .'

*'Hmmm,'* Dad responds.

'What can I do? All her friends are settling down. I worry – you know how I worry. Who's going to look after her when we are gone?'

I don't want to hear any more, so I charge down the stairs, stomping on each step as loudly as I can, clearing my throat on the way down.

Immediately, my mum stops talking. She turns up the volume on the Sikh channel.

# Chapter 33

The thought of seeing Natalie has already lightened everything, just a bit. Knowing that for a few days Mum and Dad aren't going to be walking on eggshells around me, knowing Mum won't be standing outside the bathroom door every time I shower, as though waiting for me to self-combust, or asking me questions twenty-four-seven – it has all helped me breathe a little bit more easily.

Natalie will want to do outdoorsy stuff, so I've packed accordingly – even though Nat knows me well enough not to suggest Big Nature™. I love the idea but hate the lack of facilities and the reality of it.

I always forget how far Victoria Coach Station is from the train station, and by the time I get there I'm all sweaty and uncomfortable and I'm wearing the kind of knickers that feel lovely against your skin but travel down your arse the second you put them on.

I hurriedly suck on two chalky travel-sickness tablets as I wait in the queue. A surly-looking man in a hi-vis jacket with a no-nonsense air about him is checking tickets. The queue is formed of mainly older Indian people and young European students with backpacks the same size as them, all dressed in oversized puffer jackets. I bury my nose in my scarf in a vain attempt to block out the coach fumes, which are already turning my stomach.

'Hiya!' I say cheerily to the ticket inspector/driver as I show him my ticket on my phone.

'Luggage?' he replies, in a gruff Yorkshire accent, not looking at me.

'Nope.' I tap the bag I'm carrying.

He waves me onto the coach without a word. I thought all Northerners were supposed to be friendly.

I settle into a window seat, desperately hoping no one chooses to sit next to me. As we set off I mutter, 'Waheguru,' under my breath three times. Force of habit. Any time we leave the house my mum says it. You never know what might happen on the way; it's to protect you from harm, she would say. I used to roll my eyes at her, but I've always done it. And seeing as I'm on a rickety old coach and the driver has already applied the emergency brakes twice even though we've not yet left the bus station, I'm going to need some divine protection in order to arrive in the North in one piece.

For a second, I think about Mum, sitting at the kitchen table with the two cups of cha. What would she have said if I'd told her how I was feeling? Would it have convinced her that I was cursed by black magic? Would she have told me to eat something, something to make it all better, before telling me to go on a diet? Or would she have listened?

We leave London and make our way onto the motorway. Every time the coach takes a corner, the toilet door flies open and the smell of human waste floods the air and mixes with the stench of stale body odour and peach air freshener. In that instant, I decide it's worth going deeper into my overdraft and book a train ticket for my return.

I take my eye mask out and wrap my scarf around my head so I can lean against it as a pillow and as protection from the smeared, scratched window, which doesn't look like it's ever been cleaned. I put my rucksack next to me and wind one of the straps around my arm; you can take the girl out of the Sanghera household ...

⋆  ⋆  ⋆

When I wake up, the landscape has changed. It's raining but greener and my shoulders have definitely dropped since I left Victoria. The further North we travel, the lighter my heart feels.

The coach lurches into the bus station in the middle of Sheffield town centre. And I crane my neck to see if I can spot Natalie, but the station is deserted.

As I disembark from the coach (getting ignored by the coach driver this time), I see Natalie careering around the corner, her arms outstretched in a canary-yellow raincoat, cheeks flushed and mouth open in the most joyful screech.

'BAAAAAAAABES!!!'

I squeal loudly, not caring about who is around, and half run to meet her, only vaguely sensing the disapproval of strangers but for once not caring. We squeal and hug for the longest time, pretty much Catherine-wheeling across the pavement. A woman tuts loudly as she goes past and I raise my eyebrows at her as Natalie says, 'Joyless fucker,' a bit too loudly. 'Jacket potato, pal?!' she says, threading her arm in mine.

I've not seen her in so long, I forgot how much energy she has – how *infectious* that energy is.

'Always.'

We cackle our way to a café that looks like a used tyre shop from the outside but is clean and homely on the inside.

A middle-aged waitress comes over with our giant jacket potatoes loaded with cheese and baked beans, with nothing more than a rumour of a side salad.

'Here you are, love.' She pats Natalie on the shoulder.

'Cheers, Tina, looks lovely!'

I have never known anyone so consistently enthusiastic as Natalie.

We eat in silence for a few moments until Natalie puts down her fork, leans back in her chair and looks at me. I hold my breath.

'So how are you? Really, I mean.'

'I'm OK.'

She looks at me with a half-smile until my resolve crumbles.

'OK, I'm not,' I confess.

'Come on then, let's have it.'

There's so much I need to tell her. There's so much she's missed.

'I don't know where to start.'

'Maybe start with that bellend Michael?' She smiles wryly.

'Yeah, so, that's a no-go. He's barely been in touch since we . . . you know . . .' I trail off, aware of the noisy family that have just plonked themselves next to us. Their boisterous toddler shouts, 'NO!' as he's wrestled into a high chair.

'Yeah . . . then there's the whole friends saga.' I'm afraid if I start talking about the girls, I'll start crying, and I don't want to make a scene in Natalie's local café.

But it's too late. A lonely, fat tear rolls down my cheek.

'I'm sorry,' I say, brushing it away angrily.

'Don't you bloody dare apologise. You've been mates for years with those girls, and you've been such a good friend to them. You're allowed to be upset.' She reaches over the table and squeezes my hand reassuringly. And then it all comes out: the spa weekend, the hen do, the dance rehearsal. And all the dates – Jag, in particular.

By the time I finish, we've polished off our jacket potatoes and we're finishing our second round of strong tea and I'm feeling stiff from sitting down for so long. My head feels heavy, but something inside me feels lighter. Just slightly. Barely noticeable.

As we leave the café in a flurry of goodbyes, Natalie turns to me suddenly and hugs me tightly. 'Look, let's get you to mine. But, Sunny,' Natalie looks at me, 'I'm so fucking proud of you. For standing up for yourself. In front of those girls.'

Despite the biting cold and the breeze, we drive to Natalie's house, top down, our hair plastered across our faces, Arctic Monkeys on full blast. Natalie's place is a curious tower-like, two-bedroom house atop one of Sheffield's many inclines. I stop outside her front door, savouring the clean, sharp air, breathing it in deeply.

As soon as Natalie opens the door, Aloysius runs to greet us, his tail wagging, and his steel-coloured coat and ridiculous old-man face and eyebrows make me laugh. I crouch down and pet him as he puts his paws on my thighs. His rough tongue licks my hands.

Natalie clips on his bright-teal lead and we walk across the road to the park to digest our carb feast and stretch our legs.

When we get home, we're both exhausted – Aloysius has more energy than I remembered and had us chasing him around the park, while we both screamed with glee, trying to keep up. As we slump on the sofa with yet another cup of tea, Natalie turns to me and says: 'Show me a pic of what you're wearing to the wedding!'

I groan immediately, knowing she'd ask this – she's obsessed with how ostentatious Anj's wedding is, and I half wish I could take her as my plus one just so she could see it all in real life.

'I think probably this.' I show her a picture of it on my phone – the outfit hanging up on the back of my door.

'That is *gorgeous*! The colour is going to look beautiful on you,' she says, and I can tell she means it. 'You're going to be beating them off with a shitty stick, babe!'

'I'm going to look ridiculous compared to the others!'

'Sunny.' Nat looks at me then, her eyes sharp. 'I know you've always struggled with this stuff, but you've got to let yourself see you how you see your friends, with the same kindness you look at me with, you know?'

'Nat!' I snap softly. I can't look at her for a second, and stare at the photo of my outfit – the only outfit that fits me, with Mum telling me it was too tight here, too loose here. I look at the photo and try to imagine myself, just as I am, looking and feeling beautiful. But I can't.

The next day, after a leisurely breakfast of poached eggs and avocado on toast, we visit a local National Trust property. It's a clear, bright day and when we jump in the convertible, Aloysius promptly falls asleep in my lap. I balk at the £16 entrance fee to walk around a rich old dead person's garden, and for that I don't even get to see the inside of the house. I don't want to pick up an information leaflet because chances are it is built on the shoulders of slavery or at the very least colonialism, and it will just make me angry.

As we stroll around the manicured gardens, the open air and greenery is like a balm. Natalie and I take a ton of silly selfies and I take lots of short videos to remind myself of this day, so I can watch them back whenever I need cheering up.

'So, I've started seeing someone,' Natalie says, her eyes looking straight ahead. For a second, I realise she's worried about upsetting me. 'It's early days, though, so who even knows?' She shrugs, and I can tell she means it. She's the kind of person who is so unattached to outcomes, whereas everything feels like life or death to me.

It's one of the things I really envy about her: she's not scared of anything, not even death . . . Though she is terrified of flying, mainly because of her 'poo worries', aka stress-related IBS.

'Tell me more,' I nudge. I want her to tell me; I want her to feel she can.

He's a yoga teacher. It's all casual at the moment, apparently.

'I cosmically ordered him,' she says breezily as if she had ordered a Domino's. 'I asked for a tall, good-looking spiritual type with one foot in the real world, who likes travelling and playing sports, and here he is!'

Their first date went on for hours; it was spontaneous and incredibly fun. I watch her face light up when she talks about him, and I wonder if he's The One.

She won't have asked herself that question yet.

I search my heart for jealousy and I can't find any.

But there is a small ache, just under my solar plexus; a long-ing that I wish I could extinguish by wishing it away.

When we've already moved on to other topics, Nat leaves me with Aloysius while she goes to the loo – although my mind is still on Nat, manifesting her perfect guy. And as I hold Aloysius's lead in one hand, attracting attention from all direc-tions, I look around at the families, the couples. This could be my life. If I wanted it, it could be my life too.

I feel a little flicker of something. Desire? Hope? But it disappears just as quickly as it arrives.

'Hey,' Nat says, watching me daydreaming as she returns from the loo, Aloysius already jumping up to greet her. 'Fancy going to that caff again? They do the best pies.'

'Pie sounds perfect,' I reply, and Aloysius jumps up in agreement.

I board the train the next day with a lighter heart, a picnic hurriedly purchased from the tiny M&S in the station and elevated levels of oxytocin from a whole two days of laughter, hugs and Aloysius cuddles. And the warm glow that only comes from knowing that someone else loves you for who you are, flaws and all.

As I settle into the quiet carriage and spread out my wares, my phone vibrates.

It's Beena.

I feel my cheeks lift, my mouth forming a smile once more:

*Hi, doll! How was your weekend in God's own country?! Can't wait to see you at the wedding! Let me know what time you're getting there and we can meet up beforehand, so you don't have to walk in by yourself! If you don't want to go home after, you're more than welcome to crash at mine too! Xx*

And for a moment, I'm not worried about the wedding at all. It feels like a relief. That piece of paper, with all the words that I hate about myself on it, has never been further from my mind.

# Chapter 34

'OK, smile!' Mum has me up against the living-room wall and is insisting on taking dozens of photos of me in my outfit for the wedding.

As soon as I got back from Nat's the other day, I could sense her checking me over, as if to see if I was still in one piece, but she hasn't said anything. She's been overly excited, overly chatty with me too. I don't know if she's trying to distract herself from it all, or if she's trying to distract me.

But here she is, beaming at me as though it's my first day of school, unable to get used to how to take proper photos on her newer, bigger phone. I haven't let her take photos of me since I was in my early twenties in case they ended up in the hands of a matchmaker, but here I stand, stiffly, sucking in my belly in the living room, trying to hold onto Nat's encouraging words of: 'You're going to be beating them off with a shitty stick, babe!' while Mum tries to figure out how to turn the flash off.

'Very nice. I'm going to send to Shindo.' She taps slowly on her phone until I finally lose patience with her and end up sending a photo of myself to Shindo, the Yoga Ladies WhatsApp group and my masi in America.

'Ready, Sunny?' Dad pops his head around the living-room door, noticing my outfit for the first time. 'Looking very nice, puth!'

'Thanks, Dad.' I feel my face blush; Dad never compliments me.

'Come on, let's get a photo together!' Dad exclaims, in a rare show of enthusiasm.

What on earth is going on? It feels like I've stepped into an alternate reality for a bit. Apart from my birthday and maybe Christmas, we just don't *do* photos; we're not a photo-taking type of family.

'I'm wearing my house clothes,' Mum complains immediately.

'Doesn't matter, come on!'

'Mama, you look fine – get in, I'm going to be late!'

They awkwardly shuffle themselves behind me.

'OK, smile,' Dad says through gritted teeth, his smile already on his face. 'I'm going to take a few.'

They do their usual tight-lipped smiles. Mum believes there's something vulgar about doing a big, toothy grin in photos. God knows why. She looks like a Victorian headmistress in every selfie.

'Very nice – send me on WhatsApp,' she demands, like she's concluding a business transaction.

'Yes, yes, I'll do it in the car. OK, bye, Mama!' If I don't leave now, I'm going to miss the train and I don't want to keep Beena waiting.

'Take a jacket – you'll get cold later,' she warns, already settling in on the sofa, TV remote in hand. I sense one eye and ear on me, as though she's watching the TV but really taking note of my every move.

'I'll be fine!' I shout from the hallway, grabbing my bag and checking my teeth in the hallway mirror. I quickly snap a selfie to Beena, who snaps one back, commenting, *YOU LOOK AMAZING!! LET'S DO THIS*. Even her selfie is full of energy, and I immediately feel like I *can* do this.

It's a beautiful day, the sun is shining and there's not a cloud in the sky. The perfect day for a wedding. The perfect day to face all the things I've been dreading for months.

I walk carefully along the well-manicured path lined with plump red and pink tulips to the sizeable lawn, where a collection of brightly clad guests are congregating in small groups. A fleet of smartly dressed servers glide between the groups with shiny copper trays laden with drinks. A couple of shrieking toddlers lurch into a flowerbed and are rescued by their respective parents, who already look exhausted. I slow down purposefully so I can scan the surroundings, firstly to see if I'm the fattest one here, and to see if I can spot the girls, so I can avoid them, of course.

I spot a fellow fatty and feel initially reassured, until she turns sideways and I see she's pregnant.

Great.

I suck in my stomach a bit more. I think about Mum's suggestion of shapewear and start to regret my decision not to wear it – but I catch myself before my mind jumps to that white piece of paper with all the words on it again. There's a reason I don't wear that crap any more, because it was *fucking* uncomfortable. And the last thing I really want today is to feel uncomfortable *and* out of place ... When I got off the train at Waterloo, I had a voice note from a stressed-sounding Beena: 'Sunny, I'm so sorry, I'm running late – my boiler just started leaking ... Will be there as soon as I can! No need to wait for me, but also definitely wait for me if you prefer!' I was half tempted to kill some time in Costa so I wouldn't have to arrive on my own, and I'd be lying if I said I hadn't spent most of the week thinking about just turning up for the reception, doing the dance and leaving. But that would be unfair on Anj. While I can't see our relationship ever being the same again, I don't want to upset her. It's her wedding day, and no matter what's gone on between us, and me and the other girls, I want her to have the day she dreamed of.

So, with no Beena here, I have to face the girls alone. Even though I'd rather staple my tits to a wall than be here, I'm going to be the bigger person (quite literally) and play nice.

Then I spot Charlie in a midriff-baring silver-grey lehenga, one of Chandni's cast-offs, no doubt, standing with Elena, who looks regal in a pastel-pink sari with a yellowy-gold border. That one is *definitely not* a cast-off and most likely she got it specially made for the occasion.

I take a breath, stride over to them, looking braver than I feel, grateful that my block heel is preventing me from sinking into the grass, grateful that my make-up isn't sliding off my face, thanks to the drag-queen make-up tips I got off YouTube. I'm that new girl in primary school, walking up to the popular girls to ask if I can be their friend.

I'm right beside them before they notice me.

'Hi.' My voice sounds strange and my tone more formal than I was going for. They turn and look at me, startled, and then Charlie stares at the ground.

'Hi, how are you?' Elena murmurs, polite but cold.

'You guys look *great*.' I can hear how forced my enthusiasm sounds; my voice is higher than normal, as if I'm talking to a distant acquaintance rather than the group of women I've shared my life with for over ten years.

'Thanks, so do you.' Charlie manages to look at me briefly before pointedly looking away again. It's *literally* like we're back at primary school.

'You look lovely,' Elena says. 'You should wear that kind of thing more often!' *Where?* I think to myself. *To fucking ALDI?* But I pull a smile onto my face – at least, unlike Charlie, Elena is trying to make an effort.

'How's Anj? Have you seen her?'

'Yeah, we saw her briefly. She's OK – really nervous, understandably . . .'

'Where is she? I should say hi!' For the first time, I realise how weird it is to be asking where Anj is on her wedding day. I used to imagine I'd be the friend with her when she was getting ready, helping her sister and her mum. But here I am, arriving as a guest, with no idea where she is.

'Chandni said no more visitors now – there's already too many people in there,' Charlie says flatly.

I nod, stung by her tone. At a loss for words, I look around at the other guests, aware of the sweat prickling on my forehead and my upper lip.

'Oh my God, you guys! You look amazing!' A heavily made-up woman who I vaguely remember from the hen do descends upon Charlie, who obliges her by spinning in a circle so her heavy skirt flares out.

'I feel like I'm in a Bollywood film,' she declares loudly, twisting her wrist and screwing in an imaginary light bulb. I cringe and turn away, rolling my eyes, but not before I note the look of alarm on Elena's face.

Charlie's long-term boyfriend John is suddenly standing next to her, his pink scalp shining through his pale-blond hair, making him look older than his thirty-five years.

'I'm afraid there's no booze until the religious bit is over with— Oh, hello, Sunny!' I never thought I'd be so happy to see Boring John and his receding hairline.

'Hi, John! How are you?' My voice is loud with relief, but I try to keep my smile moderate, remembering Charlie's words at the spa weekend about me flirting with their boyfriends. I know it's all a lie, but I don't want to give them any more ammunition. I don't want them to feel like they're right. He hands them each two tumblers of pink liquid, full to the brim with crushed ice. 'Sorry, I didn't know . . . I didn't get you one. I can go—' he stammers, looking nervously at Charlie for reassurance.

'No, no. I'll go grab one now. Lovely to see you. I'll . . . catch you later,' I say cheerily, backing away casually. I head off, purposefully keeping my head up, taking long, confident strides. They'll all be watching me as I walk away. I can practically feel their eyes on me as they wait to start discussing me.

I grab a cloudy-looking drink that is more foliage than liquid from a passing waiter and make my way to a bench half hidden by some sort of trailing vine. Praying it's not covered in insects, I perch on the edge, thankful for the shade.

I scan the lawn for any single men. All in all, it's a good-looking selection of guests, but that might be because they're wearing suits. I once said to an ex that men should always be dressed in a suit and he had the *audacity* to say they were too uncomfortable, while I sat opposite him in copycat Spanx, a bra that was threatening to stab me in the armpit and heels that were burning the balls of my feet.

I watch a tall, willowy woman being rescued by her husband as her pointy heel sinks into the soft ground and I try to imagine what it would be like to have a plus one at a wedding. I conjure up an image of Michael in an expensive suit, his arm resting protectively around my waist, sipping on a mocktail. But as I try to settle into the idea of it, shutting off my feelings, shutting off my hurt, I realise I can't actually picture his whole face. It's like I'm looking at him without my contacts in.

'Sunny!' I look up to see Beena walking towards me in a mustard floor-length floral skirt and matching off-the-shoulder top. Her ornate golden bangles jangle as she waves at me; she looks like the sun itself. I can't help but stand up and throw my arms out.

'You look amazing!' I say loudly, beaming, vaguely aware of people turning to look at us. I wonder if Elena or Charlie can see me.

'So do you! Green is *definitely* your colour!' She hugs me tightly and I feel my shoulders drop slightly. 'Have you been in?'

'Yeah, saw Charlie and Elena,' I say softly.

'How was it?' Beena looks at me as though she's trying to read my mind. Her expression is gentle and kind.

'You know,' I say, slowly at first, 'it was fine.' Beena nods. 'But I did it, I spoke to them. And I feel relieved.'

'Good,' Beena replies. 'Proud of you!'

I follow Beena into the hall, and the room is beautifully decorated with cream flower arrangements and fabric-covered plastic chairs. The tall, square mandap is dressed in swathes of translucent ivory fabric, with a backdrop of flowers; garlands of white and pink flowers are framing the entrance, and a harpist is seated to one side, serenely strumming an old Bollywood classic. Beena grabs me by the arm and leads me straight to the back of the room.

'This way we can make a quick getaway if we need to,' she mutters, giving me a cheeky wink.

I spot Charlie and Elena taking pouting selfies in their seats. I'm half wishing I was there doing the same. But then I catch myself, remembering how they'd only ever post the ones they looked good in, regardless of how I looked.

Ajay looks handsome, if a little nervous, walking down the aisle in his peach turban and cream sherwani. Both sets of parents are already by the mandap, looking impossibly glamorous and way too young to have three adult children. Anj's mum has forgone her usual sharp, tailored suits and is looking imposing in a blush-pink sari the exact shade of Anj's dad's turban. Anj's dad looks like he could crumble with emotion at any moment and is thankfully being comforted by a jolly-looking priest.

And there's Chandni. I can't lie – seeing her almost makes my blood boil. She's standing with her husband, Manoj, at the front, no doubt micromanaging everyone from her seated position.

Anj's little cousin toddles in, shyly scattering flowers, dressed in an ivory-and-gold taffeta lehenga, which she almost trips over. A collective, '*Awww,*' goes up from the guests and she runs towards her mum, who walks with her the rest of the way. The harpist smoothly switches from Bollywood to Pachelbel's Canon in D Major. The only reason I know this is because it's one of the music choices on my secret Pinterest board. It's also not very Anj, so this must be Chandni's doing.

Everyone's eyes are on Anj as she is walked down the aisle by her older brother – the one we all had a crush on at uni – wearing her mum's blood-red wedding sari, which she has since had customised. My mum would *never* let me re-use her wedding sari, no matter how overjoyed she was at me finally getting married, because she'd declare that 'people will say you can't afford a new outfit!' But then again, my mum got married in a very simple pink cotton salwar kameez, which she ended up throwing out years ago after she burnt it with the iron . . . But I used to love looking at her wedding photos, even if it was simple and nothing like Anj's or, I presume, her mum's lavish wedding affair.

Anj looks beautiful, though. She's like all the Disney princesses rolled into one, with her make-up and elegant low bun. I feel tears prick my eyes. I always cry at weddings – even when I don't know whether I want to, or can, be friends with the bride any more.

The short, tubby priest starts chanting in a low monotone over the fire. I can't quite see him from where I'm sitting, but nevertheless I'm hypnotised by the ritual of it all.

Most of the guests are now chatting among themselves, but I've got my eyes firmly fixed on everything that's going on. On my best friend – or at least the woman who used to be my best friend – getting married to the love of her life. Ajay. The tears that have been threatening to fall since Anj made her entrance roll down my cheeks as they place garlands around each other's necks and, unexpectedly, the guests erupt into boisterous applause. I look over at Beena, who is sniffing into a crumpled tissue. She catches my eye and smiles.

'Hay fever,' she says with a little laugh and a shrug.

After several more hours of photos and more rituals, the guests line the aisle as the newlyweds walk up hand in hand, the relief and joy evident on Anj's face as she nods and smiles shyly at the guests, before being pulled into overfamiliar hugs by aunties she's probably only met once. As she approaches me, I try to catch her eye, but she doesn't see me. She's already walking past.

I don't let the smile on my face falter. As I watch her continue down the aisle, her back to me, I beam more brightly. She's the first one of us to get married.

But then, there's no 'us' any more, is there?

There's gridlock to leave the room and I overhear Charlie and Elena behind us talking in hushed tones. I turn around to look at them, my resolve softened by the love in the air.

'I can't believe she's married. Such a beautiful ceremony, don't you think?'

Elena nods in agreement. She looks like she's been crying too.

'Hmmm ... yeah ... well, we didn't really understand it, did we?' She looks to Elena and John for support. 'It wasn't very intimate, was it? It's so formal!'

John nods obediently, then looks at the floor.

'I was balling my eyes out!' sighs Elena, dabbing carefully at her eyes.

'I just didn't know what any of it was supposed to *mean*? Like, with an English wedding, you get the vows and the kiss at the end – that's all the emotional stuff,' Charlie continues stubbornly, her eyes focusing somewhere over my head. I cringe inwardly, hoping no one else can hear her.

I shrug, trying to keep my voice light, trying to make sure my blood doesn't continue to boil. I think about her at the spa weekend, at the dance rehearsal. She knows this upsets me, she knows her dismissal of anything 'not English' makes me angry, so now I can only imagine she's doing it deliberately – isn't she?

'I don't understand Sanskrit either,' I begin, and Charlie looks at me like she doesn't believe me, like every Brown person must 'speak' Sanskrit at home . . . 'But that's why you have a programme with all the meanings written out for you. It's hardly opera,' I say with a smile.

Beena sniggers softly beside me, squeezing my arm in solidarity. I'm so glad she's here.

Before Charlie can reply, the queue shifts and we are face to face with Chandni, looking perfect as always in an elegant deep-blue sari shot through with gold thread, her bump concealed by clever draping. She won't meet my eye, even though I'm looking right at her.

'Right, we need to go to practise the dance. The other girls are already there, waiting for you.' She marches off on perilously high spiky heels. I see a flash of red sole. Of course she's wearing Louboutins. What else? Beena squeezes my arm again and mouths, 'Good luck, you'll smash it!' as I rush to catch up with the others.

\* \* \*

Chandni leads us into a cramped backstage area off the grand dining room. It's full of cardboard boxes and chairs stacked perilously high. Jo and Abi look up as we enter and ignore my cheery hello.

'OK, first positions,' barks Chandni as she cues the song on her phone.

We shuffle into our starting positions, bumping into each other slightly; me in the middle, flanked by Charlie and Elena; Jo and Abi behind me.

'Five, six, seven, eight!'

I have been practising the dance steps daily so now they are second nature. I've never been so dedicated to learning a dance routine since I was about seven, taking part in a school talent competition, terrified of becoming a laughing stock. But today I refuse to look like an idiot in front of hundreds of people – Charlie, Elena and Anj especially – and I'm all too aware that people don't expect fat women to be graceful dancers.

I will show everyone that we can be, and we are.

I can tell the others aren't feeling as confident. It feels like a shift. I sense, rather than see, Jo and Abi bump into each other a few times. Usually they walk into a room without a care in the world, whereas I try to hide myself away from everyone.

Today, I hold myself up higher. I feel proud of myself. I *am* proud of myself.

Chandni circles the room like a ringmaster; I wouldn't be surprised if she's got a whip under that sari. As we dance, the tiny room becomes even hotter and I feel a bead of sweat run down my spine.

'Sunny, pick your feet up,' snaps Chandni, still not looking me in the eye.

'I'm saving my energy for the real thing,' I retort, as I twirl and pop my hip.

But she ignores me. She has already moved on to criticising Jo for being out of time with the spin.

When we're done, Chandni barks at each of us as she stalks out of the room, but I feel her bark it especially loudly at me: 'Don't eat too much. Be ready to go as soon as the first dance is over. I don't want to have to be running around, trying to find you.' Jo is now crying, comforted by Elena, cooing words of encouragement into her ear.

In the dining room, I check the seating chart. All the tables are named after famous Bollywood films. With the biggest sigh of relief, I see that Elena and Charlie are at *Kuch Kuch Hota Hai*, and I'm seated next to Beena at *Dil Chahta Hai*. I don't know who did the seating plan, but if it was Anj, I feel that this was the kindest thing she could have done for me today.

Beena's already chatting away animatedly to one of the couples at our table as I take my seat. The other Indian couple – a distinguished but haughty-looking older pair, the man in a cravat and the woman dressed in a muddy-grey dress – look totally uninterested as they sip their wine. I get the feeling they'd rather be at home listening to some obscure vinyl, eating equally obscure cheese.

I've no doubt my mum would be telling me to scour my dating apps for single men at the party, but I don't need to. Because sitting opposite me is one of the only single men of my age here. Mukesh. I remember him from a house party Ajay threw last year. He looks just as sweaty and startled as he did then. He works in sewage control for Thames Water. And has the personality to match. I hastily pour myself a glass of white wine.

As much as I love the novelty of this elegant affair, I miss the raucous Punjabi wedding receptions of my childhood with non-health-and-safety-compliant smoke machines, a band

*and* a DJ. No heavy damask tablecloths on round tables, just long trestle tables covered in that paper tablecloth that comes in a roll and is ruined by one tiny spill of Five Alive. The only table décor: packets of crisps and KP peanuts thrown haphazardly down the middle of the table. No allocated seating or speeches and certainly *no* fucking dances. The night would end with the adults doing the 'Rail Gaddi' around the church hall before everyone got thrown out by a grumbling old caretaker. And then, depending on the combination of relatives invited and the levels of alcohol consumed, the night would end with a good old-fashioned punch-up in the car park. Happy days.

The starters arrive. Platters of lamb and chicken kebabs drizzled with pale-green mint chutney are on the table, along with paneer tikka dotted with fat wedges of lemons, mini samosas, squat little aloo tikkis and gobi pakora for the vegetarians. My mouth waters at the same time as my stomach turns with worry about the impending dance, Chandni's voice bellowing at me, 'Don't eat too much!'

The one good thing about not sitting with the girls right now is that I don't have to put up with their poorly concealed sneers while they point at the food, asking me to identify it and list all the ingredients, and then watch them poke it around their plate like they've never eaten questionable street meat after a night out, probably made up of animal arseholes and feet.

'You not eating, babe?' Beena is piling her plate high with kebabs.

'Maybe after the dance is over.'

'Sod that, you gotta have something!' She places a few mini samosas and a chicken skewer on my plate, before ladling on a dollop of chutney. 'I hope you're not worrying about that bloody dance,' she asks, chowing down on a pakora.

'I'm *bricking* it!' I say, realising for the first time how true that is. All that confidence I had earlier is gone. 'What if I forget the moves or I fall over and make a dick of myself?' I twist the tablecloth between my fingers.

'Listen, even if you fall over, bang your head and shit yourself, you'd still be better than them over there.' She nods towards the girls' table with the wickedest grin on her face, and I laugh so hard that I snort loudly. It makes the haughty couple turn away from their wine glasses to look at me with disdain for the first time since I sat down.

Which just makes me laugh even harder.

I wonder if Elena and Charlie can see me too.

'OOOOOKKKK, ladies and gentlemen, let's get this party started!' booms the DJ in a faux-American accent. 'Please be upstanding and put your hands together for the bride and groom! Mr and Mrs Vaswani!' We hurriedly get to our feet as two dhol players in matching black turbans walk in, drumming in unison. I spot Charlie at her table dancing to the beat of the dhol, whooping loudly.

Anj and Ajay enter the room to cheers and applause, radiating a happiness that's so infectious I can't help smiling along with them. Anj has changed into a pale-gold lehenga that shimmers as she walks. Ajay is in a snazzy midnight-blue suit, looking much more comfortable than he did in his sherwani and turban. He leads her straight onto the dance floor where the dhol players finish with a flourish and the DJ launches straight into 'How Long Will I Love You' by Ellie Goulding. The lighting changes and there's a spotlight on them as they dance. Ajay looks a little stiff, but Anj smiles at him broadly. I can tell she's nervous from the way she's gripping his shoulder.

As they move around the dance floor, I swallow hard to get rid of the lump that has lodged itself in my throat, threatening to choke me. I'm also desperately trying to ignore the bitterness that's unfurling in my gut, threatening to ruin my mood – the adrenaline and pride I felt after the dance rehearsal. It's sneaking up on me unexpectedly, like a jealous serpent, whispering in my ear.

*You will never have this.*

*This is only for other people.*

*Better people than you.*

When their song ends, Ajay lifts Anj up and spins her while the guests applaud. There's no final kiss, of course – no matter how modern they think they are, their families would never allow it. And that's when the DJ goes straight into a high-energy dance number, some terrible remix of a Bollywood song.

My stomach drops.

It falls so low I feel like it might actually fall out of my arse.

'That's my cue,' I mutter to Beena and I neck the last of my wine.

'Good luck. Remember to breathe! You're gonna smash it. I'll be cheering you on.' She gives my hand a final tight squeeze.

I make my way quickly down the side of the hall. Legs wobbly, heart thudding, the wine uneasy in my stomach.

There's Charlie and Jo already lined up, Elena and Abi on the other side. Elena is marking the dance steps and Abi looks like she's about to throw up.

I know exactly how she feels.

# Chapter 35

*You can do this. You can do this. You can do this.*

Fear floods my veins. But I remember that the very first therapist I saw said fear is the other side of the coin to excitement – she told me that I can *choose* excitement over fear, and as I spot Chandni's face, pinched with displeasure, checking we're all in our right places, I realise the energy zinging through me is telling me that my body is ready. I push the fear down. I can do this.

Then I kick off my shoes, tie my dupatta in a knot across my body and take a deep breath.

'OK, ladies and gentlemen. Up next, boy, have we got a treat lined up for you! The friends of the bride have been practising hard to bring you this number, so please put your hands together for these lovely ladies.'

The opening bars of the song blast out of the giant speakers and I stride onto the dance floor, chin up, remembering Vish's advice never to look at the floor. The guests cheer.

My heart is thudding against my ribcage.

But no one can tell because I'm channelling Beyoncé.

As soon as the beat kicks in, I've forgotten about the others. I have no idea what they're doing. And I don't care.

I am doing this for fat girls everywhere.

To show the fat-shaming aunties. To show Anj, Elena and Charlie. And to show me.

The song passes in a blur. Some of the guests clap along to the beat, some sing along. Out of the corner of my eye, I see two of the girls almost bump into each. But it doesn't put me off.

Every hip pop is sharp, every head turn is in danger of giving me whiplash, every hand gesture is deliberate and fierce.

I am Hema Malini in *Sholay*.

I am Helen in *Caravan*.

I am Aishwarya in *Devdas*.

I am Beyoncé in . . . anything.

I am Sunny.

# Chapter 36

We finish to applause and whoops and whistles, and I smile. I smile like I mean it. The faces in the crowd are a blur. I think of my mum, who has been cheering me on as I practised at home (once I promised to cover up with a chunni), and I wish she could've seen me right now.

Once we've all scurried off the dance floor, I turn to the other girls and we throw our arms around each other.

'We did it! It's over! We were so great!' we all chime in unison.

And suddenly Anj is there too, with tears in her eyes, hugging us all in turn.

It's the first time I've seen her this close all day, and for a second I don't know what to say.

'Congratulations, Anj,' I say. I mean it. I study her heavily made-up face carefully. She looks even more stunning up close, but I know her. I know she's overwhelmed by it all.

Before I can give her any reassurance, before I can remind her to enjoy the day, her mum swoops in out of nowhere and whisks her away, ignoring us all as per usual.

Breathless and giddy with adrenaline as we make our way back to our seats, my shoes swinging in my hand. I'm stopped by aunties and cousins: 'You were brilliant, beta,' they say. 'Such wonderful dancing moves!' One elderly woman pinches my cheek, which makes me feel like I'm eight years old again.

'You were *amazing*, best of the lot!' Beena says, presenting me with a glass of wine, full to the brim. 'The others made the Tin Man look flexible.'

I laugh breathlessly, giddy with relief. My part is done. I can relax now.

'God, that was terrifying! I don't know—'

'Beena! Beta, I didn't know you were here!' Suddenly I'm interrupted, as a plump older Indian woman in an alarmingly low-cut sari blouse and enough gold jewellery to sink a ship places a beringed hand on Beena's shoulder.

'Oh! Hi, Aunty.' Beena stands, letting herself be embraced by the woman, who pats her violently on her back.

'How are you? You are looking well.' She's looking Beena up and down, like she's a horse for sale; I'm half expecting her to check her teeth and hooves. 'Come, say hello to your uncle – he can't walk very far these days, diabetes . . .' She leads her off, one hand firmly around her shouders, the other gripping her upper arm.

Beena stumbles slightly as she turns to look at me, mouthing, 'Help!' but all I can do is mouth, 'Sorry,' back with a sympathetic frown and down most of my wine in one go, grimacing as it hits the back of my throat.

The dance floor is almost at full capacity now with portly aunties and uncles dancing together and younger couples holding sleepy babies and hyperactive toddlers zooming across it. In the middle Anj and Ajay dance, close but not too close – it's still an Indian wedding, after all. I watch as the girls dance over to Anj, forming a circle around her. Charlie is once again screwing in the light bulb, out of time to the music. For a split second, I think Anj might ask where I am, but I just watch as she twirls and throws her hands in the air.

I feel foolish for thinking that anything had changed. Suddenly, once again, I feel exposed, alone. I look around subtly to see if anyone is watching me, sitting on my own, but most of the guests are on the dance floor now. Apart from the mums soothing babies and the granddads nodding off despite the deafening music.

I can't see Beena anywhere, but my eye lands on Mukesh. He's making a beeline for me, unsteady on his feet. I drain my glass of wine, get up and walk in the opposite direction around the edges of the room to the double doors leading to the gardens, hoping he doesn't follow me.

The sun has almost set and there's a pleasant breeze; the sky is painted in candyfloss hues of lilac and pink. There's no one here but me, and I sit myself down at a bench that has seen better days, feeling the breeze ruffle my hair, cooling the sweat on the nape of my neck. The thrum of adrenaline is still coursing through my veins, but that sense of loneliness is dulling its edges. In the silence of the evening, my ears are still ringing with the music.

A group of rowdy potbellied men, pints in hand, walk slowly across the lawn, their ties loosened, foreheads slick with sweat. A little cheer goes up when another man joins them; they greet him with lots of back-slapping and laughter. He's taller than them and a bit younger. I can already tell from the back of his head that he's good-looking. His hair curls slightly where it meets the collar of his shirt. I want him to turn around so I can see his face, but I don't want him to see me sitting here. Alone.

Then he turns to the side and I pre-emptively look away, ready for him to lock his eyes on me. When I look at him again he's staring right at me.

*Well, hello there, sexy mystery man.*

Immediately, as a way to forget that I feel a bit shit again, my mind jumps to fantasy mode – I half imagine him ripping off my salwar kameez right now, the gardens completely deserted, while we indulge in a romantic naked picnic in the middle of the rose beds. There are no thorns, of course, because it's my daydream. Just pure sexiness. As I'm slowly unbuttoning sexy guy's shirt, he's whispering in my ear: *Sunny.*

*Oh, Sunny.*

'Sunny!'

I jump.

Chandni is stomping towards me like a baby buffalo in heels. I look up and the sexy guy is nowhere to be seen, in real life or in my daydream. 'I've been looking everywhere for you!'

'What's up?'

'Anj needs a blister plaster.' She stands in front of me with her arms crossed, not quite deigning to make eye contact. I forgot I was in charge of the bridal emergency kit; my bag is held close to my side.

'What's the magic word?'

'What?'

'Nope. Try again.' I can sense that I'm pushing it, but I don't care.

'Are you for real? Anj is in *actual* pain,' she scoffs, her dislike of me distorting her pretty features.

'I don't doubt that. But would it kill you not to be a total bitch to me for once?' I keep my voice deliberately calm. Her nostrils flare as she stares me down.

'I've always said to Anj that you're a *shit* friend.'

She spits the word at me – it wasn't quite the magic word I was looking for, and it stings. I stare at her in disbelief, my jaw slack with shock. I can feel tears in my eyes.

'You know what, Chandni?' I stand up and take a deep, shuddering breath. 'Fuck you.' I tip out the contents of the bridal kit onto the bench. A nail file clatters to the ground, followed by an avalanche of tampons, plasters and kirby grips. 'Knock yourself out.'

It takes all my energy not to look back as I walk past her and back into the hall. I need to tell Beena about this before I explode. I try to calm myself down, wondering where it all came from, wondering if Chandni and the girls have *finally* broken me.

When I walk in, the servers are already clearing the plates away, and there's some sort of dance-off going on. I spot Beena and one of Ajay's friends battling it out to 'Kala Chashma' while everyone looks on, cheering and clapping. An uncle emerges from the crowd and showers them with a wad of notes as they dance. They're both wearing sunglasses and he's wrapped his tie around his head, Rambo-style. Beena seems to be winning; she's throwing some pretty impressive shapes and looks like she's having the time of her life.

I want to walk up to her. I want to pull her away from the crowd. I want to have a friend, someone, anyone by my side – but everyone has their own group, and I'm forced to swallow my jealousy down as tears threaten to cascade down my face.

I walk as quickly as I can to the bathroom without running.

Thankfully, the plush, spacious bathroom is empty apart from a young woman who is repinning her sari. She looks up at me, startled, as I enter – and I pray she won't ask me for help as I rush into the cubicle furthest away from the door, drop the toilet lid down and sit very still until I hear her leave.

When the door shuts behind her, letting in a second of raucous laughter and booming music from the hall, my shoulders sag. I quickly undo my trousers' drawstring that has been digging into my belly all day. I purposefully tied them too tight – I had nightmares of them coming undone mid-dance – but they've left an angry-looking welt across my stomach.

I touch it and wince and that's when the tears come. Slowly at first, and then I crumple in on myself.

As much as I was dreading this day, I didn't imagine sitting in the toilets, crying. Beena was here. Things are OK with Anj even if they'll never be the same, and at least Elena has been making an effort – though the same can't be said for Charlie. Right now, I feel more than sadness.

Suddenly I'm back in Year 7, crying in the loo because I have no friends. Then I'm fifteen, crying in the toilet because I wasn't invited to someone's sixteenth birthday party.

And here I am. Thirty. Crying in the toilet again.

In my mind I hear Chandni's voice, and then my own, repeating her words over and over.

*You're a shit friend to Anj.*

*Shit friend.*

I see Charlie's anger at the spa weekend. I picture the vision of me they've all been clinging onto: the flirty Sunny, who enjoys getting the attention from their boyfriends. The Sunny who is there to entertain them. The Sunny who can't hold down a boyfriend or get a job she doesn't hate. I feel my heart crumble.

And then I see Mum's face – Mum's hope and her disappointment when I've been coming home alone, despondent, after the dates.

They've been talking about me, Elena, Anj and Charlie, and not just recently with all the arguments, but for longer than that. How long have they been talking about me behind my back?

I'm sobbing uncontrollably now, and I can't catch my breath – big, wheezing sobs, like a toddler having a tantrum. I'm thirty, but I'm crying like a child.

My neck is wet from the tears. I let them flow down on my face and splash onto my kameez, until finally the great, wracking sobs turn into whimpers, and I lean my head against the cubicle wall and close my eyes, too drained to sit upright any more.

They will watch the wedding DVD, Anj and Ajay. Maybe once a year on their anniversary. And they will see me, smiling and dancing away, lip-syncing my heart out. What will they say about me? When they show their kids years later, what will they tell them?

'Who's that, Mummy?'

'That's Sunny. She used to be Mummy's friend.'

'Where is she now, Mummy?'

'I don't know, poppet, we don't talk any more.'

'Why not, Mummy?'

'Sometimes that happens as you get older. Sometimes your friends are no longer your friends.'

I feel my chest burning, my neck, my face.

What about all the times I was there for them? I would pick up the phone any time of day or night, holding back Charlie's hair when she threw up hundreds of times in numerous toilet bowls, making sure they all got home safely, organising birthday parties, sending cards on their first day at work, carrying around that fucking bridal kit like a mug.

*Excited* for them. I've always been excited for them whenever their lives have been going well, even if mine was going backwards.

My shame, my sadness, morphs into anger once more.

Fuck them. Fuck them all.

I slam my fist on the toilet wall.

There's an alarmed squeak. Someone must have come in without me realising. I freeze for a few seconds, shaking my bruised hand.

There's the delicate clinking of bracelets; someone is washing their hands. The clatter of heels. The opening of the door; music booming through.

I wipe my face roughly with loo roll, no thought for my carefully applied make-up.

I start to scroll through the contacts on my phone, searching for someone to call, to rant and rage at. Someone who might understand. My finger hovers over Natalie's name, but it's Saturday night and I'm sure she'll be spending the night with her new guy. She'd still pick up, or at least text me to ask if I'm OK, but I can't burden her with all this. I don't want to hear her voice change from carefree to careful – caring.

Besides, what do I say? 'None of my friends like me any more.' 'I'm having a sad time at a wedding.'

I scroll past friends I've already lost touch with – girls I went to school with. For a second I even consider calling Dean. But then I'd have to face him on Monday morning. And he wouldn't get it. He'd probably just tell me to go home, have a Pot Noodle and a wank.

My finger hovers over Beena's name . . . The dance battle is probably over by now. We could leave together, maybe via McDonald's again. I picture her dancing, her infectious grin. I don't want to tear her away from having fun, just because I need some comfort. I know she'd drop everything – but I don't want to put that on her. I can tell her about it later. When I'm feeling calmer.

I shove my phone roughly into my bag and close my eyes again.

*What do you want, Sunny?*

I want to be in bed, in my pjs, with a cup of tea and a bar of Fruit & Nut. And then I want to sleep for ten hours straight.

I imagine the journey home – crowds of noisy, drunken people, the disappointing and expensive train picnic and then the silent judgement from the taxi-driver uncle.

My phone buzzes as a message pops up from Mum.

*Any nice boys? Take lots of photos, OK. You looked beautiful, puth.*

I picture my mum waiting at home, half expecting me to come back from the wedding with hope, some kind of hope, that I've found a guy. The last sentence, *you looked beautiful*, sticks in my mind.

I start typing out a message.

I start to say, *It's OK, Mama – no nice boys here. Having a lovely time*.

But I stop.

I hit call instead.

'Hello? Sunny?' There's an edge of panic to her surprise. 'Everything OK, puth?'

'Hi, Mama, I'm fine.' I try to keep as much sadness out of my voice as possible, but I still sound like a deflated balloon.

'Wedding finish already? So early?'

Nine-thirty has never been 'early' to my mum before.

'Um, nooo, it's still going . . .'

'How was the dance? Did everybody like?' I can hear a YouTube advert playing in the background.

'Good, everyone liked it.' I think about the dance again, the power I felt in that moment. 'I was really good. I enjoyed it,' I tell her, because that's what matters more now. The fact that I liked it, right? I try to keep that thought in my mind – I try to believe it. 'You watching TV?' I want to talk about her. Never before have I been more interested in what my mum is doing, sitting at home on the sofa. I want to be anywhere but here, in this toilet cubicle, the sounds of laughter, love and enjoyment ringing through the door every time someone wanders in.

'Just YouTube – there's a little boy singing in this competi-tion, so cute. Here, listen.'

I can barely hear a thing, but still I listen to thirty seconds of nothing before she's back on the line.

'Can you hear? So nice, he's only seven, eight years old maybe. So cute. What's the food like?'

'Really nice.' I feel calmer. I didn't expect it. Her questions, her making me listen to a child singing on YouTube, it feels comforting. 'Have you eaten?'

'Your dad is at the gurdwara until late today, committee meeting, so I thought why make roti only for me?'

'Mama . . .'

'So I just had cheese toast—'

'Mum . . .'

'Then your masi from America called and she was telling me that if you eat cheese at night—'

'Mum,' I say, my heartbeat racing now.

'Ha, yes, what?'

'I . . . can you . . .' The words stick in my throat.

'What's happened?' I can hear the fear in her voice as clear as a bell.

No words come out, but there are floods of tears again. I'm sobbing.

'Are you hurt? Somebody hurt you?'

'No, no, nothing like that,' I say quickly, my voice ragged.

'Then what happened?'

'I . . . had a fight . . .'

'Who with? Somebody hit you?'

'No, no, not like that, I'm fine, I'm not hurt.'

'Puth,' she says clearly, authoritatively. 'You're crying, I am coming to get you.'

'Mum, no!'

'Send me postcode, Sunny.' She grunts softly as she gets up.

'But you . . . I . . . I can get the train,' I say weakly. I imagine Mum wandering around the house picking up everything she needs. She hasn't driven in ages. She usually finds an excuse not to.

'Sunny, I am coming now. Postcode.' Her steely tone of voice tells me she means it.

'The wedding invite is on the fridge, the address is there,' I reply in a small voice.

'OK, I'm coming. I'm putting shoes on now.'

I can hear her ripping the Velcro off each shoe as she slides her foot in. Her driving shoes, sat forgotten for months.

'Mama, are you going to be OK driving at night?' Normally she leaves night-time driving to my dad, as she's always worried about being blinded by the lights of oncoming traffic.

A flash of fear crosses my mind – an image of her little VW Golf— I pause, forcing the picture from my mind, unable to even consider it. My heart is racing again.

'Don't worry, I'll wear my glasses.' I know she's still worried about it, but she's trying not to let it show. Now I know where I get it from. Hiding my feelings.

I panic. I don't want Mum to have to come all the way out here. For me. 'Oh no, actually, I'm OK now! No, I'll get the train, don't worry.'

'No! Stay inside, it's dark. I'll call when I am there, OK?'

I can't speak, because I'm crying again: tears of relief and tears at the thought of her leaving the house so late at night, for her, to drive across London and collect me. Without even knowing what's wrong. Just knowing that *some*thing's wrong.

'Sunny?'

'Yes, Mama. Thank you.'

Guilt gnaws at my insides. I'm thirty. I shouldn't need anyone to rescue me. I shouldn't need my mum to rescue me.

But the guilt doesn't dismiss the fact that I'm glad she is. I'm glad she's taking me home.

I think about the prospect of leaving Anj's wedding – a few months ago I'd have considered it the worst thing I could do. But right now, it's what I want.

For a moment, I also want to go back in there and slap Chandni round the face and tell her about herself . . . to make sure there's no doubt about what I think of her.

But I know it's not worth it. They are not worth my energy.

I wait for the group of young girls outside the cubicle to leave. From what I can make out, one of them has a crush on one of Ajay's cousins and is being egged on to send him a snap. And suddenly I feel very old, and incredibly young at the same time. When they finally leave in a flurry of shrieks and giggles, I tie my trousers – not so tight this time – and emerge warily from the toilets, heading along the corridor and out into the night.

# Chapter 37

I've never been so relieved and overjoyed to see my mum's VW pull up. Her face is looking stern but warm through the windscreen.

'Hello, Mama.' I climb inelegantly into the car and shudder as the warm air hits me. Mum touches my arm and gasps.

'You are *frozen*! Hai! Like ice! I told you to take a jacket! This is why you are always getting flu,' she chides, but there's a softness to her eyes. She's wearing a navy zip-up fleece over her house clothes; normally she doesn't go any further than the end of the garden in them, so she really did leave in a hurry. 'Get the shawl from the back seat,' she orders, reversing slowly out of the car park.

I nod meekly, reaching behind for the heavy green shawl embroidered with delicate white-and-pink flowers in the corners. As soon as I wrap it around my shoulders, I'm grateful for its warmth. Grateful my mum insisted I wear it.

I don't tell Mum that I spent the last hour or so sitting on a bench, not wanting to go back in alone. Not that I needed to worry too much about being seen on my own. The guests were all at the drunken-dancing-overtired-crying stage.

I crept around the side of the building, sticking to the shadows like a crap assassin, and returned to the bench I was sitting on earlier. I spotted a forgotten tampon in its wrapper on the floor ... from my bridal emergency kit. Other than that, there's no trace that I was here at all.

'How was your journey, Mama?' I'm hoping small talk will keep her busy enough until we get home and then I can safely hide in my room until morning, and we don't ever have to speak about tonight again.

'Easy! I didn't even have to drive through Dartford Tunnel. Go on M25, then around London.' I smile to myself, knowing she would have been pleased not to have paid the charge to cross the bridge.

'And you didn't feel . . . nervous driving in the dark?'

'Leh, what is there to feel nervous about?' I decide not to remind her about all the times she's insisted she's too nervous to drive at night, but I can tell she's just trying to make me feel better about her driving out here. 'You said food was nice? I bet they had those little little samosas,' she says. 'Bet they didn't even make the pastry by hand!' I giggle at the mock disgust on her face. I giggle, because every moment that passes here, we're getting further and further away from everyone at the wedding.

'I don't think anyone makes pastry by hand any more, Mama . . .'

'I do!' she says vehemently.

'Apart from you, of course. They were nowhere *near* as good as yours.'

She smiles a little at that, and for the first time today, I feel my heartbeat return to normal.

I look down at my phone; there's a message from Beena:

*Hey, love, I've been looking for you everywhere! Are you OK?? Overheard Chandni saying you lost it at her . . . What happened?! If you want, we can head home together? You can stay at mine if you need a bit of space xxx*

I smile at Beena's concern, feeling a bit sad that I didn't tell her and didn't say goodbye. But I feel safe now, in Mum's car, talking about little little samosas and judging the hosts pastry-making skills.

*I'm OK,* I text back. *I just had to leave – in the car with Mum now. She came to pick me up. I didn't want to worry you but will tell you everything soon. Xxx*

*That's lovely – say hi to Aunty-ji for me! Of course. I just wanted to make sure you were OK. Forget Chandni, and all of them. They're not worth your time. Get some rest, OK? And be gentle with yourself xxx*

*P.s. You looked* banging *today*

'What is this area?' Mum asks, turning into a quiet, tree-lined street of Edwardian houses.

'Richmond, I think,' I reply, squinting out of the window and turning my phone screen off.

'Hmmm, rich area,' she says admiringly. 'Open the glove box.'

'Why?'

'Just open!'

Nestled among old newspapers, an ancient A–Z of London and an assortment of biros is a blue cash-and-carry bag. I open it to find a packet of Hula Hoops, a Penguin and a carton of apple juice.

'I didn't have time to make anything,' she says apologetically.

'Thank you, Mama,' I say quietly as my heart floods with gratitude. A lonely tear slides down my cheek and I'm glad she's driving so she can't see my face. I haven't cried in front of Mum since I was little – not properly – and I'm not counting our weekly weep at *DIY SOS*.

'What was Anjali wearing? Lehenga or sari?' she asks excitedly.

'Red sari, then she changed into a lehenga for the reception.' I open the crisps and offer her the packet, but she waves it away.

'How many people?'

'Erm, I dunno, probably . . . two hundred, three hundred?' I say through a mouthful of crisps.

'Bas?! Is that it? Bet they spend a lot of money . . .'

I wait for the question I know she wants to ask – the question she texted me about earlier: *Any apne there? Any nice boys?*

But, as we sit in silence for a bit, it doesn't come. She doesn't ask it at all. Along with the Penguin, Hula Hoops and apple juice, I take this as another sliver of her kindness today.

'I should call Dad, let him know where you are,' I say, getting my phone out. It dies as soon as I unlock it.

'I left a note for him, don't worry. Hmm. People never sleep in London, always outside at night-time. So dangerous – too much crime.' She shakes her head slightly at the sight of a smartly dressed couple smoking outside a pub.

'Somehow I don't think crime is a huge issue in Putney, Mama,' I say as we whizz past vintage clothes shops and boutique hairdressers. Crisps demolished, I relax into the seat and ease off my heels, sighing with relief as I wriggle my sore toes. There's the beginning of a headache blossoming at the base of my skull. I think longingly of the strip of tablets in the bridal emergency kit I dumped.

'Puth, what happened? Somebody upset you?' She sounds like she's ready for a fight; her voice is edged with a harshness I haven't heard before – but it's not aimed at me. I open my mouth and close it again. I genuinely don't know where to start. So I begin with Chandni.

'Anj's sister, Chandni, she's been . . . she was awful to me. She's always been like that, but it's been worse the past few months. Barking orders at me, ignoring me, putting me down. She told me I'd been a rubbish friend to Anj.' I grind to a halt, waiting for her to tell me to get a grip or to stand up for myself.

'Why? You were helping with her sister's wedding all the time – you spent so much money going to her party!'

I feel the guilt of the months and months of lies I gave Mum about helping Anj out. It was my go-to lie.

'What did she do for you? Heh?' she continues, changing gear roughly.

'Erm, well, over the years . . . lots of stuff,' I stammer. 'But, Mama, I didn't help Anj to get something back for myself . . .' I rack my brains, trying to think of the last time they supported me in any way, but I'm coming up blank.

'No, no, it's good to help people, but they have to help back,' she says firmly, banging the steering wheel. 'Puth, you do so much for people. So much. You need people who are there for you when you need it as well.' For a second, I wonder if she's going to steer her way back to the party and give Chandni a piece of her mind.

'And the other girls . . . Elena and Charlie, they . . . they're not talking to me. We . . .' I don't know what more to say. There's so much I've not told her.

'I knew they weren't good girls,' she continues. 'Remember when they came in, they didn't take their shoes off?'

'To be fair, you told them not to . . .'

'So? They should take off anyway! Would they walk around their own house with dirty shoes?'

I laugh to myself. She's got a point there. I think back to the only time the girls visited, just after I'd moved back home. Mum had been cooking for days – paneer spring rolls, aloo tikki and sholay, two types of chutney and gulab jamun for dessert. She pestered me for *weeks* to find out their favourite foods and how much spice they could take. She even dusted off the good plates for them. Only for them to decide on the day that they'd rather eat out as it was 'easier'. I remember her face when I told her. My heart still hurts thinking about it.

'It's not just that, Mama,' I say quietly. 'It's lots of things . . . I don't want to be friends with them any more. They aren't there for me; I'm just entertainment for them – now they've got their perfect lives and boyfriends and marriages. I just don't want to be friends with them any more.' It sounds so juvenile, like a child at school saying they don't want to play with someone any more. But Mum just nods.

'That's OK,' she says simply. 'Friends are not everything.' I turn to her, confused. 'Friends are *important*, but they are not *everything*, puth,' she reiterates.

'You've got loads of friends, though: the yoga ladies and Shindo and all the women at the gurdwara!' I say incredulously, turning in my seat to look at her.

'Leh,' she says thoughtfully. 'They are ladies I know – we have shared interests, you know? But *real* friends. Real friends are people who you trust like family. I have one *real* friend; she is in India now.'

I frown. 'Who? You've never told me about her before.'

'She moved there before you were born. When me and your dad bought the house in 1978, nobody helped us. Not your grandparents or his brother – nobody,' she says, and I see she's back there – back in 1978. Her eyes are focused on the road in front of her, but I can hear the emotion in her voice. 'Soon after we moved, your dad lost his job; the factory closed down and he didn't work for three months. We only had £12 in the bank.' She tuts to herself, shaking her head gently. For a second, I wonder if she's forgotten that I'm here. 'We were so scared. The mortgage payment was high – we couldn't sleep; we kept thinking the bank was going to take away our house. Take our home. I called my friend for help. In the middle of the night. I didn't need to say more than a few words and she understood. I didn't tell your dad. I was so *ashamed*, and she said, "Don't worry, I will help." I was so relieved, I just cried. She saved us that day, and she's never held it over me since. She is far away now, yes, and we don't talk much, but I

can never forget what she did for us. A friend, puth, is someone who will help you when you need it most. Money is one
thing, yes, but the least a friend can do is be there for you when
you need them. If they are not there for you, then you do not
need to go out of your way for them.'

I think of my parents as young adults, scared, unable to
turn to anyone for help. I picture my mum, my proud mum,
crying down the phone to her friend, not only worried about
losing her home, but about being ridiculed, ashamed to ask
for help.

I turn my head away from her. I wipe away my tears.

I don't trust myself to speak, not with this lump in my
throat, so I squeeze her arm lightly. We drive in silence for a
bit. 'Puth, I know you have been sad. It is nothing to hide from
– we do not always talk about what is going on, but I have felt
that way before too. I kept it inside and it didn't help. I know
you have not been talking to your friends, because your friends
would not treat you like this if they deserved you. Sometimes,
your friends can't be there when you need them – but I
want you to feel always able to speak to me.' Mum nods; she
doesn't look at me and I keep staring ahead. Not knowing
what to say, I stay silent.

'Look, puth. It's like this turning.' She gestures at the junc-
tion coming up. 'Somebody goes this way, somebody goes the
other way; nobody is wrong. You just going different ways in
life. They have boyfriends, but you looking for someone right
for you. You are working hard for yourself, doing good in your
job. It is a good thing. Do what is right for you. You have to
always do what is right for you.'

I want to tell her everything else – because I know it's not
just about them going a different way to me. I want to tell her
about Charlie's insensitive comments at the dance rehearsal,
for starters – it's not simply a case of us going our different

ways, the fact that they're in relationships and I'm not. But there's too much; it's so hard to know where to begin. And I haven't even told her how much I hate my job. It's been an easy excuse for so long, to use my job as the reason why I'm out late or going on trips away.

I look at my mum, her face set in a resolute frown. I know she means well; she wants what is best for me. She wants me to talk to her, but if she knew the truth about everything – Michael and the dates before she got involved – she wouldn't understand. There's still a line I can't cross. And there are things I need to do on my own, for myself, first of all.

# Chapter 38

It's raining by the time we pull into the driveway, and we rush into the house. The hallway feels too bright after the comforting darkness of the car. I can hear Dad's rumbling snores.

'I'm going to make hot chocolate. I'll make cheese toast for you,' Mum says, kicking off her comfy shoes.

'No, Mama, I just want to go to sleep.'

She pauses. 'Why don't you have a warm shower first? You'll feel better.'

Normally night-time showers are a no-no, as Mum is a light sleeper, so any noise after 10 p.m. is forbidden. Unless, of course, it's her snoring. Which she vehemently denies. But I don't question it. I want to wash the day off me. Wash all memories of the girls away.

I hug her tightly.

I feel her hug me back, and she plants a firm kiss on my forehead before letting me go. I trudge up the stairs to the bathroom and take my contacts out.

I turn the shower to scalding and let the steam fill up the bathroom. I leave my outfit in a heap on the floor and climb into the shower. I stand underneath the hot jet of water, soaking my hair, knowing I won't have the energy to dry it. I dig my nails into my scalp as I shampoo my hair, leaving tender imprints all over my head. Eager to get rid of the smell of stale sweat, I shake out generous globs of jasmine-scented shower gel onto the shower puff and firmly scrub it across my body.

When I get out, I can hear Mum still pottering about downstairs. I put my phone on to charge, anxious to see if I've missed any messages. I climb into bed naked, my body heavy with exhaustion, and I'm asleep before I can even check my phone.

I wake up with a start and I lie there waiting for my heartbeat to slow down as I try to remember the terrifying dream that woke me up so suddenly.

My neck is damp from sleeping with wet hair and the T-shirt I'd tied around my hair is now threatening to strangle me.

The sunlight streaming in through the gap in the curtains seems intent on piercing my skull. I groan and roll over, feeling slightly hungover and drained, despite only having had a few glasses of wine at the beginning of the evening. I blindly paw at my cluttered bedside table, searching for my phone, sending make-up and a book clattering to the floor. I finally lay my hands on my phone. Forcing my eyes open, I see with a jolt of surprise that it's gone 10 a.m. The house is quiet, too quiet. And then I hear my mum flushing the downstairs loo and I exhale. How come she hasn't already called me downstairs yet? She never lets me lie in this long.

I check my messages – terrified there'll be something in the group chat, something from Anj, something from Chandni, but I am pleasantly surprised to see a couple of messages from Beena.

*Yesterday 22:23*
*Hi, love, thinking of you! Heading home now myself – party was no good without you. Hope you got some proper rest xxx*

*Yesterday 23:19*
*Let's meet up soon? If you ever want a bit of space, you're always welcome at mine. Promise I won't bother you if you need alone time! Xxx*

I rattle off a message to her straight away:

*Hi love, so sorry about last night. I'm OK, slept for ages. You were killing it on the dance floor last night! Yes, let's catch up soon pls! Xxx*

And there's also a message from Dean:

*Completely forgot that this was the night of the wedding. I hope it went OK – remember, do what you want to do ALWAYS. Only five more sleeps until KFC Friday!! D x*

I open up Instagram but pause. I don't want to see the photos – not yet. I don't need to look at them right now. I'm convinced that I'll block my friends, forever – on social media, in my life – but that can wait. That can all wait. It's time to put me first, I think.

I step downstairs, ready to face Mum, wondering if she's forgotten all about last night, hoping that we don't have to rehash my confession. But I pause outside the living-room door. I can hear her on the phone to someone – an aunty, no doubt. Her voice is hushed, not loud like usual.

'No, no, nothing happened with that boy in the end. Ha, yes,' she is saying. 'He wasn't good enough for her . . . No, I do not want to set Sunny up with anyone else – no boys until she is ready. Ha, yes, she is thirty, yes – it is not the end of the world. She needs time. I am not putting that pressure on her any more.' I notice Mum's voice rising in volume and in fierceness. 'She is *my* daughter – she will make her own decisions.'

I can hear Mum pacing now, which tells me it's definitely serious. Usually she's on the phone with her feet up.

'If you think there is a boy she will like, you tell me and I will speak to her when she is ready. But not today – she is tired. It is tiring for youngsters; there is so much pressure these days. It is hard for us to understand – things were different for us. World is different now.'

'Nahi, Kamal,' she says forcefully in Punjabi. Kamal is my chachi, Jasmine's mum – I bet Chachi called up specially to gloat about her future son-in-law's new business. But I have never heard my mum raise her voice to her before. Normally, they just talk about other relatives. She was the person who had already started recommending wedding halls for me and Jag before we'd even gone on our second date. Mum's always so careful around her in-laws; she never wants to give them any ammunition so will usually just agree with everything they say.

Mum's voice grows louder still. 'It is OK. Sunny is OK. I have told you. I don't need you to worry about my daughter. You just worry about your own.'

Then there's the beep from the phone. She's hung up. Mum hung up.

For a second, the house is silent – it has never been completely silent before.

I'm holding my breath in absolute disbelief.

I push open the door to the living room to see Mum on the sofa under a thick, brightly coloured blanket with a tiger's head printed on it, the *Punjab Times* open on her lap, engrossed in a YouTube video about how to grow an avocado in water. I can tell she has just set up this scene, to pretend she wasn't just talking about me.

'Hi, Mama,' I say quietly, poking my head around the door.

'Oh! You are awake. I didn't want to disturb – I knew you would be tired.'

'Shall I make cha?' I ask uncertainly. I thought she'd be in the kitchen buttering a stack of aloo parathas by now.

'No, no, come sit. We don't need to be working all the time.' She pats the sofa and I hesitate, half confused and half wondering if she's going to try to persuade me to put an ad in the matrimonial section of the paper.

334

As I sit down next to her, she pulls me closer with her arm around me until I'm leaning my head on her shoulder. We stay like this until the video ends and another one starts; this time the perky American vlogger is explaining why you should never throw banana peels away. I close my eyes and let her nasal tones wash over me.

I shift and lower myself to rest my head in Mum's lap. She covers me with the blanket, warm from her body heat, and tucks me in. She strokes my hair, making gentle little circles right in the centre of my forehead.

I exhale and close my eyes, letting my shoulders drop.

'I used to do this when you were a baby,' Mum says. 'You were so small, so tiny. You never let me do this any more.'

'Mum,' I smile, eyes still on the YouTube screen. 'I'm thirty now. Not a baby.' But as I lie there, I want her to hold me like this forever.

'Thirty or not, you are still my baby. Look, I was always there for you then and I am here for you now. See, this helps, doesn't it?' She continues to stroke my hair. 'It used to help you sleep.'

I close my eyes, unable to speak. There's so much I need to tell her.

'Rest now, puth,' she says softly. 'Let yourself rest.'

'Mama,' I say, softly at first, my voice shaking. As the word leaves my mouth, I realise I've begun a sentence that I now can't take back, and I finish with: 'I think I need to make some changes.'

For the first time in forever, I know this is what I need to do.

'OK, puth,' Mum says softly back. Her hand is stroking my forehead.

'No more dating, OK?' I begin. 'Just for a bit. I need time to figure out what I actually need.'

'OK,' Mum says firmly, nodding, understanding.

'And, Mama . . .' My voice is softer still now, barely more than a whisper. 'I think I need to move out. It's the right time.' As I hear the sentence for myself, I know that I'm right. I'm only able to grow so much here.

I wait for a response, but Mum is just quiet; her hand has stopped stroking my forehead, warm and soft on my skin. I keep my eyes on the YouTube video, but all I can hear is my own heartbeat thundering in my ears. I steel myself, running through all the potential scenarios in my mind.

'OK,' is all she says for a while, but I know she is only just digesting it. This is only the beginning of this conversation.

After what feels like hours of watching an endless loop of 'gardening hacks', like how to grow an avocado at home and reusing toilet-paper tubes as plant pots, Mum finally says: 'OK, rest for now, puth,' and kisses me on the forehead.

I close my eyes and breathe in deeply. I think about what's to come, what has changed, and I know there are some things that still need to change before I can.

'Thank you, Mama,' I reply, the words catching in my throat.

# Chapter 39

*Six months later ...*

'Keep your room *tidy* and be careful ...'

'Mama, please ...' I quickly look behind me to check if anyone has heard her. The last thing I need is for Beena to overhear my mum telling me off as though I'm some wayward teenager off to her first sleepover. The sound of her voice carries in the quiet residential street in South London.

A curious, fat ginger cat looks at us lazily through half-closed eyes as we finish unloading the car. My belongings looked meagre piled up in the street: a large suitcase, a few boxes and one of those plastic blue checked laundry bags for awkwardly shaped items.

My stomach has been in knots for the past three days and I keep forgetting I'm holding my breath. A combination of nerves, excitement and my steady companion, fear. I barely slept last night, lying rigid in bed in what I hope was my last night in my childhood bedroom.

Before I left I sat on my bed and looked around the room; it looked a lot bigger now that I'd finally got rid of the bags for life stuffed with old, shapeless clothes. In a strange sort of way, I know I'll miss it – it was the setting of many a teary moment, numerous whispered phone calls and secret binges.

The last time I left home and moved to London I thought that was going to be it. I know life is changeable, and no one knows what's coming round the corner – but I'm determined to make it work this time.

Mum wasn't exactly ecstatic about the idea of me moving out of home ('This is a silly, silly idea – you have everything here: food whenever you want it, a roof over your head, bedroom of your own!'), and I had no idea how I was going to afford London rent, but I pushed forward with the plan. I knew the longer I spent in Gravesend, the longer I spent with Mum too, the harder it would be for me to find out what I actually wanted for myself.

Mum insisted on being involved with the whole process and so the dating apps were replaced with housing apps. 'You need my help, henna. To make sure you find a good deal and what you need,' Mum kept insisting. But it soon became apparent that the only options within my budget were either sharing a house with five other people or sharing with one incredibly anal landlady who had a strict curfew of 11 p.m. and who wiped down no less than three surfaces with an eye-wateringly strong bleach solution as she showed us around. My mum had approved of that one. Not so much what *I* was looking for.

After a couple of fruitless months of looking for house-shares, Beena reminded me that she still had a spare room. It was airy, slightly bigger than my own and was being used as a guest room. Not only was it furnished, but it was clean and comfortable, and it overlooked the garden.

As soon as she mentioned it, my heart leapt at the idea. 'How well do you know her?' Mum had said, cautious as always – but I was cautious too. We'd become close friends since the wedding, because she just *got* it, in the same way Nat did. But what if we couldn't live together? What if she was a secret clean freak or, *worse*, a morning person?

'Beena,' I'd said to her. 'Are you a clean freak or a morning person, or secretly a serial killer?'

'Sunny,' she said to me, over a plate of doughnuts at some cute café in Clapham, 'I go away for work loads, so you'll have the place all to yourself. I'll only be a serial killer when I'm around.'

That swung it for me. Plus, the rent was a fair bit lower than anywhere else I'd seen in London.

Since it was all decided, Mum has insisted on freezing an extra portion of food from everything she's made for 'the move', as though I'll immediately forget how to cook as soon as I leave Gravesend.

Dad comes out of the house looking pleased with himself. Mum wanted him to dress smartly to make a good impression on Beena, but he insisted on wearing his DIY clothes. They eventually came to an uneasy compromise, so he's wearing a paint-splattered polo shirt with smart trousers, with meticulously ironed creases down the front.

'Very nice house,' he murmurs approvingly, more to himself than anyone else. He stands on the doorstep, his hands behind his back, rocking on his heels. Within half an hour of arriving at the house, he'd fixed the leaky tap in the kitchen, examined the vegetable patch and offered to come round and regrout the tiles in the bathroom. Beena had charmed both of them by laying on an impressive spread of vegetarian snacks. I'd clocked that she'd removed all of her piercings, bar one pair of discreet gold hoops and a tiny sparkly nose stud. And despite the heat, she was dressed in a demure long-sleeved polo neck and jeans, to cover up all her tattoos.

My phone buzzes in the pocket of my shirt dress. At first, I scroll over a message from Anj from a few days ago:

*Hey, Sunny, hope you're well. I saw on Instagram that you're moving in with Beena and I wanted to say good luck for the move. I think it'll be great for you. I wondered if we could catch up soon?*

*I miss you, and I'm sorry – I've started to understand what you meant about Charlie's attitude and I'm sorry I wasn't there when you needed me.*

My eyes stick on that word *sorry* for a moment – I haven't replied yet. But then I scroll over to the new message, and my heart lifts.

*Hope the move's going well, mate. Place not the same without you. Just getting everyone's orders in for KFC Friday. Will have a Zinger Burger in your honour lol – don't be a stranger. D*

I let out a little chuckle before checking to see if Mum has noticed. It'll be refreshing to be able to smile at my phone without Mum getting suspicious that I might be talking to a potential husband.

Sharon was surprised when I handed in my notice, especially as I had 'the potential to be a very good customer-service advisor', according to her. It took me weeks to build up to it, and weeks to prepare Andrew, the sexy Scottish customer, for the fact that I was leaving, though he did say: 'Good on you, stick it to that boss of yours, and if you're ever up in Edinburgh, you know where to find me.' And Mr Seedhouse's case with his discoloured footstool has been transferred to Dean – I knew they'd get along.

I almost skipped out of there on my last day, giving the building the finger as I ducked into the pub with Dean for one last drink.

I updated my CV and applied for any job that didn't look too soul-destroying and have an interview lined up for a hotel receptionist. I'm secretly hoping that I get promoted to wedding planner and get to wear a headset like J.Lo in *The Wedding Planner*. A Matthew McConaughey lookalike wouldn't be a bad thing either . . .

'Sunny!' Mum beckons me over to the car and hands me a large plastic tote filled with Tupperware boxes full of daal, sabji and what looks like enough rotis to feed me and Beena for a week.

*I will not cry. I will not cry. I will not cry.*

'Make sure you eat it all, and bring the boxes back when you next come home, OK? They're part of a set.'

'Promise, Mama,' I croak, masking the break in my voice with a cough. Dad sidles over and gives me an awkward side hug. He's carrying a small, brightly coloured box of mangoes. Their cloying scent fills my nostrils.

'OK, see you soon, puth,' he says gruffly, clearing his throat and turning away quickly.

'Come home *every* week—'

'Every *other* weekend, Mama,' I remind her gently. 'But I'll call every day.' My therapist told me I needed to set boundaries and enforce them. It wasn't the most comfortable thing in the world, but it felt bloody powerful. After the wedding, I just wanted to run away, but she advised me to involve my parents in the moving process as much as possible instead of sticking to my usual MO of being a secretive squirrel. Since then, Mum's wanted a say in everything, but she's also been helpful, and has, in her own way, been supportive of what I want.

'OK. Be good.' Mum hugs me tightly and whispers in my ear: 'Be careful, there is too much crime—'

'Why don't you stay for dinner, Aunty?' Beena is standing in the doorway discreetly wiping the sweat off her top lip, her face clammy in the muggy heat.

'No, no, we have to go, puth. Your uncle cannot drive in the dark.'

'Well, please come by any time, you're always welcome.' Beena beams as my mum hugs her tightly too and Dad follows with his signature awkward side hug.

We watch their car disappear around the corner and I wonder how many times they'll bicker on the journey home.

I put a little pack of boiled sweets in the glove box, just so Dad definitely has a sweet handy to calm her down.

'You shouldn't have said that,' I say, turning to Beena. 'She'll be around all the time.'

'She's not so bad.' Beena smiles as she takes her jumper off. 'She loves you. Even if she doesn't say it. But you're here and she's dropped you off – that's huge.' She walks into the flat. 'Come on, roomie, I've got some prosecco in the fridge. And Natalie sent you some beautiful flowers, and brownies!'

I follow her in and close the door behind me. Beena is already in the kitchen, getting out the champagne flutes.

I linger in the high-ceilinged hallway of my new home.

Finally, for the first time in what feels like years, I let out my breath.

If you loved reading

# Sunny

turn the page for bonus material
including reading group questions,
and an interview with author Sukh Ojla

# Reading Group Questions

1) Sunny spends a lot of her life hiding her whole self from her family and friends. How has this affected her relationships with the people around her?

2) Sunny's relationships with her friends vary over the course of the book. Who has been the most supportive friend of Sunny, and why? And who has been the worst friend to Sunny?

3) Do you think Sunny feels like she fits in with her friends? In what way does she, and what ways does she not? How do her friends show their love for her?

4) Sunny has a complicated relationship with her mother – are they similar in some ways? How do they show love for each other?

5) When Sunny and her friends go for dinner after their dance rehearsal, Sunny confronts them and points out their micro-aggressions. Do you think her friends responded in the most caring way? Why, or why not?

6) Sunny spends a lot of her energy dating. What does she learn from those experiences?

7) Dean, from work, is an interesting character, with lots of flaws of his own. But Sunny seems to feel comfortable around him and is able to open up to him. Why do you think this is?

8) How does Sunny's relationship with her mum change over time? What do you think was the first moment that started the change?

9) As the book progresses, we see Sunny stand up to her friends. Is there anything in particular that sparked this? Do you think Sunny was brave for doing so?

10) What do you hope is in store for Sunny after the book ends? Is it a happy ending? Is it the ending you expected?

# Q&A with Sukh Ojla

**1) Sunny is a character who readers really care about – I think many of us see bits of ourselves in her. What do you think it is about Sunny that makes her so relatable?**

I think Sunny, like all of us, is flawed. She makes mistakes, she lies, and loves a Poundshop haul. And like most of us, she curates an image on social media that is completely different/polished.

**2) What do you hope readers will take from reading Sunny?**

I hope that readers will recognise that they are not alone in their struggles and that their feelings are valid. I think so often we, like Sunny, are prone to gaslighting ourselves and minimising our problems rather than acknowledging them and I hope that Sunny can act like a mirror and reflect back to the reader that they really aren't doing as badly as they think at life . . . !

**3) Other than Sunny, of course, who was your favourite character to write?**

It has to be, without a doubt, Sunny's mum. I enjoyed sifting through my own mum's memorable quotes and foibles to create her character. I love her relationship with Sunny and how she can be brusque one minute and warm and funny the next.

## 4) Is there a character you dislike?

I don't dislike any of the characters, even the ones who are unkind to Sunny but I very much enjoy it when readers tell me they hate a character . . . for me, it's a sign that I've got it right!

## 5) Is there a moment in the book where you wish Sunny had made a different choice in her life?

I think every choice that Sunny (or indeed any of us!) makes is potentially a learning experience. She makes some questionable choices throughout the book but I think that is partly what makes her so endearing and human.

## 6) You blend humour and heartache so well throughout the book. How did you find striking that balance?

This is one of my favourite things to do, it is a fine balance and takes some tweaking but it is so satisfying when it feels right. I think life is a mixture of both and there is humour to be found in heartbreak and vice versa.

## 7) If you could give Sunny a piece of advice, what would it be?

I would give her a massive hug and tell her that she is more loved than she thinks she is and that she already possesses everything she needs to make any change she wishes to in her life. And then I'd take her out for a white wine spritzer and a bowl of onion rings.

8) *Sunny* is your debut novel, and it has already found its way into the hearts of so many readers. You've said before that Sunny is in some ways like you ten years ago. How was it writing Sunny and her journey, and looking back on your own life at that stage?

If I had to sum up the process in one word: therapeutic. But just like therapy, it definitely had its tough moments. It was gratifying to see how far I'd come in ten years, but also I felt very protective of Sunny at times. Sunny is obviously not directly lifted from my life; I like to think that I was a little bit more self-aware than Sunny is and I wasn't as harsh on myself – in a way she is a bit of an exaggeration, and the journey she goes on in under a year took me five years in reality.

But sometimes I still had to remind myself that Sunny was not me: in my mind, the line between us often blurred, especially as I was spending so much time with her when I was writing the book. It was a bit like spending months with the Ghost of Christmas Past. But ultimately, watching and writing Sunny's journey felt very satisfying and vindicating because of how different I am compared to her now – although saying that, some things haven't changed. I still love a Poundshop haul, just like Sunny.

9) How did you find writing *Sunny*? What was the process like and did anything surprise you along the way?

I had a very romantic notion of what writing a novel would be like; I thought the words would flow beautifully at all times, and I imagined waking up at 4am writing to the sound of birdsong and waves before jumping on my bike to go and get some freshly baked bread. But in reality, the only time I get up at 4am is to go on holiday, and this was written during lockdown so that wasn't even a possibility.

I like to be very frank about the process of writing, because I think a lot of people are led to believe that writing should be easy, and if it's not easy then you're doing it wrong. In truth, I found it to be anything but easy.

There's so much that surprised me, it's really hard to know where to start. But the main thing for me was that I was learning how to write a book while doing it, so it was like I was using two very different parts of my brain at the same time. Although there were moments of flow where it felt like the words were flying onto the page, those moments were very few and far between. It only really became satisfying towards the end when I was honing it, and it felt more like I was shaping something out of clay, where it had felt like a lump of clay for a very long time. It was only towards the end of the editing process where it started to feel like a vase.

## 10) What advice would you give to anyone else writing their first novel?

My only bit of advice would be to be like Fleetwood Mac: you've got to go your own way. Everyone's writing process is different and just because you're writing a novel, it doesn't mean that you don't have noisy neighbours, or mental health issues, or off days. It's about writing despite all of that. Your writing process might be writing for fifteen minutes a day while you're waiting for the bus, so don't compare yourself to authors who have beautiful offices and can hide away and write and don't have to worry about what they're making for dinner, and have their wives bring them sandwiches. Make writing work for you.

There were times when I wrote on my phone in ad breaks while I was watching TV because I couldn't bear to be sat at my laptop for a moment longer. And that is still writing, it's still valid!

## 11) Did you find anything particularly useful from your background in playwrighting and comedy when it came to writing *Sunny?*

The most useful thing is that I already knew about comic timing from my comedy, and I like to think I know what is funny. Whilst I was writing *Sunny*, I was imagining it being performed on TV, which really helped with dialogue and setting. The only drawback of having a history of writing for stage is that I sometimes struggled with putting enough detail in: for example, when you're writing for stage or screen, you don't need to describe what the character is seeing, because the set does that for you – but in a book, you have to create it all yourself. Generally, though, it was a huge help: I had a clear vision of the characters, their mannerisms, their clothes and their look – the things that can make a character. I also really loved picturing and then writing the little moments that help bring a scene to life.

My golden rule is that if it makes me laugh when I'm re-reading it, then chances are that at least one other person will too.

## 12) You narrated the audiobook of *Sunny* too, which is completely brilliant – what was it like reading your words out loud, and bringing your characters to life that way?

As an actor I have some experience of doing voiceover work, but nothing prepares you for your first audiobook, especially when you've written it. I put a huge amount of pressure on myself to get it right but at the same time I knew that I was the right person to do it because I could see it so clearly; I know all the voices and I knew the characters so intimately.

As a writer, when reading your work back, it can be almost impossible to stop yourself from nit-picking and editing as you go along, and I frequently found myself asking the question 'Is it too late to rephrase this bit?'.

It was a lot of fun being in the studio, although very intense, as we recorded the whole thing in about three and a half days, and I didn't realise how many words I'd used in the book that I didn't know how to pronounce.

Oh, and I'd forgotten that I would be narrating the saucy scenes in front of a producer, who I'd only just met . . .

## 13) What has been the best thing about readers discovering *Sunny*?

It makes me quite emotional when I think about this because writing a book can be a very insular process, and it's easy to forget that it will make its way out into the world and other people will one day be reading your words.

It seems to have struck a chord with a lot of people from many different backgrounds but especially women of South Asian heritage. Lots of readers have messaged me to say this is the first time they have ever felt represented or seen in a book, and they didn't know they needed this book until they read it. A lot of people have wanted to be friends with Sunny, and are protective of her, just like I am. I think it's both quite devasting but quite beautiful that women, especially South Asian women, have said that it's like I have put what they're thinking or feeling on the page, and *Sunny* has as a result made them feel less lonely. It's made them feel better because they no longer they feel like they are the only one going through what

Sunny goes through. It has created a connection and that's what feels so important about it.

Recently, I've heard that a lot of people have called their mum when they've finished reading the book, and it's so moving to know the book has compelled them to do something like that. There have also been a few women who have got in touch after reading the book, who have been in Sunny's position in terms of living at home with their parents, or needing their independence, and they've since taken steps to move out, or get a new job. It is the biggest compliment that something I've written has spurred someone on to make positive changes in their life, or inspired them to put themselves first.

It's been so lovely to seen *Sunny* making her way around the world: she's been spotted on the tube, she's started conversations on the Eurostar to Brussels, she's even been spotted with bunches of saag in a Canadian-Punjabi kitchen – very on brand for her.

To all the readers who have messaged me, who have read *Sunny*, who have spread the word and recommended her to friends, family, colleagues and book groups, I just want to give every single one of you a hug! And to everyone who hasn't met Sunny yet, why are you reading this bit first?! Turn to page 1 and get stuck in!

# Take the Quiz
## How Sunny Are You?

Let's find out how Sunny you are! Tick any of the following that apply to you!

☐ Do you feel like everyone has their life figured out apart from you?

☐ Are double carbs one of the few joys in your life right now?

☐ Do you spend an unhealthy amount of time fantasizing about your dream life?

☐ Have you sought happiness in the arms of another? (Be honest)

☐ Have you ever had to hide a tinny in your underwear drawer?

☐ Do you feel like you're living a double life?

☐ Have you sat through yet another boring date wondering what to have for dinner?

☐ Do you live for the weekend?

☐ If you met your Uni friends now, would you choose to be friends with them?

☐ Have you ever received unsolicited dating advice from an Aunty?


So, how Sunny are you? If you have ticked:

• 0–3: You're more on the cloudy side!

• 4–7: You're cloudy, with some Sunny spells!

• 8 or more: Very Sunny, little chance of rain!

# Sunny's Top-Ten Playlist

If you need a pick-me-up after a terrible date, treat yourself to Sunny's favourite tunes, selected by author Sukh Ojla.

1. *Bootylicious* – Destiny's Child
2. *Choli Ke Peeche* – Alka Yagnik, Ila Arun
3. *Piya Tu Ab To Aaja* (From *Caravan*) – Asha Bhosle, R. D. Burman
4. *No Scrubs* – TLC
5. *Milkshake* – Kelis
6. *At Last* – Etta James
7. *All By Myself* – Eric Carmen
8. *Taal Se Taal* – Priyesh Vakil
9. *Someone Like You* – Adele
10. *Independent Women* – Destiny's Child

# Acknowledgements

Thank you to the following:

My wonderful editor and friend Sara Adams without whom there would be no Sunny. Thank you for your unwavering belief in me and Sunny. You're my favourite Capricorn.

Everyone at Hodder Studio for your enthusiasm, hard work and talent. You are all extraordinary.

Liz Barker at Noel Gay and Charlene McManus at Curtis Brown for all their support and understanding.

Jayne Edwards for keeping me sane with long beach walks and toasties.

Penny Faith for a delightful three months at Salt Cottage.

Mrs Dickins, my year 6 teacher, who was the first person to encourage me to write. I've never forgotten your kind words.

Chris Woodley for our straight-talking Sunday morning chats, doughballs and spine rolls.

Emma Damian Grint (and Aloysius) for knowing me better than I know myself and for not laughing at my harebrained schemes.

Maddy Anholt, Abi Lumb, Tamsyn Kelly and Josh Berry for the long chats, voice notes and memes that kept me going for the past year.

Altaf Sarwar for keeping me financially solvent since 2017 and the endless supply of Twirls.

Amelie Skoda and Gemma Bowles, two of Gravesend's

finest, for keeping me grounded and sharing my love for sauté potatoes.

Juspreet Kaur, Pam Johal, Tommy Sandhu and Ravita Pannu for being my Punjabi hype men.

And to all my Instagram family whose messages and support mean the world.

# About the Author

Sukh Ojla is a comedian, actor and writer. Her first play *Pyar Actually* toured nationwide in 2017 and 2018. She has performed on *Jonathan Ross's Comedy Club*, BBC2's *Big Asian Stand Up Show* and across the BBC Asian Network. She has appeared on *Mock The Week* (BBC) and *Sorry I Didn't Know* (ITV). In 2019, she took her debut solo show *For Sukh's Sake* to Edinburgh, which received rave reviews. In 2021, Sukh went on a nationwide tour with her new show *Life Sukhs*.

As an actor, Sukh recently appeared in *Bridgerton* (Netflix), *The End of the F\*\*king World* (Channel 4), *Feel Good* (Channel 4) and as a regular role in *GameFace* (Channel 4) and *Class Dismissed* (CBBC) and appeared in feature film *Victoria and Abdul*.

*Sunny* is her debut novel.